FIVE BLOODY HEARTS

An absolutely gripping crime thriller with a massive twist

JOY ELLIS

Published 2019 by Joffe Books, London.

www.joffebooks.com

ISBN- 978-1-78931-077-1

Dedicated to Debbie Sands.
Thank you for being such a good friend, for listening to my rants and for always being there when help was needed.
Plus, I swear you know more about the books than I do!

CHAPTER ONE

Sunrise. DCI Matt Ballard had seen enough of these during his thirty years' service in the police force. Now his time, his helter-skelter, white-knuckle ride of a career was almost over. Almost. Matt sighed as he eased the car into sixth gear. He should have left the force over two months ago, but his replacement had been caught up in a high-profile court case and Matt had been asked to hold the fort. Now, an early morning call had sent him speeding across the long fen roads to yet another complication, and probably more delay to his retirement. A farm worker had discovered a body on a deserted track, miles from anywhere. More than that Matt didn't know, but he had a sense of foreboding. Would he ever be able to get away?

The empty road stretched ahead of him. Either side of his speeding car the fields of wheat and barley turned a deeper gold in the early morning light. The crops were struggling under the hot, dry summer sun. Lack of June rain had impacted on the wheat and barley. It was not going to be a good harvest for the Lincolnshire farmers.

It was going to be another scorcher — five thirty a.m., and already beads of sweat were forming around his shirt collar. A dead body on a day that threatened to be the hottest of the year. He pushed his foot down on the accelerator.

It still felt odd to be alone, with no DS Liz Haynes alongside him in the car or waiting for him at the crime scene. Their last case together had seen an end to that. He still found it hard to believe the devastation it had wrought, the damage to both of them, and Liz was still recovering. They had reluctantly accepted counselling, and now Matt had to admit that it had helped. It had taken a while, but he now appreciated that he and Liz had been the victims of two hopelessly damaged minds, and that there was nothing on earth they could have done to avoid what happened. Now, strangely, as the physical wounds healed and the psychological ones lessened in intensity, Matt felt relief. Something dark from his past had been washed away, like a ghost finally laid to rest. Aside from the nightmares, he sometimes felt almost at peace with the world. He couldn't remember ever feeling that way before.

Both he and Liz likened themselves to survivors of a shipwreck, two mariners who had battled a terrible storm to be washed up on sunlit sands, battered and bruised but somehow more intensely alive.

Ahead of him, he saw the signpost for Washway Farm Drove. He turned into a lane that ran between two fields that seemed to stretch on forever. He drove for two or three minutes, windows down, the smell of wild camomile wafting into the car, until he saw a gaggle of vehicles in the distance. One had its blue lights still flashing.

He pulled onto a small area of hardstanding close to the track where the body had been found and stared down the grassy pathway. It was deeply rutted by tractors and farm vehicles, obviously not intended for any other kind of traffic. Deep but dry reed-lined ditches ran either side of the path. A track like this went nowhere. It would peter out at the field boundary, just an access lane for farmers checking the crops or taking soil samples for analysis.

A small group of people were gathered. Matt locked his car and made his way towards them.

'It's another one, boss.' DI Jason Hammond had beaten him to it, and didn't look happy about being out on the fen at daybreak. Then again, he rarely looked happy. He was not known for his sparkling personality or positive outlook on life. Jason was a worrier. He knew, but didn't care, that some of the beat bobbies called him an old woman. More importantly, he was a bloody good and very thorough detective. Jason wouldn't have been his right-hand man for so many years if that weren't the case.

Matt looked at the body. A man, hair unkempt, wearing heavy boots and the kind of shabby clothes that the migrant farm workers wore. He pulled on gloves and knelt down. A dark stain covered one side of the man's chest, and the tear in his T-shirt showed that he had been stabbed.

'Poor guy would have bled out pretty quickly.' Jason shook his head. 'Third knife attack in as many months.'

'No ID, I suppose?'

'Nothing. Pockets empty, stripped bare. Just the usual giveaway.' Jason indicated the man's arm. Without having to move him, Matt could see the tattoo. It was the same as the one on the last two victims. The design looked almost like a pattern used in weaving, a kind of intricate tree-like cross entwined with leaves. Matt had been told it was a traditional Lithuanian motif.

'Forensics are on their way, but I think this is cut and dried, don't you? Another casualty of the Baltic mafia,' Jason said.

It certainly looked that way. There had been a massive influx of migrant workers into the area in the past few years, mostly hardworking decent people, but with them came a hard-core criminal element, known locally as the "Baltic mafia." Often Russian, but sometimes comprised of a mixture of other Eastern European nationalities, they were heavily involved in drugs, bootleg alcohol and cigarettes. This "mafia" was the silent source of the conflict between two local groups of Latvians and Lithuanians. Their method was to brutally 'remove' existing local dealers, and lay the blame at the feet of the warring neighbours. If people knew what was going on, then they were too terrified to admit it. It was easier to blame their old enemies.

Matt stood up. 'I agree with you, Jason. There's little doubt about this. Our biggest problem will be identifying him, since the migrants are so reluctant to engage with the police.' He grinned at his friend's long face. 'Cheer up. You never know, we might get lucky and a grieving loved one will come forward.'

'Sure, and just like the other cases they might be too scared of reprisals to open their mouths to anyone.' Jason sighed. 'That's the most likely scenario, isn't it?'

Sadly, he was probably right, but Matt wasn't the glass half empty type. 'Are you okay to wait for forensics?'

Jason nodded.

'Then I'll get back and set up an action programme for the team. See you back at the factory.' He hated to admit it, but Matt felt a guilty relief at this being a death resulting from a gangland fight. The bodies, if not dumped in one of the two tidal rivers that flowed through their patch, were usually just discarded somewhere on the fens. It was horrible, but it was the unfortunate outcome of dealing in drugs. Matt had feared something different, a twisted and complex case that would have meant him staying on until the investigation was fully underway. With this, they knew where to look, who to talk to, and what they were dealing with. And it was easily handed over.

He climbed back into his car, the heat taking his breath away. He lowered the windows and reversed back into the lane. He hated using the air con, but it was definitely necessary now. As he drove, he thought back to a conversation that he'd had with Liz the previous morning.

'Do you honestly think it would work?' Matt turned back from the window and stared at Liz.

'Why shouldn't it? It worked for Tommy and Tuppence,' she said

He laughed, and went over to sit on the edge of their bed. 'Tommy and Tuppence! They sound like something from Enid Blyton. Couldn't you have thought of something a little more modern?'

'I like them.' Liz leaned back into the pillows. 'But seriously, Matt, think of all the contacts we have. Okay, we can't use our police powers, but there are so many ways to find things out these days. I think we should give it a try.'

She looked animated, alive. Matt thought she had never looked so beautiful.

She was still not fully recovered from the horrible incident that had occurred during their last case, a few months ago. She wasn't ready to continue with her career in CID yet, and there was a possibility that she would have to be retired out of the force. And considering he was set for retirement, they had some serious thinking to do.

Liz had looked at him hopefully. 'What do you say?'

Of course. This was her way of cutting her losses. If she had to give up being a detective, which for so many years had been her passion and reason for living, then being a private investigator would be more like a detour than a road closed.

'I have to say it sounds like a plan,' he said. 'God! I really don't want to keel over in my vegetable patch from heart disease or, more likely, boredom. I want to keep busy.'

They had only been together for a few months, and already he couldn't remember ever being so happy. For some time before that, their relationship had been a purely physical arrangement. It had suited them both until, against all odds, they had fallen in love, and despite numerous obstacles, mainly to do with their work, they were now living together as a couple.

Matt lay down beside her. 'I have to go to work now, but,' he kissed her hair, 'your idea is looking better and better. We could *please ourselves about what cases we took on and how much time we were prepared to devote to them.'*

'No red tape. No Police and Criminal Evidence Act to worry about. No gold braid reining us in and telling us how to run our enquiry.' She looked up at him. 'Am I selling this to you, Detective Chief Inspector?'

He kissed her, on the lips this time. 'Like a pro, Detective Sergeant.' He sat up. 'As soon as DCI Anders gets herself free of the High Court and I can step down, I think we should find out how we go about setting it all up.'

'You're good with it?' Her eyes shone.

'Let's do it!'

'I love you, Matt Ballard!'

He drove across the sun-drenched farmland in a state of pleasurable anticipation. There were reasons for going along with her idea that he hadn't shared with Liz, one being that he could keep a closer eye on her. She was not yet fully recovered from a massive overdose of a dangerous drug that had been intended to kill her. It was a miracle she had survived at all. And he truly didn't want to go the same way as so many coppers he had known, who had retired and promptly dropped dead. Officers who had led high-octane lives and just stopped, very often paid the price. He'd read one report that said men leaving highly stressful jobs could expect to live a further eighteen months. Eighteen months! Well, that was not going to happen to Matt Ballard. Yet he knew that leaving the job he had dedicated his whole working life to would come as a major shock. He shouldn't underestimate the enormity of it. His life was about to change forever.

He drove slowly, taking in the green-gold glow across the fenland and sorting out his thoughts. Sadly, he had more to worry about than just getting Liz better. His closest friend had died a short while back and it still hurt like hell. They had been unlikely companions, complete opposites, but life was like that sometimes, you found enduring friendship in strange places. Now there was a void that would never be filled.

Liz's idea might just save the day.

Matt felt a slow smile spread over his face. The more he thought about it, the more the idea of becoming a private investigator appealed to him. The Haynes and Ballard Detective Agency? Ballard and Haynes? Or just Ballard and Ballard? Matt's smile grew wider. As soon as Liz's divorce was settled, he would ask her to marry him. He already had the ring and now he was waiting for the right moment to propose. He hadn't quite got his head around that yet.

The main road into Fenfleet came into sight, and he put his mind back into gear. Retirement plans could wait. Right now he had a murder to investigate.

CHAPTER TWO

Matt closed the morning meeting and, having ensured that everyone knew what they had to do, went to report to the superintendent. As he approached the lifts, he was stopped by a young civilian who worked in reception.

'DCI Ballard? Sorry, sir, but there's a lady downstairs who has asked if she could speak to you privately,' the young man said.

Matt frowned. 'Did she give a name?'

'Grace Repton, sir.'

The name meant nothing to Matt. 'Did she say what it's about?'

'No, sir. She refused. She said it's for your ears only.'

Intrigued, Matt followed the young man back downstairs.

'She's in here, sir.' He held the door of the interview room open for Matt.

He'd never met the woman sitting at the table, but he wouldn't have forgotten her if they had. She was that kind of woman. She was around forty-five, still very beautiful, with wavy, dark blonde hair and piercing blue eyes. She wore very little makeup. He introduced himself and sat down opposite her. 'How can I help you, Mrs Repton?'

'I think it's rather the other way around, DCI Ballard. It's me who can help you.'

Her voice was soft and deep, a throaty whisper, reminding him of Lauren Bacall. She had the same air of grace and self-assurance as the old movie star.

'You have some information for us? About what?' Matt felt slightly and, unusually for him, intimidated by Grace Repton. He had to make an effort to remain cool in the hot room.

She sat back and looked at him curiously. 'The thing is, it hasn't happened yet, but I believe it will.'

Matt didn't think she was a nut or a timewaster. She was just being mysterious. 'More information would help.'

She placed her elbows on the table and made a steeple of her slender fingers. 'In a month's time I'm getting married. You know my fiancé. His name is Jeremy Reader.'

Matt started. Oh yes, he knew Jem Reader alright. Some ten years ago, he had been instrumental in getting Reader convicted on five counts of murder. He stared at Grace Repton disbelievingly.

She gave a ringing laugh. 'Priceless! It was worth coming here just to see your face.'

Matt struggled to collect himself. He'd known women who had formed relationships with killers, and he'd read about them in the papers, but this woman? It was very hard to believe. 'Should I say congratulations? Would it be appropriate?'

'Of course! I'm about to marry the man I love. What else should you say?'

Why was the word that sprang immediately to Matt's mind. 'Well, Reader *is* serving life, with a minimum term of thirty years, so I don't think a happy domestic future is on the cards.'

Grace smiled benignly. 'Jem knows he must pay for what he did. And I am fully aware that he will probably never be let out. I am also aware that you won't believe me when I tell you that he is a changed man. He is, though, whether you believe it or not. I *know* he is truly sorry for his actions.'

His actions.

Matt swallowed. Jeremy Reader had murdered five young women, and who knew how many more would have died if Matt and his team hadn't managed to catch him? He was a ruthless, scheming predator, and as far as Matt was concerned, the chances of him ever repenting were pretty well non-existent.

'It's alright, DCI Ballard. I never expected you to believe me, and as I said, it doesn't matter. What does matter is that he has asked me to contact you. He wants me to warn you about something.'

Matt narrowed his eyes. He'd had more threats from banged-up villains than most people had had hot dinners, but for some reason, he took Grace Repton's message seriously.

Grace brushed her hair back over her shoulder. 'Don't worry, this isn't a warning to you personally, it's about something that Jem believes is going to happen here in Fenfleet.'

'Happen?'

'Murder, DCI Ballard. Jem believes that a copycat killer is about to launch a new career.'

Could this be true? 'Copying Reader's methods, you mean?'

'Exactly. In every detail, and if you recall, those details were very unpleasant. Jem doesn't want that happening again, ever. That's why I am here now, talking to you.'

'How does he know this, Mrs Repton?'

'As you can imagine, Jem has had his fair share of warped young men — and women — writing to him. He always disregarded them, until he received a letter from a friend of someone who had been in prison with him, a man called Reuben Grimes. Jem had talked to Grimes in some depth about the things he did, and he thinks he passed this information on to his friend.' She shrugged. 'This young man, who in his letters simply signs himself "Alex," wants to make Jem proud of him, to continue his work.'

The thought of more killings in Jeremy Reader's macabre style made Matt's stomach churn. 'Can I ask how you became involved with Jeremy Reader?'

'I was an OPV.'

'I see.' As an Official Prison Visitor she would have spent considerable time talking in confidence to prisoners.

'Naturally I had to give that up. Getting too close to prisoners isn't allowed, and it didn't take long for us to realise how we felt about each other.'

It seemed surreal to Matt: this rather beautiful, educated, well-spoken woman speaking so fondly and calmly about a sadistic serial killer. 'Forgive me, but I'm struggling with this, Mrs Repton. I've seen other women who idolise incarcerated men, but none quite like you, I must say.'

She laughed softly. 'It's Grace, please. I suggest you don't try to understand it, DCI Ballard. I don't understand it myself, so I couldn't expect anyone else to. What I do know is that Jem has reached a state of awareness, which is something I've never seen or heard of before. He now knows that what he did was heinous. He brought young lives to a premature end and although he can never make amends, he realises that he can serve his time in humility.'

'It is likely that he will die in prison. What kind of married life is that for you?' Matt asked.

'Yes, he could spend the rest of his days in prison, but he'll do that in the knowledge that he has a loving wife just a phone call away, and visiting him as often as is allowed.' She sat up straight. 'Right now, I'm simply a messenger. Jem said that I should talk to you, that you were the only one who would listen. He believed at the trial that there was something different about you. He trusts you,

Inspector, and because of that, I do too. This Alex is dangerous. Dangerous and disturbed. He wants to make his mark, to emulate the terrible things that Jem did a decade ago. Jem has written to him, begged him not to, told him to forget such harmful thoughts and seek help, but to no avail.' She handed Matt a sheet of paper. 'This is all I have by way of information about Alex, and I suspect he is no longer at the address he gave. There's precious little, I'm afraid, but it is somewhere to start.'

Her face crumpled. 'Please find him and stop him, DCI Ballard! My Jem has gone through enough emotional trauma just coming to terms with his crimes. If he thought he was to blame for another reign of terror, it would finish him.' A tear escaped her eye and moved slowly down her cheek.

Matt exhaled. His head ached. This whole scenario was bizarre. A few hours ago he had been worrying about a gangland death, and planning the right moment to propose to Liz. Now he was being forced to stop a fledgling serial killer's first step up the ladder of infamy.

He stared at the woman seated across from him. What the hell was going on? It had to be some kind of scam, but her tears looked genuine. Maybe she was being used? A woman with a good heart, duped by an evil but very charismatic murderer? Matt didn't know. 'Leave me your details, Mrs Repton. I'm not sure what I can do, but I'll be in touch.'

She handed him a rather elegant card, and he gave her his — standard police issue and not very elegant at all.

Grace Repton went to the door, where she stopped. 'He *has* changed, Chief Inspector. Ask his governor.' And then she was gone.

Staring after her, Matt realised that his heart was pounding. He recalled his earlier sense of foreboding, the fear that something twisted and dark stalked his final days on the force. Now it looked as though that fear was about to materialise.

Superintendent David Redpath frowned. 'Okay, Matt, give me an overview of the Reader case. I know the bare bones of it, but I was working in a different area when that one was running.'

'Jeremy Reader stalked and abducted five women over a period of three years. Two in the Rugby area, two in Northampton, and the last one here in Fenfleet. If we hadn't got to him when we did, another girl would have died. He already had a target in mind and a schedule worked out.'

David narrowed his eyes. 'And you were instrumental in his capture, were you not?'

'More thanks to geography than anything else,' said Matt. 'Right place, right time, that's all.'

'Not what I heard, but go on.'

'He had a particular MO, and used it on each of his victims. He used to visit their local park at lunchtime. You know, the kind of place where office workers escape to in the lunch break. Sit on a park bench, get a bit of fresh air and enjoy some peace away from the hubbub of the office.'

David nodded. 'I do the same myself sometimes. Go over to the river walk and just watch the ducks and the water. It helps me think.'

Matt had often wondered where the super sloped off to, but had never checked up on him behind his back — or simply asked. 'Well, Jeremy, who always called himself Jem, was charismatic and very patient. He bided his time before he actually spoke to them. Just a smile, then a wave, then a simple "Hi." He never pushed his target too soon. They must have thought he was another average guy on his break, but he had been watching them for weeks, maybe months. He knew everything about them, and when he finally made his move, they could never have suspected a thing of that "Good-looking, fit, older bloke from the park." That was how the girl he had just begun to cultivate put it when we interviewed her.' Matt sighed. 'Her name was Cerys Griffiths, and she was days away from death, and a terrible death too, but she simply described him as being older than her, but really sweet.'

'Sweet?'

'He was a very clever predator, very convincing indeed. No one could blame the women for being taken in by him.' Matt paused, wondering about Grace Repton. Was she also being deceived? Was she the final victim?

'And they were all stabbed to death?' David asked.

'The full details about exactly how the women died were never released to the media, sir, although they're on file, should anyone wish to examine them. It was exsanguination. He bled them to death, very slowly.'

'Jesus! And he's now telling you that there's a copycat here in the fens?'

'Supposedly.' Matt shook his head. 'This stinks, David. Jem Reader is about as likely to be sorry for what he did as hell is of freezing over. When they took him down after sentencing, I saw the look he gave us police officers. Pure hatred. So why the hell is he now saying that he wants to help us? It's all a load of cobblers, it has to be. I just don't know why.'

David sucked on his bottom lip. 'Mmm, why indeed? Right now, I think the first thing you should do is to make some enquiries about this Repton woman, then maybe have a quick word with Laura Archer, the force psychologist, about women who marry murderers. You need to know where this woman is coming from and what her agenda is.'

Her last words came back to Matt. 'And I'll ring the prison governor too,' he said, 'see what he makes of this forthcoming wedding.'

'Do that. And let me know what he thinks of it.'

Matt stared at his notes. 'Meanwhile, we have another fatal stabbing. The victim has a tattoo, the same as the others.' He told David everything he knew so far about the gangland murders, and said he would update him as they found more information.

'This just validates my plans for next week's crackdown. Operation Saturn has the go-ahead, Matt. It's a joint drugs bust using all the other divisions in the Fenland Constabulary.'

'Good. It's been a year of covert investigations. Now it's time to hit them.'

'And hard. I've got officers from other forces drafted in, and the helicopter will support us. From what we already know, we should be able to make significant arrests and find plenty of Class A drugs.'

'And a lot of other illegal stuff too, I should think.'

'We can but hope.' David raised his eyes to the ceiling. 'Now, I won't hold you up any longer. Oh, and before I forget, if you want to talk to her, Laura Archer is coming in later this morning to help me with an assessment. I'd speak to her afterwards if I were you.'

Matt nodded. 'I will. That woman really unsettled me. I could do with a professional opinion.'

He hurried back to the CID office and found Jason deep in conversation with DC Bryn Owen. 'Anything happen while I was upstairs?' he asked.

'Maybe, sir.' Bryn had a glint in his eye. 'I'm just off to check out a rumour. A Lithuanian woman has been going round the East European shops asking if anyone has seen her brother. One of our plain clothes officers overheard and he got her name and address from the shopkeeper — if it's kosher, of course.'

'Then go! Let's try to tie this up fast. We might just have another problem looming.'

Matt said nothing further. He watched the young detective hurry out. Bryn was a bright, uncomplicated guy, he had a good brain and wasn't afraid to stretch it. Maybe he could be a little too blunt, but at least it left you in no doubt about how he felt about things. He admitted openly that he missed the sarge. He had always got on well with

Liz, and Jason Hammond was certainly no substitute if you fancied a bit of light-hearted banter. If he were not leaving so soon, he would have insisted on a replacement, but it was now down to DCI Anders to select some additional help.

'Give me five then come to my office, Jason. I need to fill you in on something a bit disconcerting.'

Matt had noticed that Jason's usual hangdog expression had intensified. He sighed. The bloke was getting worse. He loved him to bits, but it would be a whole lot more pleasing to look at Liz's beautiful face instead of Jason's. Her idea of them working together was growing more attractive by the hour.

* * *

Jason didn't even try to guess what Matt was talking about, but it sounded ominous.

He closed the report that he'd been working on and sighed. It was horrible, this waiting for Matt to officially retire. It was the end of an era, and although he knew DCI Anders by reputation, it would take him a long time to get used to a new boss.

He had been offered the post himself, but had turned it down without a second thought. There was nothing to consider. Their last case had shaken him to the core. He now knew that he valued his wife and his three daughters more than anything else. Jason was no career copper willing to consign his personal life to the shadows for the sake of the job. Not anymore. He was dedicated and always would be, but not at the expense of his beloved family. After that case, he had come to believe that life was too short to put arresting villains before the ones you loved.

He stood up and made his way to the coffee machine. From the way Matt's face was set, hard as granite, he had the feeling they might need a hit of caffeine.

He pushed the door open with his shoulder, went in and set down the two paper cups of coffee on Matt's desk. Before Matt hit him with whatever bad news he had for him, Jason had a question to ask. 'Um, I was wondering . . .' This was difficult, but he needed to say it. 'Is there any news about another detective for this team? Bryn was asking me, and, well, we are pretty depleted, and . . .'

Matt looked at him apologetically. 'There's no one lined up yet, Jason. I'm afraid it's just the three of us until DCI Anders takes over, then I understand there'll be a permanent post up for grabs.'

Jason noted that Matt's voice had lost all trace of warmth. Their last case had pretty well decimated the team. No one had come out of it unscathed, least of all Matt Ballard. 'Okay, sir. Thank you. I'll pass it on, but—'

'And before you ask, it is doubtful that Liz will be returning. Keep that to yourself for now. It's not certain, but it's looking that way.'

'How is the sarge, sir?' Jason sat down in a vacant chair.

'Sometimes she's just like the old Liz, but at others . . . well, we know the drug damaged her brain, Jason. She gets blinding migraines, sometimes her coordination is impaired and it affected her lung function too. She can't run, even in short bursts and she'd never pass the Beep test. Due to her good recovery so far, the doctors are hopeful that this is temporary, but . . .' He spread his hands, 'but they've told us that we have to face the fact that it might be permanent.'

'So, goodbye to the job that she loved.' Jason shook his head.

'She's remaining positive, old friend, and so should you — for once in your life. She's alive, and that's all that matters.'

Even Jason had to agree with that.

'Now, pin back your ears and tell me what you think about this conversation I had earlier . . .'

CHAPTER THREE

Liz got up late, showered and went down to the kitchen to prepare a leisurely breakfast. She was still surprised at how comfortable she now felt in Matt's old family home. She had hated it on her first visit. She remembered telling him the place was like a museum. She poured herself a mug of tea, smiling. Now, instead of the drab paint and faded wallpaper, the whole house was light, airy and welcoming. It had been the first thing Mattie had done when they decided to move in together. She chose the colours and he got a local company in to do the work. They would have loved to do it themselves, but at the time neither of them was fit enough. Now Matt was physically recovered, but she was taking longer.

Liz was determined to be every bit as healthy as she had been before it happened. She didn't care what others thought, she considered herself to be the luckiest woman alive. First, for the fact that she was alive at all, and, second, because she had practically no memory of what had happened to her. That wasn't the case with poor Matt. No matter how clever he was at covering it up, she knew that the mental trauma would probably be with him for the rest of his life, because he recalled every ghastly detail.

She added more fruit to her bowl of muesli. She did everything possible to make herself whole again. Good food, when Matt wasn't too busy to cook, lots of fruit, plenty of exercise and mental stimulation. She spent hours doing brain-training games and crosswords. She hated Matt going off to work alone, but another part of her had already accepted that she wouldn't be going with him again. For the first time since she was a teenager, her life didn't revolve around the police force. She and Matt could still fight crime, right wrongs and bring closure to mysteries, but without carrying warrant cards in their pockets.

She smiled. Matt was onside! It was really going to happen.

She ate slowly, wondering what to do today. She had walked Tanner's Fen and the sea bank endlessly, and knew practically every inch of it by now. She wished she was allowed to drive, so that her ramblings could extend further. Mattie had suggested that they get a dog. She was tempted, having always dreamed of having a dog by her side. But she had resisted. A dog was a big responsibility, and right now she was concentrating solely on getting better. She was also afraid that if she had one of her "turns" or a breathing attack while out walking alone, she might not be able to keep hold of the leash. If he, or she, got hurt or ran away because of her, she'd never forgive herself. So, having a dog was something to look forward to as she got healthier. And right now, it was far too hot to go walking, with or without a dog.

The phone rang. Liz put down her spoon and went to answer it.

'Gary! How are you? More to the point, *where* are you?'

'Undisclosed location, honey! Still working! Just grabbed a few moments' air time to touch base. How are you doing?'

Liz laughed. 'Well, I'm certainly not the vegetable everyone thought I'd be! In fact I walked three miles at dawn yesterday, with no wobbles or after-effects.'

'Good for you! You sound really great. And how's Matt?'

Most people would think it odd, her husband asking after her lover in such a warm and even affectionate manner. But that was the way it was. Complicated, but very acceptable to all the parties involved. Gary had been her dearest friend, and she had married him simply to allow him to follow his dream and make the grade in the army. Gary was gay, not something to admit to at that particular time, and being married gave him cover. As her job had been all she ever needed, it had worked for them. Until she met Matt. However, they had always agreed that if one or other finally met someone special, they would divorce.

'He's fine, Gary, all healed and back at work. Although he's chomping at the bit right now, waiting for his replacement to take over. He just wants out.'

'I can understand that.'

'And you? When's your next leave due? We want to see you.'

'Maybe next month, but things are pretty unsettled in this "undisclosed location." I'll keep in touch. Oh, time's up. Have to go now. Take care, Liz.'

Before she could answer, the crackly line went dead. She was sorry that they hadn't talked more, but he was safe and that was the main thing.

Liz cleared away the breakfast things and looked out of the window at the heat haze shimmering over the fields of Tanner's Fen. It was even hotter than yesterday, certainly not the kind of day for a walk. She'd do her exercises and chill out with a book for a while. Then? Well, there was plenty to do, but she'd decide on that later. Whatever, it was going to be a good day — Gary was safe, Matt had agreed to becoming a PI with her. All was well with the world. So why was she crossing her fingers?

* * *

Laura Archer listened to Matt's description of Grace Repton. 'I wish I'd met her. I've never actually met a sufferer of that particular condition.'

'It's an actual recognised condition?' asked Matt.

'Oh yes. It's called hybristophelia, a paraphilia,' Laura said.

Matt was vaguely aware that there was a sexual element somewhere in it, but was too embarrassed to ask the very beautiful Laura to expand on this.

'A friend of mine wrote a paper on it once. It's not a particularly well documented subject, and little is known about why women behave in such a way. It's mainly speculation and, frankly, quite fascinating. Some people call it the "Bonnie and Clyde Syndrome."'

Matt couldn't quite see Grace Repton and Jem Reader in that light. 'So how come women want to marry a man serving life for murder?'

Laura leaned back in her chair. 'Some women see an incarcerated man as the perfect husband. If you think about it, if she makes herself attractive to him she knows that she will be constantly in his thoughts. She knows exactly where he is, and that he won't be off philandering, but neither will he interfere with her day to day life or make heavy sexual demands on her. This type of woman is referred to as "love avoidant." She wants a romantic relationship that isn't consummated.'

Matt kind of got that, but he couldn't imagine it applying to Grace Repton. 'Grace Repton seemed so, I don't know, *sensible*. Intelligent. I'm sure that isn't the case with her.'

'There are several other lines of thought. One is that the woman sees the inner child in the man, the wronged soul damaged either by some quirk of fate or a terrible childhood. Then they want to mother him and nurture him. They believe that their devotion can restore the man's innocence.' Laura looked at him enquiringly. 'Is that more her?'

'Not quite, but closer maybe.'

'Some women think that they have enough power to bring about a change in even a serial killer.'

Matt frowned. 'I got the feeling that she didn't see herself as the instrument of his "seeing the light." But she did seem to think that her support would see him through a whole life in prison.'

'Mmm. Interesting.' Laura frowned. 'So you don't think she's a woman who just wants to share the notoriety of what he's done, to get into the spotlight and make a killing herself, from a book or a film deal?'

'Not at all.' He gave her a half-hearted grin. 'Any more categories?'

'Just that she might be a do-gooder who has hopelessly fallen for a very bad boy. But whatever she is, Matt, it's aberrant behaviour. She's deceiving herself with the notion of a beautiful romance, you know, doomed. It's a kind of exaggerated version of some romantic fiction, where the women are drawn to super-dominant males.'

Matt grimaced. 'Well, I didn't think it was exactly "normal" behaviour.'

'Weirdly, serial killers and mass murderers all get inundated with "fan-mail" from groupies. Even a man like the Night Stalker, Richard Ramirez, sentenced to death for thirteen horrific murders and eleven sexual assaults. He got married in San Quentin prison.' Laura glanced at the clock on Matt's office wall. 'Oh dear, I have to go. Maybe you'd let me know if this woman wants to see you again? I'd be happy to take a look at her and give you my opinion.'

Matt opened the door for her. 'I'd appreciate that, Laura, and thanks for the insights, even if I do find it rather incomprehensible.'

She smiled and her vivid cornflower blue eyes flashed. 'Our wonderful human race is certainly complicated, isn't it?'

'You can say that again!' Matt was grateful that he didn't have to try and understand it. He just dealt with the aftermath.

* * *

Grace Repton sat in her kitchen writing a letter. On her lap was her best friend, Cleo, an exquisite smoky grey cat whose eyes were different colours, one blue and the other green.

She took her time, choosing her words carefully. This mattered. They all did, but this letter mattered more than most.

Today, my darling, I saw your detective. He is a very grey man, isn't he? From his hair that is still thick and wavy, his granite coloured eyes, to his rather formal suits.

My visit had the desired effect, of course. I should think his mind is now in overdrive. He will be desperately trying to analyse Grace Repton's reasons for marrying Jem Reader, don't you think? A waste of time, you and I both know that, but he will have to come to his own conclusions, right or wrong.

He took on board everything I told him, which was a good start. He could have dismissed me as a timewaster, but I think I rather intrigued him. He will be in touch again, I am sure, probably after he's spoken to the prison governor, and if he isn't, then I shall prompt him.

I so wish I could visit you more often. Being limited to two one-hour visits every four weeks is torture. I would come every day if I could, but at least I can write and we can speak on the phone, so we must be grateful for that.

Well, rest easy tonight, my love. The wheels are finally in motion. Now we have to pray that your grey detective believes us. I couldn't bear to think of you suffering further hurt because of someone trying to perpetuate a terrible time in your life that you have drawn a line beneath. This is not your fault, Jem. You are not responsible for this deranged young man's actions, and it is to your credit that you are trying to stop him.

God bless. I love you, and always will. Grace.'

She read it, re-read it, and then put it in an envelope. Could she have said more, better? She knew he would read it a dozen times at least, until he could recite every word of it by heart.

Grace lived in a small village on the outskirts of Fenfleet, in a row of three-bed detached bungalows that faced out across the massive flat fenland fields. Her five neighbours were spread along a lane that meandered towards the next village. All had big gardens, double garages, and plenty of room between them. To her, it was idyllic, especially under one of those big Lincolnshire skies — the dazzling fiery sunsets, golden sunrises, apocalyptic storm clouds, and every type of cloud, all ranged across 360 degrees of sky.

At such times, beneath such skies, she thought of Jem Reader, incarcerated behind thick, high walls, triple-locked doors and electronic security devices. The skies that she saw every day would be heaven to Jem, but he would never see them.

Grace picked up the letter, pulled on a floppy sun hat and set off for the tiny post office in the village, just a few minutes' walk away. If she hurried it would go in next day's delivery. It was good to feel the sun on her skin. Such an ordinary errand would be a rare treat for Jem, but he would have her letter, and that would have to be sunshine enough.

* * *

Bryn went to the address he had been given for the Lithuanian woman, but the people there swore they had never heard of her. That left him going back to the streets to make more enquiries. Bryn felt uneasy in this place, the one everyone referred to as the "Baltic Quarter." Police weren't welcome there, and he fully understood why. For almost six months now, he had been dating an Estonian girl called Juula — he called her Jules. She spoke very good English and worked as a fitness instructor at the gym he attended. She had trained as a physiotherapist in Estonia, but her family had suffered hard times. Her parents split up, and she came to England to try to make a new life for herself. Bryn had learned a lot from her. Thanks to Jules, his blinkered attitude towards immigrants had been transformed. According to her, despite the recent reforms in their own country, most people distrusted the police. Old habits die hard.

He had noticed that even though Jules was well integrated, she rarely told anyone what he did, and Bryn had never pushed it.

Right now he was running a gauntlet of stony stares and facing a wall of silence. He had made the effort to learn a few words of the various languages, and that helped a little. At least he wasn't met with hostility. Then, in yet another Eastern European store, he found a young shop assistant who was actually prepared to talk to him. He confirmed that the woman did live at the address Bryn had visited, despite what he'd been told.

'She's worried sick, man,' the young man said. 'She's a nice woman, but I reckon her brother got mixed up with some seriously bad people.'

'You know him?' asked Bryn.

'Sorry, no. It's just what I've heard.'

Bryn groaned silently. He really could have done with a name. 'I desperately need to speak to the sister.' He lowered his voice. 'A man has been found dead. It could be her brother. He had a tattoo on his arm — like a decorated tree?'

For a moment there was silence, then the young man said, 'It's traditional Lithuanian. I think it's the Tree of Life. Look, My name is Lukas, and if you like, I'll go with you. Can't promise anything, but the people in her house might help you if I talk to them first.' He shrugged. 'However, if this had anything to do with the gangs, they'll be scared of reprisals . . .'

'I understand, but I'd really appreciate your help.'

Bryn waited while Lukas told a colleague to hold the fort. Soon they were back at the dingy house on Craven Street.

Bryn listened to them speaking. He didn't need an interpreter to understand fear and anger. It wasn't looking hopeful.

Finally, Lukas made an impassioned plea to one of the older women standing a little apart from the others. Bryn watched her hang her head and mutter something.

Lukas gave her a nod of thanks and beckoned to Bryn. 'That was her grandmother. I know where she is.'

Ten minutes later they found her. She was pleading with an off-licence owner to ask his customers if they had seen her brother. Lukas spoke to her first and Bryn heard the word, *uzmustas* and knew that could mean dead, killed or murdered.

After a while, Lukas turned to Bryn. 'Her name is Lina Derus, and her brother is called Filip. She does speak English, but not as good as me. I've told her that you have found a man, maybe murdered, so she should prepare herself. She will go with you to see him.'

Bryn thanked him, and then he and the young woman turned towards his car. He spoke gently to her, but she didn't answer. He had a feeling she knew exactly what had happened to her brother, and what she would find at the morgue. He opened the car door for her and then rang the boss to tell him what he was doing. If the dead man turned out to be Filip, they'd have had a remarkable piece of luck — not that it would be lucky for poor Lina.

Bryn said slowly, '*As atsiprasau*, Lina.'

She gave him a sad smile. 'I am also sorry. Because I think I will know your dead man.'

CHAPTER FOUR

The governor of Gately Prison seemed happy to talk to Matt about Jeremy Reader. What he said next was completely unexpected.

'He came to us five years ago, transferred from HMP Frankland,' Ross Cadman began.

'Can you tell me why he was moved?' asked Matt. He knew Frankland, the prison everyone called "Monster Mansion," home to some of Britain's most notorious criminals, including Charles Bronson, Levi Bellfield and Peter Sutcliffe.

'Cat A prisoners are routinely moved from time to time for security reasons, especially if there's bullying involved,' the governor said.

Matt couldn't imagine a man like Reader being bullied, and said as much.

'Actually it's quite common. If a prisoner attacks a high-profile inmate like Reader, he'll make a name for himself. Huntley had his throat slashed in Frankland, don't forget. It will up the attacker's status, and as most Cat A prisoners will never be released, they have nothing to lose.' He gave a wry laugh. 'Then, of course, you get the other kind of prisoner who will be desperate to make friends with him.'

'I see.' Prison life was another world entirely, and Matt was just glad that their division had little to do with Her Majesty's Prisons. 'The reason I rang, Mr Cadman, was that I had a visit from Grace Repton earlier today.'

'Yes, I know. Jem told me he was going to ask her to talk to you.'

That seemed a very casual statement. Matt was temporarily at a loss for words.

'Maybe I should explain, DCI Ballard. Jeremy Reader has been a model prisoner, even in Frankland. That's one of the reasons he was moved. He volunteered for a programme in a special psychiatric unit, something that most serial killers would run a mile from. There are perks for sure, but it involves intense group psychology sessions and some very heavy in-depth one-to-one meetings with psychologists and psychiatrists who rake about in your past, especially stuff about your crimes.'

'Forgive me for saying so,' Matt interjected, 'but wouldn't that just boost their egos? Some killers like nothing better than to crow about their evil doings. Surely the attention would actually elevate their opinion of themselves?'

'Some killers, yes. But they would never be invited onto this programme. Don't forget, Reader has served ten years of his minimum term already, and in twenty years' time he will become eligible for parole. If the parole board sees that he's completed this particular course, it will count in his favour.'

'That would make him seventy-four, maybe seventy-five if the board agree to release him. And he would still be on a suspended sentence even after he was freed,' Matt said.

'Yes, he could be sent back to prison at any time. Even the slightest misdemeanour would have him inside again.' Ross Cadman paused. 'But in Jem's case, I'm certain that wouldn't happen. You'll think me a soft touch, Detective Chief Inspector, but Jeremy Reader is a changed man. I really believe this.'

So that was why Grace had said, *"Ask his governor."* Matt sucked on his bottom lip. 'And to what do you attribute this remarkable metamorphosis?'

'I don't know, and that's the truth. Even our psych team are confused. He's — how should I put it — a multi-layered person. Sometimes he seems complicated, and at others he's straight forward and very human.' Ross paused again. 'Would you like to meet him?'

'I've met him, Mr Cadman. I was the one who arrested him, remember?' Matt said shortly.

'Then you'd be the perfect person to reassess him, wouldn't you? Experience this "metamorphosis" for yourself.'

There was no answer to that.

Matt agreed and put the phone down. He sat for a few minutes, deep in thought. What on earth was Jeremy Reader up to? It seemed a ridiculously elaborate game to play, just on the off-chance of influencing a parole board thirty years down the line! There was nothing else to gain from the course other than a few perks, and they would probably be short term. Whatever his reasons, Reader had certainly done a number on Governor Cadman. And Grace Repton.

Matt didn't remember Reader as being the charismatic type. He was certainly no charmer — like Ted Bundy for example — that was for sure. But he seemed to have cultivated two loyal acolytes. Well, if nothing else, a visit to HMP Gately would be an education, though he had no intention of becoming devotee number three.

A knock on his door brought him back to the present.

'Am I interrupting anything?' Jason Hammond asked.

'Only some rather weird thoughts about a serial killer. Come in, Jason.'

'I've just heard from Bryn, sir. We have an identity for the dead man found on the fen. His sister has confirmed it, but she is too scared to say much else. Bryn said she's distraught about her brother's murder, and although he doesn't want to push her at this point, he feels she might be helpful when the initial shock has worn off.'

Matt raised his eyebrows. 'At least the ID was speedy, unlike the other deaths.'

'Remarkably, yes.' Jason sighed. 'Although I doubt it will be so easy to get any names of the people involved in killing him. Everyone clams up the moment they see a policeman.'

'I'm thinking that Bryn, with his sympathetic nature and a smattering of their languages, should stick with this one, don't you?'

'Not to mention the Estonian girlfriend. That might be a bonus. I'll get him making enquiries as soon as he gets back in.'

'Good. Oh, and Jason, make sure he does some homework on that tattoo. We know it's traditional, but who in particular wears that design, and why? I want to know everything about it.'

Jason went out, leaving Matt trying once again to fathom why a vicious, calculating and callous murderer would develop a conscience *and* embrace the idea of holy matrimony. It was hard to imagine, almost laughable.

His phone rang. It was Ross Cadman.

'He's agreed to talk to you, DCI Ballard. Tomorrow at two pm. Can you make it then?'

The sooner the better, as far as Matt was concerned. He needed to see this "saintly" killer for himself. His imagination was already running riot. 'That will be fine, thank you.'

'I'll be extremely interested to get your take on him,' said Ross.

'Don't start placing bets. I'm feeling very sceptical about the whole thing.'

'As did I, I promise you.' Ross laughed quietly. 'But don't let me colour your judgement. Meet him, talk to him, and we'll compare notes afterwards.'

'Can I ask one thing before you hang up? Do you give any credence to this threat of his about a copycat killer taking over where he left off?'

'Well, he believes it, I'm sure. And reading some of the letters that deranged and mixed up people send to Category A prisoners would make your blood curdle. So, let's just say you certainly can't afford to ignore it.'

'I won't. We are already checking out this ex-con that he allegedly opened his heart to, and also the address of this budding Jem Reader replica. Not that I hold out much hope on that score.'

'Well, good luck, and incidents, riots and prison mutiny allowing, I'll do my best to see you tomorrow.'

Matt hung up. He rather liked the sound of Ross Cadman and looked forward to meeting him. The governor's last words had been tongue in cheek, but they contained truth. The job of prison governor was gruelling, few people would cope with it. Not only would he have to contend with off-the-scale stress in ensuring the smooth running of the prison, there would also be a plethora of other jobs, like ploughing through even more paperwork than Matt. Incident management, dealing with suicide attempts, attacks and inmates self-harming . . . the governor even had to taste the prisoners' food. It was one of those jobs that required a very special and dedicated sort of person. It was certainly the last thing Matt would have considered doing. He had once read an article in a daily paper detailing a day in the life of a duty governor in a high-security prison. It had been truly shocking. He often faced massive pressure in his own working life, but he had no idea how anyone could face such stress on a daily basis.

He walked out of his office and along to the big CID room, where Jason had his desk.

His inspector was just putting down the desk phone. 'This mysterious Alex, our alleged apprentice killer, is no longer at the address Grace Repton gave us. He disappeared three weeks ago, owing a month's rent.'

Matt wasn't surprised. He had expected as much. If he was surprised, it was that the man existed at all. 'Did the landlord give any helpful info on him?'

Jason shrugged. 'Not really. He said he was quiet, a bit of a loner, and he saw very little of him. He was originally sharing the flat with another man, the main tenant, but he left and Alex stayed on, paying the full rent in cash, until last month, when he did a runner.'

'Description?'

'Vague. I'm sending a uniformed officer round to try to get more from him, including the details of this "main tenant." He might be our best bet for getting Alex's full name and ID.' He pulled a face. 'I'm guessing the landlord isn't being particularly helpful because the place is a shithole and probably illegally rented out in the first place. It's not exactly a highly sought after neighbourhood, and he didn't even know Alex's surname. Says it all really.'

'Par for the course, isn't it? Still, as you say, the flatmate could be more forthcoming. I wonder if he was the ex-con that was pally with Reader? That would make sense, wouldn't it?'

Jason stood up. 'I'll get onto it immediately, sir.'

'Who is tracking the old lag anyway?'

'Me, sir. I'm covering that as well, but I'm still waiting on answers.'

Matt watched Jason hurry out. They needed more help. Maybe he should ask for it now? With no Liz, and being one down after their last horrific case . . . With a shiver, Matt pushed the dark memories away. They were too thin on the ground to cope with much more.

He headed for the stairs. Time to talk to Superintendent David Redpath.

* * *

David Redpath was angry and frustrated. This was not what he had wanted for Matt's last days on the force. This man had suffered more than any officer he had ever met, but somehow he still remained stalwart. Where others might have thrown up their hands, he was hanging on until the final curtain.

Despite his frustration, David's hands were tied. Well, shackled was probably a better word. Budgets, targets, cutbacks and all manner of red tape prevented him from acting for the good of his officers and easing their burden.

'All I can offer, Matt, is temporary exclusive use of one of the pool detectives. Everyone else has wall to wall running cases, but I could free up DC Kim Peters for you, if that would help? It wouldn't be permanent, but she's got the smallest backlog of work on her desk.'

Matt nodded. 'That will help, sir. I appreciate it.' His face darkened. 'If I find that this weird stuff Jeremy Reader's giving us is for real, we're going to need all the help we can get.'

'Let's take it one day at a time, Matt. Go visit him, and take Kim with you. Get her to watch through the observation window. I'm not sure if you are aware of it, but her big thing is studying body language. She has a talent for it and she could be useful.'

'I'll do that, sir.'

David leaned towards his old friend and colleague. 'Matt, if this goes on too long, I'm going to suggest you back down and retire as planned. I still don't have a date for DCI Anders's arrival, and let's face it, everyone else can just step up a rank until she gets here. Jason can take over as acting DCI, he's more than capable.'

'Of course he could, but it's not what he wants or needs right now, David. Our last case affected him far more deeply than a lot of people realise. He's coping well, but he doesn't need extra pressure.'

'And you? You were affected more than anyone. Hell, man, you were dragged to the brink! What about the extra pressure you're under?'

'I'm a different animal, David, and you know it. For one thing, I don't have a wife and three beautiful daughters at home. That makes a profound difference, doesn't it?'

David raised his hands in surrender. 'Okay, okay! But if it gets too much, you come straight to me. That's an order!'

'Understood, Super.'

He reluctantly let Matt go. David knew that Matt was deeply scarred. For all his bravado, he was far less hard-boiled than he made out. He prayed that this supposedly reformed serial killer was just indulging in some kind of power play devised to waste police time and drain resources. Because if it wasn't, they could be facing very dark days. Matt had confided in him that he was planning on asking Liz to marry him just as soon as her divorce was settled. Now, instead of enjoying a quiet wedding, the detective could be facing another psychopathic killer.

Could he cope? David didn't know.

CHAPTER FIVE

PC Jack Fleet was a "proper copper" of the old school. He knew his days were numbered, but policing was his life, and after thirty years, he wanted it to continue as long as possible. His face, weathered and craggy, was a familiar sight around Fenfleet, and little went on there that Jack didn't know about.

Today, CID had asked him to make a few enquiries about a man called Reuben Grimes. Jack knew Grimes of old. He was an ex-con, who in his youth had rarely spent longer than a few months at a time out of young offenders' or prison, but for once he seemed to be keeping his nose clean. He'd been out for almost a year now without a whiff of trouble, so maybe he had learned something from his stay in HMP Frankland.

Jack wasn't convinced. Reuben was a habitual criminal, and had been since he was a kid. Jack couldn't see him keeping straight forever.

He pulled the car into the parking area and killed the engine. Reuben had moved out of the flat he'd been renting around three months ago, and since then Jack hadn't seen him. Maybe he'd gone back inside. Jack strolled up to the small complex of purpose built, low cost housing where he'd been told Reuben was now living.

Reuben had always been a bit of an enigma to Jack. Where did he get his money from, for a start? Whenever he was released, he had never had to go into a shelter, and he always seemed to be able to look after himself without working. Carefully stashed ill-gotten gains, no doubt. Oddly, considering his background, his apparent lack of formal education and his criminal career, he seemed to have considerable knowledge about a lot of different subjects. Maybe he was one of those rare people who soaked up every little thing he heard or read.

Jack made his way along the narrow passageway between the small houses, and stopped at Reuben's door. He saw at once that Reuben Grimes wasn't there.

The place was unkempt and shabby. Cobwebs festooned the doorframe and dried leaves had gathered on the step. Even so, he rang the bell, but as he expected, no one answered.

Jack looked to the next door along, that of Reuben's neighbour who would have occupied the upstairs part of the maisonette. A tiny handwritten nameplate gave the surname as Chambers. Jack knocked and waited.

He heard footsteps, the door opened, and a tall, heavily built man eyed him suspiciously.

'Sorry to bother you, sir. I'm trying to find Mr Grimes. Reuben Grimes?' Jack smiled politely.

The man's face betrayed a hint of relief. 'He hasn't been here all week.'

'I suppose you wouldn't know where he's gone?' Jack asked without much hope.

'No idea, mate. We speak occasionally, but we're not particularly friendly. He likes his own space, and I like mine.'

Jack took a card from his pocket. 'When he comes back, sir, would you tell him to contact me? It's urgent.'

The man shrugged. 'Can't see a bloke like him ringing a copper, but I'll pass the message on. *If* he comes back.'

'When exactly did you last see him, Mr er, Chambers, isn't it?' Jack pointed to the nameplate.

'Steve Chambers. I reckon it must have been Friday last week. He'd locked himself out and I gave him a hand to get his back door open. Yeah, it was Friday, because we both complained that the bin men hadn't collected the rubbish for two weeks. I'd rung the council and they said there'd been a dispute. In this heat! And they didn't turn up until this morning, would you believe? Disgusting, I call it.'

Jack thanked Chambers and started to walk away.

Then he had a thought. He turned back just as Chambers was closing the door. 'Mr Chambers? That back door that you helped him with, could you show me where it is?'

The man sniffed. 'Sure, but hold your nose. We have to walk through the area where all the bins are, and it still stinks to high heaven.' Chambers locked his door. 'Can't be too careful,' he muttered.

'Very wise,' said Jack, wondering what on earth someone living in this rundown property might have to protect.

He followed Chambers around the side of the house and ran the gauntlet of the freshly emptied but still stinking waste bins. His heart began to race. He'd been in his job far too long not to recognise that the overpowering stench was due to more than rotting waste. 'I think you should go back indoors, Mr Chambers. You can leave this to me.'

Chambers looked perplexed. 'But I know how to open that door of his.'

Jack was tempted to tell him to go ahead and open it, so he could confirm what he believed had happened, but he had spotted the flies and maggots crawling around on the inside of the kitchen window.

He gripped Chambers's shoulder. 'This is not for you, sir. I'm going to have to get some help down here anyway. You go back upstairs and I'll come and see you later.'

'He's dead, isn't he?' The man looked like he was going to throw up. 'All fucking week I've been complaining to the council about the smell from the bins, but it wasn't just that, was it?'

'Sorry, but it does look that way, Steve. Now you get yourself off, and I'll see you as soon as I've rung this in, okay?' Jack gently pushed the big man back towards the alleyway. 'I'll keep you informed, I promise.' He was thinking how lucky it was that Reuben hadn't lived above Steve Chambers. Body fluids had a nasty habit of seeping down.

While the horrified Chambers backed away, Jack radioed in and reported what he'd found.

Within five minutes, two of his colleagues had joined him, not looking exactly pleased. Suspicious deaths were not a copper's favourite shout.

'Okay, let's get this over with,' Jack said.

It took a single swing of the enforcer to gain entry, and Jack's fears were realised. The smell was nauseating.

'Oh, great!' PC Barney Woods exclaimed, his hand clamped over his mouth and nose. 'Just lovely!'

His crewmate, WPC Maggie Smithson, shook her head and groaned. 'Thanks a bunch, Swifty! I'll pay you back as soon as I can.'

All his mates called him "Swifty." It was a play on his surname, Fleet, and a bit of a dig at his slow, methodical manner. 'My pleasure, guys. I suppose it's me in first?'

'You said it,' they chorused.

They found Reuben Grimes in the last room they checked, a tiny box room, usually referred to laughingly as a second bedroom. It was time to call in CID.

Reuben, it seemed, had closed the window and sealed it with wide adhesive tape. He had not, however, secured himself to a hard-backed chair with the same adhesive tape, and then slit his own throat.

'This is one for the detectives, fellas!' Maggie said. 'Well, we mustn't contaminate the crime scene, must we? I suggest we bugger off out of here, fast.'

Barney didn't need telling twice, but Jack hung back. Despite being sick to the stomach, he remained behind for a moment, gazing at Reuben. He hadn't known him well, but he was one of the town's more familiar faces, and for all the crimes he'd committed, Jack had never thought he was a cruel man. Well, he'd certainly met with a cruel and terrifying death.

This was not an isolated incident, Jack was certain. It was part of something much bigger.

After a minute, he followed his friends back outside, pleased to get some fresh air. He knew the procedure only too well. Preserve the scene. Secure it. Instigate a log. Then it would be CID, forensics, undertaker, more forensics, and then when all that was done, bring in the clean-up team. Their American counterparts called it a "decomposition" clean-up and "biohazard remediation," but here they were called Mike and Baz from Rentokil. Not quite the same gravitas, but the poor buggers did a damned good job considering what they had to deal with.

Jack looked sideways at his pasty-faced colleagues. Today was going to be a very long shift.

* * *

Matt ducked under the cordon tape, adjusted the hood on his coverall, and made his way to the back of the small maisonette. Jack Fleet's detailed description still hadn't prepared him for what he saw in that tiny room. Maybe it wouldn't have been quite so bad if it wasn't so oppressively hot, if Reuben's killer hadn't taped the windows closed and packed towels along the bottom of the door. Matt presumed this was to keep the smell in and prevent the body from being discovered too quickly. And the council workers' dispute over the rubbish collection had played right into his hands. Even killers got a lucky break sometimes.

Matt stared at the bloated, decomposing body and wondered why a murderer would go to such lengths to slow up the discovery of his victim.

Behind him, from the doorway, Jason said, 'So, there goes our only link to Alex, aspiring serial killer. Alex's landlord was next to useless, he knew sweet FA about his tenant. I was banking on Reuben Grimes filling in the gaps, but now . . .' He didn't bother to finish the sentence.

Matt turned to speak, but saw Ella Jarvis, the forensic photographer, humping her large aluminium flight case full of equipment along the hallway. 'Ah, Ella. Bad one, I'm afraid. I really don't envy you having to take close-up shots of this poor guy.'

'Someone's got to do it. And I kind of gathered it wasn't going to be a bed of roses when I smelt the place.'

'Could I ask you to get some shots of the tape around the window frames, Ella? I'm rather hoping that the SOCOs might get some evidence off of that. It's difficult to work with adhesive tape and keep it free from fibres or skin cells. We might get lucky with it.'

'Certainly, sir.'

She stared at the subject of her next portrait, and he guessed that beneath her mask she was gritting her teeth.

'We'll leave you to it,' he said.

She didn't answer. Matt knew she was already in the zone, that world of angles, exposures and lighting. The grotesque figure tied to a chair was just a subject now, no longer a man called Reuben.

He followed Jason outside and they peeled off their sweaty protective suits.

Jason looked pensive. 'Don't you think that this adds weight to the idea that there really is a copycat killer ready to pounce? Reuben Grimes was definitely the man Reader confided in.'

'Well, we don't know that for certain, all we have is Grace Repton's word for it. The only thing we do know is that she gave us that name. Anyway, I'll clarify it tomorrow when I see the monster in person.'

'You're taking Kim Peters with you?' Jason sounded a tad peeved.

'Super's orders. Apparently she's ace at body language, so Redpath wants her to watch him from behind the observation glass.'

'Oh, I see.' Jason looked slightly mollified.

'*And* we get to keep her for the duration, which is a huge bonus.'

Jason almost smiled. 'You can say that again, boss. It's the best thing I've heard all week. She's a nice woman.'

'And a smart detective. And considering we now have all this to contend with,' Matt pointed back to the little house, 'we really need her.'

* * *

Matt arrived home that evening and went straight upstairs to shower. The smell from that tiny, claustrophobic room clung to him and no matter how much he soaped himself, it wouldn't go away. He washed his hair twice and stood for a long time under the jet of hot water. Finally, he pulled on jeans and a T-shirt and went down to see Liz.

'It's just a microwave meal tonight, sweetheart,' she said apologetically. 'I didn't know what time you'd be home, so I went for spaghetti carbonara. Is that okay?' It was ready meals all too often these days.

'You should have waited, I could have made dinner.' Matt worried constantly about her, especially when she used a sharp knife. She had those occasional hand tremors and loss of coordination less often now, but there was no telling when one would strike.

'I'm okay, Matt, honestly.' She grinned at him. 'The salad came in a packet, I just washed it, and even I can stick some slices of bread under a grill. You can't do everything, you know.'

Matt put his arms around her and drew her to him. Sometimes the realisation of how close he had come to losing her threatened to overwhelm him. For days she had hovered between life and death, and in those dark hours he hadn't dared contemplate a future for them. It was still a miracle that she was here, with him, still beautiful and bright, and positive that she'd return to full health.

Very gently, Liz kissed him. Her kiss could make time stand still. For a few seconds, his whole being became suffused with love. Matt closed his eyes.

The microwave pinged and they both laughed.

'Time out!' She smiled at him suggestively. 'Plenty of time for more of that later. Right now, let's eat!'

Over supper, Matt told her about his grim day.

'How do you feel about meeting Jeremy Reader again?' Liz asked.

'Frankly, I can't wait. I'm totally bemused at how a tough cookie like Ross Cadman, the prison governor, could be so,' he searched for the right word, '*supportive* of Reader.' He put down his fork. 'I checked Cadman out, you know. He's worked his way up from guard to governor, in places like Feltham Young Offenders Institution — and you know what that place is like. And HMP Liverpool too, that's certainly no cushy number. He can't possibly be a pushover, yet he swears Reader is a changed man.'

'And the chances of that are minimal, to say the least,' added Liz.

'Almost zero.' He grinned. 'That's why I can't wait.'

They chatted inconsequentially for a while, and then Liz said, 'Could I drive in with you tomorrow, Matt? There are some things I need to do in town and I thought I'd see if my old friend Morag is free for coffee.'

'I'll be going in early. After the day we had today, my desk will be groaning with reports.'

'That's okay. I can say hello to the team, then head off out to the shops when they open.'

'What about getting home again?'

'Morag will drive me, or if she's busy I'll get a taxi back. I'm not exactly spending my money on anything else at present.' Her smile faded. 'Damn! I really miss just jumping in the car, especially living this far out on the fen.'

Matt felt for her. She was an active woman. Being grounded must be hell. 'Just a couple more weeks before your next assessment. Hang on in there until then, okay?'

'If it wasn't for the computer and my Kindle, I'd probably be climbing the walls by now.'

'You've come a very long way, Liz, much faster than any of the doctors predicted. Just keep doing what you're doing. It's working.'

Liz cleared the dishes and stacked them in the dishwasher. 'You're right, of course. And the exercises are getting easier.' She glanced at the fitness tracker on her wrist. 'Speaking of which, I've obviously been a bit lazy today. I haven't reached my daily target.' She moved behind him and began to massage his shoulders. 'Can you think of something that might use up a few more calories?'

He felt her warm breath on his neck. 'A nice evening stroll along the sea-bank maybe?'

'Far too dangerous. We'd get bitten to death by mosquitos. Try again.'

'Chess?'

'Not nearly energetic enough. Again?'

Her tongue lapped his ear, and he closed his eyes. 'I've just thought of the very thing. Come with me, young lady, and we'll send that fitness tracker into orbit.' He took her hand and led her up the stairs.

* * *

Matt woke at three a.m., covered in sweat. It had nothing to do with the temperature or Liz's ministrations. He couldn't recall his dream exactly but it had terrified him. Thankfully, he hadn't woken Liz. Rigid in the darkness, he tried to regulate his breathing.

All the bad things that their lovemaking had pushed aside had come back, marching into his head like an army of the night. The bloated remains of Reuben Grimes. The warning that a new serial killer might be lurking in Fenfleet's shadowy alleyways. The death of a young Lithuanian. They crowded together, clamouring for his attention. In the background stood all the characters that had played a part in their last gruesome case — wraiths, silently watching him. One loomed larger than the rest, his old friend who had given his life for Matt.

'I miss you, mate,' he whispered into the shadows. He lay, straining his ears for a reply. None came.

He rested his hand on the sleeping Liz's thigh. So much for a quiet, low-key retirement.

CHAPTER SIX

The drive to HMP Gately took around an hour and a half, long enough for Matt to learn quite a bit about DC Kim Peters. Jason had been right, she was a nice woman, and very knowledgeable about the psychology of body language. In fact, she had a master's degree on the subject of non-verbal communication. Matt was impressed and told her so.

'It's something that's always fascinated me, even as a child. I could always tell when one of my siblings or school-friends was lying. It just came naturally to me, and I couldn't understand why other people couldn't see it too.'

He liked the soft lilt of Kim's Scottish accent. 'And did you always plan on using it in law enforcement?'

'Not at all. I'd intended to go down the psychologist route, but then I began to wonder where I'd be of most use. I mean, where do you meet most liars?'

'Ah. Villains.'

'Absolutely, and that appealed. So I joined the police force.'

They made their way to the visitor centre. Though he was often obliged to visit them, Matt never liked going into prisons. There was something horribly claustrophobic about a series of doors being locked and unlocked as you proceeded into the depths. It was ironic really, since he had spent most of his life endeavouring to put people in such places. Gately was not a "cushy" prison, but neither was it some ancient Victorian edifice such as Wormwood Scrubs, or a prison within a prison like the High Security Unit at Belmarsh. Gately was Cat A, but being much newer, was not as intimidating as some.

Their warrant cards and the details of their visit were checked, and they were escorted across to the main building. They passed through several series of those hated locked doors before arriving at a reception area. Here, their fingerprints were scanned and, like in an airport, they had to remove their shoes, belts and put their belongings through an X-ray machine. They then walked through a metal detector and were given a body search. It was thorough. Their mouths were examined, their ears, and even the soles of their feet. No one was exempt. Category A was the highest security, and even the guards were subjected to these checks.

The meeting with Jeremy Reader was to take place in an interview room just off the visitors' hall. Beside it, there was a small office with a one-way viewing window and a speaker system, so that Kim could both see and hear Reader.

Matt suddenly felt anxious. The last time he'd seen Reader, the man was being dragged from the dock by court officers and shouting threats at him. Reader might have been cool and calculating when he murdered women, but he had not taken his life sentence calmly. His hate and anger had erupted in a storm of vitriol.

And this same man wanted to help him? Matt was sceptical.

A prison guard escorted Kim into the office, and then unlocked the interview room door.

Jeremy Reader was waiting, sitting on the far side of a bare table, a single guard standing silently by the door.

For a long moment the two men regarded each other in silence. Then, slowly, Reader's face broke into a smile. 'I owe you an apology, DCI Ballard. Last time we met I was less than polite to you.'

Matt stared at him in silence. This was not the Reader he remembered. The man sitting before him, dressed in a smart blue-and-white striped shirt and grey joggers, his dark hair greying at the temples, he almost looked like a member of some respectable profession on their day off. His blue eyes were clear and shrewd.

Jeremy Reader looked back at him steadily. 'Thank you for coming. I appreciate it.' He seemed very much at ease. 'So you made DCI in ten years. Impressive. But you were always streets ahead of your colleagues. After all, you caught me, didn't you?'

Matt said nothing. Reader went on. 'I don't blame you for not trusting me. I told Grace that if the boot were on the other foot, I wouldn't trust me either.'

'Grace Repton trusts you, enough to marry you. That does bother me.'

'I can understand why. . I've had sackfuls of mail from weirdos, serial killer groupies who fantasise about having a relationship with a man who has committed an atrocity. Offers of . . . well, you can guess. But Grace is not one of those. She is simply the woman I fell in love with, and what anyone else thinks is irrelevant. You included, DCI Ballard.' He leaned forward. 'But that is not what this meeting is about.'

'Grace explained. You believe a man called Alex is going to continue murdering women in your name, is that right?'

'I do. I know he will.'

'You confided all your gruesome secrets to a man named Reuben Grimes. And he passed them on to a young man who was sharing a flat with him, someone obsessed with you and how you killed women.'

Matt saw Reader tense. He closed his eyes for a moment and said, 'Yes, that's exactly what I think. Ask Reuben.'

Matt decided that this was not the time to tell Jeremy Reader that someone had already made quite sure he couldn't do that.

'Okay, let's assume I believe you. Why would you want to help the police — me especially?'

'I'm a very different man to the one who committed those murders, DCI Ballard. The man I am now can't bear to think of more families going through the agonies of what those mothers, fathers, brothers, sisters and friends had to bear when I took away their loved ones.'

Matt felt the urge to ask for a bucket. 'Can we cut the pathos, Jem? Tell me, what great Eureka moment brought about this metamorphosis? This awakening to the truth about what you did?'

Reader laughed softly. 'There was no "moment," DCI Ballard. No one can rehabilitate you, no well-meaning psych doctor or do-gooder. It has to come from within you. People change when the time is right. I was kept locked up, sometimes for twenty-three hours a day, for months on end. You learn to calm your mind. If you don't, you go insane, self-harm, or top yourself. Or maybe kill someone else, who knows? But in one of those long solitary spells, I discovered a desire to understand what impelled me to do the things I did.'

Matt listened in silence, still unconvinced.

'The chaplain suggested meditation. At first I laughed, but then I tried it, and although it took years, I can now focus my mind, and I came to understand that my actions were unforgivable.' Matt saw a tear glint in Reader's eye. 'I can't go back and undo the past. I cannot raise those women from the dead, although I wish I could. All I can do is take responsibility. I fully accept that I was justly punished, and I just hope it gives those poor families some peace to know that I will never again walk under a blue sky with the wind in my face.'

'But you could. You could be released in twenty years.'

'I'll be dead by then.'

Matt had nothing to say to this.

'I will die in prison, I know that. Lifers rarely think about release, DCI Ballard. They don't dare to. We have to look inward, within these walls, to find whatever meaning life may hold.'

'And, Grace? Where does she fit in?'

'Love can't be confined in a prison. It can't be chained. Whether I'm in here or out in the world, I'll still love her, and she feels the same. We are soulmates. We don't need to be in physical contact to feel that love. It is always with us, always.'

For a man that had taken the lives of five people in cold blood, Reader spoke far too glibly about "love." Matt remained silent.

Reader seemed to sense his scepticism. 'Talk to Reuben, DCI Ballard. Please. He should never have spoken to that boy, and he knew it. But the lad was so interested. Intelligent too. He was at college and also studying online. Reuben assumed he was a psychology student wanting to understand such crimes from the perpetrator's point of view. He had no idea what was in the boy's head until it was too late. When he realised that he was obsessed with me, he'd already given him the details. He was devastated.'

'Why did you reveal so much to Reuben Grimes in the first place? Why not talk to the doctors who were helping you?'

Reader laughed sardonically. 'The doctors at that time weren't like the ones here, on this programme. They were completely desensitised. At least, that's how it seemed to me. They'd heard too much. That place was full of violence and rage, from the governor to the inmates. Reuben was a breath of fresh air. He wasn't a Cat A prisoner and he was only being held there for a short time. I forget why, but I knew he was short stay. The time allowed me for association was limited, so I made every minute count. Reuben was the best listener I'd ever met. He wasn't interested in airing his own opinions, and he didn't make judgements. He was my unofficial counsellor, my sounding board, and my friend. The only friend I've ever had. I was glad for his sake when they let him out, but I missed him.'

Matt was on the verge of telling him about his "only friend," but he kept quiet. If Reader felt that deeply about the man, then the moment he told Jem about Reuben's death, the interview would have to be terminated as Matt would get little more from him.

'Did he visit you after they moved you here?'

'Oh, yes. He's on my visitor's list. Naturally his visits are fewer now, as I have Grace to consider.' Jem smiled benignly. 'He understands.'

Even Matt was starting to feel some compunction, knowing that there would be no more visits from Reuben Grimes, *the best listener in the world*. 'This Alex. Did you keep his letters? You must have had his address to answer them.'

'I destroyed most of them, along with all the others that I found distasteful and a waste of my time. The only address I had was the one I gave to Grace.' He looked worried. 'The letters stopped abruptly after one in which he told me he was going to "let his actions speak for him." That was when I asked Grace to contact the police — well, you.' He looked Matt straight in the eyes. 'He's not there, is he? He's moved on.'

Matt nodded. 'He has.'

'Find him!' There seemed to be genuine fear in Reader's eyes. 'Or someone will die.' He slumped back in his chair.

Matt wished he knew what Kim Peters was making of it all, because he certainly didn't know what to think.

Jeremy Reader rubbed at his eyes. 'Okay, DCI Ballard, here's the deal.'

Matt tensed. 'I don't make deals, Reader.'

'You don't have to. It was a figure of speech. This is a gift, and it's not given lightly.' He leaned towards Matt, his elbows on the table. 'Everything I say to the doctors during the PIPE scheme sessions — that's the Psychologically Informed Planned Environment — is completely confidential. But, in the interests of, what do you call it, complete transparency, I will give them my permission to allow you access to all my records, all my psych evaluations.'

'Why would you do that?'

'So you can look inside my head, Detective. I want to convince you that I'm not pulling some kind of scam. I truly want you to stop some innocent losing their life in a horrific manner.'

Now, Matt wished he had Liz sitting alongside him. He had always known what she was thinking when they interviewed suspects together. Well, he would just have to wait to hear what Kim thought. He looked hard at Reader, trying to discern some hint of trickery, some other agenda. But Reader simply looked exhausted.

'I appreciate that, although I might not need to see them.' Matt hoped he looked mildly enigmatic.

'Then I'll help you out, and if this doesn't convince you, nothing will.'

What was Reader about to say? Matt swallowed, and waited.

'Going back to my trial, there was one detail that was never pursued in court.' Reader spoke in a monotone. 'There were questions regarding some of the injuries the victims suffered — abrasions and grazes in particular. I stated that they had fought back prior to being immobilised. That I dragged a couple of them across concrete, so I supposed that was how the injuries occurred.' He took a deep breath. 'I lied.'

Matt remained silent, wondering what was coming next.

'Each of those abrasions, or grazes, concealed a tiny piece of skin excised very carefully, and then the area was made to look like the result of a desperate woman fighting back.'

Matt was stunned. 'You took a piece of their skin?'

Reader nodded slowly. 'A thin slice. About one inch. In the shape of a heart.'

A trophy? Matt had read about such things.

'Five tiny hearts, DCI Ballard. I suggest that you check the findings of the various pathologists. The post-mortem reports will record a deep abrasion in these places.' He quoted: "Mary Jayne Fowler, upper arm. Denise Paul, forearm above wrist. Lindsay Richards, outside of right thigh. Betsy Gilham, left shoulder. And Lucy Packer, right breast." Reader flopped back in his chair.

'One question,' Matt asked. "Did you keep those hearts of skin?'

Reader nodded miserably. 'Only four people know about this — Reuben, Alex, Grace, and now you.' He looked up. 'Make that five, I forgot about him.' He pointed to the guard. 'If I tell you where they are, will you promise me that you'll make finding Alex your main priority? We both know that this information will mean I'll have no chance of parole, ever. I have bared my rotten soul in an attempt to stop more deaths. You must take me seriously, DCI Ballard.'

'Tell me, and I'll move heaven and earth to find Alex.'

'Alright. There's a rented garage, in Grange Road, Fenfleet. The old skinflint who owns it has the rent paid by standing order. Grace keeps an eye on my finances, so I know it's still there. My car is inside, and taped under the passenger seat is a small airtight container. A forensic check will confirm what I've told you.'

The meeting was over.

Neither man had anything else to say.

Matt stood up and drew in a long breath. He turned to the guard. 'We are finished here.' He looked back at Jeremy Reader and gave him a nod.

Reader returned the nod.

Matt had said he never made deals, well, this time he had. Reader had given away his last chance for freedom, and Matt had promised to hunt down a psychopath called Alex.

The door closed behind him.

CHAPTER SEVEN

DC Kim Peters and her new temporary boss drove in silence for what must have been at least five minutes.

Finally, Matt Ballard glanced at her. "So?"

As Kim knew, interpreting body language was more of an art than a science. The same sign or gesture can mean different things, the most common being scratching the nose during a conversation. If the person doing the scratching is the one talking, it's a classic sign that they are lying, because this increases the size of blood vessels and can make you itch. If it is the listener scratching, they may be in disagreement with what is being said. Or in both cases, it can simply mean an itchy nose.

The thing was, Kim had expected to see a devious killer cleverly conning his mark. But she hadn't. 'The main thing, sir, is that he gave no sign at all that he was lying to you. If anything, his body language indicated guilt and shame. I really didn't expect to see that. He also seemed desperate, and I think that came from the fact that he desperately wanted you to believe him.'

'But if it was some kind of elaborate hoax, wouldn't he feel that way too?' asked Matt.

'Yes, of course, but then there would have been an element of him trying to control you, and there was no sign of that at all.' She paused for a moment. 'As I see it, there is one major stumbling block here. People can learn to control their body language. It's a technique that some of those "life coaches" teach to build confidence and dispel negativity. If Reader has studied this, he could have been putting on a brilliant act.'

'And what does your gut tell you about him?'

'Frankly, sir, I understand why the governor believes him. I believe it's a rarity, but I think I was watching a serial killer who is truly remorseful about what he did. He genuinely wishes you to stop another man from taking over where he left off.'

Matt whistled softly. 'Is that possible? Really?'

'Maybe Laura Archer can answer that one for you, sir.' Kim stared down at the copious notes she had made. 'All I can say is, if he was faking the whole thing, he's a real pro. He used subtle movements and gestures that would be very hard to put successfully into an act.' She had the impression Matt was pleased that Governor Cadman had been detained elsewhere and couldn't meet them after their interview with Reader. He clearly wasn't totally convinced about their remorseful killer, and must have wanted to get his head straight before discussing it with Cadman.

'One of the first things I do will be to speak to Laura. I was certain I'd take one look at him and know, one way or the other, how I felt about him, but . . .' Matt gave an exasperated grunt.

'I was the same, sir. He was nothing like what I'd envisaged.'

'That last secret threw me completely. I could be wrong, but I think that if he ever got the chance for parole, they'd take one look at that and it'd be curtains.'

'Why, sir?'

'Two things. One, he never admitted to the taking of trophies at his trial, and if he could conceal that, what else had he concealed? Maybe more murders? Or rapes, prior to his killing spree? It makes him unreliable. And two, the taking of trophies puts him in a different league. Serial killers who keep something from their victims, especially parts of their anatomy are considered sadistic predators who want to continually "nourish" the memory of their killing. It would be thought that he would be unable to integrate back into society without a high risk of him reverting to his old ways.'

'He really didn't have to play that card so early in the game, did he?' she said. 'He could easily have waited to see if you were going to work on the information he'd given you, and if you didn't play ball, hit you with that bombshell then.'

'Exactly. I had the feeling that finally having this nasty secret out in the open was a catharsis for him. And if that's the case, it means he's on the level. He does feel remorse.'

Kim didn't answer immediately. Then she said, 'We need more than this. I think you have to ask for those psych evaluations. In the hands of someone like Laura Archer, they could be very revealing indeed. We both know what that man did, what he was capable of, so we can't afford to be taken in at the first meeting.'

'So, do we believe him or don't we?'

Kim watched the fields fly past the windows in silence. Then she smiled. 'It's not every day that you're asked to make a judgement on a serial killer's ability to tell the truth. It's a first for me, that's for sure.'

The DCI smiled back at her apologetically. 'Thrown you right in at the deep end, haven't we?'

'Well, I can't complain that working with you is boring, sir. And it's one for the scrapbook.'

'You keep a scrapbook?'

'Have done since I was a little kid. Memories fade. Looking back over the years, there are a lot of things worth remembering.'

This seemed to sadden him. Kim wondered about Matthew Ballard's memories. Clearly they weren't good ones. She didn't know much about his last case, just that he and his sergeant, Liz Haynes, had been badly injured. Other than that, it had been hushed up for some reason. Kim was fairly new to the district, and felt she shouldn't be too inquisitive. She couldn't help wondering, though.

They drove the rest of the way in contemplative silence.

* * *

As two cars sped towards the lock-up garage in Grange Road, Bryn was making his way back to the Baltic Quarter. Lukas had called the tattoos the "Tree of Life," and Bryn wanted to know more.

He decided to start at the Eastern European shop where he had first met Lukas, but the young guy wasn't there. The woman on the till pretended she couldn't understand him. Bryn was being watched, not overtly, but he could see the sidelong glances.

And this was one of the friendlier places he'd visited.

He realised he wasn't going to get any joy here today, so he headed for the door. A beefy arm reached out and closed it. Two men moved in front of him and barred his way out. They stared at him.

Shit. Trouble. Bryn tried to keep his voice steady and friendly. 'Excuse me, lads. Can you let me through, please?'

'Leave Lukas alone,' one of them said.

'Sorry?'

'You heard. You aren't welcome here, so fuck off, and don't come back.' The man's head was shaven, revealing an oddly-shaped skull. His friend did have hair, straggly and greasy. Bryn wondered where this was going to end up.

Then he got mad. This pair of shitty low-lives weren't going to threaten him and stop him doing his job. 'I'm Detective Constable Bryn Owen. I want to talk to Lukas, and when I find him, I'll talk to him. So step aside before I get my colleagues down here.'

No one moved.

'Leave him alone, policeman.' The bald one leaned closer, and Bryn could smell the alcohol on his foul breath. 'You will get him hurt,' he hissed.

Bryn frowned. 'Oh? And who's going to hurt him then?'

'Not your concern, but it'll be your fault. Now fuck off, policeman.'

Before he knew what was happening, the door was pulled open and he was shoved out into the street. He spun round, and heard a bolt ram shut.

Bryn exhaled loudly. He really wanted to charge back in, but the door was barred. Probably just as well. What had happened? Why didn't they want him speaking to Lukas all of a sudden? Bryn wondered what to do. The last thing he wanted was for Lukas to get hurt. He'd have to think again. Maybe he should try Lina Derus?

He walked back towards his car, wondering what was going on in this community. It had always been volatile, but today it felt as if a huge storm was about to break. He could feel the electricity in the atmosphere. He should check that Lina was okay after the shock of seeing her brother in the mortuary, and that she was safe. What he really wanted to do was get out of the Baltic Quarter, fast.

He started the car and headed for Craven Street, thinking about what kind of reception he would get.

Somewhat to his surprise, the grandmother asked him in straight away. She pointed towards a partly open door and indicated for him to go inside.

There he found not just Lina, but Lukas too.

'Are you both okay?' he asked, looking from one to the other.

Lina nodded slowly. Bryn saw traces of tears on her cheeks.

Lukas seemed agitated, looking angry, confused . . . and was that defiance?

'Two of the ugliest sods in town have just warned me off talking to you, Lukas.' Bryn lowered his voice. 'What's going on?'

'I think I've accidentally upset a few people, Detective Owen.'

'Call me Bryn, Lukas. What have you been doing? Those guys seemed to think that you were going to get hurt if I contacted you. Is that right?'

Lukas sat down on the threadbare sofa. 'I just wanted to help Lina, find out what happened to her brother. Seems like certain people don't think that's a good idea.' He grimaced. 'And they definitely don't want me talking to the police.'

'Do these "certain people" have names?' Bryn asked.

'Of course not. I have no idea who they are.'

Bryn looked at Lukas more closely. He was sitting with his hands pressed to his stomach, just below his ribs. 'They've hurt you already!'

'Nah, just pushed me around a bit. I took a punch that winded me, that's all.'

Bryn didn't believe him. 'Lift up your T-shirt.'

Lukas shook his head. 'It's nothing. Forget it.'

'Do as he asks, Lukas,' Lina said.

Reluctantly Lukas pulled up his faded T-shirt to reveal a large area of mottled purplish bruising. 'I bruise easily,' he muttered.

'Like hell. That's a kicking, if ever I saw one. Jesus! That's a boot print!' Bryn sat down next to Lukas. 'What did you say to deserve this, kid?'

'It was the tattoo, I think. I asked Lina about it. She said a few other men in her community had the same thing, but Filip had never said what it meant.' He shrugged. 'So I asked around about it. Bad move.'

'So it seems.' Bryn frowned. 'Did anyone give you any idea of what it means — before they started using you for football practice, that is?'

'Yeah. I think that's when someone overheard and called in the heavy mob.' He grinned painfully. 'I found another guy with the same tat, just like the picture you gave me to look at. It was the Tree of Life, but slightly different.' He looked across at Lina. 'He told me it wasn't a gangland image, or even a particularly Lithuanian design, it was a family thing. Then he clammed up.'

Bryn thought hard. Family? As far as he knew, the other three victims weren't related. He turned to Lina. 'Did you and Filip have any family connections with those men who were killed recently?'

She shook her head. 'We're a big family, many cousins and other relatives, but we didn't know those other men who were murdered. One was never named, I think—'

'Even though we all knew who it was,' Lukas interjected.

'But no one came forward.' Bryn sighed.

'Do you blame them?' Lukas pointed at his bruises. 'This was just a taster of what could have happened.'

So, what to do now? Bryn knew this was very dangerous territory, especially for Lukas. 'Those two apes who threatened me. Who are they?'

'Tomas and Otto.' He smiled faintly. 'Believe it or not, they're my uncles. I'm sorry they warned you off, but family stick together and they are only thinking of my safety.'

'Well, at least you don't look like them! Will they keep an eye on you? Are you safe if you go home?'

'No one is safe anywhere around here.'

Lina nodded. 'This was good place to be. Now the dealers make it a bad place.'

'So, it's all drug-related — the killings, the threats and this feeling of fear on the streets?' Lukas seemed to hesitate. 'You don't agree, Lukas?'

'Drugs, certainly, and we all live under the threat of the Baltic mafia, but . . .' He directed a meaningful look at Bryn. 'If you can, check out that tattoo. I think the deaths are to do with something else, and that tattoo is the connection.'

If that was the case, this young man was in serious danger. Bryn's thoughts started to race. If Lukas had been seen coming here, followed shortly afterwards by a copper, there was a pretty good chance that he'd finish up on the station whiteboard. And with the budget as it was, there wasn't a hope in hell of getting him any kind of protection. 'Is there somewhere you can go, Lukas? Somewhere away from here? Some place others don't know about, and that's safe?'

Lina gave a sad laugh. 'We only have each other around here. And if Lukas loses his job . . .' Her voice tailed off.

'Well, my man, bottom line, you're certainly not safe here. And I can't just walk out on you.' A slow smile spread across his face. 'Okay, see what you think of this — though it's going to hurt.'

Lukas tilted his head. 'Go ahead.'

'Right. I leave. You come after me. There's a scuffle. I arrest you. Even if those people don't actually see it happening, the news will travel fast, and it should dispel any idea that you're collaborating with the police.'

'Do it, Lukas,' said Lina. 'My family here will tell everyone you've been arrested.'

'Only problem is,' Bryn added, 'you're already injured. Another scrap will really hurt.'

Lukas gritted his teeth. 'I can cope with that. But what then? You can't hold me indefinitely.'

'No, but I might be able to arrange somewhere for you to go temporarily. They'll think you're being held in custody for assaulting a police officer. And if they think that and you do go back to your family, the heat should be off.' He took a breath. 'It's not perfect, but I really think you're in danger if you stay here.'

'Please, Lukas. You are good man. You try to help me find out about my Filip, and now I am sad that you are hurt. Go with the policeman. Do as he says. For me?' Lina said.

Lukas stood up. 'Okay. What have I got to lose? Just remember — I really do bruise easily.'

'Good.' Bryn turned to Lina. 'Whatever you do, keep a low profile, and don't talk to anyone about those tattoos, okay?'

She frowned. Lukas translated the meaning of "low profile" to her, and then she nodded quickly. 'I understand.'

'Okay, let's go and put on a good performance for Craven Street, shall we? Let's fight.'

* * *

PC Jack Fleet knocked at 34 Grange Road. Ron Pennell, the occupant, was a small, seedy looking man with thinning hair and a pronounced beer belly. He looked more than a little anxious when Jack asked him to go immediately to Jeremy Reader's garage and unlock it for them. 'It's all above board, Officer. I have a written agreement and the rent is paid regularly. So what's the problem?'

'Police business, sir. I'd be grateful if you would just unlock it and leave. We'll contact you later to return the key.'

Pennell went inside and emerged a few moments later with a small garage key in his hand. 'The garages are just around the back. I have three of them in the access road behind here.' He locked his own door and beckoned for Jack and his fellow officers to follow him.

At the bottom of an alley that ran down the side of Pennell's house, there was a rear-access road that led to a small block of rather tatty garages and a turning space. Reader's garage was the last one.

Pennell unlocked it and was about to open up when Jack stepped forward. 'Thank you, sir. You can leave it to us now.'

Pennell backed off reluctantly, but hovered a short distance away, keeping an eye on the proceedings.

There was no electricity, so they opened both doors wide. It was stuffy and hot inside, stinking of fuel and the mustiness of a place closed up for years. Reader's car was there, as he had said. Jack felt across the top of the front offside tyre, and found the spare key. So, he had been telling the truth about that too. The big thing now was would they find what they had come here to look for?

Jack unlocked the dark red Mazda and opened the door. He took a deep breath, knelt down and pointed his flashlight underneath the passenger seat.

Illuminated in the torchlight, he saw the plastic box, securely taped to the underside of the seat. 'We've got it!' he called to the others. 'I'll ring the DCI now, if someone else could get forensics down here.'

'DCI Ballard has just drawn up, Swifty. He's here now.'

Jack was relieved. This find was important, if it turned out to be what Reader had said it was. He'd be happy to surrender it to CID, and not have to deal with it himself.

Matt Ballard and Jason Hammond hurried into the garage and stared at the Mazda Protégé. 'This hasn't been anywhere for a while, has it?' murmured Jason. 'There's definitely something under that seat?'

'Oh yes,' said Jack. 'It's what you said, a plastic container, like a small Tupperware box.'

Matt crouched down and asked for a torch. Jack handed him his. The DCI gave out a low whistle. 'That man gets to be more of an enigma with every bloody moment that passes.' He looked up at Jason. 'Well, here goes nothing.'

He carefully peeled back the now dried-out tape and released the box.

He lifted it into the light of the torch. For a moment he said nothing, and then he stood up. 'Have forensics been called?'

'Someone is on their way, sir.'

'Jason? An evidence bag, please. I'd dearly love to open this, but we have to follow the correct channels. This is one for the lab.'

Jack hadn't been told the full details, only that if he found what they were looking for, he should get CID in straightaway. What was in that box?

CHAPTER EIGHT

Intrigued by the prospect of meeting a woman who was willing to marry a serial killer, Laura Archer phoned her old friend and mentor, Sam Page, to ask his opinion.

'Well, you do come up with some strange ones, Laura!' Sam chuckled. 'Have you met her yet?'

'Not yet, but Matt says I can sit in when he speaks with her next. He reckons she doesn't seem like a person suffering from hybristophelia. She's intelligent, quite well off and very good-looking, so she's not likely to be influenced or coerced into doing something she doesn't want to.'

'People always think it unlikely that a woman could either commit a violent crime or be associated with one, and I guess the same could be said of a woman who idolises a murderer.' He paused. 'Of course, she could be the kind of woman who believes herself to be powerful enough to "get him back on the straight and narrow."'

Laura sounded doubtful. 'I suggested that, but Matt said no. Apparently she implied that Jeremy Reader had already shown remorse before they even got together.'

'Interesting.' Another chuckle. 'Not only a woman who suffers from serious paraphilia, but one who's connected to a convicted serial killer who claims to be full of remorse! Goodness me! This is a psychologist's dream come true.'

'Actually, it's all rather confusing. I was hoping for a call from Matt Ballard today, as he was visiting Reader in prison. I'm dying to hear what he made of the man.'

Sam murmured in agreement. 'It's rare for people who kill more than once to show remorse. A person who commits one murder, maybe in the heat of the moment, can truly regret their act. It can cause them real misery, but someone who has deliberately committed more than one murder is almost never sorry for what they've done.'

'I've been looking at case histories,' said Laura, skimming down a list of names she'd written. 'I've found three instances where killers not only admitted to self-reproach and guilt, but followed this through by either accepting a death sentence or killing themselves.' She paused, and asked, 'Sam? Have you ever been involved in such a case? Directly, I mean.'

'Just once, when I was young.'.' His voice lost all trace of humour. 'If there is one case from my early years in psychology that's stayed with me forever, it is that one. It haunted me.'

Laura had never heard him speak of being "haunted" by a case before. He'd been her tutor and her mentor, almost a father to her, for many, many years. It was also odd to hear him sound anything but jovial when they spoke together. 'Can you tell me more about it, Sam?'

'Not over the phone, but I could come over to your consulting rooms. Have you got any more appointments today?'

'All finished, Sam. The last one cancelled, so I was just thinking about heading home. Do come over.'

While she waited, she rang her partner, DI Rowan Jackman, and told him she might be a bit late for supper.

Then she went and put the kettle on. This conversation with Sam sounded like it might call for copious amounts of tea.

Even though she had moved in with Jackman at his lovely old converted mill house in Cartoft Village, Laura had retained her consulting rooms and the flat attached to them. There was no question that she loved him, but they were both old enough to know that two driven professionals in very demanding careers were not always the most considerate of partners. Retaining her apartment kept her options open in case things didn't work out. And of course, she still needed an office.

She made the tea and soon Sam arrived.

'You're a sly old dog, Sam Page. You never mentioned this before.'

Sam didn't return the smile. 'It happened years ago, but it still bothers me. It was the first case to make me realise just how complex a thing the human mind is.' He frowned. 'And it also made me aware of the enormous weight of the responsibility we bear in trying to understand that mind and ease the pain of those of us who are damaged and suffering. If we fail them, who else can they turn to?'

A little taken aback at the unaccustomed gravity of his tone, Laura said nothing.

'I was privileged to accompany my original mentor as he attempted to help this extremely disturbed young man, whose name was Leon Briars. He was a studious looking young chap, with a floppy blond fringe and heavy, dark-rimmed glasses — "Buddy Holly" we used to call them. He was slight and wiry, but extremely strong. He murdered eight young men, all students, over an eighteen-month period, killing two of them in a single day.'

Laura raised her eyebrows.

'Then, one day, he turned up at the local police station with a long letter addressed to the custody sergeant. In it, he declared that there were times when a monster inside him took over. When that happened, he killed innocent young men. There was no particular reason for these murders. Like Dr Jekyll in the Jekyll and Hyde story, Leon was totally aware of the evil things he had done. He went to the police to ask them to lock him away before he killed again.'

'Surely, this is a case of dissociative identity disorder, isn't it? This guy had two distinctly different personalities that influenced his behaviour. It wasn't remorse per se — or was it?'

Sam nodded. 'That was what we originally presumed, but as we continued to work with him, we realised that it wasn't actually the case. At base, he was a complex sexual sadist.' He picked up his cup, nursing it in both hands. 'I only realised later that it's a common experience when you work with murderers. You see, he really did need to understand himself and the mental illness he suffered from.'

'So, when he confessed that he killed "for no particular reason," he was lying?'

'No, he wasn't. He had honestly believed that that was the case, and he only became aware of the true reason after many sessions. Leon's childhood had been marred by violence, and his fantasies about being in control, no longer bullied and abused, finally took over his whole life. Part of him still believed in good and evil, so he labelled the bad part a "monster," blaming it for the killings, thereby exonerating the good side. And the "good" part of him felt genuine regret and horror at what he'd done to those boys.'

Laura slowly shook her head, sipping her tea. 'Something like that must have been incredibly difficult for the young Sam to take on board.'

He laughed rather bitterly. 'It was. It almost put paid to my dreams of becoming a psychologist. I wondered if I was really up to the job.'

'Lucky for all of us that you helped over the years, that you found the courage to go on.'

Sam stared into his mug. 'That case became my yardstick. I've measured all my difficult cases against what Leon Briars showed me, and it always brings me down to earth.' He looked up. 'I'm telling you all this now because I might be able to help you with Jeremy Reader. I have first-hand experience, so if you need me, I'm all yours.'

Laura smiled broadly. 'It certainly saves me finding a sneaky way of coaxing you into lending a hand. I'll put it to DCI Ballard as soon as I hear from him, but I'm certain he'll appreciate all the help he can get with Reader — and his beloved.'

'Oh yes, I'd forgotten about her.' His smile was returning. 'Even more reason to sneak in and have a listen.' He finished his tea. 'Now, on to happier subjects. How is your lovely detective?'

After another quarter of an hour, Sam stood up. 'I must let you get home. And though I didn't think I would, I feel really pleased that I've shared my story with you.'

Laura collected up the mugs and took them through to the kitchen, 'What happened to Leon Briars?' she called back over her shoulder.

'Oh, he killed himself. He went through the courts, pleaded guilty to all counts of murder, and as soon as the trial was over, he committed suicide.'

'Why did he wait until after the trial?' Laura walked back into the room.

'He said he felt that the bereaved parents deserved to see him convicted. It was the least he could do for them. He had taken away their loved ones and could never bring them back, but could allow them to see justice served. He left a note saying that although the British justice system was very good, there were cases where the only appropriate sentence was death. So he passed judgement upon himself, and took his own life.'

'True remorse, or couldn't he face life behind bars?'

'He handed himself in, don't forget. So, I reckon death was the only way for him to find peace. He was truly eaten up with remorse at what he'd done.'

'I wonder if that's the same with Jeremy Reader? Or is he playing a very dangerous game — with the police, the prison authorities and a woman who says she loves him?'

'We'll have to find out, won't we?' Sam gave her a wink. 'Right now, I'm off to do some research on the subject. Have a pleasant evening, and give my very best regards to Jackman.'

The door closed behind him, leaving Laura wondering what they would make of Jeremy Reader.

* * *

Professor Rory Wilkinson stared at the samples from the box. 'Human skin most certainly, DCI Ballard, very carefully packed with clear film between each piece. And you can clearly see from the variations in pigmentation that they're from different people.'

'From five different women?'

'That remains to be seen. Most of the skin appears to be female, though.'

Matt produced the list that Reader had given him. 'Would it be possible to discover what parts of the body these trophies were taken from? We have a list of his victims' names and where the skin was taken from.'

'Easily. We're already retrieving the details of Reader's victims, then as soon as we've identified which piece of skin belongs to which woman, we can match where on the body they came from.' He pushed his glasses up his nose. 'I've already sourced all the PM findings for your five dead women, so as soon as I can, I'll start checking where these so-called "cover-up" abrasions were.' He looked at Matt. 'Frankly, dear Detective Chief Inspector, I'm very surprised that the pathologists who performed the post-mortems didn't pick up on something being wrong with those wounds. Us forensic coves are extremely fastidious, you know, and I'm certain there will be peculiarities about them. It seems strange that several different pathologists all failed to see something wrong.'

Matt agreed, adding that as Reader had confessed that they fought for their lives and that he had dragged them forcibly across hard floors, maybe they weren't looking for something else.

'I *always* look for something else,' said Rory rather sanctimoniously, 'and I never accept anything at face value. The body never lies, but sometimes you have to look very closely to find the truth. And here endeth the first lesson. Amen.'

Matt grinned at him. 'Will you see what you can salvage from it all for me?'

'It will be my first consideration in the morning. I will rise early, and everything else can wait.'

Matt stared down at the tiny heart-shaped pieces of skin, looking like pieces of tissue paper.

'They'd make one hell of a Valentine's card, wouldn't they?' Rory said.

'They look almost perfectly symmetrical,' Matt said.

'Reader took great care and he had considerable skill, I must say. I'm guessing he spent hours practising to attain this level of expertise. .'

Matt grimaced, and wondered how you practised for something like that. 'How would he go about that exactly?'

'Like any diligent medical student,' Rory yawned, 'but don't worry, I'll expound my theories on that matter on the morrow, now scram, because right now I feel like the busiest man on the planet!'

* * *

Reader sat on his bunk and read his letter. Grace didn't know that DCI Ballard had visited him, but she'd been right in assuming the detective would take her seriously.

72

It could have gone one of two ways, but this outcome was the very best he could have hoped for. He looked at the clock. Soon it would be time for his late afternoon gym session. It had been a long, hard slog to get into this special rehabilitation programme. Now he'd passed all the required courses, and the fact that he had made a positive change to his life had been recorded.

He was still in a cell, but it was single occupancy, and had a small en-suite bathroom with a shower. With luck he would remain in the unit for a year, before being sent back into the main prison, so every day here was a luxury, and he didn't want to waste a moment. He reminded himself that his mind remained free to roam beyond these walls, wherever he wanted it to go. Jem was determined to exercise his brain as well as his body. He was studying for an Open University degree, through a virtual campus. It was available on a secure intranet system designed especially for prisons, since inmates weren't allowed access to the internet. This allowed him access to a range of information and resources that he wouldn't normally be permitted to see.

Reader stood up and placed Grace's letter on his table, letting his hand rest for a moment on her signature. Then he changed into a T-shirt and shorts. He made sure to exercise as much as possible. It both passed the time and kept unwanted thoughts at bay. Reader had a lot of those. At least there was one less to worry about today. His plan was finally coming together.

* * *

Grace stood in the men's area in Fenfleet's only department store. In one hand she held a silk tie in several shades of silver grey and blue, and in the other, a similar one in ivory and white. It was just ten minutes before they closed, but she was still undecided about which one to buy.

Jem had expressed the wish to wear something for their wedding that had no connection with prison. She looked at the silver and blue one. Royal blue tops and pale grey joggers were HMP Gately's standard prison issue, so she returned it to the rack. Then she spotted another, in a gold Jacquard leaf design. That was the one! It brought to her mind golden sunshine, the very antithesis of a prison block. Jem wanted a plain white shirt and was still deciding on the suit.

Men! she thought. *They're far worse than women when it comes to clothes.*

She checked with the assistant that the tie had a matching pocket handkerchief, and bought them both. When he phoned her tonight, she would tell him about it. Certain he'd be delighted, she decided to pack them up and post them to him without delay. If he didn't like them, she could pick them up on her next visit.

She sighed. It was pretty difficult doing all this alone. It wasn't as if he could go online either. It was all down to her. Not that she minded. They were to be married, that was the main thing. This made her think of the vows they were to make, and was rather glad they didn't mention honesty. Jem had told her everything, every sordid, disgusting detail of the terrible things he had done. He had bared his soul to her, but she hadn't been quite so transparent.

Grace Repton had a son. Her darling Ritchie. Her big secret.

She quickly banished all thought of him from her mind. He was not part of this aspect of her life and she didn't want him to be. If he were around, Ritchie would be horrified if he knew she was marrying a convicted killer, and her husband-to-be had no idea about Ritchie. Perfect! Most people would consider this bizarre. Why not tell him? And before the wedding, surely? But Grace had no intention of doing so. She shut out all thoughts of Ritchie, and returned to thinking about the wedding.

This whole thing was surreal. Jem had talked at great length to the prison chaplain, and had made up his mind that he wanted them to be married in the chapel. It had bothered him initially, because he didn't feel worthy of being married "in the sight of God," but after much soul-searching and discussion, he had told the chaplain that he wanted God to witness his penitence and bless his marriage.

Grace had assured him that she only wanted what he wanted. She'd marry him on the block if that was his wish.

She had already completed all the necessary paperwork and bought her own outfit. Right now, her only problem was that there was no one to give her away. They were allowed five people to attend the service and then stay for their short reception, which would probably consist of a few canteen sandwiches, crisps and cups of tea. Jem wanted Reuben Grimes for his best man, and they had been encouraged to invite a couple of close family members. They were both estranged from their families, and had been for many years. Grace's first husband had died not long into their marriage, and the rest of her family could be anywhere. She hadn't kept in touch with any of them. So, Jem had asked two of the staff members on the PIPE course if they would attend, and they'd both agreed readily. Apparently they actively encouraged this kind of thing, as it made for a more stable and well-adjusted prisoner.

Outside the store, she wondered if it would be against prison rules for her to ask Ross Cadman to give her away. There was no one else she could think of. Grace was a loner, and always had been. This kind of marriage would suit her perfectly.

She liked being inside high-security facilities. It was why she'd enjoyed her job as a prison visitor. She knew this wasn't "normal," but she couldn't help finding something extremely exhilarating in the tension inside. She relished its volatility. Spats could flare up like wildfires, be quashed, then spring up again somewhere else. It was a dangerous place, but one she could walk away from when she chose. This made her feel as though she were above it all. In control.

Now she only visited Jem, and she missed all the tension. In the PIPE unit, things were much more relaxed and far less threatening. Still, Jem was by far the most important thing. She reminded herself that, once, Jem would have been the most dangerous of all the inmates. And now she was to be Mrs Jeremy Reader. She repeated the name in her head. It had a nice ring to it. Grace returned to her car, smiling.

Grace found her excitement through other people's emotions, and the more intense they were the better. Especially hate. Maybe that was why she had made such a good prison visitor. She had thrived in that toxic atmosphere, while remaining unaffected by it. It was hardly surprising, then, that she had found it so easy to form a relationship with a man like Reader. They were utterly different, yet they understood each other. As she drove home, she wondered, was this what you called being soulmates.

CHAPTER NINE

Matt arrived home with his head still spinning. Hardly noticing the re-heated dinner, he was just thankful to sit down, enjoy a large whisky and get some food inside him. As far as he could remember, he hadn't eaten since breakfast. The day had sped by, and now he was having trouble making his mind slow down. Too much coffee and too many revelations.

With Liz's gentle coaxing, he ate what she'd provided, and then he was able to sit back and tell her about his day. 'I was so certain that I wouldn't be fooled by Reader. However much of a master manipulator he might be, he'd never take in the old hand, DCI Matt Ballard. Ha.' He poured another finger or two of whisky into his glass. 'I left that place in utter confusion.'

'So, Governor Cadman hadn't been such a walkover then?' Liz said.

'He's spent years with that man. I had half an hour, and he almost had me convinced.'

'But you still have doubts,' Liz said shrewdly.

'What gets me, and DC Peters too, is that he gave me damning evidence. It will benefit our enquiry no end, should there be a copycat murder, but that same evidence will mean that Reader dies behind bars.'

He told her about the five tiny hearts.

Liz pulled a face. 'Would that make a real difference to a parole board? By the time he got that far, he could well be in his dotage, and he'd already confessed to five counts of murder. If he had demonstrated over a period of thirty years that he was a reformed character, surely this "extra" evidence wouldn't go against him? It might even go in his favour. You know, a final confession.'

'More often than not, trophy killers are considered to be too damaged to rehabilitate. I'm sure it sealed his fate.' He frowned. 'And he seemed to think it was worth it.'

'I understand your confusion. All I can say is, why not sleep on it? Don't try to unravel it all immediately. It's one of those things that needs a bit of distance to see clearly.'

He laughed. 'It'll take more than a night's sleep to make sense of this situation! But I know what you're saying.' He stretched and yawned. 'Oh dear, I haven't even asked about your day, have I?'

Liz gathered up the dishes. 'Morag and I had a coffee and a mooch round the shops, then she brought me home. Since then I've been researching how to set up as a private investigator.'

Matt brightened. 'And?'

'Basically, we've got it made. We ought to get a license from the Security Industry Authority. They aren't essential right now, but it looks like they will be in the near future, and we'd need it if our investigations ever took us out of the country.' She gave him an encouraging smile. 'Apart from that, we meet all the criteria. The days of the turned-up trench-coat collar and standing in the shadows watching your mark are over. Let alone all that whisky.' She grinned. 'We'll need to spend some money on some technology.'

'You mean I can't buy a deer-stalker and a pipe?' Matt opened his eyes wide.

'More like a hidden spy camera and a GPS vehicle tracker,' laughed Liz.

'This is sounding really interesting.' Then Matt became silent, thinking of his present workload. 'If I ever get free of the Fenland Constabulary, that is. God, there's more on my desk now than I've ever had. It's a nightmare!'

'Hey, you! It's gonna happen, so don't stress!' Liz walked around the table and gently massaged his tense shoulders. 'I'm not fully fit yet anyway, so there's no rush, is there? I'll use the time to keep working on my fitness, and to find out everything we need to know about being a PI. Then when the time comes, we'll be prepared and ready to roll.'

He nodded. 'You're right. I just never expected my last weeks to produce a case like this, if it *is* a case and not a smokescreen.'

'Smokescreen covering what?' Liz asked, perching on the arm of his chair.

'A private vendetta against me? To make my life hell until I walk.'

'Did Reader give you that impression?'

'Not at all. I'm just looking at it from all angles.'

She ran her fingers through his hair. 'I don't think it's that. If he'd wanted to, he could have done that without putting his own neck on the block. That's not to say that I don't think there's a lot more to this than meets the eye, because I do.'

'I agree,' he breathed. 'But right now, I'm so tired I can't think straight.'

'Then go grab a shower and turn in. I think we should get an early night.' She kissed him lightly on the forehead. 'And I mean for sleep. Tonight you are relieved of all duties, so make the most of it.'

'And what if I don't want to be relieved of said duties?' Matt asked. She made him forget everything when they made love.

'Sorry, but tonight I'm putting my foot down. You look exhausted, and I don't want to be the cause of you driving into a fen ditch because you fell asleep at the wheel.' She eyed him from beneath lowered lashes. 'But tomorrow night you can work a double shift if you're rested enough. How does that sound?'

'You're a man-eater, Liz Haynes!'

'And aren't you the lucky one!'

'This is no way to get me to go to sleep!' he said.

She laughed and threw her hands up. 'Sorry! I'll be good now, I promise. You go get showered, okay? I'll sort everything out down here, and I'll see you in bed.'

Matt climbed the stairs. How lucky he was. Living alone, after a day like today he would have come home, drunk far too much, fretted all night about how to tackle his workload, and then felt like shit in the morning.

Liz had turned his life around. He had always dreamed of having a relationship like this, but had never believed it would happen. If only it could last forever.

* * *

The fenlands sweltered that night, but one person remained cool.

Calm, and with a steady hand, he spent some time assembling everything he would need: surgical scalpels, all with single-use sterile carbon steel blades, new. He aligned them in their case and put it into his holdall, adding a retractable Stanley knife and a couple of recently sharpened chef's knives. This, he followed with rolls of duct tape, nylon rope, heavy-duty rope, clingfilm, a small plastic container, a leather belt and a cheap scarf. He then went through every item again and zipped up the bag.

He pulled on a pair of surgical gloves and picked up the photograph. It showed the head and shoulders of a woman in her late twenties, blonde with blue-grey eyes. Her smile looked warm and friendly. He turned the photo over and read the address on the back: Three, Wendell

Street, Fenfleet. Good, it was nearby, and she would be alone and expecting him. Probably expecting flowers too, chocolates or maybe a bottle of wine. He gave a sardonic grunt. Little did she know that all he'd be bringing was a bag of cutting tools.

* * *

Matt was sleeping, his arm heavy across her body, while Liz lay awake, mulling over her day.

She had made it sound so innocuous, so ordinary when she told him. But in fact, it had been deeply disturbing.

She had driven in with Mattie and spent a pleasant hour catching up with old friends at the station while she waited for the shops to open. Pleasant? Perhaps not. These were her close colleagues, her friends, and she cared deeply about them. But as she chatted away, she grew aware of her distance from them. She would never go back there now. While they all babbled on about how she'd be steaming back in and grabbing the reins again, the CID room began to feel like somewhere totally alien. After a while, all she wanted to do was get out of the place.

She said her goodbyes and made for the town's bookshop. Its quiet atmosphere always had a calming effect on her. After browsing the new titles, she purchased a tote bag, covered with a colourful print of bookshelves and a boxed mug decorated with the cover of Jack Kerouac's *On the Road*. It was Mattie's all-time favourite book.

Feeling confident again, she went to pay for her purchases.

Suddenly, she became overwhelmed by confusion. At the cash desk, she discovered that she couldn't work out which card to use and how to remove her credit card from her purse. She covered it well by dropping her purse on the floor, and by the time she had picked it up along with some loose change, her brain was functioning again. Brief though it was, this incident upset her. Oh, why couldn't she stop these frightening lapses? She walked out of the shop into the hot, busy street, and all she wanted to do was get home to safety. But she had arranged to meet her friend Morag.

She dragged herself reluctantly to the café, where Morag's chatter soon lifted her spirits. But not for long.

They ambled down one of Fenfleet's pretty cobbled lanes, looking at some of the older shops, when Liz suddenly gripped Morag's arm. She had no idea where she was. The town, whose streets she knew intimately, the place she had policed for years, meant nothing to her. She could have been in a strange town in a foreign country. She turned to her friend for reassurance, but saw a stranger walking beside her . . .

Lying here with her beloved Mattie beside her, Liz once more experienced the horror of it. She drew in long, deep breaths to calm her racing heart.

Morag and she had been friends for many years. They had started basic training together but while Liz found her true vocation, Morag had married and found meaning bringing up three sons and working from home as a freelance proofreader and editor.

Morag had been marvellous. She'd got Liz to her car and driven her straight home. She had wanted to ring Matt, but Liz had stopped her. It had happened once before, but only in hospital, and that was a while ago now.

Her friend had stayed for an hour, only leaving when she was satisfied that Liz had recovered. But it had shaken her badly. She had been coasting along, certain that every day was taking her further from the damage that the drugs had caused, and then something like this had to happen.

She moved closer to Matt and, despite the warmth of the night and Matt's sleeping body, she shivered. Matt mustn't find out. She had sworn Morag to secrecy, hoping that it had just been a glitch, a minor hiccup in her recovery. Perhaps something had triggered it. It could have even been her trip back to the police station, the root of her near demise. Here, at home, these episodes almost never occurred, so it must have been returning to her old environment that had sparked a reaction.

That must be it. And it was easily controlled. She'd just have to avoid going back to the station. Liz closed her eyes and felt the tension slip away. All she wanted was to be with Matt Ballard, and be well again. Was that too much to ask?

CHAPTER TEN

Bryn made Lukas as comfortable as possible, ready for his night in the cells, and went to find somewhere for him to lie low for a while. He couldn't understand why "they," whoever they were, had been so upset at Lukas making inquiries about those tattoos. They were supposedly a "family thing," yet none of the murdered men seemed to be related. He was just going to have to look at the other, older cases and see if he could find any relevant evidence. He was also worried about Lina and uneasy about the atmosphere of tension and looming unrest in the Baltic Quarter.

The previous night he had tried to get his girlfriend Jules to explain why there was such animosity between the two nationalities. Was it a general thing, or just some local war? Jules had reckoned that, despite the animosity between Latvia and Lithuania, the conflict in Fenfleet was parochial. She likened the two nations to squabbling siblings, who fought between themselves but presented a united front to outsiders.

He went back downstairs to the custody suite and found Lukas eating breakfast.

He grinned up at Bryn. 'I could get used to this. Though the cell is a bit scary.'

'Best not get too comfortable, mate. I've already had your marching orders from the custody sergeant. He said, and I quote, "This isn't a fucking hotel, Owen! You want to take up being a landlord, do it in your own bleedin' house, not my custody suite!"'

'Sorry,' Lukas said. 'I do appreciate what you're trying to do for me.'

'Can't you think of anyone outside the Fenfleet area that you could stay with, Lukas? The more I think about the beating you took, the more I believe you stumbled on something important. I don't want some angry villain deciding to shut you up permanently.'

Lukas pushed his tray of food aside. 'Maybe. I have a cousin who married and moved to Greenborough. She might help me. I can ask, but won't it put her in danger?'

'I honestly can't say, mate. Why not just talk to her? Meanwhile, a friend of mine in uniform is going to put you into a police car and drive you out of here. If anyone sees, it'll look like you're being transported to another nick, or being taken to court. In reality, he's going to meet up with me just outside town, and then I'll get you away from Fenfleet.' He looked at Lukas earnestly. 'You're my only link to what might have happened to those three dead men. The police just don't have the resources to put you in a safe house, not on a bit of guesswork.'

'I understand. Maybe I should just go back home. My uncles will keep an eye on me, I'm sure.'

Bryn shook his head. 'Not enough. They have to work, don't they?'

'Yes, they are with a gangmaster, working the fields.'

'Long shifts. No good. We'd better do this my way.'

Lukas nodded. 'Okay, but I really don't know any more than I've told you already.'

Other than the name of the second and up until now unidentified murder victim, thought Bryn. He decided to leave that one for later. 'If I do discover more, you might be able to explain the bits I might not understand, if you get what I mean? We are talking a different culture and a different language.'

'And you are police,' said Lukas grimly. 'Everyone distrusts you.'

'Except Lina. But I want to keep her well out of this.'

'Why are you taking such an interest in us, Bryn? No one ever has before. Sure, the other murders were investigated, but not like this. No one really cared.'

Bryn wondered that himself. 'I have a good boss, and he wants me to get to the bottom of Filip's death. I don't want to let him down, it's his last few weeks on the job.'

'Fair enough, but I think it goes deeper than that.' Lukas eyed him shrewdly.

'My girlfriend is Estonian. Maybe that's given me more insight into how things are for the immigrants who really want to work and get on. I've heard about the hardships of life back home. You can't blame anyone for wanting a better life, can you?'

Lukas nodded. 'We'll do it your way, Detective Bryn Owen, and if I can help, I will.' He stared at the floor. 'I have one problem, though.'

He didn't need to tell Bryn.

'Money?'

'I have very little, and if I can't find work soon . . .'

'Speak to your cousin, and meantime, I'll sort something out.' Bryn could just about support himself and help Jules when things got tough. Her wages from the leisure centre were pretty basic. But he felt responsible for Lukas. After all, it was his enquiries that had got him into this trouble. He knew the young Lithuanian was in danger, and wasn't going to send him back into the lion's den for the sake of the price of a few nights in a B and B and a couple of MacDonald's takeaways. He put a hand on Lukas's shoulder. 'Come on, let's go. We'll sort it out, one way or another.'

* * *

Matt arrived in his office to find an email from Laura Archer waiting for him. She told him she'd spoken with a trusted colleague, and discovered that he'd had dealings with a remorseful killer in the past. She believed his input could be invaluable. Matt agreed and sent her a message asking her to ring him so they could set up a meeting.

He still hadn't decided about Reader. Someone who'd already dealt with such a case would help him make up his mind.

'Morning, sir,' Jason said glumly as he passed the door.

'You're bright and early,' Matt called back. *Well, early, at least . . .*

Jason stopped and came into the office. 'That death, Reuben Grimes. It's been bothering me all night. I wondered if the forensic report was through yet.'

'Not as far as I know.' Matt sifted through the pile of reports on his desk. 'No, not yet. What's bugging you?'

'It just seems odd that he was murdered just as you were about to talk to him. And Alex has done a runner. I keep thinking that this whole thing is going to rear up and bite us at any moment. It's looking to me as if this serial killer's warning could be for real. Alex, whoever he is, has got rid of the one person who knew all about him, and is getting ready to start killing.'

'I was wondering that too, but if it was Alex, why not kill Grimes the same way that Reader killed his victims? You know, use him as victim number one? Or at least as a practice piece?'

'Because Reader only ever killed women,' Jason said immediately. 'And a very particular type of woman. I think he was just tidying up prior to getting down to the nitty gritty.'

Jason was probably right, but Matt didn't want to assume anything just yet. 'Well, Reuben was an old lag, he'd been in and out of the bin for years. There's a chance he made other enemies, or maybe had a falling out with some criminal. We need to look at all possibilities. Even if he was going straight, something unpleasant from his past might have just crawled back to sort out an old score.'

Jason sighed. 'I'm on that at the moment, sir, but so far nothing nasty has shown up on the radar. And anyway, if that was the case, why not just kill him? This murderer wanted the body to remain undiscovered for as long as possible. That would indicate that he's pushed for time for some reason.'

'True.' Always sensible and logical, Jason was usually right, but Matt preferred to listen to his gut instincts. 'Anyway, I'll let you know the moment that post-mortem report shows up.'

After Jason left, Matt's thoughts returned to Jeremy Reader. What reason could he possibly have to arrange this complicated fiasco if it wasn't true? What was the benefit to Reader? Did he want to simply cause Matt the maximum amount of irritation in his last few weeks on the force? Did he want revenge for his capture and incarceration? Matt thought back to their meeting. There had been no indication of that at all, and DC Kim Peters had agreed. So, what other reason could he have? Pure mischief? A bright mind inventing a little mayhem to pass the time and alleviate boredom? Sticking two fingers up at the establishment that put him away? But would Reader need such a distraction when he was planning his wedding? Surely not.

'Sorry to interrupt, sir.' PC Jack Fleet hovered in the doorway.

'Come in, Swifty. What have you got for me?' Matt pointed to a chair.

Taking a seat, Jack produced a couple of printout images from a CCTV camera. 'We've been checking the area around Reuben Grimes's flat, sir. There are no cameras that cover his building, but there's one outside a convenience store at the end of an alley that comes out close to those maisonettes.' He handed Matt the pictures. 'There's three people who've aroused our suspicions. One cropped up three times, on different occasions, and he's the one that interests me the most.' He pointed to a shot of a man clad in denim jeans and a dark baseball jacket with a hood. He was carrying a bulging rucksack that clearly contained quite a bit of stuff. 'I'm told he's wearing something called a varsity hoodie, much like a normal baseball jacket but slimmer and has the attached hood. They aren't two a penny, and apparently they're normally quite colourful with white arms and stripes around the cuffs and waistband, but this one is black and dark grey, which isn't common, so that could help us find him.'

Matt stared at the man in the picture, whose features were hidden under his hood. He silently cursed whoever invented the hoodie. It had to have been a criminal. 'Is this alleyway used a lot?'

'No, sir. It's a shortcut, but it's unlit and it floods in bad weather.' He pulled a face. 'A few of the nastier neighbourhood kids gather there sometimes, so decent people give it a wide birth.'

Matt looked at the other two pictures. Both were of men, or so he thought. Clothing and hairstyles made it difficult for his generation to tell the difference these days. All three looked shifty, but he knew exactly what Swifty meant regarding Varsity Man. Matt stood up. 'I'd like to see the footage, please.'

Jack led the way down to the IT room. Soon, Matt was watching the three figures swing into the alley at different times, and make their way towards where Reuben had lived.

He noticed a difference in the attitude of Varsity Man. 'Purposeful,' whispered Matt. 'That one has a purpose, doesn't he?'

'That's what I thought. He's going somewhere, he's not hanging around or dawdling like the others.'

Matt narrowed his eyes, trying to remember the landlord's vague description of Alex. It *was* possible. Was he looking at the prospective serial killer? There was no way of knowing, of course, but Matt was with Swifty on this one. His money was on Varsity Man. He looked at Jack. 'Do you know anyone in that area who might recognise this guy?'

'I've got a couple of contacts, the owner of the store for one. He'll know if he's a local. Nothing gets past Ravi.' He smiled. 'And Reuben's neighbour has lived there for a while, he might know him too.' Jack picked up a copy of the image. 'I can get out there straightaway, sir, if it helps.'

Matt nodded. 'If it's okay with your sergeant, I'd appreciate it.'

'I'll go clear it.' Jack hurried out.

Matt's phone rang. 'Ah, Laura. Any news from your colleague?'

'Sam Page is retired, Matt, and he only lives ten minutes away. He's free as a bird and suggested this morning, if that suits?'

'Perfectly. Bring him straight to my office, and thanks, Laura, it's much appreciated.'

On his way back to the CID room, Matt remembered that he should ask Ross Cadman to break the news to Reader that his only friend from HMP Frankland had been murdered. He wondered how Reader would take it. Matt stopped in his tracks. On second thoughts, he needed to witness his reaction first hand. He decided to go back to HMP Gately and give Reader the news, together with Governor Cadman. Of course, there was always the chance that the prison grapevine had already picked it up, but Reuben Grimes wasn't a "name."

Back in his office, he took it a step further. If Cadman allowed, he would take Sam Page with him to observe, like Kim Peters had. He rang Cadman immediately.

It was the first time they had spoken since Matt's visit to Gately, and the governor was anxious to hear Matt's opinion. Matt put him off until they met, and asked if he and Sam could visit, and why. Cadman agreed. They could come at midday.

'We'll be there. I really appreciate your help with this.'

'This news will affect him profoundly, DCI Ballard. Reuben Grimes was to be his best man at the wedding. He feels, er, felt great affection for Reuben. It will hit him hard.'

'I'm sure it will. It won't help that his friend was murdered, will it?'

'It certainly won't. I'm quite sure Reader will feel responsible. A whole lot of emotional baggage will surface — issues from his therapy sessions that made him confront the knock-on effects of his actions, like the trauma the friends and family of a murder victim have to undergo.'

Matt heard the governor sigh. 'I'll come with you when you tell him, if you don't mind.' It wasn't a request.

'Naturally. I'd appreciate it if you would. Reader is comfortable with you. One thing, though. I'd rather not tell him that I already knew of Reuben's death when I spoke to him yesterday. I don't want to anger him, and he talked about Reuben quite a bit, so I had every opportunity. I just knew that the moment I mentioned it, he would think of nothing else and I'd get nothing more from him.'

'It's not relevant at this point. We can say we have no details yet, but you thought he should be told before it hits the media.' Ross Cadman sighed again. 'I'd better go and get these visits sorted. We'll expect you at noon.'

This visit would kill two birds with one stone. He couldn't wait to hear what Sam Page thought.

* * *

Bryn collected Lukas from his uniformed colleague and bundled him into his Ford Fiesta. Without any clear destination in mind, he headed for the main road. Then he spotted a sign to Saltern-le-Fen, and knew exactly where he was going to take Lukas.

'I'm a real goofball! I should have thought about this first. There's this guy in Saltern who'll certainly find you a room for a little while.'

Lukas looked hopeful, and then his face dropped. 'Don't forget, I haven't got much money.'

'The man I'm talking about is called Jim Cousins. He runs a shelter for destitute kids. It's in a great big house. It's clean, and he provides food too. Short term, he won't charge you, but I'll see he's not out of pocket, don't worry.'

'That would be a big help. I'll talk to my cousin, but I'm worried for her safety if anyone finds out where I am. Maybe it's just too risky.'

'Stay with Jim for a while, then we'll think again.' Bryn headed for Saltern-le-Fen, happy to have found a solution. Jim's "guests" were usually runaways, homeless kids or sometimes recently released kids on license. No one would think of looking for Lukas there, he would blend in and be safe. 'Lukas? Can I ask you something? Well, two things really.'

Lukas nodded. 'Go on.'

'When the guy with the tattoo told you it was a family thing, did you get the feeling he meant the domestic kind of family, or something like a brotherhood, you know, or the mafia. Gang members that band together in a kind of family.'

'He meant real family, I'm sure of it.' Lukas frowned. 'Well, that's how I understood it anyway.'

'Okay. Now the other thing.' He paused. This was the big one. 'When I asked Lina if she was related to any of the other dead men, you said you all knew who the unidentified guy was. Could you give me his name?'

Lukas tightened his lips.

'I'm not pushing you, Lukas. It's just it seems awful that there's a man lying in a mortuary who doesn't even have a name, let alone someone to mourn his death. Our pathologist thinks he was only around twenty-five. It doesn't seem right.'

'It *isn't* right, Bryn, but surely that shows you how scared his family are! They are too frightened of reprisals, too frightened to even claim their own son.'

'They've been threatened?'

Lukas nodded. 'They have two more children and they've been told that if they talk to the police, the same thing will happen to them.' He stared down at his hands lying loosely in his lap. 'I would help you if I could, but if they think it was one of us that told you, you could well have two more deaths in Fenfleet. I just can't take the risk.'

'We need to catch these people,' Bryn said. 'There's no place here for the likes of them.'

'I really think the drugs are only part of it. Yes, there's a territory war over the supply of cocaine and heroin, and now guns too, but I think there's something else going on, something more personal.'

'A vendetta of some kind?' asked Bryn.

'Something like that, yes.'

Bryn thought hard. Families and communities fought over honour, cultural beliefs, or a historical injustice caused by another family. He had mostly heard of it in relation to Asian families, but could it be true of the Baltic states too? He'd have to ask Jules. Lukas was looking pretty done in, and Bryn decided he'd answered enough questions. He had just one more.

'Promise you'll keep in touch with me?' he asked.

'I will, and I know it must seem that I am repaying your kindness by being unhelpful, but I've seen what that family are living through. I can't speak out.'

'I understand. But can I just say that if I find out by other means, if I get a name, would you just confirm whether I'm right or wrong?'

'Yes. I would do that.' Lukas looked worried. 'But be careful, Bryn. Whoever is doing this is ruthless, they're evil.

Taking a life means nothing to them. I think they'd enjoy killing a policeman.'

Bryn glanced at Lukas's anxious face. He wasn't exaggerating. 'I won't go in mob-handed, don't worry.'

'Just don't go anywhere in that area by yourself, that's all I ask. You've been lucky so far, you've only met my family, and that was bad enough. So, never alone, okay?'

They spent the rest of the journey talking about Jim Cousins, the weather and sport, but an unspoken question still hung over them like a storm cloud. Who was killing young men in Fenfleet? And why?

CHAPTER ELEVEN

Jeremy Reader stared at the table. After a while, he said, 'This is all my fault.'

So Ross Cadman had been right when he said Reader would blame himself. Matt stayed silent.

'I should have realised. I should have gone about this differently. Of course there would be repercussions! It's that bastard Alex, isn't it?'

'How could you have realised?' asked Cadman. 'You weren't to know this would happen, and there's a chance it's not connected to this Alex at all. It could be something completely unrelated. Grimes had spent his whole life in the company of dangerous people.'

'Yes. People like me.' Reader looked at the governor. 'He really didn't deserve this, Mr Cadman. Reuben was a good man. Okay, he wasn't on the right side of the law, but he never hurt anyone. He never took a life, not like me. And even though he knew what I'd done, he had time for me. He listened, and he never judged. How many people do you know who are completely non-judgemental?'

No police officers, that's for sure, thought Matt. *We can be the most judgemental of all.*

'Not too many,' conceded Cadman.

'If, and only if, this was the work of Alex, Reuben brought this on himself by giving him the details of your crimes, no matter how altruistic his motives were.' Matt looked at Reader's grave face and wondered what was going on in his mind.

'He thought he was helping a student. That would be just like Reuben,' Reader said.

'Reuben had spent his whole life among dangerous criminals, yet he didn't realise he was talking to one then,' murmured Matt. 'Pity, that.'

'Alex could be very convincing, DCI Ballard. Remember that when you catch up with him. Don't underestimate him. When I read his letters, I quite warmed to him.' He gave an impatient gesture. 'I wish to God I'd kept those damned letters. They might have helped you find him.'

'Indeed,' said Matt dryly. 'Did you keep any at all?'

'Only the last one. I received it weeks ago, and then nothing more, I hoped he'd had a change of heart, but . . .' Reader looked at Cadman. 'I gave it to the governor yesterday.'

Cadman took an envelope from his pocket and handed it to Matt. 'I thought you'd need it.'

With a nod, Matt took it. It would be covered in prints and most likely useless to forensics, but it was evidence. 'Did he ever visit you?' he asked Reader.

'Never. He asked for a VO, but I never allowed it. I didn't consider it appropriate, even though I was curious about him.' He paused. 'Did he suffer, DCI Ballard? Did Reuben suffer?'

'We don't have the PM report yet, Jem. I don't know exactly how he did die, but in my opinion it was quick.'

Reader stared beyond his visitors into the distance. Matt wondered if he was thinking of his own victims. Those five women had died very slowly indeed.

'I can't even attend his funeral, can I?' he asked Cadman.

'Sorry, Jem. You're Cat A, and not eligible for ROTL. And even if you were, Reuben wasn't a partner or a close relative.'

Cadman was referring to Release on Temporary Licence, whereby, at his discretion, a prisoner could leave the prison for a short time, usually for a funeral or other grave family matter. Matt wondered who would be at the funeral. Grace Repton, maybe?

As if he'd read his thoughts, Reader said, 'I'll ask Grace to represent me.'

'I expect this has rather upset your wedding plans, hasn't it?' Matt said.

'What do *you* think? He was going to be my best man.' Reader's flash of anger subsided at once. 'Poor Grace. This isn't going to be the wedding of the year, is it?'

Unless the press get hold of it, thought Matt, *and then it'll be on the front page of every newspaper in the country.*

'Well, judging by my meeting with her, I don't think she sees the ceremony as all that important. I think simply being married to you is all she needs,' Matt said, his compassion surprising even him.

'Yes, you're right,' Reader said, 'although God knows why. But even so, I wanted it to be as special as possible.'

Matt stood up. 'I should get back. I just thought you should know before the media get hold of it.'

'I appreciate it.' Reader looked at Matt intently. 'Catch Alex, please?'

'Oh, I will.'

Reader smiled. 'If anyone can, it's you, isn't it, Matthew Ballard? I should know. You're the reason I'm marrying my Grace in HMP Gately, rather than a country church with flowers and a choir.'

'If you hadn't killed five women I wouldn't have had to hunt you down in the first place, would I?' Matt retorted.

'Touché, Mr Policeman. And you're absolutely right.'

Matt walked to the door of the interview room, and then turned back. 'I'm sorry about Reuben.'

Reader nodded. 'Would you tell Grace for me, DCI Ballard? I don't want to drop a bombshell like this over the phone.'

'Of course. I'll call in on my way back to the station.'

'Thank you.'

Matt closed the door of the interview room behind him, collected Sam, and they began to make their way down the corridor. Ross Cadman hurried after them. 'Before you go, will you let me know how it all pans out — if Alex is to blame for Reuben Grimes's death, and if you find out who this mysterious Alex is?'

'Yes, of course. As soon as I have something definite, I'll contact you.' They reached the first of the locked gates. 'And thank you for arranging this at short notice. I do appreciate your help when you're so busy.'

'No problem. Jem is my responsibility. He'd been doing very well indeed, and now I'm concerned that he'll slip back. I'll be keeping a close eye on him. The staff on his unit need to know as soon as possible, just in case . . .' He said no more, he didn't have to. Frustration in prison often resulted in violence or self-harm, even when the prisoner was considered well-adjusted.

Another door clanged shut behind them and Matt heard the scrape of a key in the lock. What a bloody miserable place this was!

* * *

"Well?" Matt asked Sam. They were on their way back to Fenfleet.

Sam shook his head. 'That man was not what I was expecting, DCI Ballard.'

'It's Matt. If we're going to work together, let's dispense with the formalities.'

'Okay, Matt. Well, he's a complicated individual if ever I saw one!'

'He has me completely foxed.'

'I'm not surprised. Even I'm not sure where to start.' Sam paused. 'It was a strange experience for me, Matt. It brought back memories of a time when I was involved with another patient like this one. He too had killed several people, and he insisted that he felt sincere remorse.'

'Laura mentioned that you had previous experience of this kind of situation, but she didn't go into any detail.'

'People like this are few and far between. Most murderers feel no remorse or empathy whatsoever. They have a very different moral sense to you and me. Many are even proud of their killings, so a man who regrets what he's done is rarer than hen's teeth.' Sam turned to look at Matt. 'Of course, saying that you feel sorry is very different to actually feeling it. Some are only sorry because they got caught and will spend the rest of their lives in prison.'

'Or if it can further their chances of parole?' Matt said.

'Yes indeed. But I understand that this man has another twenty years to serve before he can even be considered for parole?'

'And now that he's admitted to being a trophy killer, as well as providing us with the, er, souvenirs, his hopes of parole are very slight even then.'

'I didn't know that. The most common trophies take the form of either underwear or hair, although there have been some pretty gruesome ones too, like heads, genitals and eyeballs.'

Matt pulled a face. 'At least what I recovered was not quite so horrific. They consisted of small heart-shaped pieces of skin, excised very carefully from the women's bodies.'

'After death?'

'So I'm told.'

Sam drew in a long breath. 'It's hard to believe that the man I saw could have done such things. I watched his every expression and every gesture, and I really believe that his shock, grief and feeling of responsibility for Reuben Grimes's death were genuine.'

Matt nodded. He felt the same way.

'However, even though he was genuinely upset over losing a friend, that doesn't mean that he is necessarily remorseful about the murders he committed. He may still have an agenda. He could be a convincing and devious man playing a sadistic game. You must never lose sight of what he did a decade ago. The question is, if he were released tomorrow, would he kill again?'

'I'd always have to assume that he would,' Matt said. 'Personally, I'd never let him out. Never.'

'But is he truly conscience-stricken, guilt-ridden, contrite? That's what we have to discover.'

Matt glanced at Sam. 'Can you do that?'

'I think so. Would I have direct access to him? There are some very important questions I would need to ask him.'

Matt wasn't sure. They would need Reader's permission. Would he refuse? Or would he take it as another opportunity to show his cleverness by convincing an eminent psychologist of his remarkable change of heart? 'I'll inquire. To start with, I do have access to all of his notes from the PIPE unit — that's the Psychological Informed Planned Environment progression unit — plus other specialists' reports on his general and mental health since his move from HMP Frankland.'

'Ah, music to my ears, Matt! I would welcome the opinions of other professionals.'

'I'll let you have copies of them as soon as we get back to the station.'

They drove on, each lost in his own thoughts. Matt remembered he'd promised to deliver the news about

Reuben to Grace Repton. They would pass her house on their way back to Fenfleet. 'This is a lucky break, you getting to see both in one day,' he said.

Sam nodded. 'It is indeed. I'll be most interested to meet Reader's bride to be.'

'Scary thought that,' murmured Matt. 'Before I met her, I thought I knew what she'd be like, going by other women who latch on to men who've committed atrocities, but Grace was completely different.'

Sam chuckled. 'Oh, good! I do so like an enigma.'

'Well, I could do with a few less puzzles right now,' Matt said. 'I have a murder to investigate.'

'Point taken.' Sam still looked mildly amused. 'Tell me, in what way was she different to your expectations?'

'I'll leave you to make your own mind up about that,' said Matt.

* * *

Liz stood at the sink, staring down at the shattered wine glass. How had it happened? One minute she'd been polishing it, and the next she was looking at a sink full of shards.

She had only lost a few seconds, but they felt like an eternity. What was happening to her? They were small things, but they were occurring far too regularly for her liking.

Now she had the problem of clearing up, and she'd promised Matt that she wouldn't go near knives or any other sharp objects when he wasn't around. And if she couldn't even remember what had happened . . . She didn't much relish bleeding to death.

It was wonderful living out on the fen, she loved it, but having no near neighbours and being miles from your friends had its downside. Like now.

With all Matt had to contend with right now, she daren't put herself at risk. She knew he would put her first, and just jack in the job, but it wouldn't make him happy.

That wasn't the way she wanted him to end his time on the force. No, she'd keep her promise, but play down what had happened. Anyone can break a glass. She'd say she knocked it on the tap and it shattered. No big deal.

Liz went through to the lounge and turned on her computer. She would play a few games and try to forget her anxiety. She was probably blowing a simple slip out of all proportion. She'd do some brain-training tests, and some more research into setting up a private detective agency. At least she couldn't come to any harm doing that.

* * *

Grace Repton's hand flew to her mouth. 'Dead? Murdered? Oh my God! My poor Jeremy!'

'We've already broken the news to him, Mrs Repton. He wanted us to speak to you before it becomes common knowledge.'

'How is he? Reuben was his only real friend. Oh, I wish I could go to him.' She groaned. 'And he was to be our best man.'

'Mrs Repton, have you any idea who could have done it?' Matt asked, looking around the neat lounge with its superb view out across the fields.

'Why, Alex of course! Who else?'

It always came back to Alex, didn't it? The faceless man who idolised a serial killer.

'Did you know Reuben Grimes personally?'

Grace sat back in her armchair. 'I met him, of course, several times. Jem would send him messages which I passed onto him. He was a pleasant man. He didn't look like a criminal. He was softly spoken and seemed remarkably straightforward, considering the fact that he'd been in and out of prison most of his life. When you spend as much time talking to prisoners as I did, you realise that they're rarely as open and uncritical as Reuben.'

'Jem referred to him as being non-judgemental,' Matt mused.

'To be frank, Detective Inspector, I wondered if he was a bit lacking. Not that he was disturbed, but maybe he had a few learning difficulties. I think he acquired all his education in the university of life and the school of hard knocks.'

Matt made a mental note to check out Reuben Grimes's criminal record as soon as he got back. Everyone said what a gentle soul he was, so how come he'd spent time in "Monster Mansion?" He certainly didn't know of any gentle souls in HMP Frankland.

They talked for a little longer, mainly to give Sam more time to form an opinion of Grace.

'How did he die, if I may ask?' Grace enquired.

'I'm sorry, Mrs Repton, I'm not at liberty to say at present. I'm sure you understand.'

She nodded. 'Of course, of course. I just hope he didn't suffer. He was someone you just couldn't dislike.'

Someone certainly didn't like him, thought Matt. *Was it Alex?* Matt needed to put a face to the name. Logic said that if Alex existed, he would have motive and opportunity. Motive? Reuben was the only one who knew him. Reuben could describe him. So Ruben was a stumbling block to Alex's progression to becoming a killer. Goodbye Reuben. Opportunity? He would know where Reuben lived, he was well-known and had regular habits. Any smart guy could track him down and gain access easily. Knock on the door and good old Reuben, non-judgemental Reuben, would throw open the door and put the kettle on!

Yes, logic declared that it was Alex, but without proof that the man even existed, he was chasing shadows. Matt stood up, thanked Grace, said that they might need to talk to her again, and they stepped out into the glorious sunshine. She certainly lived in a beautiful spot. Not remote, like his home, but not overlooked either, and you could see for miles across the endless fenland fields. Only minutes from the village, it was the perfect spot to live peacefully, but not feel cut off from society. For a woman on her own with only a weird cat for company, she had chosen well.

As he waited for Sam to buckle up, Matt noticed that the name of the bungalow was *Nirvana*.

He recalled that Nirvana meant an ideal or an idyllic state or place. It was the final goal of Buddhism, a pure state without suffering, desire or sense of self. Had Grace named it herself? Or had she inherited the name along with the bungalow? House names had always fascinated him. One day he'd ask her.

'Ready when you are,' Sam said.

'Sorry, miles way.' He put the car into gear and pulled out into the lane. 'Okay, Sam, so what did you make of that one?'

'Has Laura met Grace yet?'

'No, but I said she could sit in next time I spoke with her.'

'Did Laura tell you anything about hybristophelia?' Sam asked.

Matt stopped at a junction. 'Well, she mentioned the different kinds of women and their reasons for wanting to be attached to monsters.'

'Then I expect she told you it's a very under-explored area of psychology.'

Matt nodded.

'Grace Repton doesn't seem to fit any category that I know of. I'd swear she felt genuine sadness for Reader's loss. I really believe she loves him.'

Matt thought hard on that. It was true that we don't always choose who we fall in love with. But a cold-blooded killer? Wouldn't you allow common sense to overrule your heart?

But Sam was speaking again. 'However, I do have another observation. If I thought Reader was difficult to fathom, that was before I met Grace. She's even more complicated than him.'

'But she appears so normal, so well-balanced. Why do you think she's complex?' Matt asked.

'Because there's so much going on in that rather attractive head, Matt. I think we were looking at the store dummy, the carefully dressed and prepared woman that she wants us to see. I still think she genuinely loves Reader, but why, and what she sees in him, or wants from him, I dread to think.'

Matt exhaled loudly. 'Just great. These two are all we have now Reuben's dead. If Alex exists and starts killing people, like they say he will, they're our only connection to him. Wonderful!'

Sam chuckled. 'Could be worse. You could have no connections at all.'

'I'm not sure which of those two scenarios is worse!'

'Believe me, Reader and Repton will be very helpful indeed, once I can fathom out how their minds work. The first step to that are those medical records from the prison.'

'So I need to be grateful that we have Repentant Jem and our Gracie, do I?'

'Indubitably, Detective! They are going to be invaluable!'

* * *

After sending Alex's last letter to Reader off to forensics, Matt made room for both Sam and Laura in his office, and then left them sorting through reams of psychological reports from the PIPE unit at HMP Gately.

He was anxious to know if Jack Fleet had had any luck tracking down any of the characters seen on the CCTV footage from close to Reuben Grimes's home. He also wanted to know what kind of crimes Reuben had been involved in, considering how "nice" everyone said he was. It all seemed rather strange. No criminal is nice, at least the successful ones aren't. Well, maybe Reuben just wasn't very successful.

'Sir, could I have a moment?' DC Bryn Owen stood up as Matt passed his desk.

'Yes, Bryn?' Matt said, taking a seat.

The young detective explained the situation concerning Lukas and Lina from the Baltic Quarter. He told Matt that the community knew the name of the unidentified dead man but were too terrified to disclose it.

'I'm not surprised about that, but I am surprised that Lukas believes these killings go deeper than a drug-fuelled turf war.' Drugs and guns were bad enough, but deaths due to something more sinister were another matter. What was going on? Once again, he felt his retirement slipping further away.

'The last thing Lukas said to me was that the men who killed Filip and the other two Lithuanians would enjoy killing a policeman. He warned me — us — to tread with the utmost care.'

'Then we'll heed his warning. You've done very well, Bryn. You've found the identity of the latest victim, and you've got a lead about this tattoo being a "family" design, but no more going it alone, understand? Two officers minimum when you go into that quarter, more if you think it's required. No taking risks, young man. Is that clear?'

'Absolutely, sir. There's a bad atmosphere on the streets of Fenfleet right now.'

'Good. Now, Jack Fleet is helping out with the search for this bloke called Alex. I've no doubt he'd be happy to tag along with you too, if you need to go back and see the migrant workers. I'll clear it with his sergeant. Swifty knows this town like the back of his hand. He could be an asset to you, and he's got a decent attitude, a bit like you, so he won't put people's backs up . . . unlike some I could mention.'

'Thank you, sir. That would be really useful.'

'Could you do me a favour, Bryn? It shouldn't take a minute. Would you pull up Reuben Grimes's record? I want to know exactly what kind of crimes he committed, and in particular, why he did a stretch in Frankland Cat A.'

'You got it, boss.'

Matt watched Bryn's fingers fly across the keyboard, wishing he was as proficient as the younger officers were these days.

'I'm homeless at the moment, they're using my office for psych research right now, but I'll be around here somewhere.'

'I'll find you, sir. As you say, it won't take long.'

Matt looked around the office. The door to Jason's office stood ajar and, inside, he and DC Kim Peters were deep in conversation. Then, to his amazement, Jason put his head back and laughed.

Matt stifled a chuckle. He tried to recall the last time he'd even seen Jason crack a smile, let alone laugh. This was good news. Hopefully, when he did retire, he would leave a close-knit group of detectives working well together as a unit. He hoped so, for DCI Anders's sake. It was bad enough taking on a new post without inheriting a bunch of disgruntled detectives with no cohesion.

Matt wandered down to the coffee machine. While it spluttered and coughed out his drink, he rang Liz.

'Just checking in to see if you fancied a takeaway tonight? It looks like I should be away on time, or thereabouts.'

Liz said she'd like that. He thought she sounded tired.

'Are you okay, sweetheart?' he asked.

'I'm fine, Mattie. I was watching an old film on TV and nodded off. I always seem to miss the last vital minutes.'

'Typical.' Matt laughed. 'Have you heard from anyone today?'

'Only Morag. We might have a day out next week. She wants to drive down to Peterborough and do some serious shopping.'

'That's a great idea. You'll get to see somewhere different from Tanners Fen for once. Tell her I'll treat you both to lunch, whatever and wherever you want.'

'That's dangerous, Mattie. You know how much Morag likes her food!'

'Small price to pay! She's being your chauffeur, and I know for a fact that she's not exactly well off.'

'Then we gratefully accept. Now, you get back to work or you'll finish up being late home again. Love you.'

'Love you too.' He ended the call.

Matt realised he was smiling broadly. He still found it incredible that he had someone in his life, someone so special. He picked up his drink and returned to the CID room.

As he entered, he almost collided with Jack Fleet. 'Ah, good, Swifty. Any luck?'

Jack looked rather annoyed. 'According to Rav in the convenience store, none of the three people on the CCTV are locals, although he's seen our number one suspect more than once. He said the man called in a couple of times last week for a local paper but he'd never seen him before that. Rav says he's not too good on English accents but Varsity Man definitely had one, though he didn't have a clue where from.'

'Not much to go on.'

'No, sir. And Steve Chambers, Reuben's nearest neighbour, was out, so I haven't spoken to him yet. I've put a card through his door and asked him to ring me. Poor bloke was gutted after what happened to Reuben. I wouldn't be surprised if he's buggered off for a few days until the dust settles.'

'Wouldn't blame him,' Matt replied.

'Me neither. Still, I've just checked the list from the house to house inquiries, and there's one particular curtain-twitcher that's certainly worth another knock on the door. He wasn't in either when I called. Apparently he's a lonely old guy who spends a good part of his life peering out of his front window. I'll go back tomorrow morning.'

'Good idea, and, Swifty? If I can okay it with your sergeant, I'd like you to give us a hand with our inquiries about the death of that immigrant, Filip Derus.'

'Certainly, sir. Sarge is in a good mood today, so you should be in luck.' Swifty's sergeant was known to be mercurial, to say the least.

'Okay, you get away and leave that with me.'

Matt went over to Bryn's desk.

'Ah, sir, I got some of what you asked for, but his stint in Frankland is still a bit of a grey area. I'm working on that now, I've rung the prison but there have been two governors at Frankland since Reuben was there so I've left it with admin to check for me.' Bryn handed Matt a printout. 'Reuben's is the usual story. The guy started life badly. Most days he bunked off school. There's reports of learning difficulties that weren't dealt with, and then, pretty young, he started nicking stuff. Went on to being a "runner" for a local bunch of villains, then joined them as a fence. That seemed to be his main line, moving stolen goods onto unsuspecting buyers.'

Matt skimmed down the list of arrests and convictions. It seemed that what Reuben lacked in intellect, he made up for with charm and being streetwise. But nothing on the rather long list warranted being incarcerated in Frankland. 'Keep at it, Bryn. I'm off to try and get the okay for Swifty Fleet to help you.'

Matt glanced at the wall clock. The day had flown by, and he wasn't sure what, exactly, had been achieved.

He could see that Sam and Laura were still engrossed in reports, deep into unravelling the twisted mind of Jeremy Reader, and probably that of his fiancée too. He wasn't sure what Jason and Kim were following up, probably something to do with identifying Alex, but they were still hard at work.

There was probably little more to be gained today. He would do what he could about getting extra help from uniform, then send everyone home.

He left the office. A dark shadow stalked him. Their one and only connection with "Alex" was lying in the mortuary. That meant the way was clear for him, if he existed at all. At any moment, he might start killing.

Or would he? As he made his way down the stairs, it dawned on him for the first time that he only had Reader's word for this. Had he in fact spent years seeking out someone who would continue his work? Had Reuben been the go-between, the understanding friend that helped groom him? After all, Reuben seemed to have spent his whole life as a middleman.

Matt was torn. Torn between his policeman's mistrust of everyone and his growing sense that Jeremy Reader — murderer, keeper of five heart-shaped pieces of skin — was telling the truth.

CHAPTER TWELVE

Ronnie Lester was a wreck. He drove home from the factory after the night shift ended, certain in the knowledge that he couldn't carry on living this way. He couldn't function. He was killing himself.

How had he got to this point? Ronnie had always dreamed of being a chef, turning out delicious, original dishes that delighted his customers. Now he was working in a big industrial bakery, helping to produce six thousand loaves an hour of bread that contained enough unhealthy ingredients to damage those who ate them. His eyes and nose ran continually, irritated by the flour dust. He wheezed, and he'd been told there was a real risk of him contracting occupational asthma. Then there were the hazards, the risks from the dangerous machinery — the silos, the mixers, the dough breaks, the sweep augers, and the slips, trips, falls, burns and abrasions that happened all the time.

And after all that, he returned home to a warzone. How had that happened? How had a happy, fun-filled marriage evolved into a warzone, nothing but snipers and fire-fights? His wife, Lisa, seemed to spend her life waiting for his slightest misdemeanour so she could take aim and shoot him down.

He drew up in the driveway of their neat little three-bed house in Sycamore Close wondering what greeting awaited him this morning. One thing was for sure, it wouldn't be a friendly welcome. There'd be no nice cup of tea for Ronnie Lester.

With a sinking heart, he put his key into the lock. It was obvious that the time had come for a parting of the ways. Trouble was, Ronnie was an old-fashioned kind of guy who believed you should stick to your wedding vows, so he kept hoping things might improve. They had been so happy once. Was there a way back?

He opened the door. The house was stuffy and hot. Why didn't she open the windows overnight, especially in this heat? She said she was scared of intruders, but he knew better. He liked the windows open, so she kept them shut. That's how it was with her these days. She liked to fan the flames.

'Lisa? I'm home.' *As if you cared.*

Silence. Maybe she'd slept in. Once, he would have climbed in beside her, cuddling her until he fell asleep. Back then, she would be careful not to wake him when she got up.

With a heavy heart, Ronnie went into the kitchen. He'd make some toast with the hated bread from his bakery, and go and face the inevitable. If he woke her, he'd be wrong. If he let her sleep on, that would be wrong too.

He switched on the electric kettle and opened the kitchen windows to clear the musty air. He went to unlock the back door, but it was already unlocked.

He stared at it for a moment. If she was so scared of intruders, this was not the best way to keep them out. He shook his head. Maybe she was up already.

He made some tea and took a loaf from the breadbin. "Freshly made loaf baked in store." What a load of codswallop. He opened the drawer for the bread knife, but it wasn't there.

He blinked. What had she done with it? He checked the sink, found Lisa's supper things from the night before, but no bread knife. He checked the other drawers without finding it and decided it was another of her little games. One morning she'd hidden the tea bags, another time she had thrown the switch on the fuse-board so that the kitchen had no power. Ronnie had had enough. It was time to sort this, one way or another.

Halfway up the stairs, he knew that something was terribly wrong.

His house had never smelt bad. Lisa might have hated their relationship, but she still kept their house clean.

A few steps further up, the smell intensified. It was a curious smell, pungent, sweet-salty.

Another step. Now he knew what it was. His chest tightened. That tang of iron, or was it copper, was the smell of the Intensive Care Unit. His brother had once been rushed there following a car crash. The smell of blood.

His head full of possible scenarios, he raced up the remaining stairs, calling her name.

He came to a halt on the landing and stood there for a moment, stock still. All the doors were closed. They never closed the doors up here. He looked down at the cream carpet. At the spreading dark red stain.

It was coming from beneath the door to the master bedroom.

His initial impulse was to rush in, but the sheer volume of blood made him stop. He pulled his phone from his pocket, dialled 999 and begged for the police and an ambulance.

Screaming about his wife and the blood, he managed through his panic to give them his address.

All he could hear was a soothing voice saying that help was on the way. That he must stay where he was or

113

go down and watch for the emergency vehicles. *He mustn't to go into the room. Did he understand? Do not go into the room.*

Ronnie edged forward, his soles squelching on the sticky, blood-soaked carpet. He turned the handle and pushed at the door. Nothing happened.

This was the master bedroom, and there was no lock on the door. So why . . . ?

He pushed harder, then realised that Lisa must be lying against the door, blocking it. God!

He put his shoulder to the door, and this time it moved. He opened it very slowly.

There was nothing on the floor, other than blood.

Ronnie stepped inside.

The room had been trashed. He saw broken ornaments, a smashed mirror, bedlinen strewn over the floor. And more blood. Streaks, splashes and splatters.

It was too much for Ronnie. He turned to run back out onto the landing, but heard a creaking. The bedroom door slowly began to close.

And then he saw her, and knew why the door had been so heavy.

Lisa was hanging on the back of the door.

Ronnie shrank back and crouched down in the farthest corner of the room, burying his head in his hands.

* * *

Professor Rory Wilkinson raised his eyebrows. 'You wonderful policemen have given me some extraordinary cases over the years, and you still come up with more.' He looked at Matt, shaking his head. 'Something new, every time.'

'Can't say it's my pleasure.' Matt, clad in a protective hooded over-suit, mask and plastic shoe covers, had taken one brief look at the crime scene, and knew that his worst fears had been realised. The copycat killer had begun his work.

The house in Sycamore Close had been sealed off. There were police vehicles from one end of the cul-de-sac to the other, access was restricted and a control point had been established.

The smell in the bedroom was overpowering, but the windows remained as they were, shut tight. It was vitally important to make sure there was no contamination of evidence, so they had to endure it. One of the SOCOs was overheard to say it was much like his teenage son's room on a bad day. It was their way of coping.

Meanwhile, Matt was trying to avoid looking at the mortal remains of Lisa Lester.

Having seen the crime scene photographs of Jeremy Reader's five women victims, he was now forced to look at the real thing. And after all these years, he was struggling.

Common sense told him that after all he'd been through in the last year it was hardly surprising that he'd had enough of death, but this felt different. Matt was frightened. It was a first for him, and he didn't like it. Rory seemed to have picked up on it, and had refrained from his usual black-humoured comments.

Matt forced himself to look. What shook wasn't the dreadful method of killing. It was the woman herself. She looked exactly like the young woman at the heart of his last, terrible case. He swallowed and fought to listen to what Rory was saying.

'Well, most of this,' the pathologist cast his arm around the room, 'is frippery.' He glanced at his two SOCOs. 'Or as you guys might say, window dressing.'

'How so?' Matt asked, rallying himself slightly.

'Well, the bread knife, for one, was never used in this attack. It just looks gory and adds to the overall picture. It has no prints at all on it, so it was cleaned by the killer — who wore protective gloves, by the way.' He then waved in the direction of the bloodstains. 'These were not caused by the attack. Blood was taken from the dying victim and thrown at the walls and over the bedlinen. Just for show.'

He looked at them with an expression of scorn. 'No blood spatter pattern ever looked like that! Ridiculous.'

'What do you make of the scene, Rory? From what you've seen so far?' Matt asked.

Rory sniffed. 'Best guess, she knew him. No forced entry. I know the back door was unlocked, but I'm sure trace evidence will support the fact that he used it to make his exit. He just walked out into the night and left the door open. There's an alleyway that runs along the back of these houses and meets up with the lane to the church a bit further down. So the neighbours wouldn't see him.' He turned his attention to the body. 'I can't say until we do the PM, but it's my opinion that he stunned her, maybe roughed her up a bit, judging from the scrapes and minor cuts on her, then strung her up. She certainly wasn't dead. Her heart was pumping most efficiently to cause this amount of exsanguination.'

Matt's head spun. He felt as if he were back in the scary world of his last case. Surely, this wasn't fair? He and Liz had suffered enough damage, hadn't they? He looked around. And what of these people — Lisa Lester and her distraught husband? What of the damage they had suffered? Poor Ronnie Lester had returned home from a night shift in a bakery, to find this! Matt shuddered.

Rory was staring at him. 'Are you alright, Matt?'

He nodded. 'Just thinking. You do know that we suspect this to be a copycat killing?'

'I do. Well, this is certainly no ordinary murder. Far from it.' He adjusted his glasses, and then pointed to a deep laceration in the back of the victim's leg. 'I should think the most important thing to note is this. Just here behind the knees lies the popliteal artery. This has been very accurately cut on both legs. It takes about as long, maybe a fraction longer, to cause exsanguination as does the femoral artery which takes five to sixty minutes. The time varies according to whether the haemoglobin saturation levels are normal, and also the kind of incision.

Ghurkhas were taught to twist the knife in order to tear the side wall of the artery and death would be very fast. ' He pulled a face. 'Sadly, as these are clean cuts, I suspect it took quite a while in this lady's case.'

'There's another thing, Rory. Remember the five skin hearts I brought you?'

'The present from the original killer. I remember, and I think I've already spotted the area where the skin has been removed from this unfortunate lady. As soon as I get her back to the mortuary, I'll be able to tell you for sure.'

'Thank you.' Matt looked at Rory, 'When are you going to get her there?'

'I've done all I can here now, and Ella has taken her photographs, so we are almost ready to go. Spike has just gone down to fetch a body bag.'

'I'll get you to tell me how he got her up on that door later. It can't have been easy.'

'Again, the PM will explain everything.' Rory's technician, Spike, came in. 'I suggest you let us deal with this, Matt. It's in our job description, not yours.'

'I'm not going to argue with that, Rory. I have to speak to the husband, if I can, and that, unfortunately, is in my job description.'

Downstairs, Matt found Jason and Kim sitting with Ronnie Lester in the back of the ambulance. Jason got out and joined him. 'They've given him something to calm him, sir, but he's refusing to leave. He's in a proper state, poor sod.'

'Has he told you anything of use?'

'I don't think he knows any more than we do. He's bothered about the fact that they'd not been getting on recently, and how he'd hoped to make things better, but now . . .'

'Now it's too late, and he'll be living with that for the rest of his life.' Matt's heart went out to him. 'Has he said if there's anyone we can call to come and be with him?'

'No kids, no close family living nearby, but he has a mate who might help. We can't make him go to hospital, but he can't stay here. Kim's trying to make him understand that his home is now a crime scene, but as I said, he's in deep shock.'

No bloody wonder, thought Matt. I'm shaken enough, and she wasn't my wife. 'Get hold of a doctor and a family liaison officer, Jason. And the mate, too. That man needs support badly. He should have someone with him twenty-four/seven until his family can sort something out.'

Jason got out his phone and began making calls.

The husband was nearly always the first suspect in a domestic murder, but the state Ronnie Lester was in told Matt that he wasn't involved. He wasn't exactly "Alex" material, and Matt was now certain that Alex existed. The proof was hanging from a door.

* * *

Back at the station, Matt found Laura Archer and Sam Page making their way along the corridor to the CID room.

'We've been discussing Jeremy Reader and Grace Repton for hours, Matt,' said Sam, 'His reports have really made us think.'

'Sam and I are of the opinion that Reader may have truly undergone a transformation,' Laura said. 'We think there's a fair chance that he's on the level, especially about trying to prevent more deaths.'

Matt sighed. 'He's too late, I'm afraid. The copycat killings have begun. That's what all the furore was about this morning. We have a butchered woman, showing all the hallmarks of the Reader killings.'

The two psychologists looked at each other.

'Oh no! That's terrible!' Laura exclaimed.

'And it could cause another problem,' added Sam grimly, 'with Reader.'

Matt frowned, 'Sorry?'

'Let's assume Jeremy Reader really is sorry for the things he did. If there's another man killing in his name, glorifying the past that Reader is desperately trying to atone for, it could cause him untold psychological damage.'

'He'll feel responsible all over again,' added Laura. 'A lot of people would say, who cares? He's a five times murderer, let him suffer. But think of all he's been through to get to this point. He now understands that the things he did were monstrous and unforgivable. If I were his governor, I'd be worried for his safety.'

'As in an attempt on his own life?' Matt asked.

'Very possibly,' Sam said.

Matt thought about this. Whether or not he deserved to suffer after wrecking those lives and families, Jem Reader was his only surviving link to Alex. He needed Reader. He might need Reader for an insight into Alex's thinking. *It takes one to know one.* Reader could be very helpful, if he chose to help them. 'I need to ring Ross Cadman. Last night's murder will be all over the press in no time at all, if it isn't on the TV already. There are enough blue lights in that cul-de-sac to illuminate the whole of Fenfleet.'

He should really pay yet another trip to HMP Gately, but he was needed here. He would have to trust Cadman to keep Reader safe until he could talk to him in person.

'Sir!'

Matt didn't like the look on Jack Fleet's face.

'We think we have another one, sir! Wendell Street, a woman named Louise Farrier. She works at Cordell's haulage company and didn't turn up yesterday, so one of her colleagues decided to call in on her way to work this morning. The back door was unlocked and the smell hit her as soon as she walked in. Sensible woman didn't go inside, just called for assistance.'

'Hell! I don't believe it.' He turned to Sam and Laura. 'I have to go, but could you hang on here?'

They both nodded. 'Whatever we can do to help,' Sam said.

Matt hurried after Jack Fleet.

CHAPTER THIRTEEN

They flew across town towards Wendell Street, Jason at the wheel. Matt rang Ross Cadman and gave him the news. Cadman promised to break it to Reader, and added, 'Will you inform Grace Repton?'

Matt said that he would. He rang Kim Peters and told her to get herself straight round to Grace's house and tell her what had happened. 'And watch her carefully, Kim. I need to know how she reacts. It could tell us something about Jem Reader's motives for helping us.'

Matt stared through the windscreen, steeling himself for what was coming. One brutal killing was bad enough, but two? He hoped he was strong enough.

They found police cars parked outside number three. Uniform had already set up a cordon and a log.

Matt showed his warrant card, signed in with the officer at the front door and picked up a coverall from the waiting pile.

After so many years, he should be used to that smell by now, surely? He knew he wouldn't be, *ever*. The smell of a violent death clung inside your nostrils for days, and stayed with you for life. The sense of smell was very underestimated.

A WPC stood on the landing and silently indicated towards a partially opened door.

This time, Alex had chosen the bathroom.

Matt stood in the doorway and saw a version of the earlier scene. The striking resemblance between the two women hit him first, even before the blood. Blonde. Blue eyes. Slight. Jeremy Reader's ideal victim.

Alex had decided to hang Louise Farrier inside the shower cubicle. He had placed a wooden broom handle across the top to support her weight. It appeared that he didn't trust the shower fitting to do the job properly.

Louise was dressed as Lisa had been, flimsy summer upper clothes intact and still wearing her underwear. Just her lower garment had been removed in order to get to the artery that her life blood had drained out of. Matt noticed a pair of leggings flung into a corner.

A fleeting thought said that there was no sexual motivation for these killings. It was something Jeremy Reader had always insisted upon, even if he was not believed at the time of his trial.

With Lisa's death still fresh in his mind, he easily saw the similarities between the two killings. And the differences. 'Almost identical,' he murmured.

'Why almost?' asked Jason at his side.

'None of what Rory called "fripperies." No window dressing.'

'This seems to have been his first killing, sir. Maybe he was finding his feet.'

'Or possibly he was disturbed before he could add the final touches,' mused Matt.

They heard the sound of feet on the stairs and Matt saw the tall, lanky
figure of Rory Wilkinson striding across the landing.

'Look here, dear friends! This is a bit much, you know. Providing me with plenty of interesting work is one thing, but this is beyond a joke!'

'You can say that again,' grumbled Jason. 'And it's not our idea of fun either.'

'Poor Spike. I've had to leave him to cope with the removal of Mrs Lester, while I hare across town to attend to whatever little delight you have for me this time.'

'Another one, Rory. With some differences.' Matt stood aside and the pathologist entered the bathroom.

'Oh my! Déjà vu.' Rory smiled grimly. 'I do hope that one day I have the pleasure of meeting the perpetrator of these crimes — in my professional capacity, of course.'

'Sick bastard!' Jason added

'I need another couple of SOCOs,' Rory said. 'My first team can't leave Sycamore Close, and I don't want them missing a thing, so they can't hurry their job. I'll call Ella Jarvis for some more happy snaps, then organise extra help here.' He pulled out his phone and called the forensic photographer, telling her briefly about her next gruesome assignment.

While Rory made his calls, Matt stared at Louise Farrier and wondered what her story was. How did Alex gain her trust? He must have done, much like Reader, the quiet friendly bloke in the park. Like Sycamore Close, this house showed no signs of having been broken into, and again the back door was unlocked. Had the women purposely left it open for him? Or had he just used it to exit, as Rory had thought? Matt knew Wendell Street. He had a friend who had lived here for years, so he knew that there were back gates to these properties too, leading out into a path that circled round a playing field. Again, a convenient way of disappearing without being seen. Was this luck? Or had Alex really done his homework? He suspected the latter. Questions swarmed around in his head. Combined with the stench in the small room, they were making him dizzy.

Rory examined the woman's body. 'Exactly the same as the one we have just seen. Same incisions into the popliteal arteries, except . . .'

Matt looked up.

'Except that I can clearly see where he excised the tiny heart of skin.' He pointed to an area just above her right elbow. 'Look, he didn't manage to conceal it too well afterwards. By the time he got to Mrs Lester on the following night, he had improved his technique somewhat.'

'And we think he either had more time with Mrs Lester, or maybe he was less apprehensive or hyped up, but there are none of your accompanying fripperies here.'

'That fact wasn't lost on me either.' Rory looked around. 'And I'm wondering about his use of the shower tray to contain the blood. He has blocked the drain intentionally, that's why it has escaped all over the bathroom floor. Odd, don't you think? Surely, he'd just let it flow down the drain?'

'Something else to make careful note of.' Matt looked at Jason, who immediately scribbled in his notebook.

'He's already deviated slightly from Reader's MO,' said Jason quietly. 'Reader only killed two women in the same area. He had already killed one before you caught up with him, sir. Lisa made it two. If he was being faithful to Reader's methods, Alex should have moved on.'

'Unless he's starting afresh. In which case he should move on now, this being his second,' said Rory. 'If you are that lucky, dear boys!'

'Time will tell,' said Matt grimly. 'Meanwhile we have a lot of work to do. We'll leave this poor soul in your care and get back. I have a murder room to set up and an investigation strategy to prepare.' He exhaled loudly. 'And try to work out the most effective lines of enquiry. God help me!'

'I have complete faith in you, dear Detective Chief Inspector. I promise to burn the midnight oil until my bleary little eyes positively droop with fatigue.'

Matt was forced to smile. Rory always managed to lighten the atmosphere at these horrific crime scenes. It was very welcome. In his time on the force, Matt had worked with various pathologists, with different approaches. Some made the job even worse. But Rory was perfect. He would miss him. Professor Rory Wilkinson was a real one-off, plus he was the best pathologist Matt had ever come across. 'Remind me to pop into Boots and pick up some eyedrops for you.'

'Sweet man! Now, run along and sort your strategies. This woman has been hanging around for far too long waiting for my ministrations. I must pay her some attention, so off you go!'

They were happy to comply.

* * *

Kim Peters sat opposite Grace Repton in her conservatory, and gratefully accepted a mug of tea. While Grace was in the kitchen, a very strange cat kept Kim company. She'd heard of animals with heterochromia, cats in particular, but had never seen one. She found it oddly disconcerting. Cleo was beautiful, a misty, smoky grey colour, but her eyes, one brilliant blue and the other sea-green, were mesmerising.

Kim preferred dogs, but this cat had charisma. She found herself tickling it behind the ears and smiling at its rumbling purr. 'She's beautiful, isn't she?' Kim said as Grace came in with the tea. 'And I should think it's quite handy to have a mouser, living as you are on the edge of the fields.'

'Oh no, Chloe is a house cat, she wouldn't demean herself by chasing vermin. She thinks she's far too classy for anything like that.' Grace sat down in a cane armchair filled with cushions. 'But cat apart, I'm guessing this is bad news?'

'DCI Ballard sends his apologies for not coming himself, but he is very much involved in a double murder investigation.' Kim put her mug on the glass topped table in front of her. 'We wanted you to know that your suspicions of a copycat killer were correct. We believe that he has struck twice in the last forty-eight hours.'

Grace stiffened.

Kim watched her. She sat motionless with a myriad different emotions playing across her face. She closed her eyes for a moment.

'I dreaded hearing this. I mean we were certain it would happen, but . . . now it's happened, my worst nightmare has been realised.' She swallowed. 'This could destroy Jem.'

'It's not Jeremy's fault that some unstable madman has latched onto his past crimes,' Kim said.

'It's Jem's belief that if he had never done such terrible things, this young man wouldn't have gone down this road.'

'No, but he would have found someone else, another murderer to emulate.'

'I've tried to tell Jem that, but he won't have it. He was just praying that Alex wouldn't have the guts to go through with it.'

Well, he's certainly doing that alright, thought Kim. 'I'm going to ask for your help, Grace. I know you came to us in the first place, and initially we were hesitant to believe you, but I think you can appreciate why that was?'

'Of course. I'm not stupid. In fact, I think it was very open-minded of your boss to listen to me at all.' She sipped her tea. 'I've been working with prisoners for some time now. Nine times out of ten, they swear they are innocent when they're guilty as hell, so why would a copper trust a murderer? And Jem fully admits that that is what he is, and that he must pay for what he did.'

'We have informed Governor Cadman, Grace, and asked him to give Jeremy every support. I'm sure he will act appropriately.'

'He's a remarkably good man, and the most unlikely prison governor I've ever met,' Grace said. 'But I still believe Jem will take this very badly.'

'Grace,' Kim said, 'you probably realise that Jeremy is the only person who has had any dealings with Alex. All those letters he received, he has to remember a lot of what they said. His insight into Alex could be invaluable in catching him. We need Jeremy on board, not wallowing in self-pity or feelings of guilt. What's done is done. He can't change the past, but he can help us catch Alex. Will you help us get that across to him?'

Chloe jumped onto Grace's lap and began to purr loudly. Stroking the cat, she said, 'Of course. It's the only way he can help himself, and also prevent more deaths. I'll do all I can to get him to cooperate. Let's just pray that these killings don't affect him so deeply that he won't be able to do so.'

Kim decided to chance her arm. 'Can I ask if you've ever had doubts about Jeremy's sincerity?'

'Do you think I'd actually marry a man I didn't trust?'

'It's not so much that. He could have started to feel very differently about himself after you and he got together. I rather meant when you first met.'

'He was well on the road to rehabilitation when I met him, DC Peters. I've had no input into that process. He's tackled all his demons alone. Our relationship came out of the blue for both of us. I love Jeremy Reader, and he loves me. I'd do anything for him, and I'm sure he would do anything in his power for me. Our marriage will be very unusual, certainly, but it won't be lacking in love. Does that answer your question?'

Kim smiled, hoping she looked reassuring. 'Thank you. I didn't mean to pry, but we could be spending a lot of time with Jeremy, so I wanted to understand exactly what you felt about him.' She stood up, thanked Grace for the tea, and took one last look at the cat with the mismatched eyes.

Kim drove out of sight of Grace's bungalow, and stopped. She took out her notebook, jotted down the main points of their conversation and set off for the station.

She thought about Grace while she drove, her comments, reactions, and most of all, her body language. Grace Repton was a very complicated woman who was trying to come across as straightforward. But she couldn't disguise the fact that plain, simple women don't marry murderers.

* * *

Superintendent David Redpath drummed his fingers on the desktop. 'Are you sure this isn't too much for you to handle, Matt? Your retirement is slipping away into the distance, and there's still no sign of DCI Anders's arrival.'

Matt rolled his eyes. *Don't go there.*

'Sorry, but I have to ask. After all you've been through, this is not exactly the slow wind-down I was hoping for you. I don't want you going out on medical grounds.'

'If I can nail this murdering psychopath, I'll go out on a high.'

'Just keep communicating, Matt. Don't shoulder too much alone. You have previous for that, as you well know.'

'I won't, and I can do with all the help I can get. We need more officers on the house to house enquiries around both addresses. We have Reuben Grimes's murder still unsolved, and I can't let the Filip Derus case slip either. So far, Bryn Owen, with possible help from Swifty, has taken that on solo, but it's getting a bit convoluted. He might need extra help if he finds any more dark secrets in the Baltic Quarter.'

'I'll need to take this upstairs and see what can be organised. Meanwhile, I'll speak to uniform. Now, I'm going to have to talk to the press. Overnight, Fenfleet has turned into the murder capital of Great Britain. They're going to want answers.'

'Can we keep it as close to our chests as possible, David? Two women murdered in their own homes is scary enough for some people. We'll have mass panic on our hands if we give them any details.'

'Don't worry. I'm a past-master of the art of talking without actually saying anything. No way can the media be told about how they were killed, and the word copycat will not pass my lips, never fear.'

Matt knew that David was as good as any politician at avoiding a straight answer, but he was going to have to be on top form to fend off the inevitable questions about four murders in a single week. Still, that was the super's headache. He had problems enough to worry about.

'Before you go.' David looked at him anxiously. 'I'm not sure where we stand on Operation Saturn. Our combined crackdown on the drug dealers is organised for five days' time. Everything is in place. It's taken years of work to get this far, but with all that's going on, can we afford to go ahead? It's a double-edged sword, and I'm not sure which blade is the right one to use. I know it's not your problem, Matt, but keep me up to speed on all fronts. It could be a deciding factor in how we proceed.'

Matt nodded. He'd hate to have David's job. He must feel as if he's balancing on a high wire with no safety net below him. 'Of course I will.'

He returned to his office and prepared some notes for the afternoon meeting at four. He had a lot to tell his officers and didn't want to miss anything out. Just as he was finishing, Jason arrived, carrying a large envelope.

'Just arrived for you, sir. Prelim forensic report on Reuben Grimes.'

Matt tore it open, scanned it avidly, then grunted and handed it back to Jason. 'Only two things of interest here. The knife that was used to kill him was a very professional, surgically sharp blade, identified as medical equipment, plus the findings from the tape that was used to seal up the windows and bind Reuben to the chair.' He watched Jason read the report.

'I see what you mean,' Jason said. 'They found a whole plethora of vegetable, animal and mineral deposits on one end of the sealing tape, as if it had been dropped and rolled along the floor at some point.'

'None of which have been fully identified yet, but when they are, they could be significant when we have a suspect banged up downstairs.' It was useless until they had someone to compare the findings against. 'Still, it will be on file when we need it.'

Jason handed the report back. 'I wish I knew why the killer didn't want the body discovered immediately. I can only think he had a set plan, a schedule to stick to.'

'That would seem right, if it is Alex. Most murderers wouldn't kill on two consecutive nights, surely? That's one hell of a battle plan, to get it right with no slip-ups.'

'For a beginner, Alex appears to be very well-organised, and very confident, to work at that speed.' Jason's brow folded into a mass of wrinkles. 'I keep wondering, will he stop now and move on, as per Jeremy Reader, or will he keep going as he is?'

'That's the big question, my friend. Only Alex knows the answer to that one.'

'Best guess, boss?'

'Not that I wish to depress you further, but my gut feeling says he'll stay here.'

'That's mine too, although I wish it wasn't.'

By the time he left, Matt was feeling almost as negative as Jason, but before his thoughts dragged him too far down, his phone rang.

'Ross Cadman here. Just an update for you.'

Matt stiffened. 'How did Reader take it?'

'Initially, much as we had expected, but the therapists have made good progress already. That's unexpected, but we've all stressed that he is absolutely pivotal in finding Alex. He's coming round, Detective Chief Inspector. I think he will cooperate fully with you.'

Matt breathed a sigh of relief. 'Great news. I want to strike while the iron is hot. I'd like to talk to him again. Will tomorrow morning be okay?'

'I'm sure he'll agree. He's beginning to realise that he might be the only person that can stop Alex from killing again. I really don't think he wants his replica out there slaughtering women.'

'Our police psychologists have studied your reports and they share your opinion. They were sceptical at first, but they are coming round to the notion that he is genuinely aware of the evil that he did and that he truly wants to make amends.'

'That's very good to hear. If they want to confer with the PIPE team, they'll be most welcome to do so. Jeremy's quite happy with that.'

'That's appreciated, Ross.'

'No problem. Shall we say ten thirty tomorrow then?'

'That's fine. Oh, and by the way, we have Grace's support. She thinks assisting us will help soothe his conscience.'

'Excellent. I just hope you get results.'

'Thanks, Ross.'

But Matt was wary of counting his chickens yet. Reader could easily have a change of heart, and there was still a chance that he was manipulating them all. Were the people involved in Jem's care so invested in the idea of his penitence that they were overlooking what he had done? Was the thought of finding a truly repentant murderer so thrilling to them that they were taken in by him? He had always trusted Laura Archer's judgement, and Sam Page was undoubtedly a first class psychologist, with first-hand experience as well. But . . . Matt had long years of experience too, and he hadn't yet met a trustworthy criminal. He dare not let his guard down.

He was wondering which of the myriad tasks before him to concentrate on, when he saw Kim Peters walking towards his office. He beckoned to her.

'You look puzzled, Kim.'

'It's Grace Repton, sir. I just can't work her out. It's messing with my head. Maybe it's because I've never actually met anyone prepared to marry into such a bizarre situation. I mean, forge a relationship with a five times killer? It's just unbelievable.'

'What do we know about her?' Matt asked.

'Very little, as far as I can tell. She must have been cleared in order to work as an official prison visitor, and she's a widow. That's all I know.'

'Dig deeper, Kim. This horror story began with Grace coming to see me with the warning, so we should start there. You work on her, and I'll go back over Jeremy Reader's trial. Hell, I was there, but I need the transcripts, every little detail. And, most of all, the forensic photographs and reports. All of them.'

One thing that bothered Matt was how far the original crime scenes matched with what Jem had confided in Reuben. Would he really have been prepared to confide every last sordid detail to a man he hardly knew?

'I'll be pleased to, sir,' Kim said. 'She has me intrigued. I really want to understand her better.'

'Then go for it. See if you can come up with something for the four o'clock meeting.'

Kim left, looking determined.

Matt called the archive. 'Right, Jeremy Reader, let's see what kind of man you really were, ten years ago.'

CHAPTER FOURTEEN

Lina Derus walked along a lonely farm track towards the place where her brother's body had been found. Nothing was left now except some abandoned police tape.

It wasn't difficult to identify the exact spot. His blood had soaked the ground and the grass was stained black.

They had been so close. Filip had been a special friend as well as her brother. Now he was gone.

Lina knelt down beside the stained patch of ground and said a prayer for Filip. Then she addressed him. Wherever he was, she told him, she would see him again and they would share happy times once more. Their family had survived the fighting between the independence movement and the Russians, and they had made the best of things in the aftermath, finally travelling to England and a chance of a better life.

Lina wiped her tears with the back of her hand. England had been a shock. She hadn't been prepared for the racism they'd encountered, but after a while they had learned to ignore the shouts of, "Go back to your own country!" and had settled into a kind of a life. They worked hard, long hours for little pay, but managed to make a home, and then the rest of the family joined them. Filip said that they'd be well-off one day. He always had plans. Big ones.

Lina broke off a stem of the wild chicory that grew along the field edge, and admired its blue flower. It was so alive, so vivid. It had witnessed the death of Filip, yet it still flowered. But Filip was gone. Lina closed her hand and crushed it.

She got to her feet and stared down at the blackened ground. Then a loud cry burst from her, in her own language. 'This is wrong! The people who did this have to pay.'

She thought of the other victims' families, clinging to the shadows, keeping silent, terrified of more violence. She just wished she knew more about what Filip had been doing during those last few months. What were those big plans of his? She couldn't believe that he'd had anything to do with drug dealing. His friend Jonas had died of an overdose, and after that, Filip had been firmly against drugs. No way would he supply them. So what could he possibly have done that was bad enough to make him a target, someone to be eliminated?

Lina stepped back, her eyes still on the dark patch in the grass. She hoped it had been quick. He was such a caring person. He didn't deserve to suffer, to be frightened.

'Filip!' She called into the blue, cloudless sky. 'What should I do? What *can* I do?'

A warm breeze ruffled her hair. It felt as if his fingers were gently caressing her. She refused to keep her head down, to stay out of it, like the others. The injustice of his killing was almost too much to bear. 'Filip,' she whispered, 'I have to have answers. I have to make sure that whoever did this to you regrets it for the rest of their lives.'

She remembered the young detective who had broken the news about her brother. He had been kind. He'd even taken the trouble to learn a few words of her language. Bryn Owen, that was his name. She still had his card.

After one last look, she turned on her heels and slowly retraced her steps along the lane.

* * *

Matt spent over an hour looking through the reports of the investigation and the transcripts of the trial. It had been a heady time for him, the break that had made his career. On the back of it, he had jumped from Sergeant to DI. He had told the super that it had been down to luck — right place, right time — but it wasn't just that. It had been damned good police work. He'd been very much on the ball, making the right call at the right moment. Luck had nothing to do with it.

He sifted through the reports until he found one that chronicled Reader's criminal history.

He had expected Jeremy Reader to have followed the usual textbook pattern of escalation. Such careers usually began with a bit of voyeurism. The peeping tom, progressing to stalking, then assault, rape, and finally murder. But this had not been the case with Reader. As a teenager, he'd had his collar felt for several misdemeanours and seemed to be heading for bigger things. Then he stopped, just like that. Until he started killing. Even then he differed from most serial killers in that he never raped or sexually interfered with any of his victims.

Matt stared at the paperwork and it came to him that Alex wouldn't necessarily follow the same path. Would he have followed the path of most serial killers, escalating? He went to his office door and beckoned to Kim Peters.

'Kim, I want a list of reported cases of stalking in this area, let's say over the last couple of years.'

'Okay, sir. No problem.' She hurried back to her computer.

Reader had never been convicted of any of the earlier murders, he had only ever been a suspect. It was only after spending some time in prison that he had admitted to all of them. He also told the psychologists that he always knew he was going to murder, but had no way of stopping himself. He planned them meticulously. Even as he chatted amicably to those women during their lunchbreak, he knew exactly how he was going to kill them. From the moment he selected someone, she was a dead woman walking. From then, all he could visualise was the moment when he cut that tiny heart from their soft pale flesh.

Matt sat in the quiet of his office with the hubbub of the CID room just a whisper behind his closed door. From what he read, Reader sounded cold, callous, and unbelievably disturbed, nothing like the calm, reasonable, contrite man he had met again in HMP Gately.

Once again, the whole situation took on an air of unreality. Reader was behind bars, probably for the rest of his life, because Matt Ballard, a lowly detective sergeant, had noticed something that everyone else had missed, a single anomaly that led him to Reader's door. And now it was happening again. Like the remake of an old film with the goodie, now an old-timer, about to tackle the same evil all over again.

He had to remember that he now had a lot more experience. Looked at like that, the odds weren't quite so bad. He thought about Liz and how she tackled everything with unshakable positivity, and it gave him heart. He could do this.

* * *

Reader sat locked in his cell, alone. He needed this lunchtime "bang up" period and the solitude it gave him. When he had been in seg, sometimes locked up for twenty-three hours a day, he had longed for company. Now he craved the quiet of his cell. He put down his spoon. The governor's news had destroyed his appetite.

It was happening. Alex had kept his word.

He needed to talk to Grace. He had asked for an extra visit but his request had been declined. Instead, Ballard was coming back tomorrow morning. He wondered what questions he would have. On the verge of losing it, Reader knew he had to have his answers ready.

He pushed his plate aside, stood up and unrolled a small exercise mat that he'd been permitted to keep in his cell. He laid it out on the floor and sat down . . .

He was in a small cave behind a waterfall. All around him was the rushing of the water, calming and soothing. He breathed deeply. In. Pause. Out. He let out a long sigh. Jem Reader was back in command of his thoughts.

* * *

DC Kim Peters took the printout of reported cases of stalking into Matt's office, and then returned to her search for Grace Repton. Kim was good at tracing people, she knew all the best routes to follow. So why was Grace Repton and her background so difficult to run to ground?

Kim wanted to impress Matt Ballard. She knew he was retiring, but she still valued his opinion. She wanted the new DCI to see her as a good detective. Kim was not over-ambitious, she wasn't about to trample over others in her fight up the ladder, but she was a single woman who loved her job. She had to rely on herself, there was no one behind her, so she needed that promotion.

Back to Grace. So far, all she had found was the result of a PNC check done when she applied to be a prison visitor, stating that she was not known to the police and was understood to be of good character. Since then she had kept her unblemished character and had had nothing but positive feedback from the various prisons she had attended.

Kim obviously wasn't going to get far going the official route. It was no good trying Special Branch either. They dealt with individuals of national security interest, and Grace certainly didn't come into that category. If anything, she was just a "do-gooder."

From the prison records, she had found that Grace had been married before, and that her husband had died young, but apart from that, she could find nothing.

She tried social media, but Grace had no presence. No cute kittens, no "friends" on Facebook, nothing. Kim tried the local papers, and then Googled the name "Grace Repton." Here, she did find a mention. It was a small part of someone's blog about homeless people in nearby Greenborough town. It went on to describe how a group of night marshals, led by Grace, had discovered a lock-up with immigrants hiding inside. So, she was, or had been, a town on-street marshal. Hmm.

Kim leaned back in her chair. She was beginning to see the woman slightly differently now. Everything she did seemed to be motivated by altruism. It took a special kind of woman to walk the streets at night, even if she was accompanied by a colleague. She didn't know much about the group, a scaled-down version of the scheme run in cities like Bath. It provided another set of eyes on the streets at night, and their early reports to the police had often led to arrests. Greenborough was bigger and busier than Fenfleet, so she doubted there'd be one here. Just to make sure, she Googled it, and surprisingly found a small group operating under the umbrella of Holy Trinity Church. And sitting squarely on top of the rota of volunteers was the name Grace Repton. Kim grinned. At last, someone to talk to about this lady. If you're pacing the pavements in the dead of night, you chat to your sidekick, don't you? Kim should know. As a probationer she'd sat in enough stuffy squad cars on a nightshift obbo and listened to the entire life history of her crewmate.

Kim looked up the contact details for Holy Trinity, and was soon in the car, on her way to chat to the man who had started the initiative a couple of years ago.

* * *

'I'm sorry to say that I've never come across your group, Mr Hedley,' she said.

Christopher Hedley threw her a beaming smile. 'Not surprised, my dear. We're very small fry indeed, and you're in CID, are you not? We rarely get attention from anyone higher than a PCSO, not that I'm knocking them, but we tend to mainly look out for homeless people in difficulties and the like.'

'You're all church members then?'

'Oh no. Some are — after all, we're street pastors, there to offer spiritual guidance if needed, but any help is gratefully received. I'm a church warden, but my fellow marshals are from all over.'

Kim liked the look of this man. His body language told her he was open and honest, with a sense of humour and an even deeper sense of duty to his parish. He had a wide nose that might have been broken once, thick wavy grey hair, a little too long for his age, which was around sixty-five, Kim supposed, and a heavy frame. He looked like an older rugby player.

'So,' he continued, 'what can I do to help you, DC Peters?'

'It's Kim, and it's information I'm looking for, Christopher. We are carrying out background checks and a name has come up that I think you can help me with. In the strictest confidence, can I ask you if you know Grace Repton?'

'Good Lord! Grace? Of course I know her. She's a stalwart of this group. Always responds to a request for assistance, never misses her turn on the rota. She's a rock, that one!'

'Excellent,' said Kim. 'Have you known her long?'

'Maybe a year, eighteen months?'

'Is she a member of your church?'

'No, and not of any other that I know of. I don't believe Grace is at all religious.'

'And you would trust her, and her judgement?'

139

'Completely. Can I ask if she's applied for a job with you? Like a civilian post as a mediator or something?' Christopher Hedley looked quite excited. 'Because I'd certainly be prepared to vouch for her, you know, provide a character reference.'

'It's a little more complicated than that, Mr Hedley, but Grace is certainly helping us. We have to do a confidential background check though.'

Hedley nodded. 'So, what can I tell you?'

Kim thought quickly. The information she wanted was not the kind of thing you would ask for in an official check, so she needed to be canny. For effect, she glanced at the notepad on her clipboard. 'You've already told me that she's reliable, as in not missing her turn on the streets, but does she work well in a team, or would you class her as someone who prefers to work alone?'

'Both, really. She's well liked and teams up happily with most of our volunteers, but if necessity demands, Grace is very happy handling something on her own.' He gave a little laugh, 'Actually she's pretty fearless! She's tackled some rather scary situations.' He looked directly at Kim. 'Don't think I'm being sexist, but for a woman, I've seen her confront some very unpleasant individuals, people that even a big guy like me would think twice about going head to head with.'

'Probably seen it all as a prison visitor,' said Kim casually.

'Very true,' replied Christopher. 'And then there was that incident with her husband. That rather sums her up, doesn't it?'

Kim scanned her bogus notes. 'There's nothing about that here.' She looked at him enquiringly.

'Oh well, yes, her husband was mugged. They were in London and returning home after some evening out, and apparently a pair of drug addicts attacked them. Her husband was pushed to the ground and hit his head on the curb. They went for his wallet but Grace fought them off.

One got away, but she managed to restrain the other long enough for help to arrive. Her husband rallied, was apparently okay but a bit dazed, so she got him to the hospital where he collapsed and died on the floor of A&E.'

'Good grief! That's awful!'

'I think that's why she spends so much time trying to help others.'

Kim decided that she'd heard enough. 'I really appreciate your help, Christopher, but I think that's everything. If you would be kind enough not to mention this to her, I'd be grateful. As far as I'm concerned, we need have no concerns about Grace Repton.'

'Glad to have helped, Kim. And if you ever fancy a few hours walking the streets with us, you'll be very welcome.'

Kim laughed. 'Thanks for the offer, but I think I've done my fair share of patrolling when I was in uniform!'

He smiled. 'Worth a try.'

Back in the car, Kim went over what she'd learned. Perhaps that incident with her husband really was the driving force behind Grace's altruistic lifestyle? She frowned. What made someone commit their life to doing good deeds? Just altruism? Religious or spiritual beliefs? What was Grace's motivation?

Guilt, she thought, or trying to cover something up. In Grace's case was it guilt over her husband's death? Did she feel that she'd let him down somehow, not done enough to save him? Maybe that fateful evening she had insisted on walking that particular route? You never knew when it came to guilty feelings.

Kim started the car. Perhaps Grace genuinely didn't want the same thing happening to other innocent people walking home after dark. She decided that this was the most likely scenario.

* * *

At around three p.m., Sam and Laura returned to Matt's office.

'Sorry, Matt, I had an urgent call to Fenchester. I left Sam here going over the psych reports again.' Laura sat down and let out a long breath. 'Not the best day for Fenfleet, is it?'

'You can say that again.'

Laura's voice softened. 'Are you okay, Matt? You've been through more in one week than most people see in ten years' service.'

'I'm coping.' He hoped that was true. 'I keep hanging on to the fact that in a few weeks' time I'll be out of here and planning my retirement with Liz.'

Laura smiled at him gently. 'Promise that you'll talk to me if you're struggling. Or even if you aren't. It sometimes helps just to offload.'

'You'd need broad shoulders, Laura, for what I saw today.'

'You'd be surprised. I'm stronger than I look.'

'I can vouch for that,' added Sam with a wry smile. 'She's very beautiful, but tough as old boots.'

Laura gave him a sidelong look. 'Thanks for the compliment, Sam — I think.'

'And if you are too gallant to inflict your concerns on the lovely Laura, you can always talk to me. I'm just as tough, but not beautiful at all.' Sam raised an eyebrow. 'And as I'm retired, I have all the time in the world. Just don't bottle it up. The days of the stiff upper lip are long gone.'

'Received and understood, and thank you both, but right now, I'm struggling with a very different problem. Jeremy Reader the killer, not the reformed character.' He pushed a file towards the two psychologists. 'How could someone who admitted that he knew exactly what he was doing, who could plan such terrible sadistic deaths for innocent women, then actually go through with carrying out those fantasies, how in God's name, could he change? I just don't understand it.'

'There are many things that could suddenly make him realise that his actions were evil. But in his case, I'm thinking that incarceration was the catalyst,' said Laura. 'Especially the time spent in segregation. He was, and still is, an intelligent man. People, even murderers, can change, and an acutely difficult situation, like solitary confinement, could have forced him to confront the horror of what he did.'

'Or did he spend that time alone learning how to manipulate people, and become a Hannibal Lecter kind of character, revealing exactly what he thinks we want to hear from a remorseful man?' asked Matt. 'Could he really have surrendered that feeling of power that came from killing someone?'

'We think so,' said Sam. 'We think he really *believes* that he needs to take responsibility for his actions, and as he can't change the past and there is no way to make amends, he's doing all he can to help you catch this copycat.'

'So it's not just him confusing self-pity with remorse, because he got caught and will spend his best years behind bars?' Matt still felt confused about the man, especially when in his company. When he was away from Reader, all his suspicions returned two-fold. 'I'm still suffering nightmares that our Jem is somehow pulling the strings and controlling this killer from inside HMP Gately.'

Sam frowned. 'To be honest, I don't think he could have gone through all those intensive psychiatric and psychological therapies without revealing some sign of a controlling trait.'

'We know what some of those sessions do to you,' added Laura. 'I'm convinced he couldn't have fooled a whole team of experts for so long and not have either burned out or given himself away. Some of those one-to-one sessions can take you to hell and back.'

Unknowingly, Laura and Sam had echoed exactly what Reader had said himself. He'd told Matt that all those hours locked up alone had changed him. He'd had to face the beast within in order to survive. He'd said too that he couldn't change the past, exactly what Sam had said. So maybe they were right. What was the point in asking experts for their advice, and then ignoring them?

'Okay, I'm seeing him in the morning. I'll ask for his help. Anything he can tell me that might lead us to understand how Alex works could mean one less death.'

'Anything we can do?' asked Sam.

'Would you be up to reading the transcripts of the original trial? You've read what the psych team have made of him, but I'd quite like you to weigh it up against Reader's crimes. It's not pleasant reading, though.'

'Certainly.' Sam picked up the big file. 'It will help us to see the man as a whole.'

'Was there any mention anywhere about his childhood?' asked Laura. 'Only that's the one thing the prison unit reports have no record of.'

'Not that I recall, no,' Matt said.

'Strange. That's usually one of the first things you find out about. Childhood experiences are often the foundation of the adult persona.' Laura looked puzzled. 'We need to check that out.'

Matt suddenly noticed the time. 'Hell! I have the four o'clock meeting in five minutes! Can we resume this after I've seen him tomorrow?'

Laura and Sam stood up. 'We'll be here.'

* * *

'Bryn?' It was Lukas on the phone.

'Lukas? Are you alright?' Bryn asked.

'Yes, but bad news travels fast, especially in the kind of place I'm staying in. What's going on in Fenfleet?'

'I can't say. We have ongoing investigations.'

'Just tell me if it has anything to do with Lina. Please, Bryn? I'm worried sick.'

Bryn realised immediately why Lukas was so concerned. 'It's okay, mate. No connection at all. That's all I can say, but you can relax on that score.'

He could almost feel the anxiety fade away down the phone line.

'I thought . . . well, you can imagine, can't you?'

He could. 'Have you settled in?'

'They're very kind here, especially Jim Cousins, the man that runs this place. I just can't help feeling that I've run out on the people that need me. I feel like a coward.'

Bryn understood how he felt. He'd feel the same, he was sure. But he wanted Lukas alive, not as another body dumped in a fenland field, or floating down the river, and he told him so. 'I need your help, Lukas, and in doing that, you'll be helping your friends and family, okay? You won't be helping anyone from a mortuary slab, and if you've really upset those guys that killed Filip, there's a very good chance that's where you'd end up.'

Lukas was silent. Then he said, 'It's hard to do nothing.'

'Keep vigilant. As you said yourself, bad news travels fast. You might just pick up something from the people at the shelter. Meanwhile, enjoy the free food and clean bed, even if the company's not what you're used to. It's pretty manic here right now, but I'll be in touch as soon as I can, I promise.' Bryn didn't want Lukas to fall off the radar. It was important that Filip's death wasn't overshadowed by the double murders of their copycat killer, but because the first twenty-four hours were so critical, they took precedence right now. 'Keep a low profile, Lukas. You're out of Fenfleet and immediate danger, but watch your back, okay?'

'I will, but please, Bryn, make sure that Lina is safe. There's bad people around her.'

Bryn hung up, wondering if Lukas had deeper feelings for Lina than he let on. She was certainly attractive. Still, he didn't have time for that right now. Everyone was flat out combing the town and surrounding villages for signs of Alex. Except for the case that had decimated this station a little while ago, he had never known it in such a state of high alert. He'd heard that officers were going to be drafted in from surrounding divisions. That brought its own problems, of course, but they needed the assistance. Right now, he was handling the Derus murder investigation single-handed. Even Swifty had been commandeered for house to house in Sycamore Close. In addition to that, he was fielding the calls that were flooding into the office.

Bryn stood up and stretched. Just time to grab another coffee before the afternoon briefing.

CHAPTER FIFTEEN

The CID room was full, with officers and uniforms forced to stand. For once, even the jokers were silent. Four deaths had that effect.

'As you all know,' Matt began, 'we are facing a tough time here in Fenfleet, and before we go any further, I'm asking everyone to please give all the time you can spare. We'll be getting help from Greenborough, Saltern-le-Fen and Fenchester. If necessary, Superintendent Redpath will bring in help from outside the area. I'm going to give you a brief update on each murder, and if anyone can add anything as we progress, they're welcome to do so.'

He took a breath. 'Okay. Our dead Lithuanian has been identified by his sister Lina as Filip Derus, of Craven Street. This might not be the straightforward drug-related killing that we first thought. Bryn here has identified a witness who thinks the tattoo linking this Filip to two previous, similar deaths of Lithuanians, is something deeper, maybe something concerning two families. Anything you hear or see in the streets of the Baltic Quarter that might be connected to a "family" issue, report your findings to DC Bryn Owen immediately.'

Matt moved across to the whiteboard. 'Now, onto Reuben Grimes.' He pointed to the official mugshot. 'You've probably all come across Reuben at some time or another, but we suspect that this man,' he pointed to a still taken from the CCTV close to Reuben's alleyway, 'could have been involved in his death. If any of you see a man wearing this rather unusual hooded varsity jacket, don't hesitate to call it in.' He jabbed his finger at the image. 'Okay, everyone. It's a crap picture but this man could be Alex, our copycat killer, the man who idolises the serial killer Jeremy Reader, and has promised to continue where Reader left off.' He pointed to a photocopy on the whiteboard. 'This is a photocopy of the last letter he sent to Reader, it's short but far from sweet.' Matt read it out:

"Dear Jeremy, it is with some sadness that I send this. I realise from your last reply that you only said the things that you did to appease the authorities who read your mail. Don't worry, I completely understood that hidden in your harsh words was your blessing, your fervent wish that I continue your work. Be assured that although I won't be in touch again, my actions will speak louder than my words. For ever in admiration, Alex."

A silence followed, while Matt allowed the words to sink in. He looked around the room. 'And true to his word, he has now killed two women in two days.' He turned back to the board. 'Lisa Lester.' He pointed to a holiday snap of a bright smiling blonde. 'And Louise Farrier.' His finger rested on the picture of the second woman, so similar to the first, with pale gold hair and blue eyes. 'And this is what he did to them.'

The next two photos were stomach-turning. Matt heard someone swallow in the silence that followed.

'Although we were called to the Lester house first, Louise Farrier was actually killed first. She lived alone, and our attention wasn't drawn to her death until a work colleague called in the following day.' He looked towards the back of the room. 'We are lucky enough to have Laura Archer, force psychologist, who you all know, and Professor Sam Page, assisting us with this. 'Laura? Sam? Could the fact that we discovered these deaths out of turn, so to speak, upset or annoy the killer?'

'I'd doubt it,' said Laura. 'He's very controlled and organised. I would suggest this might have even been his plan.' She turned to Sam, who nodded. 'If he's following his master's footsteps, he will have been grooming these women for quite a while, so he'd know that Lisa's husband would return from work to find her body, and that Louise lived alone.'

The words, *his master's footsteps*, jolted Matt's memory. 'You're right! If we look back at Jeremy Reader's first two killings in Derby, I'm pretty sure that they were also discovered out of sequence, although he didn't kill twice in two days.'

'Sir?' Bryn raised his hand. 'Why is he copying Reader's murders so exactly, then changing the times?'

Matt looked back to Laura.

Sam answered. 'He is fitting Reader's MO into his own agenda. If he is allowed to evolve, he will undoubtedly begin to make the murders his, and give them his own signature. Every acolyte wants to please his master, but as they move forward, they then want to exceed him, and become a master themselves.'

This was just what Matt didn't want to hear. 'So, if he can mess with the time frame, he could mess with the geography too. In other words, stay here rather than move on, as Reader did.'

'Most certainly,' said Sam.

'I'd say that's a given,' added Laura. 'He's got your attention, and he's going to hang on to it. Fenfleet will most likely be his hunting ground from now on.'

A groan went up around the room, and Matt felt like joining in. Part of him had been hoping that Alex would be true to Reader's blueprint, and move on to another town, another city.

'I think that just serves to highlight the fact that our priority is finding Alex. And to do that we need to know who he is. First thing tomorrow, I'm returning to HMP Gately to interview Jeremy Reader again. I need him to try to recall everything he possibly can about the letters that Alex sent him.'

'You trust that killing bastard?' muttered a voice at the back of the room.

'Whether I trust him or not is irrelevant, Officer. He's all we fucking well have! Reuben knew him, and Reuben is dead. Apart from a landlord who seems to have fewer brain cells than a tadpole, the buck stops with Reader. I have a greater regard for pond life than him, but if he really wants to help us, do you honestly think I'm going to say no? Get real!'

'Sorry, sir.'

Matt hardly ever lost his temper with his fellow officers. He made himself calm down.

'Can I ask something, sir?' Kim Peters stood up. 'We're assuming he's working alone, are we?'

'Reader did, and from what we found at the crime scenes, we are pretty sure that Alex is too. As soon as we get the forensic reports, we can confirm that.' Matt was grateful for Kim's intervention. 'Why do you ask?'

'I was wondering how he hung a dead weight up on a door, sir.'

'I asked that question myself. Again we need forensics, but Rory Wilkinson believes that for one thing the women were only stunned, so they weren't actually a dead weight. With Lisa, Rory thinks he tied a thick leather belt around her waist, passed a rope through it, then threw the rope over the top of the door and hauled her up and secured it to the door handle. He didn't have to lift her any higher than about a foot or eighteen inches off the ground, just enough to allow the blood to drain. He secured her to the hook on the door with the thinner nylon rope we found still tied around her body, and then removed the thicker rope. They are apparently conducting an experiment in the forensics lab to verify this assumption. Louise was easier, as he had placed the thick wooden broom handle across the top of the shower cubicle.'

'Both women were quite petite too,' added Jason, 'If they didn't weigh much, I think it'd be quite doable.'

'We'll get the answer to that as soon as the technicians have finished hanging each other from doors.' He looked around the room. 'Okay, does anyone have something on either Lisa or Louise from the house to houses?'

'One of Lisa's neighbours said that she often saw her going out after her husband left for his night shift. She'd been doing it for about two weeks.' The WPC looked at her notebook. 'She'd go out for around two hours, then come back, always alone.'

Matt loved nosey neighbours and curtain-twitchers. 'Sounds like she was meeting someone. Do we know what direction she went in? If she went into town, we might pick her up on surveillance.'

'She turned left out of the house, sir, so she was heading towards town. We already have a team trawling through the CCTV for the town centre and other public spaces. The thing is, she always went on foot, so she can't have been going far or she would have driven.'

'She might have been avoiding her husband noticing the mileage on her car,' Jason said. 'Or someone could have picked her up out of sight of the neighbours.'

'Take this further, WPC Stringer. Knock on doors further along the route she was taking. If it was a regular thing, someone might have noticed a car stopping, or even her meeting a man.'

'Yes, sir.'

'Louise's neighbours notice anything similar?' Matt asked.

'Nothing as yet, sir,' said Bob Jones, the duty sergeant. 'My officers tell me she was a bit of a loner, and had no particular routine, so her comings and goings rarely aroused any interest. Oh, and a neighbour told us that she had no close family alive.'

'Thanks, Jonesy. Anything from her place of work? Did she talk about meeting someone recently?'

'Same thing there, sir. Very few close friends at work, except maybe the woman who called in and found the crime scene. Her name is Tricia Shields, and she said that Louise rarely talked about her private life. She suspected she'd been either jilted or badly hurt at some point, as she hardly ever talked about men.'

'Gay, maybe?'

'Ms Shields couldn't answer that, but thought not. Apparently, Louise was very attractive, and several of her colleagues, both male and female, had made tentative advances, you know, suggesting they go for a drink and all that. By all accounts she always refused.'

'Where did she work?' Matt asked.

'The big bank on the corner of the square. She was a loan officer there,' Bob Jones said.

Matt frowned. 'Doesn't that back onto County Park recreation ground?'

The sergeant nodded. 'Yes, sir. We were thinking that too. Jeremy Reader's favourite meeting places. We're checking CCTV in that area very closely, but the system there is barely fit for purpose, it's not even digital.'

'Keep at it, Sergeant. The weather has been too good to sit in the office at lunchtime. She might well have gone into the park.'

'Ms Shields has already confirmed that. Not every day, but she certainly did go out for lunch.'

Matt looked around. 'Did Lisa work?'

Jason raised a hand. 'Not officially, boss, but her husband tells us that she did some cash-in-hand work for a local wholesale plant distributor, er, Freshland Botanica in Casey's Lane.'

Casey's Lane ran alongside a drain on the road east out of town. Freshland had a few greenhouses and poly-tunnels and a big packing shed. As far as Matt could remember, they brought a lot of stuff in from Holland and Belgium and also locally grown plants, which they repackaged and distributed to different retail outlets in the area. 'And next door?' But Matt knew what was next door — a large grassed public space, with free to use open-air gym equipment at one end, and a children's play area at the other. It had lots of memorial benches — the perfect place to enjoy a lunchtime sandwich and a chat with that pleasant guy that was always there these days.

'Before you ask, boss, there's no CCTV there at present,' Jason added. 'It's one of the areas where the digital engineers met with underground obstacles and had to reroute the planned cables. Right now it's a dead zone.'

'Then we send officers there to observe and talk to the people who use that area at the times when Lisa might have been there.' Matt was certain that Alex would have closely followed Leader's MO to start with. 'Both of those two recreation areas are good starting points. Stick with the CCTV for Louise, and let's talk to people in Casey's Lane. But,' Matt raised a hand, 'we do it quietly. No swamping the place in uniforms. One, I don't want a mass panic on our hands, and, two, we are trying to keep the way these women died out of the media. We can't afford to sensationalise it. You can imagine what the press would make of it. Every blonde, blue-eyed woman in town would be buying brown contact lenses and dyeing their hair.'

'Then we don't have long, do we?' Jason said sombrely. 'People will already be asking what happened in those two houses. You can't exactly hide such an important crime scene, and the town will already be rife with rumours.'

'Superintendent Redpath is handling the media. He'll be meeting the press, of course, and will announce the deaths, but his aim is to keep things as calm as possible. "Two women have been found dead in their own homes. Police are looking for possible connections, motives . . . You know the kind of thing." It's the best we can do, but as Jason says, we don't have long before the circus begins, and we all know that will get in the way of our enquiries, so, please be vigilant, follow every lead, no matter how insignificant it seems. We want Alex, and we want him fast. Go do your jobs.'

As the officers streamed from the room, Matt sat down, drained. He'd been here before, with the air thick with anticipation and a looming feeling of anxiety about what might happen next. He was sad that this time he had no Liz to support him. He missed her more with every hour that passed. They worked well together, there was an invisible thread binding them. They had each provided a sounding board for the other's thoughts and ideas, providing a reality check when those thoughts got too fanciful. Now, although he had the rest of his colleagues around him, he felt vulnerable, exposed, like a double act ripped in two. Matt with no Liz. Alone under the spotlight.

'You okay, boss?' Bryn Owen looked at him, concern in his eyes.

'Just thinking, Bryn.'

Bryn nodded. 'It's not right without the sarge here, is it, sir? We kind of had a routine, didn't we? Get the meeting over, then the four of us would grab a coffee, chuck everything on our minds into the melting pot and see what came out. Now it just seems, well, lacking somehow.'

Bryn was always intuitive, and never afraid to say what he thought. Matt appreciated that. 'You're right, lad. It's like playing with half a deck of cards.' He straightened up. 'But that's how it is. We can't afford to get too maudlin, can we? At least we have Kim helping us.'

'Thankfully, she's one smart lady, boss.' He paused. 'Er, is it okay if I check out Lina Derus before I finish up here, sir? She's worrying me, and especially her safety. If any of the guys who duffed up Lukas saw him in Lina's home, they might just turn their attentions to her. Lina isn't quite so afraid to talk to us as the other bereaved families. I just hope they don't know that.'

'Alright, but not alone, and don't be seen. If someone thinks she's talking to the police, you could bring trouble down on her yourself.'

'I was going to ring her and meet her somewhere.'

'Good, but still take another officer with you. Maybe Swifty, if he's not on house to house.'

'Okay, sir, thank you.'

Matt watched Bryn go, wishing they had more officers free to help him. That kid should not be handling a murder inquiry with just one uniformed constable. The problem was that they were a small station compared to somewhere like Greenborough. There was only one other DI, who was tied up with a complicated money-laundering case, and life still went on. There were always the smaller jobs to try to keep up with, the petty thefts, the drug dealers, the assaults . . . The list was endless.

Come on, Matt. This wishing for the past isn't helping, He'd told the others to go do their jobs. It was time he got on with his.

* * *

After carefully taking the scalpels from the dishwasher, he made sure they were dry, and then replaced them in their case. Spotless. Perfect. He then sat down at the tiny kitchen table and went over his checklist again, ticking off "sterilise scalpels." He must have read the list at least ten times, but everything was important, timing and attention to detail being foremost. Nothing must go wrong, everything had to be exact.

He sat back. One more thing to do, and then he could relax. He grunted. He was far too hyped up for that. All that planning, months and months of it, and now the show was finally on the road. Alex had made his mark.

The only trouble was that he had no idea what effect it was having. He'd have loved to have been a fly on the wall in HMP Gately and Fenfleet Police Station. What was going through Jeremy Reader's mind right now? He didn't dare imagine. And the police? It was the stuff of nightmares, wasn't it? Especially if you were planning on a nice, peaceful retirement! Well, he'd put paid to that.

He smiled to himself contentedly. It had all been so easy! He'd imagined a dozen pitfalls, but it had been textbook. He could hardly contain himself waiting till his next exploit, but first, he must finish his checklist.

He needed more rope.

He stood up, took a Stanley knife from the kitchen drawer and went outside.

He carefully unlocked the door and stepped into the rank, damp garage, where, amidst piles of rubbish and discarded auto-parts, there was a new coil of nylon rope on a heavy plastic reel. He measured off exactly as much as he needed, rolled it up tightly and left, locking the door behind him.

Back indoors, he placed the rope in his holdall, rechecked all the other contents for the thousandth time, then zipped it up. After one last scan of his precious list, making sure every box was ticked, he took it to the empty fireplace and set it alight. After the flames died down, he took the poker, crushed the wafer-thin burnt paper, then brushed the ash through to the tray beneath.

Attention to detail. Stay one step ahead of the Fenland Constabulary. And DCI Matt Ballard.

CHAPTER SIXTEEN

Bryn sat at the table facing Lina, while Swifty got the coffees. They had avoided the cafés the migrant workers frequented, and instead chosen a tiny artisan café that was part of the Fenfleet Players Theatre. It was overpriced and the kind of place Lina never entered.

'I had today decided to come to you, and then you ring me. Very strange, is it not?' Lina said.

Bryn rather liked the way she spoke English. It sounded old-fashioned somehow. 'Well, it was good, Lina. Very good. We were worried about you.'

'It is a bad time for us.'

'I want to help.'

Lina looked up at Jack Fleet, who was just placing a large cup of cappuccino in front of her. She smiled in thanks and then turned back to Bryn. 'I am grateful. I miss my brother very much, and now even Lukas is no longer here to talk to.'

'We had to get him away, Lina. I believe he's in great danger.'

'He is, Detective Owen. I have heard rumours that certain men are angry with Lukas.'

'Do you know who they are?' Bryn tried not to sound too hopeful.

Lina shook her head. 'It was only rumours, spoken in . . .' She frowned. 'The soft voice? Is that right?'

'Whispers,' said Jack. 'Spoken in whispers.'

'That's right.' She stared at the creamy chocolate-speckled foam on her coffee.

'I'm glad you sent Lukas away. But we used to talk, and now I have no one I trust.' She looked at Bryn directly. 'Except maybe you?'

He knew that where she came from, people rarely trusted policemen, and felt a tiny glow of satisfaction. Her words were what good policing was all about. 'You can trust me, and Jack here too. We're on your side, I promise.'

She nodded. 'The men who killed my brother must pay. Some of my brother's friends talk of revenge, but we are sick of revenge and all the blood and heartbreak it brings. This is one of the reasons we leave our own country.' She spooned up some of the froth and sucked at it, smiling at the taste.

The smiled faded. 'The older ones tell them not to make things worse, not become the next body found floating in the river, but I understand the younger men. These terrible men must be stopped.'

'We're doing everything we can to make that happen, Lina,' said Jack, 'but we need somewhere to start.'

Bryn leaned closer to Lina and lowered his voice. 'Lukas mentioned "family," speaking of the tattoos, like the one Filip had, but also the reasons for this feud. Can you help us understand what that means?'

Lina seemed to be either struggling to understand his English, or with something else. 'I think . . . I think it is something old. Something that happened when I was a little girl. People were always using the word "family" in a way I didn't understand. I remember seeing that tattoo on one of the older members of my own family . . .' She pulled a face. 'But no one speaks of it now. It is . . . oh, how to say the word?'

'Taboo?' suggested Jack.

'Forbidden?' added Bryn.

She nodded vigorously. 'Men died, many men, so there must be records? Yes? I am thinking that if I tell you where this happened in Lithuania, and the year, you could look for it on your computers?'

Bryn straightened up. They certainly could. 'What about names? Can you give us any names of the people or families that were involved?'

Lina shook her head. 'I was small. There's my own name, Derus. That would be part of it. I can tell you the first names of my father, my grandfather and my uncles, but the only other one I remember is Darius Shukis.'

Jack wrote the names down, followed by whatever dates and places Lina could recall. It seemed pretty vague to Bryn, but you never knew. All they needed was one piece of evidence showing that what was going on wasn't a purely drug-related turf war, and he might be able to make some headway. 'Lina? Do you feel threatened yourself?' he asked.

'No, not at the moment. They think I am a weak woman who will do nothing, like all the others.'

'I hope they keep on thinking that,' said Jack grimly. He handed her his card. 'I know you have Bryn's number, but here's mine as well. You can ring me anytime, day or night. Just don't be too brave, Lina. Play the frightened woman, but keep your eyes and ears open and tell us anything you think would help.'

She finished her coffee. 'I should go. I don't want to be missed.'

'Thank you for coming, Lina. Do as Jack says, won't you? Take no chances, do you understand?'

She stood up. 'I understand. Thank you very much for the drink.'

The two officers watched her go.

'She's certainly no weak woman, is she?' said Jack.

'I admire her,' said Bryn. 'But this situation is volatile. I'm scared for her too.'

'And so you should be.' Jack closed his notebook and tapped it. 'At least you've got something to get your teeth into. This could be exactly what you're looking for. A feud going back generations.'

Bryn agreed, silently wondering what kind of hornet's nest he was about to stick his nose into. Family feuds had started wars. Maybe Fenfleet had become host to two warring families who'd held grudges against each other for something that had happened decades ago. What was he going to find?

* * *

Rory Wilkinson sat alone in his office. Most of the technicians had left, and only Spike remained, busily checking the specimen store and wiping down the tables. They'd had an unusually hectic day, even without the two murders. It was a large department. The main post-mortem room held five mortuary tables, so when they were fully staffed, they could handle about ten autopsies a day. Rory himself spent most of his time working in a separate room used entirely for forensic cases. To avoid cross-contamination, the entrance was situated in a different part of the building, and it had a special UV-C lighting unit that eradicated DNA and bacteria. All his lab assistants and technicians called it "Rory's Retreat," and he had spent many long hours here over the years.

Now it looked as though it would be another late night, alone with only the dead for company. Fascinating, absorbing company, each with a different story to tell. Of course, he enjoyed being at home with his lovely David and a bottle of wine, and maybe a "golden age" musical, but David would still be there, with a kind word and a listening ear, when he finally managed to tear himself away.

'Anything I can do before I go, Prof?' asked Spike.

'One thing, dear heart. Your valued opinion, please.'

Spike leaned casually against the doorframe. 'Fire away.'

'Our two new lovely ladies. What is your opinion of the differences between the two murders?'

Spike sucked his teeth. Rory hated that. 'The first murder, Louise Farrier, was more hesitant,' Spike said. 'The incision into the popliteal artery wasn't clean, as if he wasn't sure of his anatomy. And the skin heart, that wasn't taken out neatly either. Number two, on the other hand, showed more confidence — cut done straight, directly into the artery, no slashes.' He tilted his head to one side. 'Other than that, they were more or less identical. Unless you want to include all the theatrical stuff at Lisa's home? The blood splashed all over and the room trashed like that.'

'No, it was just the killing I wondered about, not the window dressing. I suppose we must assume it was beginner's nerves with Louise. After the first one, he got more confident.'

'That's how I see it, Prof.' Spike stared at him, frowning. 'Something else bothering you?'

Rory sighed, 'Just that feeling I get. You know the one. It says, "Rory, look deeper. Something isn't quite as it should be."'

'Not again! How many times have I heard that?'

'And how many times have I been right, Spike? Eh?'

Spike shook his head, although not a hair on his head even stirred. 'Every time, Prof. Every time.'

'Tedious, isn't it?' Rory said.

'What, being right all the time?'

'No, having all these puzzles, instead of nice, straightforward, open-and-shut cases.'

'Come on, Prof! You love 'em! And you won't rest until you've found what's bothering you.' He grinned. 'I, on the other hand, have a date. So . . . ?'

Rory smiled. 'Run away and play. I'll see you tomorrow.'

'I'll be here. But don't stay all night. You have a home too, you know.'

'Yes, mother.' Rory watched Spike go. He was a good lad, and they worked well together. He'd come on in leaps and bounds in the last two years. He had developed a sensitive and tactful attitude in dealing with bereaved families, and, rather to Rory's surprise, had a knack of explaining complicated issues clearly and compassionately. He'd fitted right in, and was now almost indispensable. Spike's only problem was being so sociable. He loved to party. He worked hard, and never complained about the long hours, but Rory knew that if he wanted to progress further it would take more commitment than the lad seemed prepared to offer. He had the makings of a fine pathologist, if he only applied himself. Young Spike would need to make some serious decisions in the months to come.

Rory turned back to his reports. He wanted to get the preliminary findings ready to send to Matt Ballard first thing in the morning. The poor man needed all the help and support he could get right now. The full reports would take much longer, but even the most basic details were useful at the start of an investigation.

And what an investigation! Murder by exsanguination was a very rare phenomenon. Rory had seen accidents, certainly, when a victim bled out at the scene before help could get to them. Suicides too, although very few people who slit their wrists actually succeeded. You needed to cut deep to get to the appropriate veins. Rory had dealt with a single case of death by intravenous self-bloodletting, a singularly difficult and practically impossible way to kill yourself — inserting an IV into a vein, then drawing off your blood using a vacuum pump. You are supposed to pass out and then die in your sleep, so long as no one stops the flow of blood. The would-be bloodletter generally wakes up in A & E on suicide watch.

But *murder*? It had happened in the past, but it was an inconceivably cruel way to kill someone. Rory wondered if the people who had declared Jeremy Reader a changed man would have felt the same if they had actually seen a woman who had been deliberately bled to death. A woman who was probably conscious for some length of time, in agony, watching her life drain away. He thought not.

Rory swore quietly under his breath. He had work to do, and visions featuring lakes of blood weren't helping. 'Concentrate, Wilkinson,' he growled, 'or you'll never get home.'

He worked for another forty-five minutes. A noise outside made him pause. He looked up to see Spike sauntering down the corridor towards his office, apparently deep in thought.

'Goodness! Surely you weren't stood up?'

'I cancelled.' Spike gave a wry grin. 'Unusual, I know, but, Prof, you got me thinking. There *is* something odd about those killings. Shall we take another look?'

Rory smiled broadly. 'Let's just do that, my friend.'

* * *

Everyone else had gone home, but Bryn hardly noticed. He was engrossed in searching the internet for the slightest mention of something that happened in a small border village in Lithuania, twenty or so years ago. His biggest problem was the language. Some sites were in Lithuanian, and no translation was offered. He tried Google Translate, knowing it wasn't perfect but thought it might help him understand, but soon realised it was not that easy. There were so many references that meant nothing to him. His girlfriend, Jules, wouldn't be able to help him either, since Estonian and Lithuanian were about as similar as English and Japanese. After another hour of looking at terms that may or may not have referred to villages or surnames, he gave up.

'Still here?'

He looked up. Matt Ballard stood staring down at him. 'Oh, yes, sir. I've got a lead on the Filip Derus murder, but I've no idea how to follow it up.'

'Then go home, lad. Get some sleep while you can. When all the forensic reports start to come in, we're going to be burning the midnight oil. Anyway, things usually look clearer in the cold light of day.'

'I'm about to do just that.' Bryn stood up. 'Um, please forgive me for saying this, boss, but you look really knackered. You might do well to follow your own advice.'

'Don't worry, I will. And a bloody awful day it was too.' He sighed. 'Thing is, this Alex could strike again at any moment.'

'All the more reason to recharge while you can, sir.'

Matt nodded and turned to walk away. 'Night, Bryn, and well done for the way you're handling all this. I want you to know that I appreciate it.'

And then he was gone. Bryn missed the sarge terribly, but he was going to miss Matt too. He wondered what it would be like with both gone. He really didn't want to think about that. There'd be time enough when these cases were over, and his boss really was walking out for the last time.

With his hand on the door, Bryn stopped.

What kind of thicko idiot was he? He had the answer to all his problems sitting in a shelter for the homeless in Saltern-le-Fen. He pulled out his phone and found the contact number.

'Lukas? Do you fancy a drink? I'm buying. I've got a little job needs doing, and you're the perfect man.'

* * *

Governor Ross Cadman went down to the Harbour Unit at shift change. He wanted to be sure that the on-duty staff were aware of Jeremy Reader's condition and would keep an especially close eye on him. Although Ross had a whole prison to look after, Jeremy's well-being meant a lot to him for several very valid reasons.

One, his very successful Harbour PIPE Unit was being monitored as a potential flagship for several other units around the country.

Two, Reader was under the close scrutiny of the psychiatric and psychology departments at Greenborough University. They were interested in his case because they were working on developing a new rehabilitation programme for those with serious antisocial personality disorders. Reader was considered a rarity.

Third, Ross honestly believed that Reader was now a different person, no longer the man who had killed five women. Ross was well aware of the ridicule he had aroused, but he also knew that he had got where he was through his understanding of people, and how to treat them. He knew pure evil when he saw it, prisoners that had unleashed reigns of terror on staff and fellow-inmates. He'd known cunning, manipulative minds, expressions of anger and hatred, unsolicited violence that had made him sick to his stomach. But he had also known successful outcomes. Not many, but those few had fuelled his desire to see a better prison system at work.

If he was wrong about Jem Reader, it would be the greatest failure of his career.

'How is he?' he asked Freddie Herman, the clinical lead.

'He appears to have himself under control, Governor. He's admitted to feeling pretty shattered, so he's meditating more, and it seems to be holding him together. I had Charlie talk to him, one to one, earlier. He thinks Jem is coping fairly well, all things considered, but,' Freddie threw up his hands, 'we both know Jem can hide his feelings. I think we'll just have to wait and see.'

Ross nodded. 'I know how much his forthcoming wedding means to him, and I don't want this new development to cause a problem with it. I think Grace Repton is vital to Jeremy's rehabilitation, don't you?'

'Yes,' Freddie said, 'I think it will have a stabilising effect on him.' He smiled. 'He's asked Charlie to be his best man, now that Reuben's no longer around.'

'What did Charlie say?'

'He agreed immediately, although I know he thinks the whole thing is pretty bizarre.'

'Well, he has been Jem's mentor since he came into the unit. He must have built up a pretty strong rapport with him by now.'

'Absolutely, but it's still a bit weird, being best man to a convicted killer.' Freddie raised an eyebrow. 'I wonder what Grace thinks?'

'You're the psychologist. If you don't know, who does?'

'Only Grace, I guess.' Freddie lost the smile. 'I'm sure she really does love Jem Reader, but I still can't work her out. She doesn't match any hybristophelia sufferer that I've ever heard of. She's a complete enigma, which leaves one possibility — she fell in love with the bloke.'

Ross felt the same way. Grace was much more difficult than Jem to read. Perhaps Freddie was right. Maybe they were trying to complicate a very simple situation. There was no ulterior motive behind this marriage. These two people were simply in love.

'Did you want to talk to him, Governor?'

'No, I just wanted to check that everyone who has dealings with Reader is fully aware that he could react badly to the news of these copycat murders.'

'I've alerted all staff to the possibility, and if the worst should happen, we've got an action plan ready.' Freddie grinned wryly. 'And for my sins, I've arranged to be on duty tonight.'

'Excellent. Then I'll leave you to it.'

Ross made his way out. The Harbour Unit still had bars at the windows and triple security locks on the doors, but the atmosphere was totally different to the main prison. It was calm, quiet. Prisoners kicked off every so often, but not as often. As he passed through the last gate, he sincerely hoped that more units like the Harbour would be established. They worked.

CHAPTER SEVENTEEN

Bryn drove home and hurriedly collected an old laptop and a change of clothes for Lukas. He was soon back on the road.

When he arrived at Jim Cousin's shelter in Saltern-le-Fen, he went straight to the office to discuss the curfew with Jim. The last thing he wanted was for Lukas to get into trouble — this was such a good hiding place.

'Nice lad. Quiet, and certainly no trouble.' Jim grinned at Bryn. 'Unlike some of my other residents!'

Jim was a tough-looking guy, stocky, with short greying hair, certainly no oil painting. The kids and other nomads he looked out for respected him enormously. He was an ex-con made good, which sometimes helped. No one messed with Jim. One warning, and then it was back on the street with no re-entry pass.

'However, he goes out a lot, and from the little you told me about his history, that worries me a bit — for his safety I mean.'

It worried Bryn too. 'I'll talk to him.' He wasn't supposed to go roaming the streets. It wasn't in the plan.

'Look, Jim, I need him to help me with something, and we might miss lock-up time. Is that okay?'

'I'd rather you didn't say "lock-up," but never mind. I'll tell Marvin. He's on duty this evening. He can let him back in.'

Bryn thanked him, then in a low voice, he said, 'Nothing on the street grapevine about the murders in the Fenfleet area?'

'Lots of gossip, but nothing I'd consider worth passing on, mate.' Jim's face clouded over. 'One of those two women used to live here in Saltern, the one called Louise Farrier. She was a volunteer worker at my friend Artie's place. He's from the Baptist church, goes out every night with hot drinks and food for the homeless. Louise used to help him prepare the sandwiches and stuff. Nice girl, really good-hearted. I couldn't believe it when I heard the name on the telly.'

'I missed that, Jim. What did they say exactly?'

'Oh, you know how cagey they are. They just said two women had been found dead in Fenfleet, at different addresses. Police were asking anyone who might have seen either of them earlier in the day to come forward. They said they didn't yet know if the deaths were connected. They gave the names, and that was it.'

'I guess that's about the long and the short of it, Jim,' said Bryn. 'Do you think I could have this Artie bloke's address? We need to build up a picture of Louise, and so far we haven't found anyone who knew her.'

'You'll find him at the Saltern Baptist church on Ford Avenue. If he's not there, someone'll know where he is.' Jim stood up. 'Sorry to dash off, but I've got a new recruit to sort out. Your lad's in room seven. It's next door.'

'Thanks, Jim. I really appreciate you taking him in.'

'No problem, but don't forget to tell him not to go wandering off without telling us where he's going. Oh, and apart from tonight, remind him he's still bound by the curfew. I can't lift it for one and not the others.'

Bryn went to the house next door. Jim had recently acquired the second property in order to house his ever-increasing population of street-kids.

Lukas had been given a small room with a bed, a table and a chair, a hanging space and a set of drawers. It was all very clean. The only decoration was a picture of a boat on a beach, probably bought at B&M. 'Not bad, eh?' Lukas grinned at him. 'There are showers and toilets down the hall, and there's always someone working in the kitchen if you're hungry. If I wasn't so worried about everything, I could be quite comfortable here.'

'Probably not like your home, though, is it?' said Bryn.

'My home is a dump. It's damp, and the landlord doesn't give a shit,' Lukas said bitterly.

'Pity you can't stay longer then,' Bryn said. 'I brought you a change of clothes. They should fit. I reckon we're just about the same size.'

Lukas took the bag with a look that was both grateful and disbelieving. He wasn't used to British people being kind to him. 'That's kind of you, Bryn, I appreciate it.'

'No prob. There's a disposable razor and a few other bits and pieces in there to tide you over.' Bryn took the chair while Lukas sat on the edge of the bed.

'I need your help,' Bryn said.

'Apart from the one question I can't answer, I'll be glad to do anything I can.'

'I need a translator. I've found out some things,' he paused, 'from Lina, but it's all in your language. I tried a translation tool but it still makes little sense to me.'

'My language is English,' Lukas said proudly. 'But I know what you mean. What do you need translated?'

'First, I promised you a drink. There's a quiet little pub just off the Greenborough Road. Are you good to go?'

Lukas jumped up. 'Lead on.'

Soon they were ensconced in a tiny bar at the back of the Wild Goose. Bryn stuck to Coke. He bought Lukas a pint of East Coast Screamer.

Over their drinks, he told Lukas what Lina had said about "family," and what this might have meant.

'That could be true, Bryn. A lot went on back then, nasty stuff, especially in the more remote places.' Lukas took a long swallow of his beer. 'My grandfather used to tell me stories but I was too young to understand or really care much. I thought he was inventing tales to scare us children. Years later, I realised that he was telling the truth.' He stared into his glass. 'Something bad could have happened in Lina's village all those years ago.'

'Is it possible that people are still out for revenge, after two decades?'

'More than that, it's very probable. People have long memories, especially when a loved one has been hurt or family honour is involved. Some people swear to avenge a wrong, and if they can't get their revenge in their lifetime, it becomes a legacy for their children.'

Bryn wondered if Lukas was speaking from personal experience, but he let it pass. It wasn't his business.

'Have you got any names? Places? Dates?' Lukas asked.

'I do. I'll show you the sites that I think might be useful.' Bryn took out the laptop. 'I'd leave this with you, but there's a good chance it would get pinched at the hostel. People will think a homeless street dweller with a laptop must have nicked it, so this is our office, I'm afraid.'

Lukas raised his glass. 'Could be worse. Let's see what you've found.'

Bryn showed Lukas the sites, pointing to one in particular. 'Start with this one, if you would? I'll get you a top-up while you're checking it out. Want some crisps?'

Lukas put his hand in his pocket. 'I pay for this round.'

'No, mate. You're working. Consider it a perk of the job.'

When he got back to their table, Lukas was peering at the screen. 'That one was no good, just a kind of census record, but this one,' he jabbed a finger at the screen, 'is interesting.' He squinted. 'Dead end. But it's given me an idea of what to search for.'

'Oh? What?' Bryn watched Lukas's fingers fly across the keypad.

'There are sites that people used to use to trace missing family members. Plenty of families were split up, torn apart.' He paused, gazing at the screen. 'Those dates you've given me, it wasn't a good time. Plenty of people disappeared. Their families are still looking for answers.'

Bryn drank his coke while Lukas searched on, the screen filled with words Bryn didn't understand. He could have put in a request for an official police interpreter, but with their budget as it was, it was likely to be turned down. Plus, Lukas knew the history of this particular area, which a stranger wouldn't.

After a while, Lukas sat back, drank more beer and sighed. 'This could take some time. There are hints of things, brief mentions, but I need to go much deeper.'

Bryn pushed a packet of crisps across the table. 'I've got an idea. If you're prepared to spend some time on this, I could ask Jim Cousins if he would keep hold of the laptop, and let you work in his office. He might do it. It's worth a try.'

'Sure, Bryn, it's better than hanging around being bored to death.'

'Speaking of that, I'm told you've been going out a lot. It's probably not the best idea when there's men around trying to harm you.'

Lukas looked down. 'I know a man who lives here in Saltern. I was looking for him. He might help us if I ask him.'

'And he could tell the wrong people where you're staying.' Bryn frowned. 'You have to be careful, Lukas. These blokes aren't playing games.'

'I trust him. He's a relative of one of the dead men, so he won't be helping them, I promise.'

'Even so, best keep your head down. Don't trust a soul. Anyway, will you work on the laptop if Jim is good with it?'

Lukas nodded. 'But if he isn't?'

'I'll have to think again. I really do need your expertise on this.' Bryn was thinking of all sorts of alternatives. He would have had Lukas to stay with him, but he lived right in the heart of Fenfleet town, too dangerous for Lukas.

'I'll do a bit longer here, if you like?'

'No, mate, it's getting late. Let's see if we can sweet-talk Jim, then I really need to jog off. It's going to be a long day tomorrow.'

'If it's any use, I do think you're on the right track, Bryn.' Lukas closed the laptop. 'It makes sense, especially if you understand a bit about what it was like all those years ago. I think this is a feud. We have to find out which families were involved and what started it.'

Bryn gathered up his things. 'I'd like to shake up the people who know something about the killers but refuse to help us. They have the information, but they just won't talk to us.'

Lukas sighed. 'Think, Bryn. What's it like for them? You've never had to live with your loved ones being threatened with death.'

Oh yes I have, thought Bryn. *Not so long ago, our whole department lived like that for weeks.* 'It's just that we're trying to provide justice for those three dead men, put their killers behind bars, and protect other innocent people from going the same way, yet we're met with silence. I know about the fear factor, but we could catch the bad guys in half the time if we only had help. It's bloody frustrating.'

'Yeah, like being taken off grid when you want to be out there doing something practical.' Lukas nudged Bryn. 'No offence. I know you're doing more for me than anyone ever has. But, like you say, it's bloody frustrating.'

When they got back to the shelter, Lukas went up to his room, and Bryn went to find Jim. He found him sorting through a large box of second-hand clothing. Bryn looked at the items and was glad he'd given Lukas some of his things. He put his idea to Jim.

'Of course,' Jim said at once. 'My bookkeeper comes in once a week and she's not due for four days, so Lukas can work in the back office out of sight. There's a printer/copier there too if he needs it. I can keep the laptop in my flat, so it'll be safe. That okay?'

'Brilliant, Jim. That's a real help. I couldn't do without his knowledge of the language. I'll go over and tell him now.' He handed the computer bag to Jim and hurried out.

'That's good,' Lukas said. 'I'll get to work first thing and ring you if and when I find something.'

'Oh, I think you'll find something alright. I'm sure you will.'

He turned to go.

'Bryn? Thank you. For the clothes, and for caring about us.'

Bryn was surprised. You hardly ever heard a thank you in this job.

* * *

Matt lay awake. Night had closed in over the fens, and the bright full moon was tracing her path across the sky. He listened to the night sounds. They usually relaxed him and paved the way for sleep. Night birds called over the marsh, and small animals rustled in the garden. Sometimes, if you listened carefully, you could hear the water lapping at the banks of the nearby river. Mostly you just heard the wind, whispering or tearing its way in from the sea. You were rarely without the wind. It was a major part of living on the east coast. But tonight, the curtains were still, the air unmoving.

He and Liz lay on top of the duvet, her arm draped across his chest. She was fast asleep, making little moaning noises, occasionally jerking. He stroked her hair and whispered to her. Everything's alright. But was it? He had noticed a subtle change in her over the last two days, too slight to mention, but it concerned him nevertheless. He hoped it wasn't because he was deeply embroiled in these murders, and she, for once in her life, had no part in it. It must be hard for her, leaving the job she had loved for so long. She must feel cut off from the team that had been her working family for so many years. And now his retirement kept getting held up. Part of him wanted to say, 'Fuck it! Give the investigation to someone else to worry about, I'm off!' But he just couldn't do it. He had a duty of care, and he wanted his career to end in the knowledge that it had all been worthwhile.

He ran his hand through his hair, which was sticky with sweat. It was years since they'd had heat like this. The lawn looked like coconut matting, and no rain was forecast. He used to love the heat. Now, as he got older, he craved the freshness of autumn. Somewhere an owl screeched, an eerie, haunting sound. Matt slid closer to Liz.

If only this case could be over! Where they lived was idyllic, but it was far too isolated for Liz now she was unable to drive. Matt had the feeling that she really needed him right now, and he wasn't there for her. No matter what happened, he was determined to go to her medical evaluation with her. He wouldn't let her down at such a crucial time. She'd need him beside her, especially if the news wasn't what they'd hoped for.

'Love you,' he whispered into the darkness.

'Love you too.' She spoke in her sleep. He closed his eyes and prayed for sleep. He needed to be fresh for tomorrow. This investigation had to move forward. For

Liz's sake, for his own, and for the sake of the next poor woman in Alex's sights.

* * *

Grace Repton was also wide awake. She had thrown off her duvet and lay naked, exposed to the hot night air. She ran a hand over her body. Such a pity that Jem would never get to touch her this way. She wondered what would happen if the law regarding conjugal rights in prisons were to change. How would she feel?

She had slept briefly, dreaming of Ritchie. Her beautiful boy, full of fantastic ideas, plans for impossible adventures. But the boy had grown up. Now she preferred not to think of him at all. His absence had left a vacuum, and at last she had filled it. 'Jeremy Reader,' Grace said to herself and closed her eyes.

CHAPTER EIGHTEEN

Daily orders was swiftly dealt with, the only thing of interest being some possible sightings of Lisa on her clandestine excursions around the town. Uniform were on their second sweep of the area, visiting those neighbours who had been out the first time they called. As expected, they had received dozens of phone calls after the media conference. Jason and Kim Peters were valiantly trying to sort the possible ones from the plain mad, and were following up any that sounded hopeful.

Matt prepared himself for another visit to HMP Gately. Once again, he had asked if Sam Page could accompany him, and this time meet Jeremy Reader in person. Jeremy had made no objection, so, as soon as the professor arrived, they would set off.

He would have liked Laura Archer to meet Reader too, but couldn't face the prospect of Laura sitting opposite a five-times-woman killer. This was illogical, sexist, and just plain stupid, but he knew her presence would ruin his interview. What would Liz say to this? She'd give him hell. Well, he couldn't help it, so, with Liz's voice buzzing in his ears, he waited for Sam alone.

They drove to the prison, hardly exchanging a word. Matt wondered what was going through Sam's head. He knew he'd had dealings with repentant killers before, and that one had affected him deeply. Maybe that was the reason for Sam's uncharacteristic silence.

As if reading Matt's thoughts, Sam said, 'I'm not being my usual effusive self this morning, am I? Sorry. I've been up most of the night going over old notes and case histories, mainly those pertaining to murderers who take trophies, and also to copycat killers.'

'I admit I was shocked when he told me about the skin hearts,' Matt said. 'It seemed to place him in a different category somehow. One step further into irredeemable evil. And yet here he is, claiming he deeply regrets everything he did.'

'No wonder we're baffled,' said Sam.

'But you still maintain that he's a changed man?' Matt asked.

'So far. But I'll be more certain after today.'

They were now approaching the prison, and Matt slowed down.

His own feelings still swung between those of the diehard cynical copper, who had seen all too much of what murder can do to those left behind, to wanting to believe that there was some goodness in this hard world. Had Reader really fooled a prison governor, an entire psych evaluation team, plus two independent psychologists and an intelligent woman who intended to marry him?

They made their way inside. Matt was growing accustomed to the security doors, those locks ominously clunking into place behind him. Reader sat waiting in the interview room. Today, he was wearing a white T-shirt and jeans, but still managed to look dapper.

Matt made the introductions.

'I'm not sure how I can help you.' Reader sounded pretty low. 'If I'd kept those bloody letters it might be a different story.'

'You must have received hundreds of letters. Why should you even consider keeping them?' Sam smiled at Reader. 'I certainly wouldn't.'

Reader stared down at the table. 'Because, to be honest, I always knew there was something different about Alex, something intense and threatening.'

'How so?' asked Matt.

Reader frowned. 'It's hard to describe. Please don't misread this, but I think I recognised something of myself — my old self — in him.'

Sam nodded. 'That's very possible. You could well have picked up on something that others wouldn't have noticed.'

'That's why we need you to try to think back to those letters, Jeremy. There had to be something in them, some small detail that might tell us who he is,' Matt said.

Reader rubbed his eyes. 'I've been awake all night trying to do just that. And I can't come up with anything.'

'So, what do we know about Alex?' asked Sam. 'I've come late to the party, so forgive me for repeating questions you must have been asked already. Maybe you could tell me how you felt about him? How did he introduce himself to you?'

Reader drew in a breath. 'He was quite clever, I suppose. He began innocuously enough, expressing a wish to provide a listening ear. He claimed to believe that incarceration didn't preclude interaction with the outside world. He told me that he was pretty much an outsider himself, and would be very happy to write occasionally.' Reader sat back in his chair. 'As it turned out, he wrote often. He told me he had tried to find everything he could on me. He was impressed by the way I had evaded the police for so long. He was hoping to stroke my ego, which became obvious as soon as the letters started to get more and more, well, freaky. Some I never even opened. I was beginning to get myself together by that time, and he was extolling the virtues of the monster I was trying to leave behind. I almost hated him for keeping that monster alive.'

'Did he ever tell you anything about himself?' asked Matt, staring at the blank pages of his open notebook. He had written nothing.

'From the way he spoke and comments he made, I gathered he was quite young. I also got the impression that he'd had a difficult childhood. Some of his remarks showed a startling lack of empathy,' he gave a dry laugh, 'and I know what that can mean. The whole time we were in contact, I gave him nothing. I never spoke about my crimes or my feelings. I did nothing but try to dissuade him from contacting me.'

'And he took that as an invitation to keep writing, I suppose?' Sam said. 'His reasoning being that you didn't dare write and encourage him, for fear of the authorities reading it, so he assumed it was a coded message to continue?'

'Exactly! His last letter was proof of that. He thought he had my blessing.' Reader's face took on a cruel expression, one Matt hadn't seen since the trial. 'But he didn't have my blessing, the bastard!'

So Reader didn't want Alex killing in his name. But why? Maybe he hated the thought of someone stealing his thunder. Maybe he felt cheated that Alex could freely go around killing when he couldn't, or . . . or just maybe he wanted to stop him for the right reasons.

'Did he ever mention anyone else in his letters? Places? Anything that might indicate where our guys could start digging?'

Reader put his face in his hands and exhaled. Then he looked up. 'He mentioned his mother once, and not very affectionately. He said, "Mothers can fashion a hero or a behemoth. You can guess which one I had." But that was all.'

'He used that exact word?' Sam blinked.

'Yes. That's what he wrote.'

'*Behemoth*,' Sam repeated. 'He's educated, or very fond of words and language. People don't ordinarily say "behemoth," do they? They just say "monster."' He glanced across to Matt. 'We're getting somewhere.'

Matt scribbled it down. *Bad mother. Educated or of fairly high IQ.* Something, he supposed.

Reader nodded slowly. 'He did use unusual words sometimes. I'm no academic, but I've read a lot in here. There were words he used that I certainly didn't know.'

'Can you recall any of them?' asked Sam.

'Funnily enough, yes. I even went to the library and borrowed a dictionary. *Raptorial* was one.'

'Predatory . . .' Sam mused. 'Any other words?'

'*Haematophilia*. The little shite was trying to analyse me, and what drove me to kill in that particular manner.' Reader's face wore an expression of distaste.

'Well, he got that wrong, didn't he?' Sam grinned. 'Blood had nothing to do with why you committed those crimes.'

'You're a clever man, Sam Page. Maybe another day, we could have a talk?' Reader said.

'I would happily agree to that,' Sam said.

Matt coughed. 'He uses some very long words for a young man, doesn't he?'

'Even professors and aristocrats can be murderers.' Reader laughed. 'You should see some of the men I met in Monster Mansion.'

'I'm wondering if we're going about this the wrong way,' Sam said suddenly. 'Jeremy, why don't you tell *us* about Alex? About how he works and the way he's executed his first two murders.'

'I think Reuben was his first,' said Reader flatly.

'I agree, but the women were the first of the copycat killings,' said Sam. 'If he knew the exact details of your methods, you might be able to second guess how he's thinking, and where he might strike next.'

'I see what you mean.' Reader looked across to the guard. 'Any chance of some coffee? This could be a long session.'

The warder radioed to ask for three coffees.

'Okay. For starters, did he pick blondes with blue eyes?' Reader began.

'Yes,' murmured Matt. Suddenly he saw an image of two dead women suspended over a lake of blood.

'I would think he'll stick with that for the time being.' Reader frowned. 'Were they educated, hardworking women?'

'One worked in a bank as a loan officer, and the other did part-time work at a plant wholesaler.'

'Look deeper into their background, especially the part-time worker. They must be intelligent and educated, or he's already veering off track.'

Matt wrote that down, wishing he understood the reasoning behind it. Reader was speaking again. 'He's quite a bit younger than me, I think, so he may adapt the selection process.'

Matt shivered at Reader's choice of words. *Selection process.*

'There are recreation areas next to both women's places of work. We're assuming he'll follow your blueprint.' Matt was finding it hard to keep the dislike out of his voice.

'He should, but women are more savvy these days, so he might have had to improvise.'

'Tell me,' Sam asked, 'why two nights running? You never worked so fast.'

'I should think that in his case it was the adrenalin rush,' said Reader. 'He couldn't help himself. He had two women prepared, and after the first, he either needed more of the intense thrill, or maybe it didn't go perfectly to plan and he knew he could do better. He struck while the iron was hot.'

He stopped as another guard entered with the polystyrene beakers of coffee. Reader waited until the man had left before he continued. 'You have to realise that he must have been planning this for months — hour after hour, day after day, week after week, culminating in the final act, the taking of a life. It would have given him the perfect high.' He pushed two cups towards Matt and Sam and took one for himself. 'They're never very hot, just in case I decide to scald someone.' He smiled apologetically.

Sam sipped his and made a face. 'From what you could gather from Alex's letters, do you think it would have been sexually stimulating for him?'

'Paraphilia? Yes, I know all the terminology.' Reader shrugged. 'Probably. It wasn't that way for me, but as I said, he's young, and you can never guess what kind of physical or mental reaction committing such an act will arouse.'

Matt had suddenly had enough of this. He knew what Sam was doing, but it was nevertheless a bit too weird for the down-to-earth copper in him. 'Sorry, but this all feels a bit too Hannibal Lecter-ish for me. I can't believe that I'm consulting with one serial killer to catch another.'

Reader glared at Matt. 'This isn't easy for me either. And before you say "tough," I agree with you. I deserve to suffer for what I did, so don't think you're the only one who feels that way. But right now, try to forget what I was, what I did, and treat me like you do Sam, as an expert witness.'

Matt reminded himself of how vital this man was to stopping Alex. 'I'm sorry. I'm not handling this very well, am I?'

Reader replied in an unexpectedly soft voice. 'You're handling it exactly how any other decent policeman would. But just let me help, will you?'

Matt knew he couldn't afford to let his personal feelings get in the way. 'Go ahead. Anything else you can think of?'

Reader drank his coffee and pulled a face. 'I have dreams about drinking a decent cup of coffee . . . but back to business. Did he harvest the trophies?'

'Yes, although the first one was kind of ragged. The second was much neater.'

'Oh, it's not easy,' Reader said.

This was too much. Matt wanted out. He half rose from his seat.

'DCI Ballard! This could be important,' Reader said. 'He would have had to practise on some animal. Students often get free or discounted animal parts from a butcher. Pigs' feet in particular. That's what I did. Saying it was for medical studies gave me credence. Catch my drift?'

'Check the butchers for anyone claiming to be a med student.' Something tangible at last.

'That would be my advice. A pig's foot has thicker skin than a human, but nevertheless, it's a good thing to practise on.'

They sat in silence for a moment, Matt feeling distinctly queasy.

After a while, Reader said, 'One last thing. I think there's a chance he'll write to me again. He may not be able to resist the urge to boast of what he did, thinking I'll be proud of him. If he does, you might just pick up something from it, especially if we have all my mail stopped and bagged to block contamination.'

'That's a valid point,' Sam said. 'He's going to want his master to know how clever he's been.'

Matt stood up. 'I'll speak to the governor and see what can be done. Anything else, Reader?'

Reader shook his head and turned to Sam. 'I'd like to talk to you again, if you have the time?'

'Of course. Just say when,' Sam said.

'Maybe tomorrow?'

'We'll see if it can be arranged.' Sam smiled and held out his hand to Reader. 'Thank you. You've been most helpful.'

Matt merely grunted.

CHAPTER NINETEEN

The team spent the rest of the day chasing leads, possible sightings, finding nothing but shadows. Officers had been dispatched to all the butchers and supermarket meat departments in Fenfleet and the surrounding villages. None of the medical students, or anyone else for that matter, that they found fitted the bill for Alex.

The preliminary reports from forensics were in, and Matt and Jason went through them, comparing them to the pathologists' findings from Reader's murders. They were strikingly similar.

'Reuben had a good memory, didn't he? I'm guessing Reader only ever told him once, and he didn't miss much when he passed it on to Alex.' Jason frowned. 'Wonder how that came to be? I mean, it's all very convenient, isn't it? How did Alex get to know about Jeremy Reader being friends with Reuben, let alone getting to flat-share with him?'

Matt stared at the forensic photos. 'No matter how convincing Reader is, I keep getting this idea that he deliberately fed Reuben the information in order to pass it on to Alex.'

Jason looked up. 'As in Reader is orchestrating the whole thing? Alex is his apprentice?'

'Exactly. I know no one agrees with me, not the psych team, not our own people and certainly not the governor, but there it is. He appears so genuine, but he still makes me shiver.'

Jason seemed to ponder this. 'Okay, so Reader gets all this "fan-mail." He reads Alex's letter and recognises a fellow psycho, so he finds a way to encourage him. Maybe he gets letters smuggled out or buys a mobile from another con and grooms Alex from his prison cell. Then he tells Reuben all his secrets and gets him to pass it all on to Alex.' His frown deepened. 'That makes Reuben Grimes a willing accomplice, and I didn't get the feeling he was that kind of man.'

'Well, maybe he wasn't actually complicit in what was going on. Reader could have set it up with Alex, who then conned all the info out of Reuben by pretending to be a student, just as Reader tells us. But I'm sure he's not as innocent as he'd like us to think.' Matt couldn't shake off the thought that Alex wasn't acting alone.

'In that case, it would make sense that Reuben had to die after he'd passed on the information.' Jason scratched his head. 'Poor sod.'

Suddenly, Matt thumped his desk and let out a groan of frustration.

Jason stared at his boss in surprise. This wasn't like Matt Ballard at all.

'I'm coming at this all wrong.' Matt stood up, shoved his chair back, and began to pace the office.

Jason watched him march up and down. 'Boss?'

Matt exhaled. 'Look, maybe my judgement is impaired after all we suffered with the Goddard case . . .' He paused. His chest tightened as he uttered the name of the investigation that had almost destroyed the entire team. If he referred to it at all, he usually called it "that" case, or "that terrible case." Anything but say the name Gemma

Goddard. Now, chasing another monster, it was time to confront his demons. The Goddard case had evolved from an old investigation that Matt had been involved in very early on in his career. It had been harrowing in the extreme and involved young boys being taken and brutally murdered. They believed the murderer had been killed in a hit and run, but the Goddard case threw doubt on that, and a horrible can of worms had been opened, and Matt found that he and those he loved were being targeted and terrorised.

He stopped pacing and faced Jason. 'During that nightmare, I spent rather too much time with two twisted, dangerous killers. No wonder I'm not being exactly unbiased when I think about Jeremy Reader. That, and the fact that I helped put him behind bars. I saw the things he did to his victims. My natural copper's suspicious mind is adding to all this. Trust no one. That's not a bad thing, but it's made me too judgemental.' He drew in a deep breath. 'From now on, let's just deal in facts. Reader committed five horrible murders. Fact. Reader has stated that he now understands that what he did was abhorrent and he wants to make amends. He was indeed contacted by many weird "fans." Fact. One chilling letter from Alex remains, also fact. So,' he started pacing again, 'we accept the opinion of the experts. Reader is a changed man. He is doing all he can to help us, supported by a woman who appears to actually love him. For now, we accept all that. That means we have a copycat killer who calls himself Alex. Fact.'

He stopped pacing and turned to face Jason. 'Check the timeline. Compare when Reader spoke to his confidante Reuben Grimes with when Alex started writing to him, okay? Check when Grimes was released from jail, and check his addresses carefully. I want to know if he was already flat-sharing with Alex, or whether he took Alex in as a lodger after he was released. Alex had to have contrived it in some way, so we need the dates.'

His DI nodded slowly. 'Absolutely, boss. And with your permission, I'll come down hard on the only other person who had dealings with Alex and Reuben, and that's the landlord at that grotty flat they shared. He's been acting the innocent up until now, but he *had* to have seen Alex at some point. He can't say he doesn't remember him, everyone you meet leaves some kind of impression on you. I'll bring him in, scare the shit out of him, and see what he manages to "remember" this time.'

'Do that.' The thick clouds in Matt's head were beginning to slowly disperse. 'Accept what we're being told, then, if we discover a glaring and obvious anomaly, we have a valid reason to follow that up. Oh, and get DC Kim Peters to talk to Grace Repton again, this time about Reuben Grimes. She met him, talked to him, and probably they spoke about their mutual friend, Jem Reader. Maybe Grace mentioned something about Alex, probably something small, that she's forgotten, that could help us identify him.'

'Good idea, boss. Er, just a thought, but if Sam Page is able to discover what led Jeremy Reader to embark on his killing spree, it wouldn't help the inquiry per se, but it would allow us to trust the man more and then we'll know we're on the right track.'

'Sam's going back tomorrow, and I think that's what he wants to find out. I'll talk to him shortly about that. And you're right, Jason. It would at least stop me wasting time suspecting him of orchestrating this whole thing.'

'Or the reverse, if Sam isn't convinced after their meeting.'

'Right, let's move ahead.'

Jason got to his feet. 'Show me committed, boss.'

* * *

About thirty minutes before the late afternoon meeting, Jason received a phone call from Kim.

'Sorry, sir, but I can't locate Grace Repton. I rang to ask if I could call and speak to her, but her phone was switched off. I drove out anyway, but she's not here.'

'Oh well, put a note through the door and ask her to call you when she gets home.'

Kim hesitated for a moment. 'I will, but I saw her nearest neighbour walking her dog, and she said she hadn't seen her all day. I'm just hoping that she hasn't taken herself off somewhere and not notified us.'

'Well, she's not obliged to, is she? I shouldn't worry, Kim. She could well have gone to Lincoln or Peterborough for a day's shopping. She is getting married soon, after all. Or maybe all of this has just got to her, and she's driven up to Skeggie to get some sea air. You get back to base. We'll ring her later, then you can see her tomorrow.'

Jason hung up. He'd had no better luck with Alex's landlord. Although he hadn't answered the door, Jason was convinced he was inside. He'd always had a bit of a nose for that sort of thing. The landlord's scruffy home wasn't empty, he was sure of it. Well, the grumpy old bugger couldn't avoid him forever. He might even call back on his way home. He was annoyed that he wouldn't have much to offer at the four o'clock meeting. He'd felt optimistic about getting a handle on Alex, but now the optimism was fading. It was a bad case, and that was a fact, not one he would have wished on Matt for his last stand. Frankly, he wasn't sure how the boss was coping, after the Goddard investigation, but somehow his boss was functioning, and well, apparently.

Jason turned back to his screen. He would bloody well find Alex.

* * *

Although the meeting didn't come up with much new information, there was a purposeful air in the room. Matt was aware of having come to some kind of decision about how to proceed, and this added a positive note to his delivery.

He was just about to finish up when his phone rang. It was Rory. As he greeted him, he heard Kim Peters answer hers.

'Rory? Have you got something for us?'

'Maybe, dear heart, maybe. Would you be able to call by after the meeting that I've probably interrupted? Or failing that, I can get to you in about an hour and a half.'

'I'll come to you. Is it anything you can tell me about now?'

'Just a small thing, something odd from the crime scene photographs. Could be nothing at all, but my rather perceptive gut tells me otherwise.'

'Give me half an hour and I'll be with you.' He ended the call, and then looked towards Kim Peters. 'Anything interesting?'

'Grace Repton is back home. Can I go straight there, sir?'

'Go. And try to jog her memory. It's vital she remembers anything that Reuben Grimes might have said regarding Alex.'

She muttered, 'on my way, boss,' and hurried from the room.

Matt closed the meeting and looked across to Jason. 'I'm going to see Rory. He might have found something.'

'Good. Meanwhile, I'll go and pay another surprise call on the elusive landlord. I'll show him the photo of "Varsity Man" from that alley beside Reuben's house. Even if he can't describe Alex, he might recognise the jacket.'

Matt snatched up his car keys and left.

When he arrived at the forensic lab, he found Rory sorting through dozens of photographs, with Spike flicking through some images on a wall screen.

'Ah, Matt! I really do think we have stumbled on something. I'd like to say it was skill, but it was actually a passing comment from my trusty assistant, Spike here, that drew my attention to it.'

'What have you found?' asked Matt, staring at the heaps of photographs.

'This.' Rory stood up and pointed to one of the images. 'Enhance it, Spike, if you would be so kind.' He pointed to a picture of the room where Lisa died. 'As you know, our copycat was rather too liberal with the claret, so we could well have overlooked this.' He pointed to a small red mark on one wall.

As Spike zoomed in closer, a small heart took shape.

'Carefully drawn with a gloved finger dipped in blood, I think.' Rory squinted at it. 'Now. Image number two, Spike.'

Another crime scene photo appeared on the screen.

'This one is from Louise's bathroom. Look. Low down on the wall next to the shower. Another tiny heart.'

Nothing but a smear — until you looked closer.

'A drawing of a heart,' whispered Matt. He looked across to Rory. 'Reader never mentioned drawing on the walls, so is this another of Alex's attempts to stamp his signature on his murders?'

Rory shook his head slowly. 'Although our dear Jeremy might not have mentioned it, he certainly did indulge in a little bloody graffiti. We've pulled out all the crime scene photos from the five old murder cases and gone over them with a fine toothcomb — well, a computer — and so far we've found all of them, bar one.'

'How come no one ever picked up on them?'

'Hardly surprising, given the amount of blood. Most people would see a simple splash or smudge, and Jeremy's were even smaller than Alex's attempts.' Rory flopped down onto an office chair. 'The thing is, it's something that didn't come to light in the original investigations, and Reader never mentioned it during his trial.'

'And even though he coughed to the skin heart trophies, which were a major thing, he kept this very small, seemingly insignificant piece of information back. So, why?'

'I think you need to ask him that, Matt,' Rory said. 'Because he had to have told Reuben Grimes about these bloody hearts, otherwise Alex wouldn't have known about them.'

'How odd,' murmured Matt. 'How very odd.' *Insignificant*, he had said, but he had a strong suspicion they were anything but. He just wished he knew why that might be. 'Can you send me copies of all the graffiti hearts, please? And well done, guys, for spotting them.'

Rory nodded in Spike's direction. 'You can thank my spiky little friend here for that. "Oooh, look, Prof!" he says, "that looks just like a tiny heart!" So I did, and it was.'

As Matt drove back to the station, he remembered that Sam Page was planning to visit Reader the following day. His first thought was to ask him to challenge Reader on the bloody hearts, and then he thought again. This piece of evidence had remained unnoticed for years. As far as he was aware, the only people who knew about it for certain were Reader and Alex. Maybe he shouldn't let Reader know about their discovery just yet. Matt was sure it was important, but why?

He would keep it to himself for the time being.

* * *

Grace looked exhausted. This whole business must be taking its toll on her, thought Kim. Hardly surprising.

'I apologise for not returning your call, Detective,' Grace said. 'I had a hospital appointment and I switched my phone off.'

'Nothing serious, I hope?' Kim enquired.

'Oh, just some heart checks. An ECG, a scan and a stress test. My doctor noticed an irregular heart rhythm. He's just being cautious, I'm sure.' She gave a short laugh. 'Most likely everything that's going on at the moment. A bit stressful.'

Kim nodded. 'I'm sorry to add to it, but I really need you to think back to the occasions when you spoke to Reuben Grimes. We are finding it almost impossible to build up a picture of Alex, and as Reuben lived with him, he's our best hope, even posthumously.'

Grace sat back in her chair and began twisting a lock of her brown hair between her fingers. 'As I told the detective chief inspector, I met him because of the messages he relayed to and from Jem. We weren't friends. We didn't chat much. If he mentioned Alex at all, it was only to say that he was unusually single-minded when it came to his studies.' She gave a bitter laugh. 'Now we know why. He was obsessed with my Jem.' She sighed. 'If only Reuben hadn't been so naïve! He believed that Alex was studying criminology, and that he was helping him. Instead, he was providing him with all the information he needed to start killing people, and—'

'And in doing so he probably signed his own death warrant,' finished Kim.

'Exactly.' Grace closed her eyes for a moment. 'I think he might be a redhead. That's right. Reuben told me he missed Alex after he moved out. He reckoned he was a very good person to share a flat with, clean and tidy, very organised, unlike a lot of students, and very even-tempered, unlike most "gingers."'

'Thank you. It's more than we've heard from anyone else.' Kim scribbled it down in her notebook.

Grace sat back. 'I wish I'd listened more to Reuben, but it was just idle chit-chat, usually after I'd delivered whatever message Jem had for him. Reuben really liked Jem, and he believed that he was telling the truth about regretting everything that happened. He'd be devastated if he knew what a Pandora's box he'd opened.' She paused again, and shook her head. 'I'll keep thinking, but there's nothing more I can recall right now, I'm afraid.'

'You've been a great help, Grace. You have my number, don't you? Ring anytime. Information like this could be vital.'

'Of course. It's strange really,' said Grace. 'We always feared this would happen but now it has, it's far more terrifying than we ever dreamed. I thought when we handed the problem over to you, it would become your problem, and we'd be relieved of the responsibility, but it's worse than ever. And with the wedding . . .' She stared down at her hands.

'I'm so sorry. Do you think it will go ahead?'

Grace shrugged. 'Who knows?'

Kim left, wondering about this strange union. A confessed killer and a street pastor? Had love really conquered all?

Before she started the car, she rang Jason to let him know that Alex could have red hair. Then her thoughts returned to Grace and Jem. Day to day policing was one thing — the tough guys, the greedy, the conniving crooks. Even the violence. But in situations like this, involving the emotions, she was way out of her depth.

There had been a startling change in Grace Repton. When the boss first interviewed her, he'd said she was enigmatic and confident, almost taunting him about what she and Jeremy Reader apparently suspected. Now all that self-assurance had disappeared. Grace looked sick with worry. A possible heart condition? She wondered if Jeremy Reader knew about that. She thought not. It was doubtful that Grace would load another worry onto him when he was already teetering on the edge.

So many questions.

* * *

Jason's luck was in. So was Alex's old landlord. He seemed to have been expecting someone else, and looked taken aback when he opened the door to find Jason.

Jason stepped into the house, which smelled musty, dirty, unwholesome. His own home had a lived-in feel to it, untidy in other words, but it was still clean and he had never been embarrassed to bring anyone home. This place was a shithole. At least there was no offer of tea or coffee. The man's name was Craft. Very appropriate, thought Jason.

'Mr Craft. I'm struggling to understand how you could fail to recall anything at all about your lodger, the young man known as Alex.'

'I don't go down to that place very often,' Craft said in a surly tone.

Bet you don't, thought Jason. Not too fond of repairs and maintenance, probably.

'Anyway, the woman who lives on the top floor always collects the rent and brings it here. Has done for years. I don't think I've seen him more than twice.'

'Then I'll have her name and flat number as soon as we've finished here, please, but you *did* see him? Can't you give me some kind of description?' Jason would have liked to shake the man, only he would have had to get close to do that.

'I never took any notice.' He frowned, then relented a little, probably realising that he'd get rid of Jason quicker if he cooperated. 'Okay. I suppose he was in his twenties. Typical student type. Wore a kind of American-style jacket, I do remember that.'

'Like this?' Jason showed him the picture of Varsity Man.

'Yeah, just like that, but,' he looked closer at the picture, 'I couldn't say whether that was Alex or not, not with that hoodie up.'

'But it could be him?'

'It's the jacket that makes me say it could.'

'When you saw him, did you notice what colour his hair was?' asked Jason.

The man shifted uncomfortably, obviously willing Jason to hurry up and leave. 'He used to wear a baseball cap, with his hood over it so the peak stuck out. Tight jeans with rips in the knees, but that's it. That's all I remember. Now—'

Jason ignored the implied request to hurry up and go. 'Well, we're getting something of a picture, aren't we? Shame you didn't give it more thought earlier, but better late than never, I suppose.'

The doorbell rang again and Craft jumped.

'Expecting someone?'

Craft pushed past him and went to the door. He opened it a crack, so that Jason wouldn't see his visitor, but Jason was having none of it. He pulled the door back and saw a tall, willowy woman of around fifty, holding a batch of envelopes.

'Your rents, Mr Craft.' She thrust them towards him. She wasn't smiling. 'My tap is still dripping and Mr Edmunds's damp patch has started peeling the wallpaper off the wall, and that's apart from the wasps' nest in the eaves. When are you going to get someone in to see to all this?'

'Next week, Miss Gillespie, next week.' He smiled ingratiatingly.

'It's been next week for a month now! Please, just sort it!'

She turned to leave but Jason stopped her, holding up his warrant card. 'DI Jason Hammond, miss. Could I have a word with you?'

The woman stared at him suspiciously, and then backed away. 'If it's about that boy who lived in number six, I know nothing about him.'

Jason followed her. 'But he left his rent with you, didn't he?'

'Yes, but he just put in my mailbox, like Reuben used to. Most of the tenants do that because this lazy old sod can't be bothered to collect the rent in person.' She glared at the retreating form of Craft, who was no doubt in a hurry to count his money.

'Did you ever talk to Alex?' Jason asked.

She shrugged. 'Greeted him a few times, I guess.'

'Is this him?' Jason showed her the photograph.

She looked at it closely. 'You can't see his face, so how am I supposed to tell?'

'Build? Age? Height? Clothing? Anything familiar about this man?'

Ms Gillespie hesitated. 'Well, it could be Alex, I suppose. He certainly had a hooded jacket like that.'

'Hair colour?'

'I never saw him without some kind of headgear on. Either that hoodie or a beanie hat, or a baseball cap. Never bare-headed. He did have very pale skin though. I thought he probably wasn't eating properly.'

Jason considered this. Some redheads did have pale skin. 'What about any facial hair?'

'No. He was clean shaven.' She thought for a moment. 'Actually, even though he wore a hoodie and the hats, he just looked trendy, not scruffy. His clothes always seemed clean.'

'One last thing, Ms Gillespie.' Jason attempted a rare smile. It didn't quite come off. 'You did know Reuben Grimes, didn't you?'

'Poor man. He should have stayed here, shouldn't he? Maybe he'd still be alive today if he hadn't moved.'

'Do you know how he and Alex came to be sharing their flat? They seemed like very different people, a bit of an odd couple, if you know what I mean.'

Ms Gillespie stared at the pavement for a few moments. 'I know Reuben spent a lot of time in and out of prison. Even so, I liked him a lot. He might have been a rogue, but he was a kind man. We sometimes shared a bottle of wine out in the garden, such as it is, of a summer's evening. He used to talk to me quite a lot.'

She looked somewhat wistful. Jason suspected that she might have had more than just neighbourly feelings for Reuben.

'He told me he'd met Alex's father in prison. Said he'd promised to look out for him when he got out. Alex was living in some appalling digs and trying to put himself through university, so Reuben took him in, simple as that.'

Jason perked up. Alex's father was a convicted felon? 'I suppose you don't recall when he told you that, Ms Gillespie? Or what prison he was in at the time?'

'I do, mainly because it was my birthday and he bought me a bottle of Cava to celebrate. It was six months ago, and he told me that at the time he met Alex's father, he was in a terrible prison up Durham way.'

'Frankland?'

'That's it. Only he wasn't supposed to be there at all. It was a place where they kept the very dangerous murderers, not men like Reuben.'

'Sorry, how do you mean, "not supposed to be there?"' asked Jason.

'There was some kind of clerical mix-up. There was another prisoner who was supposed to be transferred there from a different prison. He was also called Grimes, but it was Reuben who ended up in the place, then it took over a month to get it sorted out again. He didn't have much luck did poor Reuben.'

This was exactly what Jason needed. If they could trace the prisoner Reuben had met there, they could identify Alex. They could certainly pinpoint the date on which Reuben had been transferred to HMP Frankland, then they would just need to find the man he got friendly enough with to promise to look after his son. Then, with a surname, they could find which university Alex had enrolled in. Jason began to feel a rush of excitement. He finally had a lead.

He thanked Ms Gillespie profusely.

'As I said, Inspector, he was a kind man. He didn't deserve to die like that. I miss him.' She sniffed.

He should be going home, he'd told his wife he wouldn't be late. But this needed following up. Jason drove straight back to the station.

CHAPTER TWENTY

After three hours of telephone calls, dead-end conversations and emails, Jason found himself talking to the man who had been prison chaplain during Reuben Grimes's accidental incarceration in a Category A high-security establishment. The man's name was Clifford Staples.

'I felt desperately sorry for him, Detective Inspector.' Staples had a soft, well-spoken voice. 'It was immediately found to be an administrative error, but it took weeks to sort out. But Reuben was a quite extraordinary character. He just took it in his stride. Most men would have been intimidated by the prison and its reputation, let alone the prisoners themselves, but he seemed unaffected by it all.'

'That's hard to believe, sir.' Cat A prisoners were notorious for terrifying newbies.

'No one saw him as a threat or a victim, and strangely, even some of the really difficult prisoners started opening up to him. It had taken me years to get them to talk in that way.' Staples gave a little laugh. 'He actually took a little of the strain off my back. In a couple of weeks, he became a kind of in-house counsellor.'

'I need to know who he got close to, sir.'

There was a short silence. 'Three men, one being the infamous Jeremy Reader. The other two were both lifers, one a man called Douglas Campbell, and the other a very young man called Harry Dalkins.'

Dalkins was too young to have a son of university age, but the name Campbell immediately brought to mind Scottish and red-headed. 'Tell me about Douglas Campbell, sir.'

'Dougie murdered his business associate after he discovered the man was misappropriating large sums of money from their funds. It happened at their rather posh offices, and when a security guard tried to apprehend him, he killed the guard too. He was given life. He has a wicked temper, Detective, but somehow he took to Reuben.'

'Do you know if Dougie has a son, sir?'

'Yes. Two sons and a daughter.' Staples gave a sigh. 'Sad case. Their mother was apparently a bit of a harridan who bullied the children when Dougie wasn't around. When he was sentenced she went off the rails, blaming the kids for everything. It was a torrid time, and the three siblings, all in their late teens or early twenties, got away as soon as they could. The father's assets were frozen, so things would have been very difficult for them. They must have really struggled.'

'Did he tell you their names, sir? This is really important.'

'Oh, now you are asking! Oh dear, well . . .' Staples whistled softly down the phone. 'I can't recall the girl's at all, but I think the boys were called . . . Hughie and Alex? Yes, that's right.'

Jason silently punched the air. And it was about to get better.

'Alex did visit his father once. I recall that clearly, because I saw them together in the visits room and even had a short conversation with him afterwards. The boy was the spitting image of his father.'

'Could you describe him, sir?' said Jason, trying to keep calm.

'Medium height. Slim. Short red hair, glasses. He looked academic, except for his clothes. He wore one of those American baseball jackets and ripped jeans.'

Got you, Alex! You really do exist! 'Sir? You spoke to him? Can you recall what was said?'

'Not exactly, but I found him deeply disturbing, DI Hammond. We only had one short meeting, but that young man seriously bothered me. I got the feeling that he had only visited his father on the off-chance of seeing Jeremy Reader, the man who stalked and killed five women. I spoke to Dougie about him later, and he admitted that his son suffered from a kind of OCD and was generally quite obsessive. He said he believed that he was in contact with Reader, as in writing to him.'

'He was, sir. But we can't find Alex, and we badly need to talk to him. Do you think Dougie Campbell would allow us to question him about his son and his possible whereabouts?'

'That's a moot point, Detective. Dougie died a few weeks ago, of pancreatic cancer.'

Jason groaned.

'But all of his details, his relatives' addresses and so on, will still be on record. Contact the governor. He'll help you, I'm sure.'

Jason thanked the chaplain and put the phone down. It was far too late for that now, but he'd be on it first thing in the morning. Meanwhile he'd check the PNC for details about Dougie Campbell. As a convicted felon he would be on their files.

Jason accessed the database. Campbell had lived up north in Sunderland when he was convicted, so he was not a local. He skimmed through the information on the screen. Everything was exactly as the chaplain had said regarding his crime, but as none of his family had been complicit in the murders, there was no mention of them.

He closed the screen and found the number for the Northumbria police force. Maybe someone there could help him.

Half an hour later. he gave up. Sunderland had provided old addresses that had been used by Dougie prior to his incarceration, but they had nothing on file about relatives and suggested he contact Frankland Prison. Back to square one, but even so, it was headway, at last! He wanted to ring Matt, but opted for a text. He'd give him the whole story in the morning.

A few moments later, his phone beeped with a message from Matt. *Fantastic! Good man! See you early am. Now get home!*

Jason logged off from his computer and loosened his tie.

'Ah, good. Glad someone's on duty.' A uniformed officer was hurrying across the CID room towards Jason's office.

His heart sank. 'What's up?'

'My sarge asked me to bring this to your attention, sir. I'm in the house to house on the Lisa Lester inquiry. I've found someone who saw her meet a man a couple of nights before she was murdered.'

This was worth staying on for. Jason took the memo from the constable with a name, address and telephone number.

'This lady knows the Lesters by sight. She says that Lisa met a man, who was a lot younger than her, at just before ten at night. They kissed when they met, and she reckoned it wasn't just a friendly "nice to see you" kiss either. One thing she did know for sure was that it wasn't Lisa's husband. They continued towards town on foot, sir.'

'Good work, Constable. Leave that with me, and thank you.'

The officer left, clearly delighted to have made the glum detective smile for once. Jason exhaled. This was good stuff, but again, something for tomorrow. He was exhausted, and tired policemen made mistakes

He wiped the back of his neck, hoping it would be cooler outside. He doubted it. Most of the others went open-necked in this heat, some even wore T-shirts, but Jason felt obliged to keep up standards. He was even a little mortified that a uniform had seen him with his tie undone.

But now it was home time. He pulled off the tie.

Tomorrow, he would find Alex Campbell.

* * *

'That was Jason. We've finally had a breakthrough, well, we *might* have a breakthrough.' Matt grinned broadly at Liz. 'It's certainly a viable lead.'

Liz rubbed his arm gently. 'Oh, that's a relief. You've been looking worried sick for days now.'

'I know, and I'm sorry, sweetheart. I think it's rubbing off on you too, you've not seemed your usual self either lately.' Liz said nothing. 'You are okay, aren't you? I mean, you'd tell me if there was anything wrong, wouldn't you?'

'Mattie! Relax! I've been worried for you, that's all. Worse than that, I can't help you. Can you imagine how that feels?' They were seated on the sofa, and she moved closer to him until they were touching. 'I should be out there, up to my neck in muck and bullets, not doing gentle exercise and crosswords.' She gave an exasperated grunt. 'Aargh! I know I can't, and that I have to concentrate on getting better, but it isn't easy, you know.'

'I'm so sorry.' He kissed her forehead. 'It must be purgatory for you. I'd be climbing the walls by now.'

'Well, don't look too closely, but I think you'll see footprints close to the ceiling. It is hell. I try to push it out of my mind, and sometimes I can, but often it's impossible.'

Matt turned to her. 'I know we've been here before, but would you consider going away for a little while? Stay somewhere you could occupy your time and think about something other than all the stress I bring home every night.'

'As you said, Matthew Ballard, we've been here before, and the answer is still the same. Absolutely not.'

'I don't want you to go away, believe me, but I can't help thinking that you need more stimulation — in a good way — and less anxiety.' He exhaled slowly. 'If only Gary had some leave owing, he'd cheer you up and get you out of yourself.' This made him laugh. How many men could suggest that their beloved spend time with her ex-husband in order to cheer up?

'He says he's in an undisclosed location in a major trouble spot,' Liz said. 'I can't see him coming home for quite a while.' She leant her head on his shoulder. 'I honestly do love it here, Mattie. The doctors said peace and quiet would help, and we have that in bucketfuls.'

'It's just lonely for you, that's all.'

'But not for long. This case will come to an end, and you'll be free. We'll be free. You hold on to that, because I am.'

Matt knew better than to argue with her. Maybe he was overreacting. He wasn't sure he'd have coped nearly as well as Liz if the situation had been reversed. In fact, he knew he would have been a boiling vat of frustration and worry, and would probably have made himself ten times worse. She'd been amazing, and he told her so.

Liz hugged him tighter. 'I have no choice, Mattie. I love you. I need to get better so that we can have some quality time together, have some fun, make some memories. I wish I'd acknowledged how I felt about you years before now. We wasted precious time. I don't want to waste any more.'

They sat holding each other while twilight faded into darkness. Not wasting one precious second.

CHAPTER TWENTY-ONE

Sam Page called in at the station before eight in the morning, to see Matt and discuss his visit to Jeremy Reader.

'I reckon you should just listen to him on this occasion, Sam. Let him talk, ask questions if need be, and we'll see if anything helpful filters through.' Matt told Sam about the painted blood hearts. 'Keep that one under your hat for now. I'll be very interested to hear if he mentions it to you unprompted.'

'I'll keep my ears well and truly open, never fear. They are letting us use the quiet area of the Harbour Unit.'

Matt preferred the austere, cold impartiality of an interview room, but then he was a policeman, not a doctor or a carer. The intimidating atmosphere of a barren room with an emergency alarm strip around the walls and a recording machine taping your every word was not relaxing, but it was very useful for obtaining hard facts and confessions. And that was his line of business.

Sam leaned forward. 'My main aim is to discover what drove him to kill in the way he did. Actually, I think that's why I've been invited to Gately today. I saw his face when

I mentioned the blood itself not being important. He wants to talk. I could be wrong, but I think he really wants to empty his soul of things he's never admitted to anyone, and to do it before he marries Grace Repton.'

'That could help us too. I'm not sure why, but Jason believes we need to know absolutely everything about his motives in order to know how to treat his claims.'

'He's right. Fill in all the gaps, then the picture will be clearer.' Sam nodded fast. 'But I'd better get off. I get the feeling this appointment is critical, for all parties concerned.'

'Good luck. Oh, and Sam? Would you and Laura possibly be able to come over to Castor Fen for a late supper tonight? It'll just be a takeaway, as I have no idea what time I'll finish today, but my Liz needs to see some fresh faces and hear some different conversation. I'd be very grateful if you could come.'

'An absolute pleasure on my part. Can't answer for Laura, as she's seeing precious little of her DI Jackman at present, but do ask her.'

'I will. And come anyway, even if she's tied up.'

'Love to. And I'll report to you immediately on my return from Her Majesty's Pleasure-drome!' He waved a hand and bustled from the office, crossing paths with Jason on his way out.

'Morning, boss. I've already spoken to the governor at Frankland. He's gathering all the info we need as a matter of urgency, and he's going to email me all the details of Douglas Campbell's family. We could have an address any moment now. Then, with the description provided by the chaplain, we're in business. Let's just pray that Dougie's son, Alex Campbell, is our Alex.'

This was a new Jason, and Matt was happy to see it. He was assertive, energised. Maybe his DI had finally laid the ghosts of the Goddard case to rest.

'I was also going to see if the witness who saw Lisa meeting a younger man thinks he matches the description we have of Alex Campbell — if that's okay, boss?'

'We might need to delegate that, Jason. Make Alex top priority.' Matt glanced at his watch. 'It's time for the nine o'clock meeting. Let's get that over with, and we'll get uniform to go see your witness.' He followed Jason out, noting with something approaching awe the straight back and businesslike stride that had replaced the depressed slouch of recent weeks.

Daily orders over, Matt hit the road running. Jason had set a new benchmark this morning, and Matt was hot on his heels. So, it would appear, was Bryn, who was convinced that he was getting close to finding the perpetrators of the Lithuanian killings. After the all-consuming lethargy that had spread like a crippling disease in the aftermath of the Goddard case, this new energy came as a breath of spring to Matt.

If it hadn't been for the niggling worries about Liz, he would have considered himself to be totally back on track. He'd invited Sam to supper not only to give Liz someone new to talk to, but also to get Sam's opinion on her mental state. She had been steaming ahead towards recovery, showering him with positive vibes, and now, although she was trying to cover it up, she seemed to have withdrawn. Matt was afraid that being alone at Cannon Farm, way out on Tanner's Fen, was not as good for her as she claimed. She needed the mental stimulus of friends and things going on, not word games and solitary exercise.

'Got it!' Jason didn't even knock. 'There was nothing current for Alex, but I've got an address for his sister. She lives in Lincoln, behind the Usher Gallery. Will you come with me?'

'Take Kim, Jason. I need to stay here and keep an overview. Phone me as soon as you have anything on him, okay?'

'Will do, boss. Swifty is out talking to that witness again. He's taken the photograph of that guy we think is Alex. I've asked him to report straight to you when he gets back.'

'Good. Now you get off. And take care, Jason. We have no idea what we're up against with this man. He may be staying with his sister.'

'Doubtful, sir. He'd need a base around here to be able to prepare for his killings. Lincoln's too far.' Jason flashed a rare grin. 'But I'll be careful, don't worry.' He strode out.

Matt sank down in his chair and let out a low whistle. They were making headway at last. Soon they might be knocking on Alex's door.

* * *

Sam sat on a two-seater sofa opposite Reader, who seemed much more relaxed this morning. He offered Sam a mug of tea. 'Welcome to my world, Professor Page. Not too bad, is it?'

'The Harbour is the best PIPE unit I've seen,' said Sam honestly. 'And it's Sam — if I may call you Jeremy?'

'Or Jem. I don't mind either way.'

They were alone in the quiet area, in a room painted a soft green, with carpeted floors, a selection of comfortable chairs, a well-stocked bookcase and a fish tank. Sam looked around, admiring the setting, while surreptitiously watching Jeremy.

Reader seemed very much in control, although worry lines still criss-crossed his brow. He looked pensive. Sam wondered if he'd been awake into the small hours, trying to decide how many secrets from his past life to share with his visitor.

'Thank you for coming,' Reader said, rather formally. 'It's good to talk to a new face, even in the current circumstances.'

'Sometimes it's easier to talk to a stranger, Jeremy, no matter how dire the situation.'

Reader asked Sam what his relationship with the police was. Sam explained that he was a retired psychologist who had had prior experience with cases like Reader's, so he'd been called in to help.

'Ah, cold-blooded killers,' Reader said softly.

'Yes, and particularly those who express remorse for their actions.'

'So, I'm not a one-off then? There are others like me?'

Sam smiled. 'Very few, Jeremy. You know that. The men you've lived with are usually proud of their deplorable actions and revel in going over every disgusting moment.'

Reader nodded.

'It's rare to find someone who has committed crimes that most would find abhorrent, and who wishes to make some sort of reparation.'

Reader stared at Sam over the top of his mug. After a moment, he said, 'You have no idea what a dark place I was in when I committed those crimes. I was consumed with anger and hatred. You can't live like that without something awful happening. I made it happen. I took lives. For a while, killing deadened the pain.'

Sam thought of the tiny hearts. 'Darkness such as you describe always derives from some traumatic event that happened either to you or someone close to you. In your case, I'd say to someone you loved.'

Reader put down his mug and rested his chin on his clasped hands. He took a deep breath. 'It really wasn't anything out of the ordinary. Everyone loses someone close to them. It happens all the time. The difference was my reaction to it. It was very violent and extreme.'

Sam waited.

Reader drew in a breath. 'I knew a young woman named Cheryl Court. She suffered something called a thyroid storm. It's rare, but potentially life-threatening if not treated in an intensive care unit.'

Sam had heard of it, but all he knew was that it was a complication of hyperthyroidism, in which extremely high levels of thyroid hormones are released.

Reader continued in a flat monotone, as if quoting from a medical textbook. 'The body temperature elevates, blood pressure rises, the heart palpitates, resulting in chest pain, abdominal pain, breathing difficulties, sweating.' He stopped suddenly, his face contorted, as if seeing these symptoms before his eyes.

'Cheryl died?' Sam said softly.

'Cheryl died.'

'And you loved her?'

'She was my dream come true. She was absolutely beautiful. She had skin of the palest porcelain, and soft blue eyes. I was already on the wrong path, a clever child with no direction that became a lost and confused young man. Cheryl saw what I could have been, and, had she lived, I think I would have achieved something, something good.' It wasn't easy assimilating the information while at the same time observing Reader's body language and trying to guess his intentions in revealing this hitherto untold story. Sam tried hard to give nothing away. He was starting to make connections, to understand why Reader had killed those women in that particular manner.

'We'd taken a few days away together. It was out of season and we borrowed a holiday let, a little chalet, from an aunt of Cheryl's. There were only a few other chalets on that deserted strip of East Coast shoreline. They were all unoccupied of course, closed up for the winter. You can imagine the rest. Night time. No phone signal. A young man with no knowledge of first aid . . . Even though I now know nothing could have saved her in that situation, I felt intensely guilty. It stayed with me for years.' Reader fell silent.

'Your anger at losing her that way became all-consuming. Then you started seeing other young women who bore a striking resemblance to Cheryl, and something snapped.' Sam hoped he was right.

'Ha!' Reader said. 'You're good, Sam Page! I bet you've even worked out why I did what I did. You knew it even before today, didn't you?'

Sam shrugged. 'I only made a guess. Why don't you explain?'

'Give me one more thing to prove that you really understand me.'

Sam looked him directly in the eyes. 'It wasn't the blood. It was the pale, cold skin. That's what you needed to see. That's why you took those tiny hearts.'

Reader put his face between his hands and began to sob.

Sam let him cry. After a while, he said, 'Why now, Jeremy? You could have shared this years ago.'

Reader raised his head. 'All this time I've been nothing but a guinea pig, a specimen to be analysed, prodded, stared at. I've spent countless hours talking to psychiatrists and psychologists until I was exhausted. But I have never met anyone who understands. Every action has a reaction. I was reacting.' He exhaled. 'I did those evil things because I was driven by the deranged thought that I could somehow bring Cheryl back, restore her to how she had been. Yes, it's crazy, but at the time it made perfect sense.'

Sam tried to imagine what Cheryl would have looked like to her terrified young lover — flushed scarlet with a high fever, racked with pain and struggling to take her next breath. And there was nothing this lover could have done to save her. He couldn't leave her, help was miles away, so he stayed and watched her die, burning up, her heart failing. He had wanted her back as she had been. Her skin pale and soft, not scarlet and glistening with sweat.

'You've never spoken of this at all, not even to Grace?' Sam asked.

'Especially not Grace.'

'Because of the depth of your affection for Cheryl? Or maybe because the two women connect to two different Jeremy Readers?'

Reader frowned. 'I'm not sure. Grace is a wonderful woman, and she believes we have no secrets from each other. It's probably wrong of me to keep this from her, but it makes no difference to how much I love her.' He paused. 'I may never tell her.'

'I think you should,' Sam said. 'She's an intelligent woman. I don't think much shocks her, do you? It might make it easier for her to understand your actions.'

'Possibly, Sam. I'll think about it.'

'Any more secrets?'

Reader smiled faintly. 'No. Ah, except for one very small thing, since I'm baring my soul to you. It was never noticed, ever, but I painted a tiny heart in blood on the walls. Like a lover carving initials into a tree.'

And there it was, he'd volunteered it. Sam didn't say that they already knew about these drawings.

'I've never told a soul. Not even Reuben, so you won't find our copycat Alex drawing any hearts.'

Sam found it difficult to conceal his surprise. But Alex *had* drawn them. What did it mean? He summoned a smile. 'You must feel easier now.'

'I'm not sure how I feel. It was good to know that you'd already worked it out, so I didn't have to try and explain it. I'd wanted to talk to you from the moment I saw you, but I didn't know if I'd have the courage to relive it all again. You've made things so much easier, and I'm grateful.'

They talked for a little longer, until it was time for Sam to leave. 'Would you visit me again, Sam?' Reader asked.

'Of course, with pleasure.' It seemed an odd thing to say, but Sam meant it. He had been very apprehensive about this meeting. He remembered the terrible time he had had with that old case and the murderer, Leon Briars.

Sam had feared that the same twisted psychology would manifest itself in Reader. But Reader was quite different. Did that mean he was telling the truth?

Sam told himself to be wary.

He drove back to Fenfleet, going over Reader's words in his head. How had Alex learned about those painted hearts?

CHAPTER TWENTY-TWO

PC Jack Fleet hurried back into the CID room and headed straight for Matt's office.

'Sir, she's certain it's the same man as the one in the CCTV still. She says the jacket is identical. I think it's safe to assume that Lisa met Alex just before her death.'

'It was late evening, Jack. How can she be so sure?' asked Matt.

'I asked her that. She says it wasn't really dark, sir. There's a street light right outside her house. She recognised Lisa immediately, then, when she realised it wasn't her husband Lisa was kissing, she had a closer look.' Jack grinned. 'She's a neighbourhood watch member, a retired security guard who used to work in the shopping precinct in Greenborough, so she's pretty astute.'

'And bored,' added Matt. 'And nosey.'

'Thankfully. I love nosey neighbours.'

'Well done, Swifty. Another box to tick. Now, if Jason and Kim can get an address from his family, we could be knocking on the door of his lair in a matter of hours.'

'I hope so, sir, I really do. I'm on tenterhooks every day that goes by without another death. There's no way he's going to follow Reader's pattern and move to a different area, is there?'

'I very much doubt it, Swifty. He seems perfectly happy right here in Fenfleet.'

The phone rang, and he snatched up the receiver. It could be Jason. 'Sir, we have an address. It's on the outskirts of Fenfleet.'

Matt noted down the road name and number. 'Get back here immediately, Jason. I'll prep the super, get uniform together, and we'll hit the place. Well done, both of you. Tell me the rest when you get here, okay?'

Matt put down the phone. 'Jason's found out where Alex is living.'

'Praise be,' said Jack. 'Let's just hope he hasn't done a runner.'

Jack went off to let the duty sergeant know, and Matt hastened upstairs.

David Redpath struck his palm with a fist. 'Yes!' He hesitated. 'We have no reason to believe he has a gun, do we?'

'No, sir. He's only used knives so far.'

'Good, then no need for an armed response vehicle.'

Matt briefly wondered at the changing times. In his day, there'd been no stab-proof vests, no Tasers. Officers, unarmed, were expected to deal with everything that was thrown at them. Once, when he was still in uniform, he had witnessed a WPC take on a knife-wielding attacker with nothing more lethal than her handbag to protect her. She'd disarmed him. Now the Fenland Constabulary had their own ARV (armed response vehicle), as well as a Tactical Armed Policing Team (TAPT) that supplied specialist firearms officers. Great, except that they were both stationed over an hour and a half away, and they covered four counties.

David looked to Matt. 'How do you want to play this?'

Good question. Matt thought for a moment. 'As far as I can see, we have two choices, sir. We either put the house under surveillance and wait to catch him coming in or leaving, or we get uniform to quietly surround the house and Jason and I simply knock on his door.'

'I'd go for the second option,' David said. 'What do you reckon?'

'Me too, though I need to talk to Jason first, and find out exactly what he's been told. But, basically, we've received information that Alex Campbell could be residing at that address, and we're checking it out. If we leave it under surveillance and he kills again, we'll have an awful lot of questions to answer.'

'Then as soon as you're ready, get uniform to assist and go round there.'

'Wilco, sir.' Matt turned to leave. 'I'll report back as soon as the situation's a bit clearer. You never know, we might soon have him banged up in the custody suite.'

'I'll be waiting with bated breath. And you take care, Matt. Alright?'

'I always do, sir.'

'Actually, you don't. You have history, Matt Ballard.'

Matt looked suitably chastised. 'I'll cough to that, Super, but in those days I only had myself to think about. Now I have someone else in my life.'

'Then just remember that if you feel the urge to act the hero.'

'Message received and understood, sir.'

The CID room was already buzzing with excitement.

'Can I come with you, sir?' asked Bryn.

'Not this time, Bryn. I'll just take Jason and some uniforms. He's only one guy, after all, and I want to keep it as low key as possible. Our Jason does a pretty fair imitation of a double-glazing salesman. I don't think we'll be sussed as coppers.'

Bryn looked crestfallen.

'Sorry, but I need you here, lad. Anything could happen, or something important could come in. Keep your attention on those Lithuanian murders, and don't take your finger off the pulse for a second. I have a feeling something's about to develop on that front.'

'Yes, sir. Don't worry, I'm not going to let anything slip past me.' He gave Matt a rueful grin. 'Just fancied a bit of action, that's all.'

'Well, I'm hoping there won't be any. I'd like a nice, quiet arrest, thank you.' He looked up as Jason and Kim came through the door. 'We spoke to Alex's sister, sir,' Jason began. 'She doesn't have too much to do with Alex. It turns out the siblings went their own ways after the mother went off her rocker, and now their father is dead, they hardly ever see each other.'

'The sister — her name is Fiona — says Alex has always been odd,' Kim said. 'He had OCD, and she admitted to being scared of his obsessive behaviours. She only has his new address because of something to do with probate after the father died. He's living in a small terraced house on Cadogan Street, housesitting for a cousin while she's away on some course up north.'

'Convenient for him,' muttered Matt.

Kim looked at her notebook. 'Fiona hasn't heard from him for several days. She needs to get in touch with him for something to do with the probate, but he hasn't contacted either her or their solicitor.'

'Too busy planning his next murder, no doubt,' added Jason dryly.

Matt drew himself up. 'Ready to pay him a call, Jason?'

Jason's eyes lit up. 'Does the sun rise in the east?'

* * *

It was lunchtime, and Lukas had been working on the laptop since eight that morning. Having made sure he was drip fed coffee, Jim now presented him with a large cheese and pickle sandwich.

'Any luck?' asked Jim.

'Not sure.' Lukas stretched. His shoulders ached. He wasn't used to this kind of work, sitting still for hours on end. He humped groceries around, stacked shelves, and drove the van for the store where he worked, or used to. He couldn't see them taking him back after this. 'I think I'm getting close, but there's so much secrecy.'

'Then don't let me hold you up.' Jim patted his aching shoulder and left, closing the door behind him.

Lukas took a bite of the sandwich and tried a new search. He had been looking for Darius Shukis, the name Lina had mentioned, and couldn't find it anywhere. But he had found another name, mentioned in connection with Lina's family name, Derus. He vaguely recognised it, but couldn't recall why or where he'd heard it before. The name was Backus.

Lukas narrowed his eyes and chewed thoughtfully on his sandwich. Gradually, he began to forget about his aching muscles. At last he was on the right track.

* * *

The house in Cadogan Street was smart and well maintained, with clean windows and fresh paintwork. With the uniformed officers close by but out of sight, Matt and Jason approached the front door.

They chatted casually as they walked up the short path to the front door, although they were both as tense as taut electric cables.

The windows were in UPVC but the door was solid wood, painted a rich green. It sported an old-fashioned brass knocker.

There was still no response after the second knock, and Jason was growing annoyed. Alex wasn't at home. Or he had no intention of answering.

Before he could say anything to Matt, the next door neighbour appeared. 'She's away. Can I take a message?'

He was overweight, dressed in ill-fitting shorts and a faded T-shirt that announced that he'd been to Disneyworld, although from the state of it, Jason guessed it hadn't been anytime recently. True it was very hot, but Jason couldn't disguise his look of disapproval. In his book you didn't dress like a dropout, no matter what the weather, and you *never* told strangers that your neighbour was away.

Jason and Matt presented their warrant cards. 'We understood her cousin was housesitting for her? It's him we've come to see,' Matt said.

'Oh, him. I think he's buggered off. He was here for a while and then he disappeared. Haven't seen him for days . . .' The man scratched himself. Jason tried not to wince.

'Yeah, he had a visitor a couple of weeks or so back. I think they had a bit of a barney. I never saw him again after that.'

Jason glanced at Matt.

Matt thanked the man, and they made their way back down the path. They stopped at the gate. 'I don't like the sound of that, do you?' asked Matt.

On an impulse, Jason walked back to the door, bent down and lifted the letterbox flap.

He recoiled with a gasp. 'Sir!'

Matt was immediately by his side. 'Shades of Reuben Grimes?'

'Oh, yes.' Jason swallowed hard. 'A dead body. Once smelt, never forgotten.'

Matt pulled his mobile from his pocket, told uniform what they suspected and asked for assistance in gaining entry. Once again the neighbour flung open his front door, but this time they gave him short shrift.

'Go inside, sir, and stay there, please. Someone will be sent round to see you in due course.' The man retreated. A police officer carrying a heavy enforcer approached them.

'I'm not looking forward to this', muttered Matt. 'Me neither,' Jason said. You had to be some kind of weirdo to want to be the one to find a decaying corpse. He knew it happened, it came with the territory, but he found the whole thing quite horrific. 'I'll just take a look around and see if we can find an open window or back door, sir.'

'Yes, do.' He beckoned to a PC. 'Go with the DI, would you, Adrian? See if you can find a way in so we don't have to batter the door down.'

A narrow alleyway ran between the houses, leading to the tiny, fenced back gardens. The gate was bolted, but the police officer was over it in a flash.

Jason tried the back door. It was locked, but a pair of old-fashioned French windows that led into the dining room were not so secure. He rattled them and felt some give. 'Do you think you can pop this lock, Adrian?'

PC Adrian Lovell eyed it up. He nodded. 'Think so, sir. It's pretty old, isn't it?'

Jason watched the young man put his boot to the lock and kick out. The door swung open. 'Nice one, Adrian.'

The police constable stepped back, allowing Jason to go inside first.

'Wait here. We need as few people in or out as possible until we know what we're looking at.'

He went inside, trying to ignore the all-pervading stench and dreading what he would find. An enthusiastic Rory Wilkinson had once told him that, in addition to various gases, a dead human body produces around thirty different chemical compounds, and they all emit distinct odours. He had gone on to list smells — rotten eggs, stale garlic, rotting cabbage, musty mothballs, and a lot of other waste products that Jason preferred not to remember.

Carefully he walked through the rooms until, finding nothing untoward, he opened the front door for Matt with a gloved hand.

As SIO, Matt had already set up a scene guard to restrict entry. From the awful stench, it wouldn't take them long to establish that they had a crime scene on their hands. But who was dead?

'Downstairs is clear, sir, although nothing around to give us an ID on who was living here.' Jason said.

'Right. Let's see what upstairs has to offer — as if I didn't know,' Matt said. They mounted the stairs.

The two bedrooms and the tiny box room were all neat, and empty. Not so the bathroom.

'What the . . . what *is* that?' Matt exclaimed.

Jason stared at the bath. And what it held.

Initially it appeared to be a bundle of dirty laundry, until you saw the white hand reaching up through the discarded bath towels.

'Jason, call Rory Wilkinson. We need the lot down here.' Protective gloves on, Matt tentatively reached forward and peeled back one corner of a duvet. A decomposing face stared sightlessly up at him — that of a young man, framed by red hair.

Staring at the scene before him, Jason rang forensics and explained what they needed.

He saw a pair of glasses, lying broken on the tiled floor. A small pile of neatly folded clothes on a small white stool in the corner. On the shelf above the sink, a wristwatch with a metal strap, alongside an unopened bottle of shampoo.

Matt drew the duvet back across the dead face. 'We need to get out of here,' he whispered. 'Preserve the scene.'

Jason nodded, only too happy to comply.

At the door, they signed the scene log and noted the time, while the officer on duty made a note of exactly what they were wearing, to eliminate them from any trace evidence the SOCOs might find.

Outside, Jason breathed the fresh air. 'Do we think we were looking at Alex Campbell, sir?'

'I'd say most certainly, Jason.'

'Then . . . ?'

Matt beckoned to him and they moved away from the police officers who were setting up cordon tape and sealing off the road. 'I need to stay here until Rory arrives.' He lowered his voice. 'If that is Alex, we are in deep trouble. It's pure guesswork, but I'd say he's been dead a couple of weeks. That means Alex isn't our killer.'

Jason's brain was reeling. Well, he'd found Alex Campbell alright. Then who was the murderer? 'Before we decide anything, we need absolute proof that our dead guy really is Alex.'

'Why don't you get the ball rolling by going and asking the sister for a DNA swab.' Matt grimaced. 'One thing's for sure, we won't be asking anyone to identify this guy from a post-mortem photograph.'

'Good idea. I can be back before the SOCOs have finished. By then they might have found something that will help confirm his identity.'

'Off you go. I'll suit up and go in with the pathologist when he gets here. I'll bag and tag anything I think might help us.'

'Sir?' Jason said. 'What's going on here?'

Matt shook his head. 'I wish I knew. I was so positive, and now, if that really is Alex in there, we're well and truly fucked.'

CHAPTER TWENTY-THREE

The news of the discovery of the body filtered back to Bryn just after Lukas had sent a message saying he had some interesting news for him. He swore loudly. He wanted to get to Lukas, but now he would have to stay where he was and wait for instructions.

He texted Lukas to say something had come up but he'd get there as soon as he could. Lukas sent back a thumbs up. Kim was watching him from her desk. 'You look a bit tense, Bryn.' Yeah.' He frowned. 'I need to be in two places at once.'

'Can I help?'

Bryn explained his predicament.

'Tell you what. Let me go over to Saltern-le-Fen and collect whatever he has for you. I'll be back in an hour.' Kim glanced at her tidy desk. 'It'll be ages before the work starts to trickle in from the crime scene, and I've nothing else to do.'

'Would you?' Bryn brightened up. 'I'd really appreciate it. I'd send a uniform, but that would draw attention to Lukas, and I need to keep him well under the radar.'

'No problem.' Kim stood up. 'It's in Bridle Street, isn't it?'

'That's the one. Jim Cousin's place. Lukas is staying in room four in the second house, but he should be working in Jim's back office right now.'

'I'll find him, don't worry. See you in around an hour.'

* * *

At last, Rory Wilkinson. Matt had been waiting with his head bursting with suppositions and guesses. He wondered what effect this news would have on Jeremy Reader and Grace Repton. In a single stroke, Reader's acolyte, his disciple, had been eliminated, as dead as the women who'd supposedly been his victims.

Finally, Rory had taken everything he needed from his Citroen, and was now hurrying towards him.

'Rumour has it you have a stinker for me.' Rory raised his eyebrows.

'"Fraid so.' They signed in at the door and went inside.

'What a nice little place! Apart from the pong, it's delightful.' Rory gazed around in admiration.

'I wonder if the owner will feel the same when she gets back home.' Matt was pretty sure he'd be seeing a For Sale sign at the gate before long. 'He's in the bathroom.'

He led the way up the stairs.

'Oh my!' Rory stared at the heaps of towels and bedding piled into the bath. 'Thoughtfully done, isn't it? All the bodily fluids nicely contained in the tub. No mess, no fuss.'

Matt felt mildly nauseous.

Rory called down the stairs. 'Is my beautiful photographer here yet?'

A voice answered that she had just arrived and was unpacking her equipment.

'We give our Ella some choice subjects for her photo shoots, don't we?' Rory said.

'Poor woman.' She had told Matt that having a lens between her and the deceased made it less real, less sordid. Still, he would have hated her job.

A few moments later, Ella Jarvis's slim figure appeared in the doorway. If she was daunted by the smell, she didn't show it. Matt knew that, like Jason, he was particularly sensitive to odours, but some officers seemed to take them in their stride.

'Lots of shots please, Ella, of the whole room as it is before we start to uncover this unfortunate soul,' Rory said.

Matt went and stood in the doorway, so as not to get in her way.

'Now, let's see what we've got here, and pictures all the way, please.'

Rory began lifting away the towels and the duvet, placing them in evidence bags. It was hard to piece together what had happened but initially, at least, it looked as though he'd been preparing to take a bath, had removed his outer garments, folded them and placed them on the stool, then been attacked from behind.

After a closer examination, Rory corroborated this. 'It looks like a single blow to the back of the head with a very heavy blunt weapon. Then I suggest he was pushed, or fell back, into the bath, where he was suffocated.' He pointed to a bag containing a pillow that had been lying alongside the body. 'Most likely with that. The forensic tests will confirm it, I'm sure.'

This was Alex Campbell. Everything about this young man, clad only in boxer shorts and a T-shirt, told Matt it must be him. 'Can we get fingerprints, Prof?' he asked hopefully.

'Maybe. It's not impossible, but he has undergone extensive decomposition.' Rory looked up at Matt, now standing just behind him. 'Rule of thumb says they remain viable for around four days in hot weather and up to fifty days in winter. This hot weather has speeded things up,

I'm afraid, even though this room is cooler than the rest of the house.' He looked closely at the man's hand. 'However, we've got rather clever at this over the years, you know. We have several advanced techniques that could work. I'm assuming you're asking for a quick identification, Matt?'

'Oh yes,' he replied grimly. 'Until an hour ago we believed that this was the man who'd murdered Lisa and Louise Farrier. Alex Campbell, Jeremy Reader's pen pal.'

'Tut-tut. Not like you to make such a massive balls-up.'

'Tell me about it!' Matt shook his head.

'All I can say at the moment is that this young man was well on his way across the Styx when our two lovely ladies were executed. I'm thinking he died between ten and twelve days ago.'

Despite the horrific state of the body, Matt was finding it hard to tear his eyes away. 'How on earth are you going to get him back to the lab?'

'Let me worry about that, huh?' Rory grinned. 'I've had worse. Do you know, once, way back, I recall—'

'Enough!'

Rory grinned. 'Maybe you'd like to check out his clothes before we bag them up. Jeans pockets are a pretty good place to find the odd identifying item.'

Of course. Rory was right. In one of the back pockets of the victim's denims, Matt found a folded sheet of paper. He opened it out and saw it was a half-written letter.

Dear Jeremy . . .

Matt read on. It seemed that Alex had had a change of heart. Now he wasn't sure if Reader had meant it when he begged him not to kill. Either that, or he had found that the taking of a life was beyond him.

Matt tried to picture the handwriting on the last letter Alex had sent to Jeremy Reader. He was pretty sure it was the same. He'd check when he got back — no, wait. He could do it right now.

Outside on the landing, he rang Bryn.

'Do me a favour, and take a photo of Alex's last letter — there's a copy on the whiteboard — and send it to my phone. As soon as, Bryn.'

A few moments later he received the attachment. He checked it against the one from Alex's pocket. They were identical. This was Alex.

He exhaled very slowly. There was a killer loose in his town, and he had no suspect at all. He was back where he started.

* * *

Sam arrived to find the CID room almost deserted, the only occupant being a sombre-looking Bryn Owen.

'Goodness! What's happened? Where is everyone?'

Bryn told him.

Pole-axed, Sam went over to the whiteboard and stared at it. 'So, who is it? Who is killing in the manner of Jeremy Reader?'

'We have no idea.' Bryn sounded uncharacteristically downbeat. 'The boss wants a big campfire when he gets back. Will you stay?'

'Try and stop me,' said Sam. 'Someone is being very devious indeed. But who?'

'If our dead man is identified as Alex Campbell, it will have blown the whole investigation out of the water,' Bryn said.

'Not necessarily,' said Sam thoughtfully. 'After all, a lot of what you have here,' he pointed to the whiteboard, 'still stands, doesn't it? This guy you call Varsity Man still exists, it's just not Alex Campbell. Whoever it is, Alex must have told him in detail all about Jeremy's MO before he was killed, don't you think?'

'Yeah . . .' Bryn nodded slowly. 'Most likely. I guess it's the fact that we thought we had him, and he'd be in custody by nightfall. It's thrown us — well, it's certainly thrown me.'

'Naturally. But when you talk it through at your campfire, I don't think it will seem quite so dire. It's more of a setback than a disaster.'

Bryn smiled. 'You're a good man to have around, Professor Page.'

'Call me Sam, please. And I'm just being logical.'

Bryn took a phone call, and Sam saw the anxiety return to his expression.

'Another problem?' he asked.

'Not sure. It could be.' He stared at nothing, thinking. 'I'm getting a young Lithuanian man to help me with my inquiry into some local killings. He was threatened, so I spirited him away. He rang earlier to say he had something for me, and Kim went to see him. He's left a letter for me, and now he's gone missing.'

'Missing as in taken?' asked Sam.

'More like buggered off to do a bit of private sleuthing, if I know Lukas, but that puts him in serious danger, especially if the silly sod starts speaking to the wrong people.' Bryn drummed on his desk. 'I told him to stay put!'

Sam smiled. 'He's a young man, like you. Would you stay shut up behind a locked door if you thought you were onto something?'

'I'm a copper. He's a grocery shop assistant, and he's already been beaten up!' His frown deepened. 'I wonder what he's found out.'

'Well, at least he's left you a note. So you'll know soon, won't you? Patience, Detective.'

Soon afterwards, Kim was back with the note. 'Jim Cousins said that Lukas asked him to lock up the laptop, and then he went out.' She handed Bryn the envelope.

Bryn ripped it open. 'It's a name. He says he thinks it holds the key to all the deaths, and more too. But it's nothing to do with the people we suspected. Does he mean the Latvians?' He groaned. 'Damn him! Why didn't he just wait?'

'What's the name?' asked Kim, logging into her computer.

'Just a surname — Backus.' Bryn spelled it out.

'Nothing more?' Kim typed it in and pulled a face. 'We have a Brewery, a hospital, a city, a scientist and heaven knows what more. I'll try the PNC, shall I? See if he's known to us.'

'He, *or* she,' corrected Sam.

After a while, she said, 'Joris Backus. Lithuanian national, arrested last year after a raid on an illegal cigarette factory. Oh, he's serving time, so I guess it's not him.' She shrugged. 'He's the only Backus they have.'

'And Lithuanian, not Latvian? Hell. Where are you, Lukas?'

'He said he'd ring you. You just have to wait,' Kim said. 'I asked Jim Cousins to get hold of you if he heard anything from him.'

Sam sipped his coffee. All they could do was wait — for Lukas to get in touch, and for Matt Ballard to get back from the crime scene. He glanced at his watch. This was going to be a long afternoon.

CHAPTER TWENTY-FOUR

Matt and Jason returned mid-afternoon and went immediately to report to Superintendent David Redpath. Twenty minutes later they were back in the CID room, Matt standing in front of the incident board. 'Okay, everyone! Ten minutes' time, I want all officers involved, and you too Sam, if you don't mind, in here for a special four o'clock meeting.'

Kim went off to notify uniform while Matt went into his office and closed the door. He needed a few minutes of silence, and to make a phone call, before he tackled the briefing.

Liz answered almost immediately. 'Is something wrong, Mattie?'

Without taking a breath, Matt poured out the whole story.

When he'd finished, she said, 'Maybe you've been coming at this all wrong. I think you're going to have to step back and take another look from a different viewpoint. Are you going to have a brainstorming session?'

'After the meeting. First, I want everyone fully aware of exactly how things are. I'll take the whole thing back to page one. Then I'll get together with the team and Sam and we'll throw around a few ideas and see if anything sounds reasonable.'

'Do that. It worked for us in the past.'

Matt heard the hint of nostalgia in her voice and wanted to walk straight out and go to her. Sighing inwardly, he said, 'I'll be bound to be a bit late, so I'll bring a takeaway. Any preferences?'

'Indian.'

'Indian it is. I'll ring you when I'm on my way. Maybe you'd mull over what I've told you?'

Liz snorted. 'As if I'd do anything else! See you later, and,' she blew him a kiss down the phone, 'thank you for sharing it with me.'

'Who else would I share it with?'

'Love you, Mattie.' She hung up.

Matt sat back. She was right. It was slowly beginning to dawn on him that someone might have been manipulating the whole investigation from the start. And who else but that master manipulator, Jeremy Reader?

He stared at his screen, and the badge of the Fenland Constabulary emblazoned across it. Could it be that he, his whole investigation and the prison governor, had been hoodwinked by a very clever murderer?

He looked up at the clock. Time to go. Back to the beginning. Back to mistrusting everyone, meaning Jeremy Reader.

* * *

Matt described what he had seen in the house in Cadogan Street, and again asked for the officers' support in giving some extra time. The woman who owned the house had been notified. She would travel back at once, and would be staying with Alex Campbell's sister, Fiona, in Lincoln.

'I want her interviewed immediately on her return. I want to know when she made the arrangement for Alex to housesit, and why she trusted him with her home. We need the exact date when he moved in, and anything else she can tell us about him. We need to know who he was closely involved with — friends, fellow students, work-mates. I assume he had a part-time job to help with his college fees?' He looked at Kim. 'DC Peters, would you go and see Grace Repton and tell her what's going on? It'll be all over the news in no time, so she'd better hear it from us first.'

'Yes, sir. I'll go after the meeting,' Kim said.

'I'll speak to Governor Ross Cadman. He can tell Reader — if he doesn't know already.' He knew he sounded bitter but sod it, they'd been led a dance. 'There is a chance that Jeremy Reader has been behind it all from the start. We can't rule it out.'

He caught Sam's worried glance. He obviously still believed in Reader. Well, he'd discuss that with him later.

'The fact remains that *someone* knew all about Jeremy Reader's methods — the type of women he preyed on, how he attracted them, how he got into their homes, and how he finally killed them. Some of that stuff could have been picked up from the media, but an awful lot couldn't. Up to now, everything pointed to our murderer being Alex Campbell, a disturbed young man suffering with an obsessive disorder who idolised Reader and often wrote to him. He had declared that he would take up the mantle and continue killing as a tribute to Reader, but an unfinished letter found in the deceased man's clothing shows that he'd had second thoughts and that he never went through with his intention.'

Matt blinked, trying to clear his tired eyes.

'Someone, who we will continue to call Varsity Man, has been impersonating. Alex. He must have got Alex to give him all the details, then stole his signature jacket and began killing women. The jacket, which his sister told Jason was his pride and joy, was not among his things. In fact, he had very few clothes and shoes with him, but there were empty hangers suggesting that some of his things might have been taken. Varsity Man is probably the same size as Alex, but may not have red hair. Alex's baseball caps and beanie hats have also gone. Varsity Man always had his head covered.'

He pointed at the picture taken from the CCTV camera near Reuben Grimes's maisonette. 'We have to find out who this man is, because he certainly isn't Alex Campbell.'

After a few questions and answers, Matt delegated the tasks, called the meeting to a close. While the officers streamed out of the CID room, Matt called his team, plus Swifty and Sam, to his office. Inside, he said, 'I was going to hold a brainstorming session now, but I'm going to let you digest this overnight. Then we'll hit it hard tomorrow. We're going to have to look at the main players in this drama again, along with everyone connected to them. I want you to consider different scenarios, even if they seem bizarre at first, because we're not looking at this right. I'm going to suggest that you all get off the minute the shift finishes, grab some down time, think this through, and come back to me tomorrow. It could be a tough week, guys. We have to make some sense of this, and fast. He will kill again, I'm certain of that.' He looked at Kim. 'If you'd just call in on Grace on your way home? Like now?'

Kim stood up. 'On my way. See you tomorrow.'

Bryn raised his hand. 'I have another problem, sir. It's not to do with this case.'

'Then, Jason and Swifty, off you go. Sam? Still on for a takeaway?'

Sam Page nodded. 'Certainly, and I'll tell you about my visit to the prison. I've just got a few calls to make.' Soon, only Bryn remained behind.

'So. What's bothering you?' Matt said.

'Lukas. He's done another disappearing act,' Bryn said glumly.

'Ah, now, listen. You've done all you can, more than most would have. But you can't wrap him in cotton wool, Bryn. He probably doesn't realise just how dangerous these drug-running gangs can be. You see it on a regular basis, so it's no wonder you're concerned for him, but you know what they say about horses and water.'

'But I think he's discovered something, sir. Look.' He passed Matt a folded piece of paper.

'Backus? And he doesn't think it's to do with the turf war?' Matt pulled a face. 'I see why you're worried. What *is* it to do with then?'

'I need to find him, sir. Can I get off now, and go to Jim's place? If Lukas isn't back, I can at least get hold of my laptop and check the search history. It could indicate where Lukas has gone rushing off to.'

Reluctantly, Matt gave his permission. This lad was taking on too much single-handed, but he had no spare hands to offer him right now. Bryn Owen was a good detective and had a sensible head on his shoulders, but Matt wasn't so sure about Lukas. He sounded impulsive and maybe a bit naïve, which could be dangerous, both for himself and those around him. 'Just go carefully, Bryn. We're getting into unchartered waters here. We have no idea what's behind these deaths. Stay sharp, and if you find Lukas, read him the riot act, okay? And do nothing on your own, understand? If there's a lead to follow, ring it in and get assistance.'

Bryn nodded. 'I'll keep you up to speed, sir.'

'You'd better phone me even if nothing comes of it.'

Matt watched Bryn leave, tidied his desk and shut down his computer. Tomorrow was going to be hell, so he might as well take his own advice and get away. He was also very keen to hear what Sam had to say about his visit to Reader. He shut his office door and waved to Sam. 'Hope you like Indian food. I've had my orders regarding supper.'

'Perfect.' Sam smiled. 'I'd better follow you in my car, I have no idea where you live.'

'First stop, the Kerala Palace in the Market Place, then on to Cannon Farm. I promise not to lose you on Tanners Fen.'

* * *

When Bryn arrived at Bridle Street, Lukas still had not returned. He had rung his mobile several times, but it was switched off.

'If he's not back by curfew, he has to go. I've made sure he understands that.' Jim looked anxious too. 'I don't want to do this, considering the situation. He's a nice lad, Bryn, but rules are rules.'

'I think he may have discovered something important, Jim. Could I have the laptop, please?'

'Sure. Come with me.' Jim led the way upstairs to his flat. He unlocked the door and they went inside. 'Lukas said to make sure it was safe, so I'm thinking your guess is right. He had found something.' He indicated to the sofa. 'Take a seat, and I'll go and get your computer.'

Bryn looked around the room. From the look of it, Jim spent very little time there. Apart from the sofa, a low coffee table, a bookcase, and a big TV, the room was bare. No photos, pictures or ornaments. Bryn didn't like too much clutter, but this was going a bit far.

'Here we go.' Jim returned and placed the laptop and charger on the coffee table. 'Want to check it out here, or down in the back office?'

'Downstairs, if that's okay? Just in case he comes back.'

It only took a few minutes to realise that he'd made a major oversight. All the sites that Lukas had accessed were in Lithuanian, and even using Google Translate, the scanty information meant little to him. Lukas must have seen something he actually recognised personally. He cursed under his breath, then took out his phone and rang Lukas's number again. As he listened to the recorded voice, he scrolled down the sites. Again and again, the names Derus and Backus were mentioned. He pushed his phone back into his pocket and returned to the computer. He clicked again on the most informative site. It was a kind of e-zine, dealing with unsolved murders from decades ago. It was vague, only hinting at dreadful occurrences that may have taken place in the towns and villages close to where the Derus family came from. The details were hazy, consisting mainly of rumours and suppositions about disappearances and violent deaths, but again the name Backus appeared along with the familiar name of Derus.

Bryn closed down the computer, and stared blankly around Jim's little office. He trusted Lukas. He totally believed that he would ring him, just as he had said he would. If he could. He was terrified that someone, somewhere, had Lukas's name on a hit list. Matt Ballard was right. Lukas didn't fully appreciate how ruthless these people were. That, or he believed he was clever enough to outwit them. Both assumptions could be fatal.

After a few minutes, Bryn took the computer back to Jim. 'Sorry to be a pain, but could you lock this up again? If Lukas comes back, I need him to explain exactly what he discovered on these sites, and it won't help if I have the laptop with me and I'm miles away.'

'No problem,' said Jim. 'And I've been thinking.' He rubbed his chin thoughtfully. 'Just this once, I'm prepared to take him back. I get the feeling that he's vital to whatever you are trying to do, and I don't want to put a spanner in the works.'

Bryn heaved a sigh of relief. 'That's a weight off my mind, Jim. Thank you.'

'Just ring me. I'm on night shift here tonight. I'm expecting a late "guest" you lot have asked me to take under my wing.'

'You're a good bloke, Jim.'

His smile broadened. 'Never thought I'd hear a copper say that. An old lag like me!'

Bryn handed over the laptop. 'I think I know where Lukas has gone, but if he comes back, tell him to call me immediately, would you?' Bryn took a deep breath and hurried back to his car.

There really was only once place Lukas would go, and that was to Lina Derus. He just prayed that she was safely at home, and that he could get to them in time.

* * *

Grace sat upright on her sofa, facing Kim, the cat close beside her. She seemed to be in a trance.

'Can I get you a cup of tea, Grace?' Kim touched her arm gently. 'I know it's a shock. I'll go and make you a drink, okay?'

She went to the kitchen and made tea. When she returned to the lounge, Grace was pacing the floor, her hands clenching and un-clenching. Kim hadn't expected this. Grace was usually so controlled.

Kim put down the tea. 'Talk to me, Grace.'

She said just one word: 'Jeremy.'

'The governor has been notified. He will tell him.'

After a moment or two, Grace seemed to regain control of herself. She sat down again and let out a huge sigh.

'I just don't understand. It makes no sense. In his last letter, Alex intimated to Jeremy exactly what he was going to do, so how can he be dead? Everything Jeremy told you was true. He really believed Alex wanted to carry on killing, in Jeremy's honour. He wanted to make Jeremy proud of him.'

'I'm wondering why the prison allowed Jeremy to receive that letter,' said Kim, 'without censoring it.'

'All mail is removed from the envelopes, in case of enclosed contraband or money. Mail is always read in Cat A prisons, mainly for the sake of security, and always in

239

the prescence of the recipient.' Grace knew the ropes. 'Prisoners have to be told if their mail is being censored or withheld. Don't forget, Alex was considered by most to be just another nutter, it was Jeremy who recognised something darker in him. The authorities had heard all this empty bragging before from a multitude of "fans." I'm not surprised they gave it to him.' Her expression became angry. 'Now answer my question, Detective, how can Alex be dead? He has to have been the killer!'

'We suspect Alex confided all he knew about the earlier murders . . . Jeremy's murders, to someone else. Just as Reuben had to Alex. And, like Reuben, he paid with his life.'

'But why?' Grace was almost shouting. 'This will finish Jeremy. He's tried so hard to do the right thing, make amends, but it all backfires on him! He'll take this as an omen that he'll never be forgiven, doesn't deserve forgiveness. I know him, DC Peters. This will be the end of him.'

'If you think that's the case, he'll need you to be strong for him,' said Kim. 'You're a strong woman, Grace, unless I'm very much mistaken. You've been through a lot in your life.'

Grace Repton looked at her askance. Kim could not read that look. 'You are right, of course,' she said. 'I am strong. But this isn't about me, it's about Jeremy. He isn't strong, not now. Facing your demons leaves you weak and vulnerable.'

Kim wondered about their forthcoming wedding, but chose not to mention it.

'He'll ring me this evening, I hope. I'll do my best to support him, of course, but even I am completely nonplussed by this news. You are sure it is Alex who has been found dead?'

'Everything points to it. We are awaiting forensic identification, but there is little doubt.' Kim sipped her tea. 'Please think very carefully about anyone else who might possibly have a reason to want to take up where Jeremy left off. Anyone at all, no matter how slight the connection.'

Grace picked up her mug and stared into it. 'Other than Alex, I don't have a clue, Detective. Not a clue.'

'Think hard, Grace, and contact me or the DCI if you think of anything. It could be someone with a grudge against Jeremy, or who even opposes your marriage. There are many reasons for revenge.'

'Oh, I know. I've spent a lot of time talking to some very bad people. I've heard some unbelievably strange reasons for taking a life.' Grace's face was set like stone.

'As have we,' Kim said. 'So, please help us if you can.'

'I'll do my best.'

Kim stood up. 'I'm sorry to bring you news like this, but we wanted you to know before the media gets hold of it.'

'I appreciate it. And I'm so sorry for the way I acted. It's just . . . it was the last thing I was expecting to hear. You've been very kind.'

'Just keep in touch,' said Kim, 'and I hope your conversation with Jeremy goes well.'

Grace held the front door open for her. 'At least I'll have time to consider what to say to him. Thank you again.'

Kim drove away. Grace's extreme reaction puzzled her. For someone with a history of tackling muggers and walking confidently into a prison block, it was extraordinary.

Maybe she'd try to get a word with either Laura or Sam Page, and see what they made of it.

CHAPTER TWENTY-FIVE

Their meal over, Matt, Liz and Sam sat in the conservatory with their coffee. All the windows were open and the ceiling fan was on, but still the night was oppressively warm.

After the usual comments about the weather, Matt asked Sam to tell them about his talk with Jeremy Reader.

Sam looked at Matt. 'I got the feeling at the afternoon meeting that you've reverted to your earlier opinion of Reader.'

He nodded. 'I have, Sam. Someone is playing us, and Reader's my first choice for the part.'

'Well, sorry to disappoint, but I still think that man is repentant.'

Sam told them about Reader's past history.

'Maybe he never spoke about it before because he's only just invented it,' murmured Matt, still unconvinced.

'Anything's possible,' said Sam. 'But I had a bit of time to wait before you got back for the meeting, and I got Bryn to do a little checking for me. We didn't delve too deeply, but we did find an obituary for the girl called Cheryl Court, and a small piece in an East Coast local newspaper about a young woman suffering a collapse and dying before help could get to her. I think it's kosher.'

'Maybe.' This still didn't change Matt's mind.

'Now, the biggest thing I uncovered was about your bloody hearts, Matt.' Sam emptied his cup. 'He offered that information freely, without prompting, and he swears he never mentioned them to Reuben, so Alex was never told about them. Jeremy said he hadn't told a soul.'

'So how did Varsity Man get to know about it?' asked Liz.

There was no answer to this.

Matt got up. 'I'm going to make another pot of coffee and allow my poor aching brain to digest that particular item.'

Coffee made, he was putting it down on the table when his mobile rang. 'Bugger!' He glanced at the screen. 'Oh, I'd better take this. It's Kim Peters. Would you excuse me?' He hurried back into the kitchen.

* * *

Liz and Sam chatted casually for a few moments until Sam asked, 'Are you sleeping properly? You look very tired.'

Liz wasn't sure what prompted it, maybe just Sam's kind face and understanding expression, but the floodgates opened and all the episodes she'd been experiencing recently poured out of her. It was lucky that Matt's call was taking time.

When she'd finished, he said, 'My dear Liz, none of this is even slightly surprising. You're recovering from a major trauma, not only to your body but your entire nervous system. It's a miracle you've come so far so soon. There will be glitches. You must learn to forgive your body and your mind, they're still working hard to get you back to where you were before, or at least to an acceptable level.'

'You really think I'm not regressing?'

Sam's smile widened. 'Not at all. But worrying won't help. Stress can trigger these episodes, plus they will make them seem worse than they really are.' He paused. 'Would you like to see me, maybe once a week, for a chat? Tell me your worries, and I'll see if I can make sense of them for you.'

'I'd love that, Sam!' Then her face fell. 'Oh, but unless I get through my assessment, I can't drive.'

'I'll pick you up, or see you here, whichever you like. It would be my pleasure. And don't panic if you do fail your assessment. They are very strict, they have to be for everyone's safety. But I promise you that it won't be too long before you have your freedom back.'

Liz could have hugged him. Just those few words had made her feel so much more relaxed. Maybe she could even be of some help to Mattie, because he certainly needed all the help he could get.

Matt came back in and flopped into his chair.

'What have I missed?' he asked.

'Sam has just offered to give me some of his precious time, sweetheart, to help me understand the healing process.'

'That's really kind of you, Sam,' Matt said. 'Thank you.'

'Right, Mattie,' Liz said. 'On to your case. Drink your coffee and let's have a bit of a practice run before your brainstorming session tomorrow.'

'First off, Liz, if you were running this case, where would you start looking?'

'Hmm, let's see. What Sam just said about Reader not telling anyone about those bloody hearts makes it rather difficult to know. I guess I'd start thinking laterally. We know your killer is the same height and size as Alex, and you have a CCTV shot of him, so you are looking for a male of a certain build and type. You have a witness who saw him meeting Lisa. She said he was younger than her, so that gives you an approximate age . . . I'd look at young men closely connected to both Reader *and* Grace.'

'Good point,' added Sam. 'What if someone hates Reader enough to want to blight his life all over again, and put a stop to his marriage? Maybe it's not about idolising the killer but hating him.'

'I wonder if we should look at the staff from the Harbour Unit?' mused Matt.

'That's a possibility!' Liz nodded vigorously. 'He's been opening his heart to them for months. Someone there might not be as altruistic as they make out.'

'Or,' Sam said softly, 'what if it's not about Jeremy at all? What if someone doesn't want Grace to marry a murderer?'

'Someone who loves her?' said Liz.

'Maybe. She's mixed with some very odd people in her life, some of them very dangerous. She might have attracted a wrong-un.' Matt sounded almost elated. 'And I've just heard from Kim. She's pretty confused about Grace's reaction to the news that Alex isn't the copycat killer after all. She thinks it will finish Reader off.'

'And that could be exactly what someone wants.' Sam placed his cup down as if to emphasise the point. 'This could be all about Grace Repton. What do you actually know about her?'

'Probably not enough. Kim knows more than any of us. She went off on a fact-finding trip the other day and got quite a bit of her history. Apparently she was a street pastor, a kind of night marshal.' Matt's eyes lit up. 'I know exactly where we'll be starting tomorrow. With Grace Repton.'

Although she wasn't working the case, Liz had one of her intuitions. This was the right direction to go in. Someone wanted that wedding stopped, Reader destroyed and . . . what? What was the end game?

* * *

Lukas and Lina walked at a steady pace down a shadowy street in Fenfleet. He had his arm tightly around her waist and stopped every so often to whisper something in her ear, making Lina laugh softly.

It was all a pretence. Lukas hoped it would convince anyone watching that they were just another young couple out for the evening together. If they were recognised, they'd be in serious trouble.

After contacting Lina, he'd cadged a lift from Saltern to Fenfleet with a guy who'd been delivering charity clothes to Jim Cousin's place. He had met Lina in a café attached to the local theatre. Her idea, because no one she knew would be likely to go there, and she'd met Bryn there. Over a shared cappuccino — he couldn't afford two — Lukas told her what he had discovered earlier that day. Slowly it began to dawn on her. She had heard of Backus, but only in whispered conversations that she hadn't been supposed to overhear. Then she remembered someone who could give them the answers they needed. They were going to see him now.

'How much further?' Lukas asked.

'Not far now. He lives in a bungalow in an old people's complex close to the health centre. It's called the Maples.'

Albert Matonis answered his door on the second ring. He was probably well into his eighties but was still wiry and upright, with a surprisingly strong handshake. 'Lina! I haven't seen you for months, girl! I am so very sorry about Filip . . . well, we'll talk about that later. Come in! Come in!' He greeted her in their native Lithuanian.

Lina introduced him to Lukas. 'I call Albert my uncle. He was really my uncle's best friend, but he's always been family too.'

Lukas took to Albert immediately. He readily accepted the offer of tea, and glanced around the room, which was full of photos and knickknacks, quite different from Jim Cousin's Spartan residence.

The old man made a pot of proper leaf tea and produced three mugs, all different, and all with humorous mottos. Lukas's read, 'Keep Calm and watch Judge Judy.' Albert produced a sugar bowl in the shape of a fat lady, and placed it on the table next to a plate of chocolate biscuits. He then sat back. 'I haven't met you, have I, young man? My memory isn't what it was.'

Lina leaned forward. 'Uncle, we need your help. It's about Filip's death.'

Albert stared down into his lap, his expression sombre. 'You young people should keep away from anything to do with these murders.'

'It's too late for that, Uncle. My brother is dead, and I won't rest until I point the finger at those responsible.'

Albert shook his head. 'You always were a feisty one, Lina. Ah, Filip . . . He mixed with some bad people, and he wasn't a match for those Latvian drug dealers.'

'His death had nothing to do with the Latvians, Albert, and I think you know that.' Not wanting to upset the old man, Lukas spoke softly. 'Please, tell us all you know about a family named Backus.'

Albert picked up his "Present from Alcatraz" mug and blew into his tea. After a long silence, he said, 'The Backus and Derus families were close, like brothers and sisters until the troubles began. It was a terrifying time for us all. People disappeared, others were found mutilated, murdered.' He shuddered. 'Then one of the Backus women was attacked and left for dead. Unspeakable things had been done to her. Before she died, she said one word.' He swallowed. 'Derus.'

Lina looked aghast. 'She accused one of *our* family of the attack?'

'That's how the Backus family took it. Everyone knew that a young Derus boy was very fond of her. Her name was Serena and she was a beauty. I can see her now. People thought she was out of the boy's league and came to the conclusion that she refused him, so he took her by force. He denied it emphatically.'

'What did the Derus family think had happened?' asked Lukas.

'They thought he had found her and tried to help her. I still believe that. Maybe she loved him in return, and died with his name on her lips. He disappeared a few days later, and was never seen again.' Albert took a long drink of his tea. 'That was the beginning of a war that went on until we got out of the country and went our separate ways.'

'What about that tattoo, the Tree of Life? Where does that fit in?' Lukas asked.

'The Derus boy had one on his forearm. Many people in the family, as well as other local men who believed him to be innocent, had one done after he disappeared. Even generations later, they still do.' Albert rolled up his sleeve to reveal a faded tattoo — the Tree of Life.

'But Filip?' Lina said.

'Oh yes, he knew the story. He was a staunch Derus, if a little misguided in his choice of friends.'

Lukas scratched his head. 'But what about the threats from the Latvians? The drug-related crimes? The dead men's families really do live in fear of reprisals. I've seen it.'

'They do, but not from the Latvians or the Baltic mafia. That's smoke and mirrors. It's the Backus family they are terrified of. About a year ago, they found us — well, found the community that supported the Derus family.'

Lukas saw that Albert's hands were shaking.

'There's a rumour that there's a young Backus leading them now, who's clever and ruthless. He's used the situation with the drugs and the Latvians as a cover, in order to finish what his predecessors started. They say he has a list of names, and he will only consider the war to be over when the last name is crossed off.'

'What's his name, Uncle Albert?' Lina asked urgently.

'I don't know, and that's the truth. I don't think anyone does.' All at once, the old man looked his age.

'Are you on that list, Albert? Are you in danger?' Lukas asked.

'I don't think so. The Grim Reaper will dispose of me before they do. I think he is taking out the younger ones, the rebels, anyone who dares stand in his way.'

Lukas felt a stab of guilt and fear. If someone had seen him and Lina come to the house, Albert was in danger. They were dealing with something far bigger than he'd imagined. This was no mindless turf war over drugs and guns. This was assassination.

'Is there a back way out of here, Albert?' he asked.

'Only over the fence and into the neighbour's garden,' Albert said.

'That'll do.' He took Lina's hand. 'We must go. We have to get in touch with Bryn Owen.'

'Ring him.'

'Lina, we need to be out of here right now, for Uncle Albert's sake. Come on.'

Albert opened the back door and they stood for a moment, looking out into the garden. Twilight had fallen and the shadows had a menacing air.

'Lock the doors and windows, Albert. Keep yourself safe,' Lukas whispered.

The old man gripped his arm. 'It's not me you have to worry about. You just keep that girl from harm, understand?'

He did. Finally, he really did understand.

* * *

Bryn got the call at ten thirty that night. Lina and Lukas were safe — for the time being.

On enquiring at Lina's house, he had been told that she had received a phone call and had hurried out without saying where she was going. Remembering their own meeting, Bryn had asked at the theatre café, where they had indeed been seen. After that, he had no idea where to look, so he was very relieved to hear Lukas's voice.

'I've cleared it with Jim, and you can go back to the shelter. He's on nights tonight and he'll let you in.'

'Don't think I dare, Bryn. Maybe I'm being paranoid, but we saw some scary blokes earlier, cruising round in a car, real slow. We hid, but I'm not trying to make it back to Saltern tonight.'

'Where are you, Lukas?'

'On a bench down on the river walk, close to where the river taxi moors up. We're well out of sight.'

'I'll come and get you both and take you back to Jim's place.'

'Would you? That'd be great. First, just in case anything goes wrong, let me tell you what we know.'

Bryn wrote it down. So they had got it wrong, been led up yet another blind alley. It was nothing to do with a war between Lithuanians and Latvians at all. It was an honour killing.

* * *

It was midnight by the time Bryn got home, and he suddenly realised that he had let Jules down yet again. He had promised to take her out to dinner, but like so often before, their date had never happened. He couldn't help feeling guilty, although he'd made it clear how things stood with his job. He'd make it up to her, as soon as he discovered who this vengeful Backus was.

Jim had been good enough to find Lina a bed for the night. Tomorrow they would work out some sort of plan. When Bryn found them he could see how scared they were. At least Lukas was aware how dangerous the situation was. No one had followed them back to Jim's place. He quickly showered, dried himself and climbed into bed. So much for a romantic dinner and an early night! Before settling down, he sent a text to Jules.

A few seconds later, his phone buzzed, and he saw a row of kisses. Forgiven. He smiled into the darkness. Maybe they should live together. It was a big step to take, but even so, he was considering suggesting it to her. He had an idea she was thinking along the same lines.

He just had to find Backus.

CHAPTER TWENTY-SIX

'Well, today has started with a bang. He's called off the wedding.' Matt had gone straight up to see David Redpath. 'I've just heard from Ross Cadman, who's really worried about him. He's put him on suicide watch.'

'I see,' David said slowly. 'That's either another bit of clever acting, or someone really is trying to destroy him.'

'We are pursuing the idea that Grace Repton is the pivotal factor here. Someone wants to stop her marrying Reader. This morning's news from Ross Cadman only serves to validate that supposition, sir.'

'It's a very real possibility, Matt. Take her life to pieces and examine every shred. If there's someone lurking in the shadows, find him.'

'We're already on it, sir. Jason and Kim are checking her background, and uniform are out talking to some of the people she used to work with when she was a night marshal on the streets. We're looking at this area, and Greenborough and Saltern are checking out their patches for us. As soon as a few answers start filtering through, we'll get her in.' Matt was sure they were on the right track at last. Someone couldn't bear to see a considerate and very beautiful woman wedded to a killer. 'The last thing I want to do is frighten Grace, or draw too much attention to our enquiries. I don't want to push Varsity Man into killing again.'

'From what I've seen in your reports, Grace Repton seems tough enough to withstand a lot.'

'I would've agreed, sir, but DC Kim Peters saw her last night, and she is concerned about her reaction to the news that Alex couldn't have been the killer. She said she went almost catatonic for a few moments. Then she got really agitated. She calmed down after that, and became herself again. Kim said it was really weird.'

David Redpath said nothing for a while. 'Okay, Matt, play it as you see fit. Just keep me notified all the way. Oh, and anything on the Filip Derus murder?'

Matt nodded. 'Young Bryn made an important discovery last night. Jack Fleet has been assigned to him this morning, and they are following a very interesting lead.' He told the super about Lukas and Lina Derus's visit to "Uncle Albert."

'Are they safe enough in Saltern, do you think?' David said. 'Our budget won't extend to protection unless this information is reliably corroborated. Even I can't get around that one.'

Matt shrugged. 'We have no idea how much this Backus family know about Lina and Lukas's efforts to get justice for Filip Derus and the other young men who wore the Tree of Life tattoo. They might not even react to his distraught sister creating waves, unless they find out about her sudden association with Lukas, then she could be in real danger. The odd thing is, we can find no trace of anyone in this area called Backus.'

'You've put out an attention drawn across all forces?'

'Yes, sir. Bryn has the pool detectives watching the incoming messages on that.'

'Good. Very good actually. If we are pretty sure they aren't involved in the tattoo murders, I think Operation

Saturn can safely go ahead.' He exhaled. 'Thank God! I cannot begin to think how much money and time has been spent getting everything in place for that.'

'One person worries me, sir. Lina's uncle, the old guy, Albert Matonis. He's key to the history of this ongoing war. In fact, he's the only key. Could we afford an officer to keep an eye on him for a while?'

'Give me his details, and I'll do what I can. I think uniform can probably spare one officer to keep him under surveillance — short term.'

Matt felt somewhat relieved. One less thing to worry about.

'Before you go, Matt, how is Liz? I heard she called in, but I missed her.'

How was she? Until last night, he hadn't realised just how anxious she had been about her recovery. After Sam left, she'd told him that she hadn't wanted to worry him but she had been experiencing episodes of confusion. Appalled that he hadn't noticed, he recalled the broken glass in the sink, and her unusual reluctance to talk about herself of late.

'She's not finding it easy, David. But Sam Page is going to spend some time with her, and she's already looking better after one short conversation.'

'It can't be easy for her, can it? Your life turned around in an instant. I'm not sure how I'd cope with that, or indeed, if I would at all.'

'She's been amazing, honestly. Sam says she's just expecting too much of herself. Given the drugs that monster injected her with, recovery usually takes a great deal longer. All things considered, she is quite a miracle. Oh, and she had a text last night. Gary has a couple of days leave soon, so that will cheer her up no end.'

'Ah, Lieutenant Colonel Gary Haynes. A very nice man, and brave too. He's still in Iraq?'

'No idea. He's in an undisclosed location, so he tells us.'

David smiled. 'And you and Liz are both happy?'

'Never more so,' Matt said.

'Then tie up this case and walk off into the sunset with your lady.'

'I have every intention of doing just that, David.' Matt stood up. 'So, I guess I'd better buckle down.'

Back in his office, he saw that he'd missed a call from forensics. He phoned Rory.

'Good news! Well, depending on who you are and what you want to hear, I suppose.'

'Get to the point, Rory.'

Rory sighed. 'Impatient as always. Well, you'll no doubt be thrilled to hear that I have a fingerprint match for you, and I can confirm that our dead man is Alex Campbell.'

'I am seriously impressed! You'd said they might not be viable.'

'We have a new technique called thanatopractical processing. I took fluid from other parts of his remains and used it to restore firmness and volume to the fingertips. They plumped up nicely, and I got a pretty perfect print.'

'But where did you get any prints to compare them with? He wasn't on our database.'

'From his sister, Fiona, number provided by dear Jason, see, you are not the only one around here to think like a detective! She said Alex had visited her regarding their father's death. If you remember, he had OCD, and his sister recalled him rearranging some glass ornaments into straight lines. One of your uniformed officers kindly retrieved them for me, and hey presto! A beautiful print.'

'Genius!'

'You flatter me, but I have to concur. As you say, pure genius! Ta-ta for now.'

Matt called Jason and Kim to his office. 'First off, I've had a message from Rory and he's positively identified the body as Alex. Now we know for sure that he wasn't our killer, so I'd like your opinions, please. If you were Varsity Man, assuming you were aware that we'd found Alex's body, what would be your next move?'

Silence.

Kim stared at her feet. Then she looked up. 'Kill again, so as to really push Reader over the edge.'

Jason frowned. 'Maybe. But I'm thinking he might make a move on Grace Repton. If I was besotted with her, I'd try to become her best friend at this time of crisis, a shoulder to cry on.'

Kim nodded. 'That's a fair point.' She looked at Matt. 'Maybe we should make her aware of that possibility? Ask her to keep her eyes open for anyone trying to get close.'

'Do it, Kim,' Matt said. 'And get her to give you a list of people of Varsity Man's approximate height and build that she worked closely with in any of her jobs, including the prison visiting. Don't ring her, and don't frighten her. Go see her face to face.'

She hurried back to her desk to get her bag. Jason said, 'I've had another idea. What if marriage was never on the cards? What if he's just used Grace, manipulated her into believing he was a reformed character so as to make himself seem more believable?'

'And Varsity Man is his real disciple, carrying on the master's work?' added Matt.

'Controlled by Reader. It's a thought, isn't it?' Jason said.

'A very scary one. Could he really have deceived the prison governor, Grace, Sam, Kim, and the whole psych team at the Harbour Unit?'

'Improbable, I know, but not beyond the realm of possibility. Think of Harold Shipman. If he really was responsible for the more than five hundred killings that he "confessed" to in prison, then he deceived rather more people than Reader has,' Jason said.

'We need to keep all our doors open,' Matt said. 'Until we get some evidence to tell us where we're going, I'm not dismissing a thing.'

Jason went back to chasing up Grace's past.

Matt went over to Bryn's desk. He told him the super was trying to arrange someone to keep an eye on Albert. Bryn was as relieved as he had been. 'Lukas is still working on tracking down the Backus family and where they might have gone after they left Lithuania. I could do with having him in here with me. He's pretty restricted by just having Google and social media to work with, and his language skills and local knowledge are invaluable.'

'I can put in a request for a translator, Bryn, but it won't be Lukas. It might be safer for him.'

'It's just that his background knowledge is a real help. A stranger wouldn't know which piece of info was valuable.'

Bryn was right. 'What about Lina?' Matt said. 'Is she on the run too?'

'She wants to go home, but I know damn well she'll be straight back out there, ferreting around. And that could be fatal.'

'Can Jim put her up for a while?' Matt asked.

'He says yes, as long as she chips in and helps around the place. But she has none of her things with her, and I can't go and collect them. I gave her some money for toiletries and the like, but that won't last for long.'

'I'll cover that. Don't you be out of pocket.' Matt took a twenty pound note from his wallet and handed it to Bryn. 'We need to work out a proper solution, and soon. As you said, they'll get fed up with being cooped up, and next thing they'll be off again, causing heaven knows what trouble for us.'

'I'm open to suggestions, sir,' Bryn said.

'I'll think on it.'

* * *

Once again, Kim parked outside the neat bungalow. 'Nirvana,' she muttered, looking at the sign at the gate. She shook her head.

This time Grace seemed very much in control. 'I have ten minutes, DC Peters. I really need to go out.'

'This won't take long,' Kim said, 'but I need your help.'

'Of course. Come in. I have to collect some things for Jeremy. I have an appointment with the tailor in town to discuss his suit. Men! They either couldn't care less, anything will do, or they're too picky. You can guess which one Jeremy is.'

It wasn't her place to tell Grace that Reader had called the wedding off, but nevertheless Kim felt awkward. It was sad that the bride to be was the last to know. It was like being abandoned at the church door. She swiftly moved on. 'Grace, we've had confirmation that the murdered man was Alex Campbell. Now we have to look elsewhere for our killer. We're concerned that someone from your past might be trying to destroy your relationship.' Kim tried to avoid using the word *wedding*. 'This person might try to befriend you in some way, get close to you.'

Grace laughed. 'Fat chance of that! I love Jeremy. And it's been a long time since anyone tried to come on to me.'

'Nevertheless . . .' Kim produced the CCTV image of Varsity Man. 'If you know anyone who looks like this, especially someone who's being friendly, or over-friendly, you will tell us, won't you? Maybe someone in your past, especially when you were a prison visitor? It's important, Grace.'

'But that man looks so much younger than me. It's hardly feasible, is it?'

'It's a poor quality shot, and men do get crushes on many different types of woman. I worked in vice, I should know,' Kim said.

'As soon as I get back, I'll think about it, I promise.' Grace sighed. 'It could be someone with a grudge against

Jeremy, you know. He'd be the first to admit he did some terrible things. Maybe someone can't let it go.'

Would you, if your daughter or wife had been brutally murdered? Kim bit back the retort. 'Whatever the motive is, we need to find this man.' She pointed to the photo. 'He's wearing Alex's clothes. He stole them after he killed him. He's very dangerous, and we need to get him behind bars as quickly as possible.'

'I'll try my best for you, Detective, although no one springs to mind.' Grace held the door open. 'And I'll certainly contact you if anyone starts chatting me up.'

'I'm deadly serious, Grace. I don't want to scare you, but we're concerned that it's you that this is all about, not Jeremy at all.'

Grace smiled sadly. 'You're wrong. Someone wants to make my poor Jeremy pay, and go on paying until he can't take it anymore. But I'll be there for him. I'll see him through this.' Kim thanked her and returned to her car, bemused again. That woman was more changeable than the bloody weather!

* * *

Matt was starting to feel the heat. Maybe they were on the right track in focusing on Grace, but in truth, they were groping in the dark. They had nothing concrete — actually nothing at all — by way of evidence. Bryn Owen was making more headway with his complicated investigation, and he was flying solo.

He looked out of his office window. Hunched over his computer, Jason was scanning through screen after screen of information. Kim sat staring at her notebook, gnawing on her bottom lip. The pool detectives were either on the phone or scrolling though data. Behind them loomed a dark, malevolent figure in a varsity hoodie, laughing at them.

'Who are you?' Matt whispered.

He stared at the busy CID room, suddenly visited by terrible memories of his last case. He thought back over his career. An early case had sent him scurrying off to a remote Greek island to recover, where peace, quiet and good advice had given him direction and put him back on track. Then, approaching retirement, he had taken on the Goddard case. That investigation almost broke him. It did break Liz, and now she wasn't here to support or advise him. He felt lost and lonely.

'Boss? Are you alright?' Jason said.

Jason and Kim stood in the office doorway. 'Of course. Just trying to fathom out our next move, and not having much success.'

'Kim has something that might help with that, sir.' Jason's eyes were bright with excitement. 'You need to hear this.'

Matt gestured for them to come in. 'Sit. Talk to me.'

Kim took a breath. 'Grace Repton has a son, sir! His name is Richard. He's somewhat elusive, but Jason's chasing him up. From comments I found on social media, it seems they're estranged. The posts refer to him as being rather an odd kid, but I've only just scratched the surface so far.'

'She never mentioned him, did she?' murmured Matt.

'No, she certainly didn't. We need to find out why, and whether there really is a rift,' Jason said.

'Probably his mother's choice of company,' added Kim. 'Murderers and Cat A prisoners aren't everyone's idea of a great stepfather.'

Family disputes could be toxic, even deadly. Matt thought of Bryn's case. 'Is he roughly the right age to be Varsity Man?'

'Twenty-five, sir. Quite possible.'

'A vengeful son,' Matt said thoughtfully. 'Unable to reason with his mother, so determines to stop the wedding at all costs. Hell, if he's mentally disturbed, far lesser things than that have led to murder. And Grace could have inadvertently led him to Reuben Grimes *and* Alex Campbell. Oh, shit!'

'There's more, boss.' Kim took out her notebook. 'When I saw her today, she rang all sorts of alarm bells. She was saying one thing but her body language was saying something very different. And she was a far cry from the woman I saw last night.' She stared at her book. 'She was adamant that we are wrong about her being involved, that it's all down to someone from Jeremy's past out to destroy him. She's going to see him through it she says. She was on her way out to order his wedding suit.'

'So, he hasn't told her yet? About the wedding being cancelled?' Matt frowned. 'Or is she in denial?'

'I'm asking myself the same question, sir. Frankly she confused me, but there was definitely something going on inside her head that she wasn't sharing with me. She couldn't wait to get away.'

'We need to go and talk to her again, don't we?' Jason said. 'When was she getting back, Kim?'

'She said she had an appointment with the tailor, but no more than that.'

'There's only one men's outfitters in Fenfleet, and that's Rutherford's on the corner of Barley Street, just along from Iceland.' Jason liked his suits tailor-made. 'They do wedding outfits.'

'Kim? Ring them. Ask what time Grace's appointment was, and also if she'd mentioned going on anywhere else. Do we have a mobile number for her?' Matt was gradually getting back into gear.

'She only gave us a home number, sir.'

'Damn! Still, track her down, then both of you pay her another visit. Tell her from me there's going to be no more secrets or omissions. Lives could depend on her being open with us.'

'Will do, boss.'

Matt stared after them as they hurried out. Then he picked up the phone and rang Ross Cadman.

'I know this will sound a bit odd, Ross but, strictly between you and me, did you know Grace Repton had a son?'

'A son? Really? No, never, and I'm pretty sure Jeremy doesn't know either. Are you sure?'

'Yes. My guys have just checked it out.'

'That's odd, because when we were arranging the wedding, she distinctly said that she had no close relatives. Now I'd call a son pretty close, wouldn't you?' Ross Cadman sounded genuinely surprised.

'And the wedding is still off, I presume?' Matt said.

'Jeremy hasn't spoken to a soul all day. He hasn't eaten, and he won't get off his bed.'

'I don't know if you are aware of it, but he hasn't told Grace about his decision,' said Matt grimly. 'Apparently, she's out ordering his wedding suit right now.'

'Oh, damn it! He told me he'd tell her immediately. He can't leave her believing it's all going ahead. That's not fair.' Cadman gave an impatient sigh. 'I'll go and see him.'

'Maybe he's having second thoughts about his decision?'

'No, Matt, you didn't see him. He's determined to cancel. In fact, I'd say he's just a few steps from the edge of the parapet.'

'Then for heaven's sake, don't mention this son,' Matt exclaimed. 'That could really push him over.'

'No way. That's strictly between us.'

'Keep me up to speed with his condition, will you, Ross?'

Cadman said he would. As Matt hung up, he saw Jason hurrying towards him.

'Sir, I've just spoken to the men's outfitter. Grace never arrived for her appointment.'

'Get round to her home, Jason. Maybe she's found out about Reader pulling the plug on their wedding.'

'Or maybe—'

Matt cut him off. He didn't want to hear any more suppositions. 'Just go! And take Kim.'

CHAPTER TWENTY-SEVEN

In a small hamlet just outside Fenfleet, the man was clearing up. He did this meticulously, following his checklist to the letter. It was why he had remained on top of his game. He checked his equipment for the third time, then his watch, looking around the spacious hallway. All in order. He gathered up his bag and let himself out.

He strode out into the warm afternoon air with a sigh of satisfaction. Perfectly executed, everything according to plan. This type of work called for a cool head and almost military timing, whereas his previous jobs had been rough and sometimes opportunist. This was more to his taste, it called for more finesse. He whistled quietly as he made his way back to where he had concealed his vehicle. He was moving on.

* * *

Soon after Jason and Kim left, two uniformed officers entered the CID room and made their way to Matt's office.

He knew that look, he had seen it so many times before. He was about to be asked to attend something very unpleasant.

'Blacktoft Village, sir. Carrington Lodge. The owner returned home to find his daughter murdered. Will you attend, please, DCI Ballard? The duty sergeant says it looks like your copycat.'

Matt's mouth went dry. 'Give me everything you have so far, and I'll get over there.'

One of the constables handed Matt a brief memo. 'Address and name of the owner and the daughter, sir. The crime scene has been established and secured, sir, and forensics have been notified.'

Matt looked around the room. Only Bryn was left, and he didn't want to go to Blacktoft Village alone. 'Bryn! With me, please.'

Was he up to this? He'd been praying that they would get a breakthrough before another innocent victim lost her life, but clearly whoever was up there had been busy elsewhere.

'Are your two Lithuanian PIs still safely tucked away in Saltern?' he asked Bryn.

Bryn nodded. 'I heard from them around half an hour ago, sir. Lukas is still digging around on my laptop, and Lina is helping Jim with something. They say they were scared shitless last night, so I reckon they'll stick it out a bit longer.'

'Good. That just leaves this.'

* * *

The house was fairly modern, set in a generous plot of well-maintained garden. It said money.

'Nice,' said Bryn.

'Very nice. Pity about the blue lights, all the uniforms and those emergency service vehicles.' Matt could feel the sweat gathering. He was dreading walking into Carrington Lodge.

In the open porch, a pile of disposable hooded coveralls with masks, latex gloves and boot covers awaited them. They suited up, and the officer guarding the door logged their time of arrival.

'Where is she, Constable?' asked Matt, hoping his voice was steady.

'Right here, sir, in the hall. Er, I know you're the SIO, sir, but forensics haven't arrived yet . . .'

'I know, Constable. We're only observing. We'll touch nothing.'

Matt took a deep breath. At least the mask gave him a sense of anonymity, some distance from what he was about to see.

They went in.

He didn't see her at first. Then he looked towards the stairs.

He felt Bryn's hand grip his arm. 'Oh, my God! She looks exactly like . . .'

Gemma Goddard, all over again. The short, blonde hair, elfin features, eyes that changed from pale blue to slate grey as the light altered. The slender build. Bryn let go of his arm. 'Sorry, boss. Sorry, I, I just . . .'

'It's alright.' Matt didn't know how he found the breath to answer. 'Let's just remember that lots of young women have those looks. This is Penny Carrington, daughter of Henry Carrington, who's sitting in the back of the ambulance outside.'

'Yes, sir,' Bryn whispered.

'Do you want to go out for a moment?'

'No, sir. I'd have to come back in then, wouldn't I? I'm okay now, really.'

For what seemed an age, neither man spoke. Then Matt dragged himself back to the present. 'Same MO by the look of it, but a simpler method of allowing the blood to drain.'

The stairs to the first floor didn't run straight up. They ended in a small landing area, then turned before they reached the top. They were covered in a rich, thick-piled carpet that was now drenched with the young woman's blood.

Penny Carrington lay on the staircase, on her back, feet pointing downwards. Her arms had been secured to the decorative wooden newel posts on the small landing halfway up. It looked like some form of crucifixion.

'The incisions are in the same place,' Bryn said, 'but this is a major departure from Reader's methods.' He pointed to a large heart, drawn in blood, high on the landing wall above the body.

Matt hadn't even looked that far. He was still transfixed by the sight of the girl that so closely resembled Gemma Goddard.

He raised his eyes. Yes, this was different. Another kind of message was being sent.

Matt wanted out, but it seemed wrong to leave her alone.

'Bryn? Go and see if we have an ETA for forensics, would you?'

He nodded. 'Are you okay, sir? Considering the—'

Matt cut him off. 'I'm fine, son. It's just . . . Someone should take care of this poor kid as soon as possible. Go check on Rory, and you'd better ring Jason too. I'll stay here.'

After Bryn had left, Matt wiped a tear from the corner of his eye. He'd had enough of death, especially deaths like this one. It felt personal somehow. The shock of seeing her had reopened half-closed wounds. He was only grateful that Liz hadn't been here to see this girl's body. Her face.

* * *

At around four, Superintendent David Redpath arrived. Matt and Bryn had been at the scene for two hours and had done just about all they could. The most harrowing part had been talking to the father, Henry Carrington. It transpired that he was a single parent, and although Penny was in her early twenties, they had been very close since her mother left them some five years previously. Penny had been contemplating going back to university, and Henry was about to put the house on the market. It was too big to live in alone, and now he would be alone always.

Matt could do nothing to comfort him but promise to get the bastard who had killed his precious daughter. He handed him over to a victim support officer and left, emotionally drained.

'Are you holding up, my friend?' David asked him.

'By the skin of my teeth, David, but I'm seeing this through if it fucking kills me.'

'I won't let it go that far. I can get you extra help. DI Nikki Galena in Greenborough has pledged her team's support if you need it. You only have to ask.'

'Thank you, I appreciate it. Let's just sort this mess out, and get some facts from forensics. Rory said he'll give us an update as soon as he can.'

'He thinks it could take a long while to process all the evidence from the scene,' David said. 'The kid had lots of friends, who often visited, and the father has business colleagues and friends around all the time. Our SOCOs won't be in and out like they are in the movies, that's for sure.'

Matt nodded. He'd known crime scenes with high traffic areas take a week. It was painstaking work, sifting the detritus to find just a speck of evidence.

'Have you had any news about Grace Repton?' David asked.

'Jason rang me a few minutes ago. They haven't tracked her down yet. We're starting to get more than a little concerned about her.'

'Specifically, what are your fears?'

'Initially, I was scared that Jeremy had told her he was cancelling their wedding and she had taken it really badly. Now I'm thinking more sinister things.'

'Like?'

'If the son is the one behind all this, he won't know that his plan has succeeded and Jeremy has thrown in the towel. He might have abducted his mother to stop her going through with it. I'm wondering if that's why Grace was in such a hurry to get away from Kim, *and* why she missed the tailor's appointment.' Matt looked at his watch. 'We need a lot more info on this Richard. So far we know next to nothing. The moment I get back to base, I'll find out where we are.'

David looked towards the door of the big house. 'Rory is coming out.'

Rory came towards them, removing his mask and hood. Matt didn't like the look on his face.

'Matt. David.' Rory said. Even his voice had lost its normal light-hearted tone.

He held up an evidence bag. Through the clear plastic, Matt saw a white envelope with writing on it.

'I'm not sure what this means, but we found it tucked beneath our murdered girl's body.' Rory looked at him steadily. 'It has your name on it, Matt.'

'*My* name?' Matt replied.

David Redpath took a pair of latex gloves from his pocket. 'Rory? I need to open it, okay?'

Rory handed over the envelope. It was evidence, but they had to know what the letter said. 'Use this.' Rory took out a scalpel. 'Slit it along the top, so as not to disturb any DNA or tissue samples that might be on the adhesive seal.'

Very carefully, David slid out a single sheet of folded paper. He put the envelope back into the evidence bag and unfolded the note. He looked at it, and then held it out for Matt to see.

It read: *Because you haven't suffered enough.*

Matt stared at it, uncomprehending. No one spoke.

Rory put back the note and sealed the evidence bag. He coughed. 'She hasn't been dead for long. She's still in the rigid stage of rigor mortis, but this heat has speeded up the process. I'm thinking it was rapid onset rigor, so my best guess for you would be that she's been dead for around four hours.' Matt had never seen him so serious. 'It's the same killer, as I'm sure you are aware. The skin heart trophy was taken from her upper arm, but this time little was done to cover the wound. And no doubt you saw the wall art. That is certainly a new innovation. It's a real statement piece this time.' He frowned. 'Although I have no idea what it's telling us. That he loves his work, maybe?'

A hint of the old Rory. Oddly, the humour made Matt feel easier.

'Who on earth would think I haven't suffered enough?' he mused, trying to keep a tremor from his voice.

'A lunatic? Someone from your past?' Rory said.

'But why?'

'You know there's no answer to that just yet.' David Redpath was looking at him, his eyes full of concern. 'So don't even try to find one. Now will you accept help from outside?'

'No, sir. Let's do as I originally planned. Wait for Rory's post-mortem report, collate everything we have, and find Grace Repton. If I can't cope, I'll tell you.' With every word he spoke, Matt regained strength. 'I'd never jeopardise an investigation out of sheer bloody mindedness, but I need to put this one to bed myself before I bow out. I really do.'

'A few more days, then we'll reconsider.'

'I do have one little gem that might shed a ray of light on your darkness, dear hearts.' Rory gave him a knowing grin. 'Mr Carrington, owner of this rather splendid house, was about to install some rather sophisticated home security cameras. Sadly, as I said, only 'about to,' and his old system had already been deactivated. Disaster, I hear you say! But no, actually. I suggest you get your boffins to take a look at a couple of nifty little ones concealed in the garden, close to the road. They are on a separate system to the house cameras, are pretty well undetectable, and dead bloody clever. I'd bet a month's supply of my gorgeous and horrendously expensive French moisturiser that the killer never noticed them.'

'Now that's the kind of news I *can* cope with.' Matt thanked Rory, then turned to David. 'I'm going back to the station. There's a lot to do, and I'm of very little use here. If that's okay?'

'Of course. Uniform have everything under control here. But, Matt? Every step of the way, understand? I want to know exactly what's going on.'

'Yes, sir. Absolutely.' Matt called to Bryn, and they made their way back to the vehicle. As they went, he told Bryn about the envelope.

Bryn said quietly, 'So it's aimed at you? Because those girls look so similar to her, could there be a connection to the Gemma Goddard case?'

Matt had to face the question, he had no choice. 'But that case was closed. No loose ends, no unanswered questions. Nothing was left in the air.' He unlocked the car and they got in. 'I just can't see how there could be a connection, can you?'

They drove back, both deep in thought. Neither could find any answers.

* * *

The CID room, usually emptying as the day shift finished, was still a hive of activity. Grace was still unaccounted for and fears were mounting. Matt was adding a new name and photo to the whiteboard when he heard his office phone ringing.

He hurried in and picked it up. 'DCI Ballard.'

'Matt, it's Ross Cadman. Just an update on Jeremy Reader. He's much improved now. The quack gave him something to relax him, and he's finally more himself.' There was a short pause. 'Thing is, he can't get hold of Grace. She's not picking up. She's not with you, is she?'

Matt groaned. 'I wish she was, Ross.' He explained everything that had happened since they last spoke.

'Jesus! That is going to set the cat among the pigeons again! Apart from the alarming fact that Grace might be in danger, Jem can't possibly cope with another bombshell. What the hell do I tell him?'

'Does Grace have a mobile phone?'

'Yes. Jem rings her on it. They gave me the number for emergencies. Haven't you got it?'

'No, she only ever gave us her landline, but I'd appreciate that mobile number, please.' Matt wrote it down. 'As for Jem, I suggest you buy yourself some time and tell him we have her here, say there's been a development and she's helping us. I'll ring you the moment I have anything concrete.'

'Best I can do, I suppose.' Ross Cadman sounded exasperated. 'You'd never believe that I have a whole prison full of problem-ridden men, but just one single man occupies a good two-thirds of my time. Look, I hope you find her, Matt, and I hope she's alright. She's a good woman. I know it's an odd thing to say, but I think she and Jem make a great couple. It could have been one story from HMP Gately that had a happy ending. You know what I mean — a real feelgood, tearjerker. Bad boy makes good.' He gave a grunt. 'But it's turning into a bloody horror story.'

'I have to get on, Ross, but I'll be in touch, and try to keep Jeremy calm. She might, just might, have buggered off for the day and forgotten to charge her phone.'

Another grunt. 'Excuse the analogy, but pigs might fly!'

Matt hung up, hurried back to the CID room and gave Grace's mobile number to Kim. He then rang Liz, and told her as much as he dared without upsetting her. He was alright, he said, but would no doubt be very late. Just hearing her voice made him feel better. He had to keep on top of everything for her sake. More than anything now, he wanted to be done with this job forever. He'd served the force well, given a lot more than some. It was his time now. His and Liz's.

'Sir!' Bryn called out. 'We've got him on screen. The prof was right. He strolled right past two of the garden security cameras!'

Matt dashed out and stared at Bryn's computer screen.

'Varsity Man,' he breathed. 'Look, the guy filmed near Reuben Grimes's home. The bag he was carrying, his build, the walk, all match up, but he's ditched the jacket.'

'Doesn't need to try to look like Alex anymore, does he?' said Jason.

'And this time we have a partial face shot! This is him, guys, our copycat killer!' Matt spun around. 'Jason, it's not a perfect image, but see if we can get it cleaned up and run a check to see if he's on our files. Bryn, get it onto the PNC, the local systems, the press, the media, anywhere you can think of. I want every police officer in this country to see that photograph.'

'So, is he Richard? Grace's son?' asked Kim, peering at the figure on the screen.

'He could be, but let's not jump to conclusions. Let's ID him, and find him.' He smiled at Kim. 'Then you can ask him, can't you?'

Kim grimaced. 'Just gimme the chance. But, sir, how did someone so calculated not see those surveillance cameras? These images are pretty clear even if they are not full face.'

'I think he went in fully expecting to find a system in operation,' said Jason. 'Don't forget, if he had already chatted Penny up like the other women, and she was expecting him, she would have let him in herself. I can just see him admiring the house, asking if she was nervous there on her own, and giving her the old "Sweetheart, I worry about you" spiel.'

'Yes, and poor unsuspecting Penny would have said, "Don't worry, Daddy is fitting smart security soon."' Kim raised her eyebrows. 'He must have thought all his Christmases had come at once.'

'And looked no further.' Jason stared, unblinking, at the image. 'Look at him! Cocky bastard.'

'Well, he's made his first big mistake,' added Matt. 'Hopefully, a fatal one.'

* * *

Bryn set about his tasks, still shaken by the uncanny resemblance between Penny Carrington and Gemma Goddard. And by the fact that the killer had sent a direct and personal message to Matt Ballard. The boss was playing it down, but it must have hit him hard. The whole Goddard affair had been aimed at Matt, so this message must have come like a bolt from the blue. No fucking wonder he wanted to retire.

Bryn rubbed at his temples. No matter what the boss said, there had to be a connection between the old case and the present one. Bryn wanted to talk this through with someone, but who? Both the DCI and the DI had been too deeply involved with Gemma Goddard to be impartial.

'Evening, everyone. Looks like you're ready to burn the midnight oil.'

Laura Archer and Sam Page strolled in.

'I'm finished for the day, but we wondered if we can help here in any way?' asked Laura.

Bryn grinned. Here were the perfect counsellors. While Sam went to talk to Matt, he asked Laura if she had a moment.

'If you buy me a coffee. I've just given a lecture at Greenborough University, and I'm gasping.'

At the drinks machine, Bryn told her what had happened, and his fears that Matt wasn't taking the connection seriously.

Laura stirred her coffee. 'I think he's fully aware of it. He just isn't ready to face it. He's going to want to keep his mind strictly on the known facts and set aside any conjecture.' She leaned against the wall. 'If you're certain that there is a link, it could be up to you to try to find it.'

'I'm up to my neck, Laura. I have the Filip Derus murder to try to keep on top of, and now this. I'm stretched to capacity.'

Laura smiled at him. 'Oh dear. But you know this will bug you to distraction if you ignore it.'

'Tell me about it. I keep thinking that there's some small thing from the old case that I should remember. Something that someone said? Or did? Oh, I don't know!'

'My advice would be to try and forget it. Just concentrate on what you're doing now. It will come to you, but not if you keep struggling to remember.' Laura smiled. 'Easier said than done, I know. But concentrate on your other work, and it will surface. I promise.'

'I hope so, because it's driving me nuts.'

CHAPTER TWENTY-EIGHT

At seven thirty, Kim's mobile rang. She recognised the voice immediately. 'Grace! Where on earth are you? Are you alright?'

Behind Kim, the office fell silent. She turned the phone on to speaker.

'Sorry? Is there a problem?' Grace sounded surprised.

Kim squeezed her eyes shut. How should she put it? 'We were worried about you, Grace. You never turned up at the tailors, and your phone was off when we tried to talk to you.'

'Oh, I'm so sorry! I ran into an old friend, someone I used to do some voluntary work with. We had one or two gin and tonics, then went for a meal to soak up the alcohol. I . . . left my phone in the car.'

'I see. Well, are you at home now? We do need to speak to you.'

'No, uh, look, is it really important?'

'Yes, Grace, it is, and it's not something we can really discuss over the phone.'

'Oh dear, this is difficult. You see, I'm on my friend's phone, and I've left my car in town rather than get picked up for drink driving. I'll come in first thing tomorrow, I promise.'

'Grace! This is urgent. Where are you? We'll come to you.' Kim was both annoyed with Grace and worried about this rather odd conversation. Who was this friend?

'Is Jeremy alright? Is this about him?' Grace said.

'Not directly, but we really do need to talk.'

'Tomorrow. Nine thirty. I'll be there.' There was a pause, and Kim thought she was going to hang up. Then Grace said, 'You asked me to think about men who looked like that photo. There is only one man that I can think of, and it was my friend who reminded me about him. His name is John Baker. I met him when I was a night marshal in Greenborough. He did try it on with me, Detective, and to be honest, he wasn't easy to put off. I had to get tough with him in the end.'

'Is he still in this area?' asked Kim.

'Oh yes. In fact I saw him the other day, right here in Fenfleet. Luckily I spotted him first and avoided him.'

'Do you have any more details about him?'

'Sorry, no, except he lives in the town. I really do have to go now. I'll see you in the morning. Goodnight, Officer.'

Kim was left staring at her phone. 'Anyone any idea of what to make of that?' she asked the room at large.

'She certainly sidestepped telling you where she is, didn't she?' said Jason.

'That whole conversation didn't sound right to me at all,' Sam Page said.

'I agree.' Kim frowned. 'One minute it was vital she get to that tailor's appointment, then suddenly she just buggers off and gets sloshed with some old friend. Does that sound like Grace Repton? I don't think so.' She tried to call back. 'Switched off.'

'I'll try to trace the call, but I don't think she was on any friend's phone at all,' Bryn said slowly. 'I don't know what her game is, but I'll bet that phone wasn't connected to a network.' He picked up his phone and asked for a trace.

'She's with her son, isn't she?' said Jason. 'No one is supposed to know about him, so she's inventing some "old friend."'

'The worrying thing is, does she know he's the copycat killer?' Jack Swift added.'

'If we knew more about him, it would help,' grumbled Bryn. 'And do we follow up this John Baker that Grace has suddenly so conveniently remembered?'

'Can't afford not to.' Matt had appeared in the room. 'Run a check now.' He turned to Laura and Sam. 'Did you pick up anything from that call that would lead you to think she was being held against her will and was being forced to say what she did?'

The two psychologists looked at each other.

'I'd say she wasn't alone when she made the call,' said Laura, 'and she was certainly lying, especially about going for drinks.'

'And about leaving her phone in the car,' added Sam. 'And what about the way she just casually mentioned Jeremy? We've seen her almost distraught about him, but he only got a desultory mention, didn't he? Something was well out of order there.'

'So was she being threatened?' Matt asked.

Laura shrugged. 'I couldn't say for sure, but it could be the case. She wasn't speaking easily. She ummed and ahhed a lot. And that's not a good sign. '

'In my opinion,' Sam said slowly, 'the entire purpose of that call was to give you the name of John Baker.'

'To what end, I wonder?' murmured Matt.

'I've got three John Bakers in this area,' Bryn called out. 'All addresses in and around town.' His printer whirred into life. 'And we can't trace the call from Grace to Kim's phone. As we thought, unregistered sim, no way to triangulate.'

'Shall I get a crew together and go visiting, sir?' Jack Fleet asked.

'I think that's a good idea. We now have a picture of the killer. See if anyone fits the bill, and if he does . . .'

'He'll be in the slammer before you can blink, sir.' Swifty grinned, took the addresses from Bryn, and hurried out.

'Be careful!' Matt called after him. But Swifty had gone.

Matt began to pace the room. 'What are you thinking, sir?' Kim asked.

'Grace Repton. Tell me everything you actually know about her. Hard facts.'

Kim opened her notebook. 'Born Grace Repton, in Shoreditch, London. Married Clive Emery and moved to Greenborough. Shortly after their marriage, her husband was mugged and died from his wounds. She reverted to her maiden name. She had one son, Richard, and from the dates, she must have been pregnant when her husband was killed. Richard was registered under her married name of Emery. We are struggling to follow them while he was growing up. It seems she moved about a lot.' Kim nodded at the pool detectives. 'The lads are trying to find a medical history and where he went to school, but it isn't easy. Richard seems to have vanished from her life by the time she settled back in Greenborough. Finally, she moved here, to the house in Fenfleet. She was vetted when she applied to be an official prison visitor, and was cleared. She's done a lot of voluntary work here and in the neighbouring towns.' She looked up. 'And that's all we have.'

'And then she fell in love with the five times killer, Jeremy Reader.' Matt heaved a sigh. 'Hell, we need to find that son!'

'Holy shit! That's it!'

This sudden outburst from Bryn Owen made Kim jump.

'Sir! There *is* a connection between the copycat killer and the Gemma Goddard case. Gemma had some guy following her around. Not exactly a stalker, but it got bad enough for her to report it. His name was Richard Emery! Grace's son was obsessed with Gemma Goddard.'

'That explains the social media comments that he was a bit weird,' said Kim excitedly. 'He's an obsessive!'

'And if he can have an obsession over one thing, why not another? Like stopping his mother marrying a killer.' Jason looked really alive now, almost incandescent.

'That all makes sense,' said Matt slowly. 'But . . . the note with my name on. He blames me for what happened in the Gemma Goddard case. Hence, he thinks I haven't suffered enough.'

'And he's only copying Jeremy Reader's murders because of his mother's proposed marriage,' said Sam. 'Two birds with one stone.'

Kim tried to sort out all these separate pieces of information. Gradually she put the story together. A mentally unstable young man idolises a young woman. She is taken from him. He needs someone to blame. He decides to get back at one of the police officers. Then his mother says she is remarrying. Maybe he thinks he will finally have a proper father, but discovers the man is in prison for murder. Chaos ensues. Richard Emery goes into meltdown, and so begins a killing spree.

She looked up. Everyone seemed to have come up with the same answer. The only person who didn't seem satisfied was the boss. Had she missed something? The only thing that jarred with this seemingly perfect scenario was John Baker. Who was he? And why had Grace made sure that they would check him out? She voiced her concern.

'Because Grace wants him in the frame for the murders, not her son.' Laura Archer spoke softly. 'She delivered you a scapegoat, a decoy to put you off the scent.'

Kim had to agree, and she didn't like the conclusion this led her to. Grace knew her son was a killer, and she was trying to protect him.

That, or . . . What if Grace's "loving" son had taken her prisoner and had forced her to make that call? What would happen next?

CHAPTER TWENTY-NINE

Bryn phoned Lukas, wanting to make sure that he and Lina were still safely ensconced with Jim Cousins.

'You're a mind reader. I was just about to phone you.'

'Have you got something more for me?' Bryn asked, hearing the excitement in Lukas's voice.

'Yeah! Listen to this. When the Backus family arrived in this country, they worked in Cornwall, doing seasonal work there. They decided to settle here permanently and after a while, two of the younger men changed their name in order to fit in. That's why I was struggling to find Backus.'

'Ever thought about a career in CID? That's amazing, Lukas. So, what did they change it to?'

'Baker. Their surname is Baker. There are still some of them in Fenfleet.'

Bryn's jaw dropped. Baker? But hadn't Grace Repton just mentioned a Baker? It was a common enough name, but twice within an hour . . . could it just be coincidence?

'Are you still there, Bryn?' Lukas asked.

'Sure, sure. Listen, do you have any first names for these Bakers?'

'Sure do. Two brothers, called John and Markus. Oh, and they are descendants of the most vengeful side of the Backus family. The ones who haven't forgotten.'

'How on earth did you find this out?' Bryn said.

'Albert Matonis. He says these senseless deaths have to stop. He's spoken to some of the older members of the Derus family and convinced them it's time to speak out. He managed to get us a few contacts, and gave them to Lina. Now it's up to me to talk to them.'

'Do you know these two men?'

'Sorry, Bryn, we don't. Neither Lina nor I have heard of them before. Apparently they live just a few streets from the railway station, not in the Baltic Quarter. Albert says they think of themselves as English now, not migrants, and they both speak very good English.'

What were the addresses Swifty was going to? Wasn't one in Mallard Street? And Mallard Street was quite close to the railway . . . 'Shit! Lukas, mate, I'll get back to you.'

He ended the call. 'Sir! We need to contact Swifty! He could be walking into trouble.'

'He's expecting trouble, Bryn. He's looking for the copycat killer,' Matt said.

'There's a very real possibility that John Baker could be the man who killed Filip Derus, and maybe the others who died too. If it is him, he's a vicious assassin. Swifty and the others are only making enquiries about a bloke who used to fancy Grace Repton. Sir, you have to get hold of him!'

After a brief glance at Bryn's expression, Matt picked up the nearest phone and called Control, ordering the officers to take a cautious approach to the Mallard Street address.

As he replaced the phone, he turned to Bryn and said, 'Uniform are on to it. They'll keep us informed.' He paused. 'Just for a moment, let's suppose that Grace's son has nothing to do with it, could one man really be responsible for both sets of killings?'

Bryn was nonplussed, but pointed to Laura and Sam. 'They are the ones to ask that, sir.'

Laura took a breath, then said, 'In a way, the first deaths were also honour killings, weren't they? Whoever carried out the killings was avenging a wronged family member. It would depend if he believed that he was an instrument of justice.'

'I agree,' added Sam. 'If that is the case, then the answer is no. The man would not see himself as a murderer, as he is only carrying out a sentence.'

'The possibility of reverting to mindless killing would only arise if the man had a predisposition to murder,' Laura said.

'As in, he enjoyed what he did and wanted to take it further,' concluded Sam. 'So the answer to your question is that it's a possibility. We couldn't rule it out, in case the first killings gave him a taste for murder for its own sake.'

Looking unconvinced, Laura said, 'Even so, the odds are very much against it. People who kill usually have a particular method, and they stick to that. So, I can't see the slightest reason for the Derus killer to suddenly start copying someone else. It doesn't make sense. Kill again? Certainly, if it had become an addiction, but I would have thought he would develop his own MO, with a personal touch, not turn copycat. And why Jeremy Reader? The killer would've had to be closely connected to either Reader, Reuben Grimes or Alex Campbell in order to have discovered how the murders were committed. I can't see how any of these points fit together.'

Bryn couldn't either. But he couldn't stop thinking about Jack Fleet. What would happen when he knocked on the door of that house in Mallard Street?

* * *

PC Barney Woods and WPS Maggie Smithson were looking at the second address on Jack's list.

'Hope this one is more like John Baker than the last one we visited,' said Maggie. 'A bloke with his arm in plaster doesn't quite fit the bill for Mr Copycat.'

Both officers kept up their usual banter. It was what they did, their way of coping. Take the piss out of a bad situation, and it seems less threatening. It wasn't Jack's way, but he understood.

Barney chuckled. 'You can ring the bell on the next one, Mags. I've got a feeling in my water that this John Baker is the guy we're after. So, you can go first.'

'Chivalry is alive and well,' she retorted, 'but obviously not living in Fenfleet.'

'You lot wanted equality,' Barney said.

'I still wear a bra, thank you, and I like a bit of gallantry.' Maggie said. 'But I fully realise I won't find much of it in a partner like you.'

'Okay, kiddies, party's over. We are approaching Mallard Street. How shall we play this?' Jack slowed the car. 'And I mean it. What approach are you happy with?'

They got serious.

'If this guy is the one Grace Repton was talking about, I can't see him kicking off, can you?' said Barney. 'If he's our killer, he's a very cool, calculating customer. He won't be answering the door with a double-barrelled shotgun in his hand. Most likely he'll think he can talk his way out of it.'

'He'll deny everything,' added Maggie. 'He'll know we have no evidence, since it's just us. I'd play it down. How about you and I have a friendly word to establish his identity, Jack? Find out if he admits to knowing Grace. Barney, you hold back and observe in case things go pear shaped. If it does, you can call for backup.'

Jack drove slowly down Mallard Street, looking out for the house number. 'I'm okay with that. You, Barney?'

'Sure. I'll have your backs.'

Jack parked a couple of houses away, and they got out. For all their chat, they were a good crew to have at his side. They'd done this sort of thing a hundred times before, and it was never like the movies. Aware that Grace had probably offered them this guy as a red herring, Jack was alert, but not over-concerned about what they'd find.

The house was a semi-detached old-style property in a fairly quiet residential road. Jack noticed that it was well looked after, compared with some of the other houses along the street. It looked like a decent road to live in, but he hadn't expected to find it quite so immaculate. Most of the places they dragged felons out of were pretty rough.

Maggie rang the bell.

Jack waited by her side, listening for the sound of someone approaching the door.

There was definitely somebody inside. He could hear the sound of movement, but no one answered.

Maggie rang the bell again. She looked at Jack, her head slightly to one side. 'I thought I heard someone, didn't you?'

He nodded, and peered through the front window. He could see an open-plan lounge/dining room, and at far end, open French doors.

'He's heading out the back way!'

Maggie immediately called for Barney, then saw him running towards them, waving frantically.

'Don't approach him! Back off! We've got to wait for backup!' Barney panted. 'The bastard's suspected of the Derus killing too, and the other migrant deaths. He's dangerous.'

'He's just ahead of us. Look!' Jack ran towards the side entrance. 'I'm damned if I'm letting him get away!'

Maggie glanced at Barney, who nodded. They set off after Jack. At the end of a small garden, the back fence was around four feet high. Even old Swifty was over it in seconds.

Jack could see the retreating figure heading across a small area of waste ground towards a path that led to the railway station. Jack upped his speed. Despite his age, the name Swifty was still appropriate. He often went running along the fen lanes.

'Police!' he yelled out. 'John Baker! Stop right there!'

The man glanced back over his shoulder. There were three of them after him now. He slowed his pace.

'Hold it! Right now! Down on the ground! Good man. Now, down! Then we'll talk, okay?' Jack reached out to take hold of him, and just caught the glint of metal.

The next thing he knew, he was on the ground. It was as if someone had cut his legs from under him with a whip. Just above the knees, were two clean slices across his uniform trousers. Then the pain kicked in.

'He's got a knife!' he shouted. 'Maggie! Barney! Knife!'

Through a blur of pain and shock, he saw his two colleagues pause above him, and then they charged.

They hit the retreating figure like two wrecking balls. The knife flew from his hand and slithered across the weeds. Game over.

Lying in a pool of his own blood, Jack heard the sweet sound of handcuffs snapping shut.

* * *

Everyone at the station waited anxiously for news of their fellow officer. It would be a while before they heard about the extent of his injuries. Meanwhile, the super was on his way to the hospital. John Baker was securely locked away downstairs in the custody suite, where Matt doubted he'd be receiving much in the way of care and consideration.

The courage Maggie and Barney had shown in arresting a very dangerous suspect had been overshadowed by the wounding of the third officer. Swifty was a popular man.

'I've just had a call from Christopher Hedley, sir,' Kim said, 'the church warden from Holy Trinity. I rang him earlier to ask if his flock would keep an eye open for Grace Repton.'

'And?' asked Matt.

'Someone spotted her earlier today. She was with a man, close to the church. The woman waved, but Grace pretended she didn't see her.'

'So? Maybe she didn't.'

'Oh, she did. Grace is very well-known and popular with all the people she did voluntary work with. This particular woman was on her team, and they were good friends. She said that Grace seemed distracted. She wasn't sure, but she thought that she and the man were arguing.' Kim looked down at her scribbled notes. 'She said Grace looked straight at her and gave her the strangest look, either of anger or fear, and fear wasn't something she associated with Grace Repton.'

'Description?' Matt asked.

'Younger than Grace, medium height and build, and he was wearing dark clothing. Nothing more than that.'

'Could be anyone, three-quarters of the male population of Fenfleet. Or it could be John Baker.' Matt thought for a moment. 'But that wouldn't make sense. If he had taken Grace and forced her to make that phone call, he certainly wouldn't have got her to walk right by the church where everyone knew her.'

'Then it sounds very much as though she was with her son,' Kim said.

'You're right,' Matt said. 'Kim, would you work out a timeline for Grace's movements, as far as we know them?'

'Sure, boss. From yesterday?'

Matt nodded. 'Please. I'm just going to ring down and see if John Baker, or Backus, has been processed yet. I can't wait to sit across that table and question him, and, more importantly, see if he matches our image from the last crime scene CCTV.'

'The arresting officers said it certainly could be him, although they can't be certain as it's just a partial facial image. And if it is him, what a brilliant collar,' said Kim. 'If only Jack hadn't got hurt. Why on earth didn't he wait for backup?'

'Swifty isn't the kind of copper to stand by and watch a villain leg it without doing his best to stop him. And I doubt many of us would have done any different.'

'True.' Kim sighed. 'I just hope that bastard hasn't caused any serious damage to our Jack.'

After hearing what Maggie and Barney had said, Matt feared for Jack's life, but he didn't pass that on to Kim. He was dreading hearing what David Redpath had to say.

He went to his office and phoned downstairs. He was told the man had vomited and had insisted on seeing a doctor. That would hold things up for an hour at least. Mmm, thought Matt, he knows his way around a police cell. It was an old trick. Make yourself hoop up, then insist on medical attention. The clock ticked on while there was no way they could be interviewed.

Who did they have in the cells? The Filip Derus killer? Did they have the copycat as well? Even if he did resemble their CCTV mugshot, Matt didn't think so. He was in agreement with Laura Archer about that. Killers had particular ways of working. An arsonist didn't suddenly think, 'Oh, I reckon I'll give strangling a try today.' They stuck to their chosen methods. Besides, no one got that lucky. No. They may have their Lithuanian killer, but not Jeremy Reader's acolyte. But why had Grace Repton fingered Baker? How would she know a Lithuanian murderer? Common sense dictated that a ruthless killer bent on vengeance wouldn't be wasting his time coming on to some older woman. It didn't make sense.

Matt stuck his head out of his office door and called to Jason.

'What do you think, Jason?'

'I've been wondering if Grace knew who the Tree of Life Killer was, and was trying to draw our attention to him without actually coming out with it. She did mix with some pretty insalubrious characters, both in the prison and on the streets. Maybe she'd heard something.'

'But why not simply come to us?'

'I think she used him to draw our attention away from her son, who she believes, or knows, is the copycat.'

'Alternatively,' Matt said, 'the son is holding her against her will and told her to find him a fall guy.'

Jason looked at him, 'Do you think she'll show up tomorrow, boss, like she said?'

'Not a cat in hell's chance, Jason. Although I don't know whether it will be because she is being held against her will, or because something else is going on with this prodigal son.'

Jason raised an eyebrow. 'He's proving to be a right pain in the arse, boss. The lads are working flat out trying to trace his history, but they're coming up empty handed.'

Matt's phone rang.

'Matt? It's Ross Cadman. Just to say that Jeremy Reader is cooperating again. I think Grace's call put his mind at rest.'

'She called him? When?' Matt couldn't hide the surprise in his voice.

'She rang me at around eight in the evening, and I arranged for her to call back. I allowed Jeremy to take the call in the Harbour Suite. They talked for around ten minutes.'

'Did you get the number she phoned from?'

'Yes, we keep a log of all calls.' After a moment, Ross gave Matt a number.

'Thanks for that, Ross. You don't know what she said to him, I suppose?'

'Oh, apparently she was pretty upset about all that was going on at the moment, so she'd gone to stay with an old friend for a few days. She said she'd dropped her phone and smashed the screen. She'd be buying a new one and he mustn't worry if she was out of contact for a day. She said she was using her friend's phone to make the call.' Ross paused. 'Jeremy didn't mention the wedding, and to be honest, even though he had been adamant about cancelling it, I get the feeling that he might just be having second thoughts. Anyway, it's late. I'd better go, but at least you know Grace is safe and well.'

'Actually, we don't, Ross.' Matt paused. 'We have no idea where she is and we are seriously concerned about her. She's playing some sort of game. What we don't know is why, but we suspect she is being forced to feed us lies, the lot of us. All that stuff about a friend and damaging her phone is a crock of shit, but as to whether she's doing it under duress or to protect someone, we have no idea.'

'Oh hell bloody fire! Just when I thought . . .' Ross hesitated. 'It's easy to speak from hindsight, I know, but now I think of it, I did think she sounded, well, odd, when she spoke to me.' He swore under his breath. 'I thought she was stressed out by the copycat killings, or maybe she'd heard about the wedding being called off. I never thought any further. I should have done.'

'Don't blame yourself, Ross. She has us all tied in knots.' Matt told the governor about John Baker and his arrest.

'It's perfectly possible,' Ross said thoughtfully, 'that she got to know about the Lithuanian killings right here in Gately. Prison is the perfect place to get inside information, believe me. The inmates get the lowdown before a crime even happens. But she's a good woman, and intelligent, why not go straight to you?'

'Maybe she would have, under normal circumstances, but we suspect she gave him to us as the copycat killer — even though he isn't — because she suspects her own son is the real one. The son who Jeremy doesn't know exists.' Matt took a breath. 'We think the son, Richard Emery, is doing it to stop the marriage.'

Ross let out a low whistle. 'Hence the web of lies.'

'But she's not being consistent, is she? She told us she'd left her phone in her car, but she told you and Jem it's broken. She would know we'd collaborate.'

'Maybe she wanted you to know that something is very wrong?' suggested Ross.

'That's what we are thinking.'

'Well, I'll pass on anything I get.'

'Appreciated, Ross. And I'll keep you in the picture too.' Matt ended the call and called Kim to his office. 'What time did Grace Repton call us?'

'Seven thirty this evening, sir.'

'Well, she called HMP Gately at eight o'clock, then again a few minutes later.' He handed her a note. 'This is the number she rang on, supposedly the "friend's" phone. I'm guessing it won't be the number she rang us from. Can you compare it, and try to get a trace, please?'

'I'm on it, sir.'

As Kim left, Matt realised that no one had eaten yet. He went out to the CID room. 'You lot must be starving, so what's it to be? Pizza or KFC?'

They agreed on KFC, and one of the pool detectives volunteered to order and collect it. 'I've got one last report coming through, boss, and then I'll go pick it up.' The detective, a young woman called Rita Kindred, didn't take her eyes off her screen.

Then, over the general hubbub, Matt heard an exclamation of surprise and a loud expletive.

'Rita? What's up?'

Rita stood up. 'We can take Grace Repton's son out of the equation, boss. He's dead! I've just got confirmation from the Nottinghamshire force. It was suicide, sir, six months ago. Richard Emery hanged himself.'

Matt's head dropped to his chest. What next? The way this was going he had more chance of having a heart attack than enjoying a peaceful retirement. He had a man in the cells who had answers, but he was playing the system to hold up the interview, and now his theories about Grace had been stymied. And all the time, three dead women and three dead men were crying out for justice. Could he hold on long enough to give it to them?

Someone touched his arm, and he slowly raised his head to see Jason looking down at him anxiously. 'Boss? We've just heard from the team working John Baker's house. They've found a bag containing knives, medical scalpels, latex gloves, rope . . . everything the copycat used on his victims, plus the bag itself. It's exactly the same as the one on the CCTV pictures of Varsity Man. They also found the varsity jacket stuffed in a black sack outside with the bins, all ready for the dustmen to collect.' He shook his head in disbelief. 'I know it sounds incredible, but John Baker is the copycat killer! Grace was right to point us in his direction. It had nothing to do with using him as a fall guy either. We'd asked her who might have had an interest in her in the past, and she told us. Simple as that.'

He wasn't elated. He felt no relief. What Matt Ballard felt was suspicion. He was very, very worried.

Kim came in. 'I've just had confirmation from some of the street pastors from Holy Trinity. There was indeed a young man who used to fancy his chances with Grace. They used to refer to him as her toy-boy, and the description they gave me matches John Baker. And, sir, the phone she used is a different number. It's unregistered, so is the sim. I tried triangulation to find a location, but it's switched off and not connecting to the nearby cell towers. I'm guessing that if we do find it, it'll be in a rubbish bin somewhere.'

'Or in the river,' muttered Jason. 'So, if whoever she was seen arguing with in the street isn't Baker, and it isn't her son, who was it? And where is she now?'

'What if she's simply had enough, couldn't take any more?' asked Bryn. 'I wouldn't blame her for throwing in the towel, would you?'

'The cat!' Kim suddenly exclaimed. 'The cat with the two different eyes. It wasn't there when I called last, when Grace was in such a hurry to get away.'

Jason stared at her. 'So?'

'It's a house cat. It never goes out. It pretty well lives in the lounge and always greets you when you go in. It wasn't there.' She frowned. 'So you could be right, Bryn. Maybe she'd already put the cat in kennels, and was just about to take off.'

'That's quite possible,' added Jason. 'And all that stuff about coming in tomorrow was just buying her some time to do a runner.' He turned to Matt. 'Whatever, surely the main thing is that we have a multiple killer sitting downstairs in the custody suite?'

Matt nodded slowly. While the room dealt with the more important issue of popping out to collect the KFC, he phoned downstairs to find out if the interview could go ahead.

He slammed the phone down. The slippery little bastard had claimed he needed rest, and as it was approaching ten in the evening, the interview would have to wait until morning. 'Sodding PACE!' he muttered. How were they supposed to operate when all the rights were on the side of the criminals? Everything was stacked against them. Food, sleep, toilet breaks, legal advice, studying the codes of practice . . . a canny villain could string out their twenty-four hours very easily if they knew how to play the game. Most of them did.

He was just about to go back to the CID room when his phone rang again. It was probably Liz. He'd managed one or two quick calls earlier, but it was getting late, so maybe she was planning on turning in early.

Instead of Liz, he heard Rory Wilkinson's voice.

'No peace for the wicked, is there, Matthew? And we must have been very bad indeed. I'm positively aching for my super king-sized bed!'

'Me too. Not the best of days, is it?'

'Well, this could cheer you up. My lovely assistant Spike has isolated a fingerprint. We are thinking the killer used a latex glove and it tore when he took up wall art.'

'Excellent. We're holding a suspect now, so that could be very useful indeed.' It was what they needed. Viable evidence.

'It's a strange case though, Matt. This murder scene is somehow different to the last two. Oh, I don't know, it just feels over-dramatised if you know what I mean. Staged. Spike feels the same. And it wasn't just the big bloody heart either. The cuts in the woman's legs were deeper, and there was more attention to detail. Oh, I know we've seen it before — the need to shock, to outdo all those who went before, but . . .' his voice trailed away.

'Not like you to be so perplexed, Rory.'

'It isn't, is it? We just feel that we're not seeing the full picture. Either of us. So here we are. Me not nestling close to my darling David, and Spike unselfishly forgoing his nooky for the third night running. I'm hoping our sacrifice will be recognised at some point. Hopefully in financial terms.'

In the midst of all his turmoil, Matt was forced to smile. 'I'm sure it will. I assure you that I, for one, appreciate it very much, and the fingerprint is brilliant news.'

Matt hung up, and thought of Jack Fleet. He decided to give the super another half hour, and then he'd contact him. The waiting was affecting them all. He could only hope that no news was good news.

Bryn stuck his head around the door. 'Grub's here, boss.'

'No news about Grace?'

'Nothing at all.'

'Then I reckon we eat, and go home. John Baker can't be interviewed until the morning, so there's nothing I can do here. We might as well all grab a few hours' sleep.'

'If it's okay with you, sir, I'd like to go to Saltern-le-Fen to see Lukas and Lina. By the looks of it they will be able to go home tomorrow. Their killer can't threaten them from our custody suite, and they were instrumental in putting him there.'

'What about his brother? I thought there were two of them?'

'I've made inquiries about him, sir. The one called Marcus won't be bothering anyone for a good long while. He had an accident and he's in hospital. He'll be there for some time, it appears. Then I'm reliably told that he is moving from our area.'

'An accident, Bryn?' Matt raised an eyebrow. 'Sounds rather convenient, doesn't it?'

'Probably was, sir, but I'm not asking too many questions right now. We've got our hands full with looking for Grace Repton, haven't we, boss?'

'Absolutely.' Matt grinned. He was proud of Bryn and the way he'd handled the situation in the Baltic Quarter. Never once had he complained about having little or no support, and he had come up trumps. Matt would put in a very glowing report when the case was closed, and hopefully his new boss, DCI Anders, would treat him well. 'Now grab some food and go see your two private detectives. Oh, and Bryn — say thank you from me.'

'I will, sir. I'm hoping that with continued support this could make a difference to how people in the Baltic Quarter view the police.'

'Possibly how some of us view them too. Now, off you go, or Jim Cousins will be locking you out.'

Matt went out to the main office, found himself some chicken and fries, ate them at his desk, and shut his computer down. It had been a very long day, and all he wanted now was to sit down with Liz, share a couple of glasses of wine, and offload.

He threw the rubbish in the bin and gathered up his jacket. One call to David Redpath, then it was time to go home.

Five minutes later, he was posting a notice on the wall of the CID room. Swifty had come through a long operation, and it was hoped he would make a full recovery after the knife attack. However, he would be on sick leave for some time while he recovered. A collection would be set up in the morning.

Matt heaved a sigh of relief, told everyone to bugger off home, and finally drew the curtain on a very strange day.

CHAPTER THIRTY

Matt drove across the night-enshrouded fenland, his mind a maelstrom of suspicions, doubts and wild surmises. He should have been elated. He should have been itching to get home to Liz. He should have been looking forward to telling her that he was just a short step from retiring and they would soon be together, free to do whatever they wanted. But he couldn't shake off the sense that he'd got something terribly wrong.

Rory had only added to the feeling. If both he and Spike were convinced they were missing something, then he, Matt, must be too. Maybe Liz could help? He would lay it all before her, and see if a fresh perspective might set them on the right track. Liz had always been astute. A sombre thought crossed his mind. But was she now?

Matt turned on the radio. As the sounds of an orchestra filled the car, he was reminded of some words he had once heard: *"The function of music is to release us from the tyranny of conscious thought."* Wasn't it the famous conductor and impresario, Sir Thomas Beecham, who said that? If only he could be released from his own tyrannous thoughts.

Matt turned into the long lane that led out to Tanners Fen. It was a perfect night, still hot, with not a breath of wind. He sniffed the salty ozone air. The indigo sky was lit with a myriad of stars.

He should be feeling good right now. Instead, he cursed the Police and Criminal Evidence Act for holding up the interview with their suspect. He'd left the station with everything up in the air, and no line drawn. And Grace Repton was still missing.

He groaned. She could be in terrible danger, and here he was, blithely driving home to be with the one he loved. Then again, as Jason said, having delivered them their killer she could be miles away, cutting her losses and heading for the hills. Wherever she was, he needed to know or he wouldn't rest. An attention drawn had been put out, and with every officer in the county looking for her, there was no more he could do. She would either walk into the station at nine thirty tomorrow morning, or she wouldn't. Only then could he act.

Liz had said that listening to classical music could have a significant impact on your mood, productivity and creativity. He grimaced. Well, it wasn't working too well tonight. He switched the radio off, just as the dark silhouette of Canon Farm appeared on the horizon, a light shining from the lounge window. So Liz hadn't turned in early. Thank goodness! He desperately needed to talk.

He parked the car and ran up to the front door. Matt had insisted that she lock the doors for safety, so he unlocked the door and went inside, calling out her name as he went. There was no answer, but Liz had a habit of falling asleep in front of the TV.

The lounge door was wide open. He hung up his jacket and went in. 'Sweetheart? Oh, what a pig of a day! I'm so glad to be home! I—'

There, seated on the sofa was, not Liz, but Grace Repton.

She jumped up. 'DCI Ballard! Please forgive me for coming here. Your lovely Liz said it would be alright if I waited here for you. I just had to see you!'

'Where is Liz?' he said.

'She has a really bad headache. Migraine, is it? She took some paracetamol and she's resting now. She told me to tell you that she'd be down as soon as it eased.' She sat back down. 'I'm sorry. This is a terrible imposition, I know, but I have so much to tell you, and I didn't dare go to the station.'

His first impulse was to go to Liz, but actually seeing Grace, after all the angst and surmise about what had happened to her, and knowing Liz had regular migraines, his curiosity got the better of him. 'I need a drink. Can I get you something?'

'No, thank you. Liz kindly made me a cup of tea earlier. I'm fine.' She indicated the two empty cups still on the coffee table.

Matt went to the sideboard and poured himself a generous measure of Scotch. Then he added another shot.

He sat opposite her, took a long swallow and waited for the fiery liquid to trickle through him. 'What's going on, Grace?'

She seemed suddenly to have become smaller. 'Oh God, what a mess. I don't know where to begin.'

'Where have you been? And this John Baker — or is it Backus? What is it with you and murderers, Grace? John Baker killed — no, brutally assassinated, three young Lithuanian men, all because of some decades-old feud. Now everything points to him being the copycat killer as well. How on earth did you get to know such an evil man? You really do mix with some choice characters, don't you?' All the anger he felt toward this exasperating woman poured out. He couldn't help himself.

He saw her wipe tears from her eyes, and knew he had gone too far.

'Oh hell! I'm sorry, Grace. Are you sure you wouldn't like that drink?'

She shook her head. 'No, I'm driving. And I mustn't stay too long.'

'Driving? I didn't see your car.'

'I parked around the back, out of sight, just in case . . .'

'Who are you scared of, Grace? Because we can protect you, you know.' He took another gulp of whisky, which so far hadn't had the usual effect of calming his racing thoughts. He drank again. 'Did you know that Baker was the copycat? Was that why you deliberately sent us after him?'

Grace looked so lost that she seemed like a different woman to the confident deliverer of Reader's warning. It seemed so long ago now.

Then it hit him. Jeremy Reader!

He stared at Grace. She'd been used, hadn't she? And now she knew it. The master manipulator, Jem Reader, the oh so remorseful killer, still playing games from his privileged position in the Harbour Unit. Of course, he wanted to call the wedding off! There was never going to be any wedding in the first place, was there? Grace had been a means to an end, that was all.

Once again, Matt remembered the look of utter hatred that Reader had given him as he was taken from the dock. He had sworn to get his revenge, and now he had. The bastard.

'Oh, Grace! I'm so terribly sorry. This is all down to him, isn't it? Jeremy.'

He felt almost light-headed. Suddenly, the pieces of the puzzle were falling into place. Thinking back, it must have been set in motion by those letters from his acolyte, Alex. Using them, and then meeting up with kind, naïve Grace, and using her too, he had orchestrated the perpetuation of his work. From the contacts he made in

301

prison, it would have been easy to find a successor. After all, he had access to a whole pool of savage killers.

He drained his glass. How could he have allowed himself to be so stupid? He'd always had reservations about Reader, but everyone else had seemed so certain of his sincerity. A truly repentant criminal! What crap. And he'd gone along with it.

He remembered Grace, began to get to his feet and sat down again. The whisky had hit its mark. 'I've let you down, Grace. Why on earth didn't I see it before?'

'See what? Has the penny dropped?' She had an odd expression on her face.

'Oh yes,' he said, 'but rather late, I fear.'

'Actually, I doubt that, DCI Matthew Ballard. I doubt that very much indeed.'

Matt screwed up his eyes and tried to focus on her. The whisky had gone straight to his head.

'I'd better tell you this fast, because in a few minutes you won't be able to comprehend much at all. It's not the Scotch, it's the small sedative I added to the bottle. Helpful of Liz to tell me how you liked a whisky after a bad day.'

'Liz?' Matt began to panic. 'Where's Liz?'

'Where I said. Lying on the bed. But it's not a headache. She's tied up securely, so forget about her and listen to me while you can. Believe me, you are going to want to hear this.'

He could do nothing else. 'What did you give me?' he managed.

'Just roofies. Rohypnol. Easily available on the streets these days, or in prison.' She laughed. 'My favourite places. You're a bit too big to overpower, so I chose an easier way.' Her expression hardened. 'Now, shut up and listen. You know how Rohypnol works as well as I do. You can see and hear, but you are incapable of movement, and sometimes you lose consciousness, so let's not waste time. You'll recover in about eight hours, but you won't be able to remember what happened. All this will have disappeared, along with me.' Grace sighed. 'It has been an extraordinary journey. Many lives have been lost and damaged, and all because of you, Matt Ballard.' Coiled in her chair, she spat out his name like a cobra emitting venom.

Matt stared at her blankly. Even without the drug he wouldn't have been able to comprehend what she was saying.

'You couldn't be allowed to drift off into a peaceful retirement, Matt Ballard. I had to make you pay. And I think I've been successful, although nothing will bring back my son, my darling Ritchie.' She leaned forward and peered closely at him. 'I can see I need to hurry. It's simple really — Gemma Goddard. It was your fault that she died, and when he heard what had happened to her, my darling boy hanged himself.' She swallowed. 'My very special son. He loved her, and you took her from him. And so you took him from me. My little lackey, John Baker, will no doubt give you all the boring details when he decides to talk. I used him, like I used all the others. I killed those women, Matt Ballard. I took the scalpel to them and watched their blood flow. Dear little John was the perfect assistant. So careful and methodical! A very helpful trait when you're trying to get rid of evidence. Then off he would trot, taking along all the tools of the trade.'

Matt could no longer move but he managed to whisper, 'Jeremy?'

Grace exhaled. 'Jem. Ah, the only thing that didn't go to plan. He is my only regret. But needs must, as they say. I hope one day he will be able to forgive me.'

Abruptly, Grace stood and looked down at him. 'Yes, a fitting end for the man who destroyed my boy. I'm not going to kill you, Matt Ballard. I prefer to remain with the thought that you live on with the deaths of three women haunting your every waking moment. It won't be very peaceful.' Grace turned and walked away. 'I really do have to go now. It's time for me to move on.'

The last thing that Matt saw and heard before the drug overcame him was a figure appear behind Grace Repton, and the words, 'Like fuck it is!'

There was a grunt and a crash, while Matt reluctantly drifted away.

* * *

Liz knew she had landed one almighty crack on the back of Grace's head, courtesy of the storm lantern they kept on the landing in case of power cuts. But somehow she had got up and was coming for her.

A quick glance into the lounge told Liz that Matt was going to be of no help to her, but she was determined not to let this woman escape. Help was on its way, because the first thing she did after she freed herself was call the situation in. She just needed to stay alive long enough to see those blue lights.

'Bitch! I should have killed you too,' Grace hissed.

Liz couldn't afford to consider her weaknesses, her lack of coordination. Worrying about that could cost her her life. She had to find the quickest way to incapacitate Grace and buy herself some time.

Liz ran into the lounge, and Grace lurched after her. She was surprisingly fast, and almost caught Liz off guard.

Almost. Liz grabbed the heavy iron poker from the fireplace and swung round on her attacker. 'Back off, Grace! It's over!'

Grace threw herself at Liz.

Liz sidestepped the charge, flung her arm around Grace's neck and the two of them hit the ground. Liz didn't even hear the sirens drawing closer.

When PCs Maggie Smithson and Barney Woods hurtled through the door, they found Liz sitting on the floor, holding the poker pressed down on Grace Repton's windpipe.

'Blimey! Nice one, Sarge!' Barney exclaimed in admiration.

'Get this mad cow out of here, and get an ambulance for Matt!' Liz yelled.

'Paramedics are already here, Sarge,' said Maggie, hauling Grace Repton to her feet. She pulled Grace's arms up behind her back and snapped the handcuffs on. 'What are we charging her with, Sarge?'

'Murder, attempted murder, assault on a police officer, take your pick! Just throw the bloody book at her.'

Liz crawled across to where Matt lay slumped on the sofa. His eyes were open but he gave no sign of recognition. She'd seen kids high on roofies a hundred times and knew the signs. That weird state of suspended animation was scary to see, but he was alive. Grace could so easily have killed him. She raised herself from the floor and flopped down beside him, cradling him in her arms.

CHAPTER THIRTY-ONE

The following morning, Jason and Bryn finally received the go-ahead to interview John Baker. Thirty minutes later they were outside in the corridor, staring at each other. Then they burst into laughter.

'Jesus Christ! That man is well pissed off at Grace dobbing him right in the shit, isn't he? I've never seen anyone so angry.' Bryn shook his head. It had taken four officers from the custody department to restrain and calm Baker.

Since Matt Ballard would be allowed nowhere near Grace Repton, she having drugged him and assaulted Liz, it had been deemed advisable to send her to Greenborough, where DI Nikki Galena would interview her. Probably a good move, considering what Baker was threatening to do to her if he ever saw her again.

Jason led the way down the corridor. 'Not sure what his brief thought of that outburst, but at least we have someone prepared to tell us everything about Grace Repton and how she organised the copycats.'

'And no way is he going to go down without taking her with him,' added Bryn. Kim called out as they entered the CID room. 'We've just heard from the hospital about Swifty. He's going home the day after tomorrow. They were deep lacerations but there's no permanent damage, or so they hope.'

'Excellent,' called back Jason. 'Looks like things are finally getting straight again.'

'Any news on the boss?' Kim asked.

'Discharged into Liz's care. Usual thing — don't drive, operate heavy machinery or make important decisions for twenty-four hours.' Jason raised his eyebrows. 'That should be quite a relief to him after this last week.' He glanced around. 'Kim? Have you got a few minutes? Laura and Sam are waiting in the boss's office. Bryn and I were about to get their opinion on a few details from our interview with Baker, and perhaps you can shed some light on Grace Repton.'

They all trooped into Matt's office.

When they were seated, Jason said, 'It seems we have a problem with Grace. John Baker paints a picture of this terrifying, controlling woman who had a terrible hold over him. Sounds a bit unbelievable when you consider the fact that he's carried out a few ruthless assassinations on his own account. And then we have Kim, who's met a group of people who think Grace is nothing less than a selfless pillar of society.'

'That's right,' said Kim. 'They really appreciate her work as a street pastor. Salt of the earth, I'm reliably told.'

'You saw more of Grace than any of us,' Jason said. 'How do you square all her volunteer and charity work with being a cold-blooded killer? It just doesn't add up, does it?'

Kim shrugged. 'That's a question for Laura and Sam, but she always confused me. She'd say one thing, while her body language was saying something else. I never felt like I'd met the real Grace.'

'Lucky for you that you never did,' said Laura. 'But I understand Sergeant Haynes did meet the real one, and finished up fighting for her life.'

'How can one person have two such different sides to them?' Bryn asked.

Sam sat back. 'We've come to the conclusion that Grace Repton became mentally unstable when she took on the muggers and her husband died.'

'The whole thing must have affected her terribly,' added Laura. 'And then she had to bring up her child on her own. We now know that right from birth he had serious psychological problems. He was difficult to handle and, although she idolised him, he was wild and with no father around to help, she really struggled.'

Bryn could understand that she'd suffered, but he couldn't see why this would cause her to commit murder. What had sent her down that road? He asked Laura what she thought.

'Until more facts emerge we can only guess, but we think that the mugging was the catalyst.' Laura glanced across to Sam for confirmation.

'It was the danger element. It was night. She tackled two drug-fuelled junkies that were intent on robbing them, and she succeeded. I've seen cases before where the affected person starts going out at night, looking to replicate that danger and the feeling of excitement it gave them.'

'Ah,' mused Kim, 'so Grace took up with the night marshals in Greenborough, and then the night street pastors here in Fenfleet.'

'And then she took herself into high-security prisons, where the whole place is a powder-keg of violence,' added Bryn, now beginning to get the picture.

Laura nodded. 'She needed that dangerous atmosphere. Mixing with serial killers would have felt like the ultimate thrill.'

'I can think of safer ways to get my jollies,' snorted Bryn.

'Then her son killed himself,' Sam said, 'and as Grace was already unstable, it pushed her over the edge. Imagine it. Her husband dies in front of her, and then her twenty-four-year-old son hangs himself. Grace needed someone to blame.' 'Matt Ballard,' whispered Jason.

'It could have been anyone,' Laura added quickly. 'She needed an outlet for her rage and grief, a scapegoat. Killing randomly wouldn't have been enough. She needed more, so she invented a fictional scenario with DCI Ballard playing the villain. She was suffering, and she needed someone connected with the Goddard case to suffer too.'

'Poor Matt,' Jason said with feeling. 'What a way to leave after thirty plus years devoted to this job.'

'At least he's still alive,' said Kim. 'She could have murdered him.'

Bryn was still puzzled. 'And the thing with Jeremy Reader? I still don't understand what was going on there.'

Sam said, 'Oh yes. His telling her about Alex and his fears that the young man would become a copycat sparked the whole train of events. Then the unthinkable happened. Grace Repton fell in love with Jeremy.'

'Was she capable of love?' asked Kim.

'Oh yes,' Laura said. 'One side of her. Then she was the faithful fiancée. The calculating killer was completely separate.'

'That's why I saw such swings in her body language,' murmured Kim. 'No wonder I thought she was complicated. She was!'

Bryn had a sudden thought. 'So, if she is found guilty, which she must be, will she go to prison, or will she claim diminished responsibility and finish up in a secure hospital like Rampton?'

No one answered immediately, then Sam said, 'It's my belief that she'll be proud of what she's done. She'll want the world to know about her crusade for vengeance for her dead son. She certainly won't want to be sent to a psychiatric hospital. She'll want to take her place among the high-profile murderers.'

'And who knows what'll happen in court?' said Jason morosely. 'If she comes over as all sweet and light, it'll be game over for a life in prison.'

There was a long silence. 'By the way,' Kim said, 'all that stuff she fed me about having a heart problem and going to the hospital was a load of crap. I contacted the hospital and there was no such appointment. She was probably out preparing her next murder.'

'One thing I'm looking forward to hearing about is why she drew that massive bloody heart on the wall above the last victim,' said Jason. 'That wasn't part of Jeremy Reader's method. He drew tiny ones in places that weren't obvious.'

'Best guess, it was a message to Jeremy,' Sam said. 'Jeremy admitted his tiny bloody hearts were for that girlfriend of his who died, like a heart carved in a tree trunk. I think she did it for him, to proclaim her love.'

'And provided us with a nice piece of evidence by way of a fingerprint.' Jason smiled smugly. 'Thank you, Grace.'

Bryn stretched. 'And now my new friends, Lukas and Lina can go home to their loved ones, knowing that a very old feud has finally come to an end.' He smiled. 'I feel really good about that. There are no more members of the Backus family left with the slightest inclination to continue the fight, so anyone wearing the Tree of Life tattoo will be safe on the streets.'

'You did well, Bryn,' said Jason. 'And the boss is very pleased with you. Keep on like this and you'll be a sergeant before too long.'

Bryn wasn't bothered about that, he was just happy to have done some good and made things a bit easier in Fenfleet's Baltic Quarter. He'd gone up in his girlfriend's estimation too. Jules was suddenly telling people her boyfriend was a detective, and actually sounding proud of it. Win, win, he thought. Hell, I love this job!

EPILOGUE

Two weeks later, Grace Repton had been charged on three counts of murder, and John Baker five, as it transpired that it had been he who killed both Alex and Reuben, along with the Lithuanian men. Now Matt was travelling, hopefully for the last time, to HMP Gately to see Jeremy Reader. He was going at Jeremy's request, but he also felt he owed the man something.

Liz had no recall of what had happened in the Goddard case, and now it was his turn to have a missing piece in his life. What Grace had told him was a blank. Liz's quick thinking in recording the whole thing on her smartphone when she had crept down the stairs had enabled him to hear it all, first hand, so to speak.

As he drove, he thought back to Liz's words after the Rohypnol had worn off and he was back home from hospital.

'She was so nice! I bought the whole bloody story!' Liz shook her head in disbelief. 'I can't believe that I even made her tea. Worse than that, I even bought into the story that you had told her to come to the house and wait for you. What a plank I was! She was so

convincing, Mattie. We chatted. She admired the house, so, like a fool, I gave her the grand tour of all the improvements we'd made. That's when she clobbered me. She caught me completely unawares, and I knew I was no match for her with all my neurological problems. I had to think fast. I was close to the bed, so I pretended to fall on it. I acted unconscious, but was only dazed. She tied my wrists and gagged me, but she was in a hurry in case you came home, so she didn't make the best job of it. She sure wasn't a girl guide — her knots were rubbish.'

'How did you get free?' he asked.

'There was a pair of scissors in the bedside cabinet. It took ages, and I kept praying you wouldn't come back before I'd got myself loose. I was certain she wanted to kill you.' Liz moved closer to him. 'I rang it in immediately, and asked for a softly, softly approach. Then I crept down the stairs with my phone switched on to record anything I heard.'

'Nicely done, Detective.'

'Private detective, darling, remember?' Her smile faded as the memories of that night flooded back.

'In thirty years of policing I've never come across such a convincing liar,' said Matt. 'I truly believed you were lying down with a migraine. I cannot understand how two supposedly "experienced" police officers could be so taken in.'

'She's the best there is,' Liz said. 'She's learned her profession in some very dark places, hasn't she?'

'Mmm, and unless there's no justice in this world, she'll be going to spend the rest of her life in one of them.'

'Then she'll feel right at home.' Liz looked up at him anxiously. 'It is over, isn't it, finally?'

Matt held her tightly, 'Yes, it is, and as soon as I've handed over to DI Anders, I'll be out of that station for good.'

Matt pulled into the car park and dragged himself back to the present. He'd refused a leaving party, much to the disappointment of all those guys keen to have a piss-up with a free bar. As far as Matt was concerned, he had failed to solve his last case. It was galling. But he couldn't go back and have another try at it. He'd got it wrong, and only the fact that Grace had misperceived Liz's supposed fainting fit, and of course, Liz's quick thinking, had brought the case to its conclusion. For his part, Matt considered it a failure.

Even the success of the combined Operation Saturn, which had gone ahead as planned and netted them a whole fistful of drug dealers, had done little to cheer him. He hadn't been part of it, so it meant little to him.

The only thing that had made him smile during the last couple of weeks had been a conversation he'd had with Rory Wilkinson. Usually it was the pathologist who shed a light on apparently unsolvable crimes, but on this occasion, it had been Matt. Something about the crime scenes had nagged away at both Rory and his assistant Spike, until Matt told them that there had been two killers — Grace and John Baker. Rory had squealed in delight. 'Fuck my old boots, as my dear departed grandmother used to say! Not one killer, but two, working together. Of course! Matthew, you're an angel! Now dear Spike and I can finally get back to enjoying our snuggles and nookie — not together, you understand. No wonder there were discrepancies. Why on earth didn't we see it? Especially me. I was so certain there was *one* copycat killer that I ignored my usual motto — you know the one: doubt everything, look from all angles. What an idiot!' He'd continued to castigate himself for several minutes, until the tirade finally brought a smile to Matt's anxious face.

He locked his car and made his way slowly towards the main building, putting thoughts of Rory aside. It seemed that he'd got Jeremy Reader wrong too. Or had he? He still couldn't bring himself to believe it. His years working with criminals had left him with a deep suspicion of every word that emerged from a villain's mouth.

Well, he had promised Ross Cadman that he would try to set aside all his prejudices. It wouldn't be easy. After Grace Repton, he doubted his every judgement.

Exhausted, he passed through the series of locked gates and searches, hardly aware of them. He felt as if every weekend on duty, every night shift and early morning of the past thirty years had finally caught up with him.

Jeremy Reader and Ross Cadman were seated together in the quiet area of the Harbour. Reader stood up and offered his hand. Before he knew what he was doing, Matt had accepted it.

'Thank you for coming, DCI Ballard. I appreciate it.'

Matt surveyed him discreetly. Reader seemed much calmer than when they'd last met, but he also seemed hollow. There was no passion left in him now.

'She wrote to me, you know.' He handed Matt an envelope.

'That's personal, Jeremy. There's no need to show me.'

'I want you to see it. Please, read it.'

Matt took it from him. It wasn't long:

I write this in sadness. You were collateral damage. I used you, and I manipulated you, all to ruin the life of the man who stole my son from me. I planned it meticulously, from the moment you told me that you had a young disciple called Alex. It seemed like a gift.

The one thing I'd never banked on was falling in love with you.

You always told me that after what you did, you deserved every bad thing that would befall you in your future life. Maybe you could accept this terrible deception as a last punishment, then forgive yourself and move on. I, on the other hand, have only one regret, and that is you. Grace

Matt stared at it for a long time, not knowing what to say.

'I've been a naïve fool,' Jeremy said. 'I believed her, it was that simple.'

'Join the club,' said Matt bitterly. 'We all did.' Except DI Kim Peters, he thought to himself. She'd always claimed that Grace didn't add up.

'In fairness,' Ross Cadman added, 'she has said that she loved you. I believe she honestly thought she could complete her mission, and still marry you.'

Jeremy pushed the letter away from him as if it were contagious. 'You believe this crap, do you?'

'Actually, yes, I do,' Ross said.

'Well, I no longer trust a word that comes out of those treacherous lips. I never will.' Jeremy spoke through gritted teeth. 'What do you think?' he asked Matt.

'She drugged me, Jeremy. I have no memory of what happened when I got home to find her there, but I've heard a recording. There was real regret in her voice when she spoke about you. She had no need to lie, she knew I would hear what she had to say and then forget it. She had no idea she was being recorded or overheard, so,' Matt ran his hand through his hair, 'I think you really were her Achilles heel. Grace Repton truly cared about you.'

Almost imperceptibly, Reader seemed to relax. Was it hope? Or maybe it was just relief that not everything she'd told him was a lie.

'Jeremy, did you ever know of a man named John Baker? Or John Backus?'

Reader shook his head. 'Not that I can recall.'

Matt was mildly pleased. Grace Repton, at interview, had declared she sourced and groomed Baker during her time as a night warden on the streets of Fenfleet. He hadn't lusted after her, but she had made it seem that way. She pursued him, in order to tempt him into taking part in her murderous campaign. She swore he had nothing to do with her prison visiting. Jeremy appeared to be completely uninvolved. 'I probably have no right to say this, but I am still profoundly shocked by the extent of her cold-blooded determination to destroy you.' Reader looked at Matt almost in awe. 'You must really have made an impression on her.'

'Well, she was wrong on all counts.' Matt didn't tell Jeremy, but the idea that Gemma Goddard would have ever looked twice at Richard was laughable. She was totally wrapped up in someone else. 'Grace's son died because of an unhealthy obsession, Jeremy. I had nothing to do with it. She believed that she could lay the burden of guilt for the women she killed at my door, but the guilt lies with her and I'll never feel otherwise.'

'So, it was all for nothing?' Reader asked.

'All for nothing,' Matt replied flatly.

A silence descended.

It came to Matt that Grace had indeed succeeded in damaging him. Not in the way she intended, but nonetheless, the damage had been done. He wasn't about to admit this to Reader, but even if he hadn't been on the point of retiring, he would have handed in his warrant card. He had been so sure that he had made it through the Goddard case and emerged from it the policeman he had always been. He had been terribly wrong. Throughout this case, his judgement had been impaired and he should never have taken it on. It was just as well that he was about to retire.

'If there's anything I can do, DCI Ballard. I'm not sure what, but if I can help when it comes to court, just ask.' Reader looked sincere.

Ross Cadman cracked a smile. 'Now that'd be some trial, wouldn't it? The key witness for the prosecution a lifer, testifying from HMP Gately.' He stood up. 'I'm sorry, guys, but I must go and catch up with the rest of my work.'

'I'd better go too,' said Matt.

'Can't you stay a little longer?' Jeremy asked Matt. 'The tea is awful but the coffee is just about drinkable.'

Matt refused a drink, remembering the last one he'd accepted, but stayed where he was, watching Ross Cadman depart.

'Perhaps I shouldn't ask you this, but would you be able to tell me a bit about how Grace set all this up?' Jeremy finally asked.

'I'll try to tell you what I can, off the record.' Matt knew that if he refused, Reader would torment himself trying to understand. 'Ask away.'

Jeremy hesitated, then asked, 'Why me?'

'To be brutally honest, it was because of the type of victim you chose. From what we gather, Grace spent some time with you as a visitor, and then looked up all the old news reports of your trial. Your crimes fitted her requirements perfectly, since they involved blonde women with blue eyes.' Matt paused. 'Before this one, Jeremy, I had a very bad case in which a young woman died. Her name was Gemma Goddard, and it turns out she was the girl Grace's son was obsessed with. Grace knew exactly what Gemma looked like — very much like your victims — so she decided to screw with my mind. Her idea was that every time I saw one of her murdered women, I would see Gemma all over again.'

'I see. And did you?'

'It was the last one that got to me.' Matt saw again the crucified figure of Penny Carrington and shivered.

'I'm sorry.' Jeremy sounded genuinely sympathetic.

'She admitted that she couldn't believe her luck when you told her about Alex. It gave her the idea of the copycat murders. When she worked as a night warden, she met an evil man called John Baker, formerly Backus. She discovered that this Baker had murdered several Lithuanians, so he was sufficiently ruthless to kill. She groomed him for the job, and he turned out to be the perfect disciple. She found the victims, and then he stalked them, chatted them up and finally gained access to their homes, all the time posing as Alex.'

'Whom they had already killed,' Jeremy added. 'Along with poor Reuben.'

'Exactly. We found the skin hearts that she excised from the victims along with the tools she used. Her assistant kept it all at his home. At the scene of the last murder, she drew a bloody heart on the wall but her glove must have torn and she left a fingerprint.'

Jeremy sat bolt upright. 'I should have known!'

Startled, Matt said, 'Known what?'

'I said I never told anyone about painting those tiny hearts on the walls, but it's just come to me. I'd forgotten, but I did tell Grace. I only mentioned it once, when we were having one of our soul-searching talks. Ha! What a fucking farce they were! That woman played me like a violin. Me, the cunning manipulator of minds. It's unbelievable.'

'Ah, I see. She made a few mistakes though. The fingerprint was the biggest one, but we also found fibres on the tape that she used to seal Reuben's windows — cat hairs to be precise. We've confirmed that they came from her cat.' Matt didn't tell Reader that they'd found the odd-eyed cat buried in her back garden. When she was ready to disappear, she had tidied up and left no loose ends at her home. Nirvana. Matt couldn't think of anything further from the truth. 'At the very beginning of this case, I wondered if someone was carrying out a vendetta against me, and I thought it was you, Jeremy. Turns out I was right about the vendetta, but wrong about the perpetrator.'

'You never totally believed me, did you, DCI Ballard?' Jeremy smiled at him.

'No. All through the entire case. But I seemed to have cocked up on that too.'

Reader looked around. No one was within earshot. 'Actually, you didn't. Well, not quite.'

Matt stared at him, waiting for what would come next.

'Seeing what this case has done to you, maybe I can offer a straw to cling to. Look, between you and me, until I came here and met Grace, all my actions were entirely selfish. I spent years listening to and learning all the psychological jargon, and I decided to play a game with the system. I knew that if I didn't challenge my brain, I'd go mad, plus I wanted privileges, some kind of freedom, even if it had to be within these walls. I decided to talk my way into a unit like this.' Reader narrowed his eyes. 'And I succeeded. Then a strange thing happened. I started talking to one of the OPVs, a delightful woman called Grace Repton, and everything I'd been pretending to feel became real. By the time I made it into the Harbour Unit, I'd become the repentant criminal that I'd always pretended to be.' He looked down at his hands, resting on his knees. 'So I suppose I do have something to thank her for.'

Matt thought about this. 'Then you fooled an awful lot of people to get here. Are you proud of that?'

'Initially, yes, I was. I had taken on the system, and beaten it. Now? Well, now I feel differently about everything.'

'Tell me something, if you can.' Matt leaned closer to Jeremy. 'If we hadn't caught you, or if they'd found you innocent at your trial, would you have gone on killing?'

Reader returned his gaze. 'Back then? Without a doubt.'

'And if you were to be released at any time, would you kill again?'

Reader blinked slowly. 'Now, there's a question. I've asked myself that over and over. I don't expect you to believe this, but no, I wouldn't. After my girlfriend died in that horrible way, and so needlessly, it drove me mad. The things I did were all because I was driven by a compulsion, an uncontrollable need to see that pale, pale skin again.' He groaned softly. 'But now? I've come a long way since then, I'm through it, I no longer have that need, that burning desire to kill.' He smiled sadly. 'But don't worry, they'll never let me out. This is where I belong, and this is where

I'll be staying until I'm dead and gone.' He took a deep breath. 'I salute you, DCI Ballard. You were the only person who never really bought into my game. You were right not to trust me. Take heart from that. As to Grace, well, others have made bigger fools of themselves than you, and you are looking at the biggest one sitting right here.'

'I'm sorry, Jeremy. You really loved her, didn't you?'

'For my sins, yes, I did.'

'The governor thinks you are on the level, so do all the psych team, including my own psychologist, Sam Page.' He fastened his eyes on Reader. 'Are you still fooling people, Jeremy Reader?'

'Not now. I meant what I said, DCI Ballard. Since I came here, I am everything I claim to be. I deeply regret what I did. When the copycat killings began again, the guilt sent me spiralling down to a very dark place indeed. It all came falling in on me, all the terrible things I'd done, the lives I'd wrecked, the pain I'd caused. It was starting all over again, and again, it was my fault.' He put his head in his hands. 'And to think, it was Grace all along.' He looked up at Matt, his eyes misty. 'You can see why I can't allow myself to believe that letter, can't you? You couldn't love someone and do that to them. You couldn't send them to the brink of the abyss, could you?'

'I guess not, but Grace is a woman like no other I've ever met. Nothing about her would surprise me. Talk to Sam Page, see what he thinks. He told me he'd like to visit you again.'

'I will, he was a good person to talk to, but he won't change my mind about Grace Repton.'

Matt stood up and found himself putting his hand on Reader's shoulder. 'Thank you for your honesty, Jem. I appreciate it.'

Jeremy Reader smiled, 'Pleasure.' The grin widened. '*If* you believe me.'

Matt grinned back. 'You get the benefit of the doubt this time, Jem, but this time only.'

'Sensible man. Never trust a villain, DCI Ballard. Lies are a way of life. For some of us, they are an art form.'

* * *

Matt drove back to Fenfleet, smiling to himself at the thought that Jeremy Reader, a confessed murderer, had just admitted to a senior policeman that he'd been playing the system and making a mockery of the rehabilitation programmes. Matt could feel nothing but mild amusement and almost a sneaking admiration. He was also rather gratified to know that he hadn't totally misread the man. And indeed, who was to say that Reader wasn't still playing the system? He'd been fooling people for years, maybe he still was. That was something he'd probably never know for sure.

Exhaustion washed back over him. Grace Repton might have failed in what she intended, which was to make him feel guilty for her crimes, but she had succeeded in other ways.

Apart from the fact that three lovely young women and two men had died needlessly, he now doubted his own judgement, and she had stolen what should have been a very special time — his farewell to the job that he had given his all to for the last thirty-five years. There would be no going out in a blaze of glory. He would simply close the door and slink away. As a young man, he had come in like a lion, and now he would bow out like a lamb.

As he took the road back to the station, Matt sighed and shook his head. 'Nice one, Grace,' he muttered. 'As leaving presents go, yours certainly takes some beating.'

He put his foot down. All he wanted to do now was hand in his warrant card and go home. Home to Liz. She too needed cheering up. She had failed her assessment, and although she'd been told she'd be sure to pass in three months' time, it had upset her that she still couldn't drive.

He hoped what he had in his pocket would put a smile on her face. The little box containing the ring was still there. He'd been hesitating for too long, waiting for the right time, for that perfect, special moment. Now he knew that moment would never come. The right time was now, and always had been.

Still smiling, he passed through the police station security gates. Grace Repton was a part of this place, part of his life as a policeman. He was going to leave all that behind, and start again. And that meant he could leave Grace Repton behind as well.

This wasn't the end. This was the beginning.

THE END

Thank you for reading this book. If you enjoyed it please leave feedback on Amazon or Goodreads, and if there is anything we missed or you have a question about then please get in touch. The author and publishing team appreciate your feedback and time reading this book.

Our email is office@joffebooks.com

www.joffebooks.com

ALSO BY JOY ELLIS

THE BEST-SELLING NIKKI GALENA SERIES
Book 1: CRIME ON THE FENS
Book 2: SHADOW OVER THE FENS
Book 3: HUNTED ON THE FENS
Book 4: KILLER ON THE FENS
Book 5: STALKER ON THE FENS
Book 6: CAPTIVE ON THE FENS
Book 7: BURIED ON THE FENS
Book 8: THIEVES ON THE FENS
Book 9: FIRE ON THE FENS

JACKMAN & EVANS
Book 1: THE MURDERER'S SON
Book 2: THEIR LOST DAUGHTERS
Book 3: THE FOURTH FRIEND
Book 4: THE GUILTY ONES
Book 5: THE STOLEN BOYS

DETECTIVE MATT BALLARD
Book 1: BEWARE THE PAST
Book 2: FIVE BLOODY HEARTS

STANDALONES
GUIDE STAR